HITLER
STOPPED BY
FRANCO

OTHER TITLES BY THE AUTHORS

Yes I Can
by Sammy Davis, Jr,. and Jane and Burt Boyar

World Class
by Jane and Burt Boyar

Why Me?
by Sammy Davis, Jr., and Jane and Burt Boyar

H.L. and Lyda:
Growing Up in the H. L. Hunt
and Lyda Bunker Hunt Family
by Margaret Hunt Hill and Jane and Burt Boyar

Sammy: An Autobiography
by Sammy Davis, Jr., and Jane and Burt Boyar

HITLER
STOPPED BY
FRANCO

Jane and Burt Boyar

MARBELLA HOUSE

Library of Congress Control Number: 2001117170
ISBN: 0-97103-920-8 (alk. paper)

First Edition.

The paper used in this book meets the minimum requirements of
ANSI/NISO Z39.48-1992 (R 1997) (Permanence of Paper). The
binding materials have been chosen for strength and durability.

AUTHOR'S NOTE

I AM NOT AN HISTORIAN. ON THE CONTRARY, I WAS A BROADWAY COL-
UMNIST AND BEGAN WRITING BOOKS AS SAMMY DAVIS, JR.'S BIOGRA-
PHER (YES I CAN, 1965). MY ONLY CREDENTIALS AND MOTIVATION FOR
writing this historical account are that my wife, Jane, and I visited Spain
in 1969 as guests of the Australian tennis player Lew Hoad, who lived
there. We found it a beautiful, peaceful place where it took a few years to
get a telephone (at that time), and it was therefore better suited for writing a book than the red-hot center of Manhattan, where we had time-
consuming family obligations. So we rented a house for nine months to
get a good start on a novel set in the world of tennis, later published by
Random House as World Class. We stayed for twenty-eight years. At the
beginning we had no clue that our "landlady" was the Chief of State's
daughter, Carmen, or that we would become intimately friendly with
Carmen and her husband, Cristóbal, their children, and their circle of
lifelong friends. During those nearly three decades, which included many
long weekends with Carmen and Cristóbal at their home and at ours, we
became aware of Spain's quiet and inadvertent role in World War II. Being
writers, and Americans who had been brought up to believe: General
Franco—Dictator—Bad, we saw it as an eye-opening, little known World
War II story. With our Spanish friends' help we researched it and were
given extraordinary access to former Ministers and others who had been
there. Among them were General Franco's wife, his brother-in-law
Ramón Serrano Suñer, who had been his Foreign Minister and was the
only surviving attendee at the meeting between Hitler and Franco in the

Führer's train at Hendaye, and his daughter Carmen, who has an extraordinary memory and sense of history. Those who know her refer to her as *Franco con falda*. Franco in skirts.

When we asked Carmen and Cristóbal to help us make appointments to interview former Cabinet members and high-ranking military, they said, "If we call they will, of course, receive you with courtesy. But there is a better way . . ."

Franco owned a *finca*, a farm half an hour out of Madrid called Valdefuentes where once a year he held a *cacería*, a partridge shoot, attended by his intimates, the very people we wanted to interview. Franco had died in November of 1975, and it was a few weeks before the spring *cacería* would take place, for the first time without him.

Carmen continued, "If we invite you to Valdefuentes for the shoot they will see you with us and understand that you are *de confianza*. When you speak to them later they will be much more forthcoming than they normally would be with foreigners." And so it happened. At lunch at Valdefuentes, a sad occasion as Franco's absence caused many a moist eye; Jane and I were pointedly seated beside Mrs. Franco and Carmen. The message was sent and received. All doors opened.

With such friends we are virtually assured of being called "apologists" and accused of "whitewashing" Franco. But the facts are the facts. History does not change by the opinion or the gesture of a friend, not to the right or to the left. I repeat, we Americans, as well as most of the world, were taught to view Franco as a Fascist-anti-Semite-friend-of-Hitler.

Decide for yourself.

PREFACE

"GENERALÍSIMO FRANCISCO FRANCO, THE CAUDILLO OF SPAIN, WAS THE MOST TENACIOUS AND MOST SUCCESSFUL OF TWENTIETH CENTURY DICTATORS. HE IS REMEMBERED WIDELY AS THE ASTUTE GENERAL under whose leadership the Nationalist cause was victorious in the Spanish Civil War, and the Communist threat exterminated, and as the head of state who successfully negotiated safe passage for Spain through World War Two, played Hitler off against the Allies, modernized his country and orchestrated the Spanish economic miracle of the 1960s. Having deftly schooled the young prince Juan Carlos to be his successor, by the time of his death in 1975 he had steered a unified Spain to world-wide respectability and envy. To many, the Caudillo was Spain incarnate—a heroic figure to match his predecessors El Cid, Charles V and Philip II . . . "

— FRANCO by Paul Preston
HarperCollins (dust-jacket copy)

The above is historical fact. Our book deals with the element of playing Hitler off against the Allies and keeping Germany out of Spain and Spain out of World War II. This is the story of how Franco did it. It was difficult for him, and dangerous, but the record stands: Germany was not able to use Spain to win the war against England in 1939.

We have "novelized" this story in order to make history more readable and, one hopes, more widely read. But our material is drawn from interviews and conversations with primary sources, family members who were privy to tightly held information. Personal details such as Hitler's physical gestures, Franco's comments and manner, were told to us by Ramón Serrano Suñer, Franco's brother-in-law and Minister of Foreign Affairs at that time. They were: Hitler and Franco; their foreign ministers, Serrano Suñer and von Ribbentrop; and one interpreter each.

Among other people we interviewed were personal friends, and their help went beyond normal interviews. An example: the Marqués de Santa Cruz spent many hours with us at dinner in our home in Marbella reminiscing about his life as Counselor to the Duke of Alba, Spanish Ambassador to London during World War II, who was also a cousin of Winston Churchill. These conversations have been used in the scenes with Alba and Churchill.

Much other information came to us from Mrs. Franco, their daughter Carmen (today the Duchess of Franco), some of General Franco's papers and an eight-page letter written by his interpreter at the meeting, the Barón de las Torres, and interviews with the Barón's son.

The only departure from documentable nonfiction occurs in four scenes with invented dialogue such as Hitler alone with von Ribbentrop, or in his office with his General Staff. Enough has been written on Hitler's manner, dialogue and pendular mood swings for us to portray him with reasonable accuracy. And the historical facts supported by his own letters to Franco concerning those moments make it clear as to what he would have been saying.

Other than those four instances (and the Prologue, which is patently fiction, a nightmare scenario intended to alarm the reader with what might have been) every other statement, every scene, every conversation is faithful to historical fact and is supported by unquestionable sources.

PROLOGUE

May 8, 2005

P UBLIC SCHOOL 81, NEW YORK, N.Y. *"GUTEN MORGEN, KINDER,"* THE
TEACHER SAYS, WELCOMING THE CHILDREN BACK FROM TWO WEEKS
VACATION IN CELEBRATION OF ADOLF HITLER'S BIRTHDAY, APRIL 20TH.
Forty-five years earlier the National Holiday had replaced Easter, Christ-
mas and any other celebrations of God or Jesus Christ. Also abolished and
long forgotten are the birthdays of George Washington and Abraham
Lincoln and other once-traditional American holidays such as Thanks-
giving and the Fourth of July.

The teacher and students extend their right arms in stiff salute to the
crimson flag with a black swastika in its center, and they all sing the
national anthem, *Deutschland Über Allus.*

This routine start of the day is taking place in every school in every
city in the United States of Germany. English, French and Spanish have
not been taught in fifty years. Since the Third Reich conquered the world
in 1941, the only language spoken is German, except for Japanese throughout the Orient. There are still some people who remember English, and
speak it behind closed doors, but they are dying out, as are the elderly who
dare speak French in what had been France.

Hitler, Goebbels, Goering and Himmler died of old age and were
given funerals befitting their leadership of the world. Hitler's tomb is a
glass-enclosed shrine atop his favorite mountain in the Bavarian Alps.
These leaders and shapers of the New World have been replaced by young,

well-schooled Third Reich party-liners. The print press, Hollywood film industry and all radio and television are strictly controlled by the state under the *Reichsaussenminister* of Culture, Goebbels, a nephew of Hitler's late propaganda chief. There are no synagogues because there are no longer any Jews, an extinct race. In New York's Manhattan, St. Patrick's Cathedral has been renovated into a mansion for the appointed Governor of the Eastern Seaboard. By law, all government officials, including schoolteachers, must be of pure German descent for three generations. Other churches have been turned into office buildings, gymnasiums and meeting halls or into mansions for lesser political leaders. There is no organized religion, only "devotion to the state." All Negroes have been "repatriated" to African countries. Only a few hundred Jews remain in the world, all elderly or ancient. There have been no young Jews born since 1948, when all male Jews were sterilized by castration. In Hitlerton D.C., the Washington Monument, the Lincoln Memorial and other American shrines were razed to make room for a massive concentration camp to house the Jews whose lives were spared for humanitarian reasons. Soon they will be extinct. There are no dollars, pounds, francs or pesetas. The world currency is the Reichsmark.

It began sixty years ago . . .

1940

THE SWASTIKA FLIES OVER THE WHITE HOUSE, AS IT FLIES ABOVE BUCKINGHAM PALACE, THE PALACE OF ELYSÉE AND ALL WORLD CAPITALS. ON THE THRONE OF ENGLAND SIT THE FORMER DUKE AND Duchess of Windsor, brought back from Mr. Churchill's "out of harm's way" exile, where the Duke served as Governor of the Bahamas, and appointed King and Queen of England by Adolf Hitler.

In Hitlerton D.C., Joseph P. Kennedy, the outspoken isolationist, German sympathizer and former American Ambassador to the Court of St. James, is now Hitler's appointed President of the United States.

Franklin Delano Roosevelt, Winston Churchill and Charles de Gaulle, their wrists bound by barbed wire, wearing barbed-wire collars around their necks linked together by short chains, and crowns of barbed wire drawn tightly around their heads, blood dripping from their foreheads, are forced to stand in the rear of an open touring car flying swastikas on its fenders, as they are paraded through New York City, Chicago and Los Angeles as Criminals of War. On their chests are cardboard signs reading: "I Killed American Boys," "I Killed English Boys," "I Killed French Boys." Crowds of silent, helpless Americans watch them. When the vilified wartime leaders of the United States, England and France have been seen throughout the country, they will be returned to Hitlerville, where they are sentenced to be hanged for "irresponsible villainy and war crimes" on scaffolds erected in front of the former Justice Department. Even if they are dead by then. The nooses will be made of piano wire, Hitler's method of "twisting the knife," reserved for special enemies.

In New York City an unknown American patriot shoots a storm trooper in the leg. Immediately, 100 Americans are arrested at random, dragged into the ice-skating rink at Rockefeller Center and machine-gunned to death in reprisal. On NBC radio H.V. Kaltenborn reads: "For every German attacked in any way, 100 Americans will be executed immediately. If this lawlessness continues the quota will rise to 500 Americans executed, or 1000 . . ."

The Third Reich has "nationalized" all media. NBC Radio's David Sarnoff, a Jew, is imprisoned. CBS Radio's William Paley, a Jew, is imprisoned. *The New York Times* owner and publisher Arthur Hayes Sulzberger, a Jew, is imprisoned. All editorial directors are removed as "unreliable" and imprisoned.

Concentration camps are being hastily prepared in New York State, Illinois, Florida and Southern California for the dangerous Jewish population until a final solution is reached.

From the White House, President Joseph P. Kennedy speaks to the nation in a manner reminiscent of ex-President "Roosenfeld's" Fireside Chats, using all the facilities of American radio: NBC's Red and Blue Networks, CBS Radio and the Mutual Broadcasting System, reading an address written by Hitler's chief of propaganda Joseph Goebbels: "My countrymen," he intones, "and you *are* my countrymen, stay in your homes, surrender your arms if you have any. Do not be troublemakers. We Americans have nothing to fear from our friends the Germans and particularly from their benevolent, humanitarian leader, the *Führer* who dreams and works only toward peace in the world. He has sent his people here to protect our freedom from the eternally troublemaking subversive elements . . ."

There will be no World War II.

The map of the world is black.

1939

A DOLF HITLER GAZES OUT THE PICTURE WINDOW IN HIS "TEA HOUSE" AT THE *BERGHOF*, HIS FORTIFIED MOUNTAIN CHALET AT BERCHTESGADEN, A QUIET TOWN IN THE SOUTHEAST OF BAVARIA. Behind him stand his naval chief Grand Admiral Raeder and the chief of his land forces General Jodl, who has just given him the news that France has fallen with hardly a shot fired, that the "invincible" Maginot Line was a farce, and at that moment twenty divisions of *Wehrmacht* are rolling through France, climbing the Pyrenees mountains toward the border towns of Hendaye and Spain's Irún.

"Jodl," Hitler smiles, "I am looking at my beautiful snow-covered Alps, but what am I seeing?"

"The world, *Führer*."

Hitler beams. "And that, my dear Jodl, is why you command our magnificent *Wehrmacht*."

Happy to be in the good graces of his master, still Jodl understands the time pressure. England is fighting alone with only economic help from the United States. But one day, soon, there will be the dreaded American presence in Europe. Germany needs to win the war before America arms herself. Despite the strong America First movement, German Intelligence has learned that Roosevelt is secretly planning America's physical entry into a decisive war. Germany does not want such a potentially formidable foe.

"*Führer*," Jodl ventures delicately, "our glorious march to world victory is predicated on the condition that General Franco will cooperate . . ."

"Cooperate? COOPERATE you say? Little Franco? He will lick the boots of all German troops entering Spain. If I order it, the *Generalísimo* will personally carry us piggyback across Spain to Gibraltar."

"But *Führer*, he has not been notified of the *Führer's* wishes."

"The sight of twenty divisions will notify him. He will know his duty to the Third Reich. He knows who won his Spanish Civil War for him. He knows that if I had not intervened he would have lost his petty conflict and would be in a Communist prison today. Or executed." Hitler smiled benevolently, "No, Jodl, have no fear. Little Franco is a friend who will perform his historic role . . . "

And so it passed. The black mass of twenty divisions of the *Wehrmacht* arrived at Hendaye, and as the vast clouds of dust from all those tanks and personnel carriers settled, the Spanish customs officials at the town of Irún raised the barrier, saluted and gestured for the Germans to enter.

Just inside Spain was a car sent by *El Caudillo* in which his brother-in-law, Ramón Serrano Suñer, Spain's Foreign Minister, waited with the Barón de las Torres, Franco's personal translator.

Serrano Suñer put his arms around the German commander, hugging him in the traditional Spanish *abrazo*. "*Mi General*," he said, aided by the Baron's fluent German. "I greet you in the name of the Spanish Chief of State, General Francisco Franco Bahamonde, and bid you welcome to our poor country. What little we have is yours. *El Caudillo* has provided troops to escort the great *Wehrmacht* safely through Spain's hazardous terrain to Gibraltar. And eternally grateful Spaniards wish you and the *Führer's* mighty soldiers Godspeed."

The black column snaked its way down the mountains to the coast, and then traveled the dirt road along the Mediterranean through Málaga, Torremolinos, Fuengirola, Marbella and Estepona. At every *pueblo* the streets were lined with Spaniards waving miniature flags of the Third Reich. The German might rolled through La Linea and onto British-held Gibraltar, which, contrary to general perception, is not an island but part of the Spanish mainland. The few lightly armed British soldiers and English Bobbies offered no resistance to the tanks and personnel carriers, of the *Wehrmacht*.

German U-boats had arrived and closed off the Mediterranean to British shipping. Now, as Hitler had planned, the British would be unable to supply themselves without this inland sea, as the alternative long route to their colonies was impossible. America's foreign aid was only money, and they could not fight without food and raw materials imperative to military supplies.

Contrary to British bluster that if needs be the Government would move to Canada and carry on the war against Hitler, Churchill sued for peace and signed a surrender with Germany's Foreign Minister Joachim von Ribbentrop. The ceremony took place at Buckingham Palace and was followed by the raising of the Swastika atop the historical home of the British monarch. The entire Royal Family was removed to prison in Berlin.

Events moved quickly. Now the Master of Europe and Great Britain, Hitler ordered his troops through Africa, where with nothing to oppose them they gained the land, slave labor and vast mineral wealth of the continent. From Africa they swept over South America and Australia, and quickly the map of the world was dominated by black swastikas. There remained only the United States of America.

By January of 1940 the ships of the French and British navies, sailing under German flags and German command, arrived on the coasts of the United States: Boston, New York, southern and northern California and Norfolk, Virginia. Some, for dramatic impact, sailed up the Potomac River to Washington D.C.

The American navy was almost entirely deployed in the South Pacific. The United States had a standing army of 150,000. Half of them carried twenty-two-year-old rifles from 1918, from World War I, with no ammunition or spare parts. The other half had wooden rifles, for marching. The Third Reich had just landed half a million heavily armed soldiers, battle hardened, and victory hungry.

Facing history's greatest firepower were only the state troopers and municipal police departments, who watched in silence as tanks, personnel carriers with light cannons, 50 mm machine guns and an endless mass of soldiers landed on the shores of the United States . . .

7

Note

What you have just read is, of course, fiction. It is what might have happened.

The following is what *did* happen.

PART ONE

CHAPTER ONE

1936

A MAN APPEARED ON THE ROAD NEAR THE GATES OF THE PALACE OF EL PARDO A FEW MILES OUTSIDE OF MADRID. HE WORE A WIDE-BRIMMED HAT AND A BLACK MUSTACHE AND GOATEE. HIS SKIN WAS VERY white. Even though it was nine-thirty in the evening he wore tinted glasses, commonly used by Mediterranean people. His suit was gray. He had no topcoat. It was May, and the Madrid weather was comfortably warm.

Two Moorish Guards on horseback outside the closed iron gates stood still as the man approached, staring directly ahead as if they had not seen him. On foot there were two sentinels of the Spanish Army. At once their rifles snapped from their shoulders and were held at port arms. A door within the gate opened, and two *Guardias Civiles* stepped out, members of the federal police force under army command. They wore tri-cornered patent leather hats, belts and holsters. The color of their uniforms, instead of dark green, was khaki, indicating that they were in the personal service of the Chief of State.[1]

One, a sergeant, spoke to the stranger. "Your name, please?"

"Reed Rosas."

"Who do you wish to see?"

"*El Generalísimo, por favor.*"

The sergeant looked at his subordinate, who with a shrug confirmed that they had not been advised of any further visitor. "Are you expected?"

"No."

The sergeant looked at him with curiosity. People did not "drop in" on *El Caudillo*, meaning The Leader, as did *Führer* and *Duce*.

The man said, "Telephone to the office and inform his Excellency that Reed Rosas would be grateful for an audience." He spoke gently but it was a command. His accent was odd. Southern, yet not true Andaluz, though similar . . . probably South American.[2]

The sergeant returned to the gate. Inside he telephoned to the palace, to the Captain of the *Guardias Civiles*. Then he waited for the Captain to telephone to *El Generalísimo's* aide, who, if he felt it appropriate, would speak to the Chief of State.

Spring rain began to fall. The two mounted Moorish Guards turned their horses toward the sentry boxes on either side of the gates, which had been built to accommodate both horse and rider. Their vigil continued through large windows.[3]

There was the sound of horses' hooves, and two more Moorish Guards approached from the left, while two others approached from the right, all at an easy canter. They passed each other and continued on the ceaseless round-the-palace inspection.

The sergeant returned and escorted the stranger through the door in the gate. In the courtyard were a full company of Infantry and two squads of mounted Moorish Guards, sixteen horses in all.[4]

The tight security was not gratuitous. It was impossible to be too careful, considering that *El Caudillo* could be assassinated only once.[5]

After the Spanish Civil War members of the Anarchist Party made attempts on the life of the man who had won the war and put them and their Popular Front Party out of power. At the end of the war Franco's headquarters had been in Burgos. When he elected to move to the traditional capital, Madrid, his wife, Carmen Polo, selected the Palace of Larios in the city proper, but the Chief of Security vetoed the site because it was surrounded by higher buildings from which a sniper could shoot at the *Generalísimo*, his wife or daughter as they walked in the garden. The home that could be protected most efficiently would be outside the city where there was less population; a residence that stood alone and could be completely surrounded. The Francos chose the Palace of El Pardo, which had been built in 1547 by Emperor Carlos I as a summer home and shooting preserve.[6] The palace was made independent of outside services with the installation of emergency electrical generators and a Captain of the Army Engineers whose sole work was maintaining the telephone lines.

A Moorish Guard stood before each of the three entrances to the palace. The Ambassadors' Entrance was almost always kept closed. The second, to the left, was the normal visitors' entrance and only the family used the third, to the right.[7]

A man wearing the livery of the *Casa Civil*, the organization of domestic servants who operated the homes of the Chief of State, approached the stranger. "I will escort *el señor* to the office of His Excellency."

They passed through the visitor's entrance and went up a flight of stairs. Then, instead of approaching the office of *El Caudillo* in the usual way, which would bring them through the aide's office where someone was waiting for an audience with Franco, the guide led the way into a library, which provided a different entrance to the office of the Chief of State. There were four: two leading to offices of his aides, one to the *Sala de Consejos* in which Cabinet meetings were held, and this one through the library that also led to the living quarters. A Lieutenant Colonel of the Army, seeing the stranger approach, used a key to open a door that, like the other entrances to the office of *El Caudillo*, had no handle or knob.[8]

Francisco Franco stood in the center of the large room, his body erect, his eyes impenetrable. He wore an army officer's uniform, his waist encircled by the red sash, which denotes the rank of General. There was nothing to show that he alone held the rank of *Generalísimo*: the General of all Generals. It was hardly necessary. All coins from the Spanish mint bore his right profile and the legend *"El Caudillo de España por la G de Dios,"* the leader of Spain by the grace of God; his portrait was on postage stamps of all denominations; the legend is that as he passed through a *pueblo* and people turned out en masse for a look at their Chief of State, a peasant asked his five-year-old son, "Do you know who that was?" and the boy replied, "The man from the stamps." His photograph was displayed in every governmental office in Spain and in most private homes, even those in which he was little admired. There was not a *pueblo* or city in Spain without a principal plaza, park or avenue named Franco or *El Generalísimo*. He held supreme power. In his own words, by edict, "The *Caudillo* is responsible only before God and history."

The crystal lamps and chandelier in his office had been made by the Royal Manufacturer of La Granja, and dated back to the 1700's, the reign of Carlos IV. The tapestries depicting the battles of Carlos I in Tunis were made in Flanders in the sixteenth century while it was still Spanish territory, ordered by Carlos I for this palace, which he then had under construction. The furniture, all the product of the Royal Cabinetmakers was old, fine and comfortable.[9]

There were no personal photographs in Franco's office. On a marble radiator cover behind his desk were autographed pictures of Adolf Hitler, Benito Mussolini and Pope Pius XII.[10]

On the right and left of his desk were piles of papers ranging from reports from his ministers to Orders of Execution and Pardon, which required his signature. It was orderly disorder in which Franco knew almost precisely where each document rested. On a table were all newly published books in which an aide routinely underlined passages that El Caudillo would find interesting.[11]

He was accustomed to reading with a pencil in hand, blue or red, the red for underlining what he disliked or saw as danger, the blue indicating favorable reaction. He was a pencil biter while reading or pondering, his teeth touching only a half-inch section in the middle.[12]

When the door closed behind the visitor and the two men were alone, Franco's facial expression softened immediately and he walked toward his guest. Reserved, even when feeling effusive, Franco's abrazo, the hug which close friends exchange in greeting, was only a strong handshake, a rapid, solid, patting of the man's shoulder with his left hand, combined with a brilliant smile.[13]

They sat on a sofa and "Reed Rosas" peeled off his mustache and goatee, rubbed his face, soothing some of the itch of the adhesive. He slipped off the dark glasses and black wig, revealing blue eyes, which few Spaniards have, and slightly thin silver hair on a head that seemed too large for his body.[14]

"Excellency, soon Hitler will turn to a friendly and indebted Spain as his key to the Mediterranean. That is part of the reasoning with which I convinced him to lend aid to the Nationalist cause in 1936. Now he is studying a proposal for the taking of Gibraltar and will want to know if your Excellency is interested in re-integrating the Rock of Gibraltar into

Spanish territory, in return for entering the war at his side by allowing him access to Gibraltar and North Africa from your southern shore. All studies on the taking of Gibraltar indicate a near-absolute necessity that the attack be launched from Spanish soil."

Franco made no comment, but he had to be thinking: Hardly a year past a civil war, the country decimated, hungry, and now threatened with another conflict. Of course the return of Gibraltar was alluring, but allowing German troops to pass over Spanish territory for such an attack would end his declared neutrality and officially make Spain a belligerent, at Germany's side.

"Your Excellency's knowledge of this document could be useful." Reed Rosas handed a paper to Franco. "It is a summary of a series of reports Hitler is studying. They were filed by the Condor Legion regularly between 1936 and 1939, and they include details on the terrain and weather which the Legion encountered here and how it effected their efficiency. They concentrate especially on the north—where the German troops coming through France would have to enter—as being terrible for flying and worse for infantry and mechanized cavalry. The essence is that if Germany had to *invade* Spain in order to pass through to Gibraltar it is estimated that to get one fighting man over the Pyrenees and into Spain would require losing from six to seven others who would not survive. Clearly it would be more convenient to be invited to enter.

"Failing such an invitation, one must confront the unknown, the erratic nature of Hitler's personality. He is emotional, radical and extravagant when it serves him . . ."

Reed Rosas was re-applying his disguise, using the polished inside of a silver cigarette case as a mirror. "Excellency, when one day your guards inform you that there is at the gate a pathetic, disheveled-looking person claiming to be Don Ignacio Moreno de Talavera, a monk who has traveled from Toledo on mule, I hope that you will not turn me away."

It was ten minutes past ten o'clock. Franco's wife and daughter would be expecting him for dinner in twenty minutes. He went to his desk and wrote a résumé of the conversation.

If Hitler was examining the cost and hazards of invading Spain did that mean that he was not confident of Spanish friendship? Or was it simply appropriate prudence?

Ready to leave, Franco rang for the aide who was responsible for the key to his office, who locked and unlocked it only for *El Caudillo* himself, and the maids who cleaned it in the presence of the aide.[15]

At Puerta del Sol, Madrid's Times Square, Reed Rosas got out of a taxi and disappeared into the densely populated streets, threading his way to the Royal Theater. At midnight, when the performance was over, a silver-haired, fifty-ish gentleman with a rather large head and very white skin left the theater and got into a waiting chauffeur-driven Mercedes-Benz.

Franco met with his Council of Defense: Admiral Moreno and Generals Vigón and Varela, Ministers of Navy, Air and Army. Speaking principally to Varela he described his information on Hitler's desires with regard to Spain. "The *Führer* could become impatient and decide to enter without our permission. It would be prudent to anticipate that possibility with a force of infantry in the north. Bearing in mind the large number of *Gestapo* and *Abwehr* agents in Spain, this would be observed and interpreted accurately as to our intentions. Therefore . . ."

The toughest combat soldiers and officers from the garrisons in the south, Seville, Málaga and Granada as well as less southerly cities as Valencia were given "furloughs." Wearing civilian clothes, they carried suitcases concealing rifles and ammunition, knives, dynamite, grenades and other weapons of guerrilla warfare. A team of three men carried the parts of a dismantled 50mm machine gun; the suitcases of four others together concealed the components of an antitank gun. They traveled individually by bus and train to San Sebastian and Bilbao and to all the *pueblos* between these cities, posing as civilians looking for work. They stayed in rooming houses and pensions and followed a plan of daily contact with the garrison at San Sebastian.

Simultaneously, work gangs appeared in the north under the auspices of the Ministry of Public Works for the declared purpose of repairing the roads and bridges damaged during the Civil War. The Spanish press explained that this was a two-fold effort to rebuild Spain and to provide work for its idle young men. These "idle young men" worked with picks and shovels on the much-needed reconstruction. Concealed were the arsenals for their real work: guerrilla warfare.

At the Ministry of Foreign Affairs, the Minister, Colonel Juan Beigbeder read a cablegram from the British Foreign Secretary, Lord Halifax, delivered to him minutes before by the British Embassy's *chargé d'affaires*.

IMMEDIATE, MADRID   LONDON, 15 MAY 1940
CONFIDENTIAL

PLEASE ASCERTAIN WHETHER NOMINATION OF SIR SAMUEL HOARE AS AMBASSADOR TO MADRID WOULD MEET WITH ACCEPTANCE OF THE SPANISH GOVERN-MENT. SIR SAMUEL HAS SERVED FOR THIRTY FOUR YEARS IN THE HOUSE OF COMMONS; FOUR TIMES AIR MINISTER; FIRST LORD OF THE ADMIRALTY; SECRETARY OF STATE FOR INDIA; SECRETARY OF STATE FOR HOME AFFAIRS; SECRETARY OF STATE FOR FOREIGN AFFAIRS; LORD PRIVY SEAL OF THE WAR CABINET.
     PLEASE INFORM SPANISH GOVERNMENT THAT AN EARLY REPLY WOULD BE APPRECIATED.

HALIFAX[16]

El Caudillo listened as Minister Beigbeder read off Sir Samuel's pedigree.

"Excellency, they wouldn't be sending somebody of such category unless there was something of commensurate value to be accomplished here. And what could it be other than to assure our neutrality in order for them to preserve their hold on the Mediterranean? This could answer all of our needs, Excellency. The British Empire could provide or get from America everything that Spain lacks."

"You may advise them that he is acceptable."

Ambassador and Lady Hoare left London on May 29, 1940, destination Madrid via Lisbon. The British Airways plane was occupied only by the Hoares, their butler and a bodyguard from Scotland Yard. As they made conversation their eyes remained fixed on the sky beyond, peering at clouds for the planes of the *Luftwaffe*.[17]

In Lisbon they were met at the airport by Hoare's old friend of Oxford and Foreign Office days, Walford Selby. "You'll be staying on with us for a while," he said giving Sir Samuel a telegram.

IMMEDIATE, LISBON   LONDON, 29 MAY 1940

PLEASE PASS FOLLOWING MESSAGE TO SIR SAMUEL
HOARE: AWAIT FURTHER INSTRUCTIONS BEFORE
PROCEEDING TO MADRID.

HALIFAX[18]

As they drove to the embassy Selby said, "All of Lisbon sees the
Nazis occupying France within a week. That would bring them to the
Spanish border in the Pyrenees in a fortnight."[19]

When the Hoares had left London thirty-six hours earlier, Spain had
been five hundred miles from any fighting front. Sir Samuel asked,
"What is the consensus as to what Franco will do when the Nazis reach
his border?"[20]

"Nine out of ten Spaniards consider Hitler invincible. And Franco is
among them. I have not spoken to a soul who has the slightest doubt that
Franco will immediately welcome the Germans into Spain."[21]

Hoare reflected: Why would he not? How could he refuse passage
through Spain to the army that had fought at his side on that same
ground? To do so would be a provocation Hitler would not tolerate, in
which case the troops, which had conquered nearly a continent in six
months, would simply invade Spain.

"Here in Lisbon there is nothing but terror. When Franco allows the
Nazis into Spain then it's just a matter of hours before they'll be here.
One might say that the moment the Germans pass onto Spanish territory
the war is over and Hitler has won the map of Europe.[22] Worse, having
occupied Portugal and Gibraltar, he will continue into North Africa and
the Middle East, gathering momentum with nothing to oppose him.
With two continents and all of their manpower and resources he could
become the ruler of the world."

One man, Francisco Franco, was in the position to win the war and
two continents for Germany simply by allowing the tanks, artillery and
infantry of the *Wehrmacht* to pass through Spain. All he had to do was:
nothing. And who would fault him for not taking up his country's pitiful
arms against Hitler's forces?

But, if he had the desire, and if somehow he could manage to refuse to allow the Germans onto Spanish soil—if he were successful, he could keep the Mediterranean open and thereby confine Hitler to Europe.

But how could he oppose the Nazi might?

And why should he try? Wasn't the first rule of statesmanship to be on the winning side?

Waiting in Lisbon, sitting in the garden of the Embassy and listening to the radio, Sir Samuel heard of the disaster of Dunkirk, the French seaport where the Germans had just chased 325,000 British and French troops across the Channel, fleeing with their lives, abandoning hundreds of tons of military equipment. It was the defeat that four days later caused Winston Churchill to broadcast to the British people:

". . . Everyone who had a boat of any kind, steam or sail, put out for Dunkirk. There came to the rescue of the army, under the ceaseless air bombardment of the enemy, about eight hundred and fifty vessels of which nearly seven hundred were British and the rest Allied. Of course, whatever happened at Dunkirk, we shall fight on. We shall go on to the end, we shall never surrender . . ."[23]

But the radio reported only continuing bad news, and Sir Samuel expected that his mission, which had seemed so urgent, so vital, would end before it started.[24]

Ramón Serrano Suñer, Franco's brother-in-law and his Minister of the Interior, slender, handsome, prematurely gray, dressed in a well-tailored black suit, sat in the Cabinet Room, at the Palace of El Pardo, addressing the Chief of State. "Excellency, now is the time. If we declare ourselves at war, as our German friends desire, we can name our terms: Gibraltar, everything that should still be ours in Morocco, plus more. Why are we waiting?"

At the head of an oblong table, Francisco Franco presided over a weekly cabinet meeting. At the beginning of the Franco government, during the war in 1938, there were eleven ministers. Now, in June of 1940, more ministries had been developed and there were thirteen. The cabinet was delicately balanced; a conservative traditionalist offset each radical Falangist. Each civilian minister by an Admiral or General. Even within the Monarchists he balanced the Carlists and the liberal Monarchists.

The balance failed only in regard to Anglophiles versus Germanophiles, the latter being a strong majority except the Ministers of Army, Navy and Air, who were respectively pro-English, pro-English, pro-German.

The meetings began at ten A.M. every Friday. At two-thirty there was a two-hour break for lunch. A buffet was prepared for the Ministers in an adjacent room, while Franco returned to his quarters to lunch with his wife and daughter and to give the Ministers a break from his presence. After lunch they resumed without stopping for dinner even if the meeting should continue until four in the morning.[25] There were no ashtrays, no pitchers of water and glasses on the table; the only amenity was dishes of hard candies. Though Franco was a nonsmoker he never forbade it. Yet, no Minister ever smoked during a cabinet meeting. If one wished to leave the room he first attracted *El Caudillo*'s attention and received a gesture of permission.

Franco spoke little, listening to the Ministers' reports and needs, occasionally making a note. He gave no immediate answers, by practice. Everything would be answered, but never at the moment. When he did speak, he was one of the rare people with the capacity of beginning and ending a subject, pursuing a single line of thought to its conclusion without digressing.[38]

When a Minister had completed the business of his Ministry he was free to leave, with permission, and smoke or have a drink in the adjoining room. Franco remained throughout the business of each Minister. He never left the room during a cabinet meeting. [(26)]

Though Ministers were not required to stand while speaking, the urgency of Serrano Suñer's feelings had brought him to his feet. "Why are we waiting before joining a war that is virtually won?"

Lt. General José Varela, the Anglophile Minister of War, retorted, "Our army is not in condition to fight a war that lasts more than two days. Our soldiers are well disciplined and they have infantry arms fit for war, but we have ammunition for two days of combat, our artillery pieces are mostly worn out, we have two hundred light tanks but no spare parts.

"As for personnel our army consists of twenty-seven divisions, we have 340,000 soldiers but few officers. Civil War losses have left our scheduled positions short of Majors by fifty percent, Captains ninety percent and Lieutenants nearly one hundred percent. If our troops are placed in the intolerable position of having to fight without leaders, without ammunition or food, without even proper shoes on their feet . . ." He gestured to indicate futility. "We need eight years to train officers, to equip ourselves . . ."

"The *Führer* will provide what we need," interrupted Serrano Suñer, "once we prove that we are his allies."

"So will the British," said the Anglophile Beigbeder. "Great Britain would not be sending Sir Samuel Hoare if they did not intend to help economically to make our neutrality possible. The British have never lost a war. The English bull has not yet come into the ring."

"Poetic," Serrano Suñer snapped, "but the fact is that the English bull has his tail between his legs. Dunkirk was a slaughter." Turning again to *El Caudillo*, "Excellency, Hitler was our friend in '36. He has a right to expect us to respond to his needs as a debt of gratitude."

Franco listened, his large, brown eyes fixed on the speaker. He rarely interrupted. His responsibilities had made him a good listener.

Beigbeder argued, "We should stay out of the war until someone has it won, and hope that we are on good terms with that side."

Serrano scoffed, "'This 'someone?' Who can resist the German forces? History has never known such armies. *El Caudillo* himself told me that he believed the Germans to be invincible."

If Franco had wanted to be quoted he would have said it himself. He gave Serrano Suñer a *mirada,* a glare that withered the recipient like a bolt of lightning. His brother-in-law sat down. Even those Ministers who did not like Serrano Suñer were sympathetic. Franco never raised his voice. He never had to; if annoyed he just looked at the offender in a way that said it all.[27]

The expression on Franco's face softened. "Ramón, Ramón, Ramón . . . out of a total population of some twenty-three million we have hardly a woman who isn't dressed in black. Ramón . . . there are no tears left . . ."

Franco did not command his Ministers, preferring always to convince, willing to sit in the meeting all night if necessary until he knew that they had been fully persuaded over to his point of view and would work *with* instead of for him.[28]

Now he turned his attention to those pro-German Ministers, notably Serrano Suñer and General Vigón, Minister of Air. "Ramón is correct. I believe that Germany is invincible. *At this moment!* But other men have been invincible: Charlemagne, Alexander the Great, Napoleon. Then they made mistakes, or encountered surprises, and each eventually lost. We should not allow ourselves to fall into a state of collective amnesia to which we dreaming *Hidalgos*, the sons of Don Quijote, are so prone. The only way to be sure to win a war is to stay out of it."[29]

He addressed his brother-in-law. "You called Hitler our friend, Ramón. He is a friend to no one but Germany, as we are friends only to Spain. Let us stick to the realities and avoid the Utopian such as friendship between states.

"You also referred to Spain's debt to Hitler. Both issues are false. Hitler sent help to us to prevent Communism from taking over Spain, that would have eliminated his hopes for the Mediterranean and Africa. His help was entirely self-serving.

"I, who was conducting the war, appealed for the specific weapons we needed: machine guns, tanks, anti-aircraft batteries to protect the cities we held, and most important: antitank artillery to combat the heavy Russian tanks.

"Why, then, did he elect to send the Condor Legion: forty-eight bombers, forty-eight fighters, plus a total of fourteen reconnaissance planes and three anti-aircraft batteries?

"He sent the Condor Legion to practice aerial warfare and new bombing techniques on the Spanish people. Spain was the *Luftwaffe*'s training ground. They arrived here as green pilots who had never dropped a bomb. In two months they had received their training and were replaced by more green pilots.[30]

"And, to add a touch of the ludicrous, they have sent us a bill of three hundred and eighty million Deutschmarks to pay for those bombs, and the air fuel and their soldiers' food and salaries while training them.

"The only reason I do not flatly deny a debt to Hitler is because this is not the time to ruffle him. We will pet and pamper him, but let it be understood in this meeting: there is no debt.

"Further we did not go to war and kill our sons and brothers to keep out Communism, only to now accept Nazism.

"We will continue to buy peace with words. Have the press continue to flatter the Germans and the Italians; let the Falange display enmity to the Allies—but keep that under control. Let's not anger the mad dogs *or* the Englishmen. Continue giving the Germans full police cooperation . . . anything Hitler wants that has little meaning. But no German troops will cross Spanish soil."

Every Minister, even the most Germanophile, General Vigón, was in agreement with *El Caudillo*. Only Serrano Suñer seemed doubtful. Shaking his head slowly, he looked at Franco. "You always used to say, 'War was my job.' Why do you stand back now?"

No one but his brother-in-law would have dared challenge *El Caudillo* like that. Franco's face showed nothing. He replied, "Was! Now peace is my job."

The *Generalísimo* looked from face to face, into the eyes of each of his thirteen ministers. "Today my job is to end four and a half centuries of an invertebrate Spain, of countless civil wars, chronic famine, military coups without number—all failures, as were the Republics. My job is to stop Spaniards from killing Spaniards. My job is to end the secular oligarchy so that for the good of Spain there will be rather fewer very rich people and rather fewer very poor. My job is to keep the Comintern out of Spain so that we never again see the hammer and sickle and red flags flying over our soil, reflecting the desperate state of the nation that caused the uprising and cost us one million Spaniards. One million dead in a single three-year period. What must the number be over four hundred and fifty years of more war than peace? If blood could enrich the soil, you could grow wheat on every square meter of Spanish land."

The intensity of Franco's feelings dried his throat and he stopped speaking for some seconds. "Granted, it would be nice to have Gibraltar, it would be nice to have the riches of Africa, but what is *imperative* is to return Spain to health from within. If we can accomplish that, and we can, we will enjoy the greatest riches of all: peace."

At two-thirty the Ministers left the meeting and Franco returned to his office. An aide awaiting him with the key opened the door. Franco kept his own key in his night table, not needing to carry it because there was at least one aide on duty twenty-four hours a day. They passed through his office, to the library. There, his wife and daughter and the other aide were waiting.[31]

He was happy to see Carmencita's best friend, Maruja Jurado, and kissed her hello. The Francos were always more comfortable when Carmencita was safely within the palace grounds and they encouraged her friends' visits.[32]

If she had been a boy she would have gone out to school, but in 1940 a girl married and raised a family, so the private tutor, Señorita Blanca Barreno, who lived at the palace, was quite adequate and made it unnecessary for Carmencita to leave every day. Never was she forbidden to go outside, and often she did, but always with plainclothes police in the car with her and another car with four more policemen directly behind.[33]

Franco and his wife sat across from each other on the sides of the oval dining table, the ranking aide sat on the right of Doña Carmen, the other on her left, and Carmencita normally sat on her father's right. But Maruja was given the seat of honor and Carmencita sat on her father's left.[34]

The aides on duty were always invited to lunch and dinner with the family as a military courtesy because they held ranks from major to colonel. Every General had two aides. The *Generalísimo* had six, one from each branch of the Army and one each from the Navy and Air Force. They rotated, providing around-the-clock, seven-day service. At lunch there were always two; one at dinner, there being only one on duty through the night.[35] But they entered into the conversations only minimally. After the meal the aides excused themselves and the Franco family enjoyed privacy over coffee in the adjacent Yellow Room.

The butler, Alejandro, had been with the Francos since Burgos, Nationalist Headquarters during the war, and he along with two others who were from the household of King Alfonso XIII belonged to the *Guardia Civil*. The three chefs, who rotated command of the kitchen, were members of the *Guardia Civil*, were all helpers, waiters and buyers of food, and were of special confidence, each of whom was known personally by the Chief of Security.[36]

Franco looked up with interest as Alejandro brought in the main course, and he smiled with pleasure at seeing that it was Galician soup, a stew of potatoes, vegetables, ham and pork fat, known as poor people's soup, to him a sort of soul food on which he had been raised in his hometown El Ferrol in Galicia. The menus at the Palace of El Pardo were distinctly more "soldier food" than "palace food."

"Let's save the rest of this for dinner," he told his wife.

The chef would be pleased to hear that, because Friday dinner was always a problem, there being no fixed hour to end the meeting. It could be at eleven P.M. or at three A.M., whenever the work was finished. The only certainty was that when dinner could be served, it had to be ready. Sometimes Friday dinners were good, sometimes they were not so good, and sometimes the food was cold, but it was always ready. At El Pardo food waited for people; people did not wait for food.[37]

IMMEDIATE, LISBON   LONDON, 30 MAY 1940
CLASSIFIED

PLEASE PASS THE FOLLOWING MESSAGE TO SIR SAMUEL HOARE: CONTINUE ON TO MADRID. HOLD THE PLANE THERE FOR USE IN THE LIKELY EVENT OF THE GERMANS ENTERING SPAIN AND YOUR NEED TO RETURN IMMEDIATELY TO LONDON.

HALIFAX[40]

Airborne again on June 1st, Sir Samuel and Lady Maud gazed downward at Portugal, green and flowery. As they flew over Spanish territory the change was abrupt. Brown and gray, the Spain of Extremadura and Castile yielded hardly a tree; long stretches of untilled land, craggy mountains and little sign of life between the scattered villages.[41] It was three in the afternoon when their plane landed at Barajas airfield outside of Madrid. The "aerodrome" looked like a small garage. Several *Guardias Civiles* in dark green uniforms were on duty as customs officers. They had been expecting the Hoares and passed their luggage without inspection.

Among those who had come to the airport to greet the new Ambassador was the British Embassy's Counselor, Arthur Yencken.[42] He rode back to Madrid with the Hoares in the Ambassador's Rolls Royce. The Ambassadorial pennon, a Union Jack with a coat of arms in its center, would not be unfurled on the right front fender until the Chief of State had received Hoare and his presence in Madrid had been made official.

"Your Excellency missed a nasty greeting the Falange had prepared for you. They were out en masse, surrounding the Embassy, shouting 'Gibraltar for Spain.' When you hadn't arrived by two-thirty the whole thing fizzled. It was deathly hot and they went off for lunch."[43]

"Not very dedicated, are they?" But Hoare recognized Gibraltar's return to Spain by a victorious Germany as a persuasive argument for Franco to join Hitler.[44]

Yencken said, "As the Embassy is partially dismantled and largely occupied by offices, I took the liberty of putting you up at the Ritz. It's still one of the best hotels in Europe."

Sir Samuel commented, "I haven't noticed a single car on the road since we left the airport."

"You are not likely to see many, sir. There's very little petrol and it's tightly rationed."

In Madrid they turned onto *El Paseo de la Castellana*, the city's splendid main artery. Yellow trolley cars ran along both edges. The broad center of *La Castellana* was well provided with benches from which nursemaids wearing long, plaid dresses with high, white lace collars and cuffs, beautifully starched and ironed, watched their equally starched, ironed and immaculate children.[45]

Sir Samuel was staring ahead. "I believe that I see a flock of sheep walking up the avenue."

Yencken confirmed it. "They're being brought to market."

Turning to his wife, Hoare observed, "Can you imagine a flock of sheep walking through Mayfair?"

Yencken said, "The expression 'Europe ends at the Pyrenees' is quite factual."[(46)]

"I daresay."

"Spain is not 'modern.' You will find no Coca-Cola, no modern materials such as plastic and nylon. But that is more than made up for by the quality of the people. With no tourism to speak of, they have not been contaminated by the outside world. They're still well-mannered, even the most humble, least educated. And generous and kind. If you were to ask how to get to a given address they would think nothing of leading you there even if it takes half an hour, and distinctly with no motive of being paid for their trouble. If, on a train, they were to open a package of lunch you would be invited to share with them.

"The majority are terribly poor; there's hardly a leather shoe among them. They wear *alpargatas*, a canvas, cord-soled shoe. In the country-side, they wear a sort of sandal that they make themselves using a slice of an old rubber tire for the soles. But they are gay and happy, the rich and the poor, because the war is over, the killing has ended."

"I've been informed you were here then."

"It was ghastly, your Excellency. Even for an observer. Nearly an entire generation of male heirs was lost. The official figure is a million dead. A woman I know lost thirty-two male relatives."

"Did you form any opinions that are not generally held?"

"Only, Excellency, that it would be simplistic to say that one side was all good and the other side all bad. The rights and wrongs, which caused the passions to rise so sharply, were not as visible as the end results. One's point of view is crucial: those who fought on what became Franco's Nationalist side tend still to call the enemy 'the reds' because they were backed by Soviet Russia. Russian Army Generals were a fixture in Madrid's best restaurants, and the International Brigade carried red flags. On the other hand those who supported the Popular Front Government, the Republicans, referred to the enemy as 'Fascists' because Hitler and Mussolini openly aided them.

"Indeed, what became the Civil War started as an uprising for law and order when a large number of Generals rose against what they considered a deliberately ineffective and Communist-directed government. With most of the Army on the Generals' side the Popular Front Government, to defend itself from being ousted, sent truckloads of rifles to the trade unions, where the members showed their cards to get a rifle and become a militiaman.

They were largely members of the Anarchist Party and once armed, their duty to defend the duly elected government gave way to personal grudges and prejudices. They burned hundreds of churches throughout Spain, killing the priests and nuns, even the altar boys. Being caught wearing a crucifix or any indication that you believed in religion, or that you had some money, sent you to prison or to death right on the spot as a 'Fascist.'

"Being titled was another death-sentence. The rich and the aristocrats fled Madrid for their lives. The militiamen moved into their homes. Not educated to such luxury, in winter they used fine antique pieces for firewood. The paintings were looted. And most of those collections contained several portraits of ancestors done by Goya and Velázquez. If they weren't sold they were disfigured; some slashed, some with a hammer and sickle splashed on them in red paint.

"When the present Christopher Columbus returned to his home after the Civil War he found his ancestor's archives—which had been assiduously catalogued, documents dating back to 1492, relating to the voyage itself—in the fireplace to be burned as trash. Their backs had been used as scorecards in card games.

"You'll find the Ritz filled with people who returned to Madrid and found their homes had been turned into nightclubs and youth hostels; destroyed or ransacked. The Duke of Alba's bed was discovered in the fifth-floor apartment of a militiaman. There's a flea market where these people search for their heirlooms and furniture, which they buy back."

They turned a corner and were approaching the Ritz. Sir Samuel commented, "What a lovely looking old building . . ." Then he gasped, "My God!" He was staring at the flag of the Third Reich, flying above the entrance, side by side with the flags of Spain and Italy.

"Startling," said Lady Maud, "to be looking for the first time at a swastika, in the flesh, so to speak."

Sir Samuel bristled, "Is this what Franco calls neutrality?"

"Your Excellency, I would suppose the hotel is simply pleasing its best clients. Perhaps your presence will cause them to raise our colors."

"Alongside the swastika? I shall urge against that courtesy."

Inside, very large men were grouped together, talking, filling the lobby with the sound of the German language.

"Gestapo," Yencken said.[47]

The Hoares had been checked in earlier, and it was only necessary for Yencken to show them Sir Samuel's passport as official identification. He returned from the reception desk, holding an envelope. "You've had a letter."

It was from the American Embassy in Madrid. Hoare pointed to the back flap. "This letter has been opened and resealed. It's completely obvious."

Yencken showed no surprise. "Your mail will almost certainly be opened and read, possibly even censored by the Spanish police. And it is likely that the Gestapo will be given a look. The Nazis will also listen to your phone conversations and search your rooms. You'll be followed by plainclothes policemen,[48] ostensibly to protect you, but in fact to report everywhere you went and to whom you spoke, to the Gestapo and to the Minister of the Interior, Franco's brother-in-law, Ramón Serrano Suñer, the *Cuñadísimo*."

"The what?"

"In Spanish the addition of 'ísimo' creates the superlative, as in *Generalísimo*; the General of Generals. *Cuñado* means brother-in-law, which one would never normally make into a superlative, so 'the *cuñadísimo*' is a bit of a whack at him because he's so powerful and not everyone's in love with him."

"His two names, Serrano Suñer? Refresh my memory on how that works, would you?"

"Serrano is his father's family name, Suñer is his mother's, which the Spanish add as a courtesy. As Serrano is a fairly common name, the addition of his mother's name helps identify him. Both names are used in written addresses. However, in person it would only be "Sr. Serrano . . ."" Yencken added, "How's your Spanish? Shall I get a tutor for you?"

Looking around with distaste, Hoare said, "It might be more useful to learn German."

Yencken guided the Ambassador and Lady Hoare through the lobby, toward glass doors that a pair of bellboys opened, and they passed into a salon. "This is the gossip center of Madrid. All the spies are here every day keeping an eye on each other: Czechs, Italians, Germans, Japanese—every nationality." He continued walking to the right. "Here's the dining room. It's excellent."

A dramatically tall and elegant couple, just leaving, passed them. The man was gray haired and six feet, six inches, the woman over six feet and blonde. Yencken murmured, "Baron and Baroness von Stohrer, the German Ambassador and his wife." Then, with sudden enthusiasm, gesturing to within the restaurant, "The man at the corner table is the bullfighter Manolete."

Sir Samuel looked at his wristwatch. It was nearly five o'clock. "They actually are still lunching? Incredible. I'm almost ready for dinner."

Lady Maud had been smiling, listening to the string music that was being played. Abruptly she frowned. She had always enjoyed Wagner. But here, with all those Germans, the *Führer's* favorite music offended her.

Alone in his office, at his desk, Franco was drafting a letter on a pad that bore the coat of arms of the Chief of State printed on each page. He studied the sentence, crossed it out and rephrased it. When he was finished he rang for the aide to have the letter typed. Then he telephoned to General Vigón. "Juan, I have a letter that I would like you personally to deliver in Berlin."

El Pardo, 3 June 1940

Dear Führer,

At a time when, under your guidance, the German armies are bringing to a glorious conclusion the greatest battle of history, I would like to offer to you the expression of my enthusiasm, as well as that of my people, who have been following with great emotion the glorious prosecution of a fight that it feels to be its own, and that realizes

*the hopes that were kindled in the days when your soldiers were
fighting side by side with ours in a war against the same, though
hidden, enemies.*

*I need hardly assure you that it is my sincere desire not to stand
aloof from the matters that preoccupy you, and that I would be deeply
gratified to render you at any time, such services as you might consider
most valuable.*

Francisco Franco[49]

"The British Ambassador is now in Madrid," Beigbeder said. "When would your Excellency like to receive him?"

"Let us give the new Ambassador the opportunity to do some sightseeing."

"Excellency?"

"I have always had the mentality of a fisherman and a peasant. The adequate use of time has been my most faithful instrument of action." Seeing that Beigbeder still did not understand, *El Caudillo* explained, "Juan, let us not appear eager. If I need a horse and I go to a man who needs to sell a horse, then despite our mutual need to strike a bargain the price is going to be higher than if he has to come looking for me and convince me to buy his horse. In this case, though we are not selling our neutrality we are encouraging the British desire to buy it."

It was a tea at the American Embassy, at six o'clock in the afternoon, or at six in the evening, depending upon one's nationality and customs.

The talk was exclusively of the oncoming German army and what would happen when its soldiers reached the Spanish border. Would they go straight down the coast to Gibraltar? Would they occupy Spain? Take over the capital?

An Allied diplomat commented, "There are probably ten thousand packed suitcases in Madrid, my own among them." He asked Sir Samuel, "Are you going to unpack?"

"Certainly. As long as we are in Madrid we intend to be comfortable. We have no intention of living in our trunks."[50] But indeed he and Lady Maud had brought only summer clothes, anticipating prompt German occupation of Spain, or Spanish declaration of joining the Axis, either of which would make a British Embassy in Madrid superfluous, if not impossible.

"But you've kept an airplane here, just in case."

"The plane was sent back yesterday."

The American Ambassador, Alexander Wilbourne Weddell, asked, "Do I understand correctly that you have found a house on La Castellana?"

"Quite. The atmosphere of the 'Reich Ritz' is not tolerable."

"But is it a fact that your house is immediately next to Ambassador von Stohrer's?"

"Yes. We are separated only by ideology and a single wall."

Despite feigning indifference, Sir Samuel had been less than delighted by the idea, but there was little choice with Madrid's best homes either occupied by their owners or dilapidated and pillaged during the war. He had finally found this very good house, and in addition to Lady Maud's liking it very much Sir Samuel viewed the proximity to the Nazi Ambassador as a propagandistic virtue.[51] He was now aware that the Spanish press never published anything positive about England, leaving Spanish readers knowing only of German victories. He reasoned that part of his work, therefore, must be to conduct himself with an air of such assurance of British strength as to convince the Spaniards that there existed an alternative to entering the war on the side of Germany. The presence of a "getaway plane" would be contrary to that illusion, which is why he had returned it.[52]

Hoare shrugged, "What does it matter that the Nazi Ambassador lives next door?"

"Don't you think it dangerous?"

"For me or for Baron von Stohrer?"

"I would not worry about von Stohrer. He goes nowhere without six immense Gestapo bodyguards, even when he walks from his car into his own Embassy."[53]

In fact, von Stohrer did not emerge from his car until the two bodyguards who rode in his front seat and four more from a car behind him had arranged themselves at his door in two files of three men. When he stepped out he was surrounded by his Gestapo officers, none of whom was less than six feet, six inches, in height.

The Nazi envoy always carried a black satchel-shaped briefcase that opened from the top. It contained, in addition to documents, a pistol and a hand grenade. The only place he did not carry it was into the Palace of El Pardo, where he left the satchel, and his bodyguards, at the gate.

Von Stohrer himself was so tall and generally large that when invited by *El Caudillo* to hunt *cabra hispanica*—a species of mountain goat whose habitation can only be reached on horseback—he brought along his own outsized stirrups because his shoes could not fit into normal ones.

Ambassador Weddell said, "Von Stohrer was here in 1918, as First Secretary, and the Spanish Government demanded his recall because the police found evidence that the Baron was involved in a plot against the life of Prime Minister Romanones."

Concealing his dismay, Hoare asked, "Then how in the world does Franco accept him?"

"Hitler would not view it as friendly if Spain refused von Ribbentrop's choice of Ambassador. If Franco was going to say no to Hitler about anything he would not have turned the Spanish press and police over to him as he has done."

Hoare said, "This is my first Ambassadorial post. Is there anything I should know in advance of the presenting of my credentials?"

"It's strictly according to protocol. When the ceremony is over General Franco always has a private chat with the Ambassador from any country of importance, but that's purely informal, you needn't prepare anything for it."

Hans Lazar, the German press attaché at the Madrid Embassy, awakened to the smell of incense. His bedroom was decorated as if it were a chapel, with twelve figures of saints surrounding the altar upon which he slept.[54]

A man of surprising tastes, Lazar was a Jew. Born a Turkish subject he wound up in Vienna serving as a fanatical worker in support of the

Anschluss. He served Hitler so brilliantly that despite his tainted blood he continued as one of the Nazi party's most talented propagandists.

Lazar lounged comfortably in bed, enjoying his saints while his mind began focusing on the day's work. Fear was his business. His boss, Joseph Goebbels had said, "If people are scared to death, we are spared the cost and bother of having to kill them." Lazar's job was to keep the Spanish people in a constant state of fear, the theory being that men off their emotional balance would almost always act foolishly. By keeping them in confusion, hopefully hovering on panic, he was most likely going to be able to cause them to behave as Goebbels wished.

In order to make them dislike the British he invented stories of British sabotage, preferably against women and children. To make them fear the Germans he wrote vengeful horror stories describing the torturous enslavement of nations that had stood in Hitler's way. Even though he had the cooperation of the Minister of the Interior, Serrano Suñer, who controlled the press, Lazar was generous in entertaining the Spanish journalists to whom free and lavish dinners were an immense luxury.

In his office at the German Embassy, Lazar took care of his deskwork, then pondered how he might make use of Sir Samuel Hoare's arrival. When he had formulated his plan he strolled from the Embassy to the Ritz and took his regular table in the bar from which he conducted a principal part of his daily business.

Despite being physically unattractive, somehow he was popular with ladies and was much in demand in Madrid society.[55] Even before the waiter could bring him a *café con leche* the press attaché from the French Embassy came by and sat down.

Lazar asked him, "Have you noticed anything odd about the selection of the new British Ambassador?"

"Well . . . only that he *is* a heavier gun than they've been used to sending here."

"Exactly. He's a big man in England. Far above Ambassador. Cabinet level for years."

Now curious, the other asked, "Then why would you suppose they'd send him as an Ambassador?"

"I don't suppose. I *know*. Now keep this to yourself, but 'Ambassador' is just a cover. He's come here as a negotiator. In her desperation to keep Spain neutral England has authorized Hoare to offer the immediate return of Gibraltar to Spain, as well as all British colonies in Africa. England knows it's all over for her." Lazar smirked, "So much so that Hoare has a British Airways plane waiting for him to get out fast when Franco joins with Germany in the war."

The Frenchman left and was replaced by others to whom Lazar confided the deal Sir Samuel was going to offer.

The "news" traveled so quickly that by evening it had circled Madrid and returned to Lazar when at a dinner party the hostess said, "Hans, have you heard? The British are going to return Gibraltar to Spain."

"No . . . " breathed the seemingly astonished Lazar.

"It's the truth. The English Ambassador is here in Madrid for the sole purpose . . .

> . . . of returning Gibraltar to Spanish
> rule.[56] Informed sources say that the
> new British Ambassador . . .

Sir Samuel gasped. The news story was on the front page of the Falange newspaper *Arriba* and was accompanied by his picture. Abandoning his breakfast he went to the telephone. But he put it down. It was only nine o'clock. His outrage was doubled by the need to wait at least until ten before he could reach the Spanish Foreign Minister.

Trying to use his time well he got off a note to his friend Lord Hankey, including the comment: "Your and my orderly mind cannot help being shocked by a mode of life that gets up very late, never has luncheon before two, nor dinner before ten and sleeps for most of the time between luncheon and dinner . . . "[57]

At ten o'clock he placed a call to the Foreign Minister. Still without official status Hoare was not at all certain he would be received. To his great pleasure he was invited to come over immediately.

Four police bodyguards were stationed outside his house. A car of four other policemen followed Hoare wherever he went.

Arriving at the Ministry of Foreign Affairs, in the Palace of Santa Cruz, once used by Spanish kings as a prison for nobles, Sir Samuel was immediately received by Minister Beigbeder, an army Colonel of Breton extraction who, like most Spanish officers of the day, including Franco, had made his name and achieved his rank in Morocco. He was fifty-two years old, with black hair and mustache, and wore black-rimmed glasses. He was dressed in his army uniform. "I have been looking forward to the pleasure of meeting you. Are you comfortable?"

"I confess that I can best describe my condition as confused," Hoare sighed. "General Franco declared Spain's neutrality as long ago as 1938, a courageous and quite marvelous thing I thought at the time since he was in fact renouncing the belligerent actions of Nazi Germany while at the same moment he was still literally dependent upon German help during your Civil War. Then, when world war actually broke out in 1939 he again declared Spain's 'strict neutrality.' After being here for only a few days it strikes me that this 'neutrality' is a curious one. Beginning with the press, the attitude toward Great Britain is openly hostile. There is not a day without news stories insisting that Germany will have won the war in a few weeks. I have been told that nine out of ten Spaniards believe that. But certainly you and General Franco know more about England than to imagine her even near defeat."

Colonel Beigbeder nodded, "Having studied her history, I have observed that while England has the unfortunate habit of losing the first battles of every war, she always wins the last.[58] My opinion is that the British bull has not yet come into the arena. Will it fight? And if so, how well will it fight? No one can say until the *corrida* is over." [59]

Sir Samuel rejoiced. This important man was the first Spaniard he had met who not only did not believe England to be finished, but seemed not to hope for that.

The Foreign Minister continued, "I regret that I must add that the *Generalísimo* does not share my optimism for England. He is most impressed by the German might. And the *Generalísimo* is a great soldier."

Depressed again, Sir Samuel returned to the subject of the newspapers. "I do not understand a totally pro-Nazi press in a neutral country. And such trash. It's virtually unreadable."

"But find solace in the fact that *because* it is virtually unreadable it is also virtually unread."[60]

The stifling hot Madrid air was suddenly softened by pleasant winds from Africa, and Colonel Beigbeder's attention seemed to remove itself from this moment and this office, to the days of his life when things were simple, when you knew who your enemy was and you rode out on your horse with a gun in your hand, as the enemy rode at you, and the better man won. He kept an illuminated *Koran* on his desk, and turning to it the Foreign Minister began an Arabic chant.[61]

A moment later he gestured an apology to his visitor, who had taken it all in, fascinated, thinking him one of the most romantic figures he had ever known, a thin, dark, Quixotic man who seemed more in keeping with the Riff and the desert than this small, stuffy room in which he now worked.[62]

Colonel Beigbeder said, "Those of us who understand the liberties that are being allowed, also understand the reason: 'We are paying Germany with words the price of our peace,' a phrase coined by *El Caudillo*. And a low price at that."

Opening his copy of *Arriba*, Hoare pointed to the story about himself. "This is totally false. It is pure German propaganda calculated to create a lot of hope and then a huge anticlimax and resentment toward Great Britain when it turns out that nothing of the sort happens."

"You're quite right." Beigbeder suppressed a desire to laugh. "Imagine the faces of Churchill and Lord Halifax when they read you are giving away Gibraltar."

"I was hoping the story would die unnoticed here in Spain."

"Not a chance. This is the work of Hans Lazar, the German press attaché, and he is cunning. It will be picked up by all Spanish newspapers. He has unlimited funds with which he subsidizes, or bribes, four hundred and thirty-two journalists working in every publication in Spain.[63] When they receive his stories they run them prominently. Next, Lisbon and Gibraltar, both of which are crazy for rumors, will take up the story, and the wire services of Great Britain and the United States upon seeing the same story coming from so many sources will assume it to be true and they will send it humming around the world."

Weakly, Hoare said, "My press attaché finds himself impotent with the press. Could you be of any help to us?"

"Lamentably, not the slightest. The Minister of the Interior, Ramón Serrano Suñer, who is also the head of the Falange, has jurisdiction over the press. He is extremely Germanophile. He has the power to fine an editor for printing something he doesn't like. Further, the Falange controls the newsprint monopoly and allots paper according to the editorial point of view of the newspaper. The less *Falangista* the point of view, the less paper they get to print it on."

Beigbeder paused, then said, "As an Englishman you'll be fascinated to learn that Don Ramón has recently accepted an invitation from Adolf Hitler to attend a victory cocktail party the *Führer* is planning to give on September 15th—in London."[64]

Indignant, Hoare could not even come up with a sarcastic remark.

"To further render me useless to help you, Don Ramón is strongly anti-British because at the outbreak of our Civil War his two brothers sought asylum in the British Embassy here in Madrid but were turned away and subsequently found by the militia, which shot them dead in the streets as Fascists.

"Finally, I can't help because Don Ramón wants my job."

Hoare moaned with discomfort at finding so many cards stacked against him. "This whole situation is impossible. A lie such as my keeping a plane here because England believes the war is lost completely undoes my mission. The plane was returned two days ago. Yet with nothing but lies in the press how can the Spanish people be aware of the fact that siding with Germany is not the only open course, that there is in fact a better one?"

"Fortunately, *El Caudillo* makes the decisions and he does not rely on our press for his information."

"I'm extremely eager for my meeting with him, to have a serious talk. Obviously I need his help."

CHAPTER TWO

A T TEN O'CLOCK IN THE MORNING A SQUADRON OF SEVENTY-TWO MOORISH CAVALRY, FRANCO'S BRILLIANTLY COSTUMED PERSONAL ESCORT, UNDER THE COMMAND OF SIX OFFICERS, FIVE SPANISH AND one Moorish, arrived at the British Embassy to escort the designated Ambassador and his staff to the royal palace, where *El Caudillo* would receive his Letters of Credence and he would officially be recognized as the British Ambassador to Madrid.

It was a gray day, almost cold, with intermittent rains. The British staff was in uniforms or morning dress. Sir Samuel wore the blue, red and gold of an Elder Brother of Trinity House with gold epaulets, a gold stripe down the trousers and a sword at his side, and on his chest he displayed his numerous decorations.[1]

British and Spanish flags were mounted side by side on the front bumpers of five automobiles provided for the Embassy's staff that Sir Samuel noted with distaste were Mercedes-Benz. He rode in the lead with the Barón de las Torres, the Foreign Ministry's Chief of Protocol and First Introducer of Ambassadors, who would also serve as translator.

The procession began. A squad of scouts led the way at a gallop, two rows of four horsemen each, preceded by a corporal, a Moor with jet-black beard, black eyes and dark skin. He and his men rode matching black horses whose hooves were painted silver, and they wore uniforms of brilliant red with long, flowing capes of the same vivid red, lined with white satin.

The scouts were followed by trumpeters, four horsemen to the row, three rows deep, their uniforms bright orange with long orange capes lined with white, riding white horses whose hooves were painted gold.

Behind the trumpeters the automobiles were interspersed with, and finally followed by, members of seven more squads of Moorish cavalry in sky-blue uniforms with sky-blue capes lined in white, riding perfectly matched chestnut horses with silver painted hooves.

All of the men wore turbans under gleaming metal helmets topped with spikes, and all the soldiers except the trumpeters carried lances. The officers wore sabers and the normal uniform of the Spanish cavalry except for a red cap, traditional for African campaigners. The four Spanish Lieutenants rode sorrel-colored horses; the Moor Lieutenant had a black horse, and the Captain in command, situated to the right of the Ambassador's car, rode a palomino, a great beige animal with silky white mane and tail.[2]

The sound of the horses' hooves on the concrete, the trumpets, the color, the streaming capes, attracted a large and animated crowd that applauded as the procession passed.

"How nice," Sir Samuel observed. "So not every Spaniard is Germanophile!"

The Barón de las Torres did not explain that the applause was not a welcome to the British Ambassador but that *El Caudillo*'s Moorish escort was so popular that it provoked applause even when *El Caudillo* himself was not in the procession.

Contentedly, Hoare smiled, "What a very good show."

Evading the issue of whose show it was, the Spanish diplomat said, "Your Excellency would find it even more dramatic if the coaches were in condition for use.[3] Before the war we used horse-drawn golden coaches. They are still being restored and teams of horses are being trained, but it will be another year before they can be put into service."

Looking out the window Hoare said, "These Moors are a striking lot."

"The pomp is only a part of it. They are all veterans of the Civil War. All known to be loyal and fierce fighters. As *El Caudillo*'s personal escort they are primarily a security force. Their theatrical appearance is diverting but while the crowd is watching the Moors, the Moors are watching the crowd."

He added, "They are employed to escort *El Caudillo* himself on major state occasions, with the only exceptions being foreign ambassadors and visiting chiefs of state."

Again Sir Samuel was pleased. Staring out the window, here and there he observed stiff-arm fascist salutes. Along the entire route he noticed an exceptionally large and watchful contingent of soldiers and *Guardia Civil*. He commented to the Barón, "Rather heavy security."

"*El Caudillo* is aware that not everybody in Spain is pro-British."

"A masterpiece of diplomacy on your part and understatement on his."

"In truth, and seriously, it is not overly cautious. We Spanish are a violent people at times." Glancing out the window he said, "We will soon be at the Palace of the Orient."

"Why would your Excellency use that name instead of 'The Royal Palace'?"

"Spain is not a monarchy today. It was improperly referred to as the 'Royal Palace' when it was occupied during the Republic. When it was the residence of Spanish Kings from the time of Philip V to Alfonso XIII it was indeed the 'Royal Palace' but without a king in residence it is more appropriately referred to by its other name, the Palace of the Orient.

"Also, your Excellency will observe that your reception will take place in a small salon to the side of the Throne Room, as opposed to the Throne Room itself, where monarchs traditionally received ambassadors. *El Caudillo* opts not to use the Throne Room."

"But, of course! He's a General not a King. He couldn't possibly use the Throne Room."

The Barón de las Torres said nothing. It would have been gratuitous to point out that in Spain General Franco could do absolutely anything he wished.[4]

Arriving at the Palace of the Orient the procession turned into the courtyard, an area covering approximately four acres. The horses' hooves clattered on the stone surface and the trumpeters announced the arrival of the new Ambassador.

Sir Samuel and the Barón de las Torres walked in the lead of the Embassy staff, entering the Palace and mounting a staircase five yards wide. The stairs were of a gray marble quarried in Granada, the center part carpeted in red and gold.

Reaching the landing of red Spanish marble at the top of the first twenty-eight stairs, the Barón de las Torres, experienced with Ambassadors who had passed middle age, paused to point out two large stone lions, discoursing on their origin. He was rewarded to note Sir Samuel listening with keener interest than would be likely. Rested, they continued up fifteen stairs to another platform and then up ten more stairs to the first floor, where they would be received by *El Caudillo*.

The party entered the *Salón de Alabarderos* and passed through it to the *Salón de Columnas*, through it to the *Salete de Gasparini* where they were met by the Chief of Protocol of the *Casa Civil*. In his charge they continued, passing through the Throne Room to the ante-Throne Room.

General Franco was flanked on one side by his Cabinet plus senior military and government figures; on the other by the Bishop of Madrid and a contingent of church hierarchy.

The Barón de las Torres entered with Sir Samuel, followed by the staff of the British Embassy.

Sir Samuel read a speech in English that *El Caudillo* had previously been shown and had approved. Then he listened to Franco's reply in Spanish, which his staff had received earlier and translated for him.

As the Chief of State spoke, Hoare was studying him, seeing him, amidst his Ministers, Generals, Admirals and the Bishop, as a small, bourgeois and insignificant figure. Franco's voice, though rather high pitched, was different from the uncontrolled shrieks of Hitler or the modulated bass of Mussolini; it was soothing, even reassuring, and Hoare thought that he might have been listening to the voice of a doctor with a good bedside manner, a big family practice and an assured income. Hoare found it difficult to see this paternal-seeming fellow as the brilliant young officer in Morocco whose exploits read like the best of Rudyard Kipling, or as the Commander in Chief who won the savage Civil War.[5] Hoare was all the more eager to get past the ceremony and into a long, personal talk with him.

Franco lowered the paper from which he had been reading. Smiling pleasantly he extended his hand, which Hoare shook. Then he stepped one pace backwards, clearly awaiting the departure of the British Ambassador.

Hardly believing that it was over, that there would not be a personal interview, Hoare led the British staff from the room, down the staircase, outside to their cars and the cavalry that would escort them back to the Embassy.[6]

Flashes of the overall negative picture in Spain reappeared in Sir Samuel's mind. And now this graphic illustration of General Franco's disinterest in even entering into a conversation with the representative of Great Britain. He thought of his conversation with Neville Chamberlain, whose advice he had sought, and who had told him: "I doubt whether it is worth your accepting this mission. You may never get to Spain and if you do you may never get away. The French army is in a hopeless rout, our own army is being evacuated from France and is leaving behind most of its equipment. Go to Spain if you wish but do not expect that in the midst of these defeats your mission can be successful."[7]

Sir Samuel began to wonder whether Chamberlain had been right; that perhaps his mission had begun too late.[8]

But no. He would not fail! Yet, clearly, it was going to take more than words and his presence to get anywhere with General Franco.

Deeply involved in thought he was not aware that they had arrived at the Embassy until he heard the trumpeters proclaiming the return of the Ambassador. Hoare got out of the car. The Moorish guards were lined up on both sides of him, and he waved to them with appreciation. The Captain and his Lieutenants had dismounted, and Hoare thanked them for the courtesy of escorting him. Then, following the protocol, he asked, "Will you gentlemen please join me for a glass of champagne?"

To which the Captain replied, "Thank you, *Señor Embajador* but the discipline of the Spanish Army forbids its officers or men from drinking any form of alcohol while on duty."

"Well, then, again my most sincere thanks," and with the appropriate courtesies having been exchanged they took leave of each other.[9]

On June 10th, as France was tottering and about to fall, Mussolini declared war on her, linking Italy's destiny with Germany and officially forming the Axis.

The Falange press was ecstatic, extolling the "historic act," evoking the camaraderie of the Civil War.[10]

At El Pardo, Franco confided to his wife his disappointment in Mussolini. "The incorporation of Italy into a victory already decided, over a beaten France—*Ningun hidalgo Español hubiera hecho eso. No Spanish gentleman would have done that.*[11]

"The *Duce* has been humiliated at seeing the *Führer* taking away his thunder? All that glory that used to be his. So when he saw the Germans walk across France virtually unopposed, thinking it a safe bet, the *Duce* made a last minute jump to join the victor. It was *¡imprudente!* The worst crime a Chief of State can commit is to bring his nation to war." He sat down on the bed. "But that's *his* problem. Mine is that now there will be all the more pressure on us to enter."

"Paco, if you let the *Führer* come through and take Gibraltar mightn't that end the war? Wouldn't the English then be forced to negotiate with him?"

"That's how it would seem, and that's what the von Stohrers have told you . . ." she nodded as he spoke, "and that's what they have told me, and Ramón repeats it in the papers every day, but . . . there is something about the British . . . I have the instinct that they will never surrender." He reached for a stack of papers on his night table and extracted one. "Alba," Spain's Ambassador to London, "sent me this report on a meeting von Ribbentrop had with Churchill in 1937, when he was the Ambassador to London, and he described the *Führer's* plans, which called for England to let Germany have a free hand in Eastern Europe. Churchill was not Prime Minister then, but he said he was certain his country would never do that, to which Ribbentrop threatened, 'In that case there will be war. The *Führer* is determined.' Churchill told him . . ." and Franco read from the report, "'When you talk of war which no doubt will be a general war, you must not under-rate England. She is a curious country and few foreigners can understand her mind. Do not judge by the attitude of the present administration. Once a great cause is presented to the people all kinds of unexpected actions might be taken by this very government and by the British nation. I repeat, do not underrate England. She is very clever. If you plunge us into another great war, we will bring the whole world against you like the last time.'"

Franco told his wife, "I have little doubt that the British will bring the Americans into it. Churchill is such a superb propagandist that he has taken the catastrophic defeat at Dunkirk and made it into the most glorious 'retreat' in military history. Germany has won a lot of battles because battles can be won by military superiority. But wars are won by politics.

"Roosevelt is already thinking of his third term. The election is five months away. The American people are passionately against intervention. 'No more wars on foreign shores'. He is too skillful a politician to work against public opinion." Franco took another report from his night table, "This is from a speech he made last month, May 11th. '. . . the United States finds itself each time more distant from Europe's war, and the people can consider themselves safe. Our country and the twenty-one American republics are pacifists.'"

Franco looked over his reading glasses. "That's what the voters want to hear. Listen to this from his Secretary of the Treasury, Henry Morganthau: 'The ten billion dollar debt from World War I is uncollectable. I very much doubt that the American people want to repeat the experience.'"

He removed his reading glasses. "The strategy is clear: stay out until the election is over. Therefore the *Führer* has five months in which he must win the war. After that, if he hasn't, the Americans could very well come in.

"Spain's situation is: if the Allies win they won't treat us well because of our form of government. But if we allow the Germans in we'll never get them out. We will be an occupied country. We saved ourselves from being owned by Stalin. My mentality cannot tolerate the image of a Spain in slavery to Adolf Hitler."

El Caudillo had called a meeting of the Chiefs of Staff at nine A.M. He had invited the Foreign Minister, Beigbeder, and the Interior Minister, his brother-in-law, to attend.

Serrano Suñer quickly said, "With Italy at war now it could be over in days and we'll be left standing uncommitted. Excellency, this is the moment. I know it. Now is the time to enter the war."[12]

Franco replied, "It is easy to know when to begin wars but not how to end them.[13]

45

"Spain stands between two swords.[14] If we are clever and lucky she will survive. If we are imprudent or unlucky, within ten years the name *España* will not exist on the maps of the world. Spain will continue her policy of skillful prudence."

"But what will I tell von Stohrer? As soon as this happened he told me 'Now we will be expecting Spain to demonstrate her friendship.'"

"You may tell von Stohrer that Spain is discarding her position of 'neutrality' in favor of our Italian friends' former 'non-belligerancy.'"

"How does that translate into friendship?"

"It doesn't. It translates only into a bit more time."

With that subject closed he turned to his military men. "The Tangier Statute of 1928 under which we, Italy, France and England share control of the city has been made meaningless by Italy's entry into the war. We, as the sole remaining neutral, should occupy Tangier with a heavy mission of Spanish troops in the name of the Sultan, ostensibly to preserve order. England has few troops available to turn us out. Nor would she wish trouble in Morocco that might bring Hitler through a 'friendly Spain.' With Melilla, Ceuta, our own coast line and now Tangier we will have considerable influence concerning the Mediterranean should it be necessary one day to exert it."[15]

On June 14, 1940 the German Eighteenth Army occupied Paris, the swastika flew from the top of the Eiffel Tower and Marshal Henri Philippe Pétain, who was serving as France's Ambassador to Madrid, was recalled to head the Vichy Government. He requested that Franco receive him so that he might bid him farewell.[16]

When Pétain had gone, Franco sat at his desk and with a quill pen he covered a map of Europe with black ink over each country that Germany and Italy dominated. When he had finished, only Switzerland, Sweden a small part of France, some of the Balkans and the Iberian Peninsula remained.[17]

CHAPTER THREE

CARS, SMALL TRUCKS AND BUSSES FILLED WITH FRENCH JEWS AND JEWS WHO HAD FLED FROM OTHER COUNTRIES TO SUPPOSED SAFETY IN FRANCE BEGAN ARRIVING AT THE SPANISH-FRENCH BORDER AT IRÚN-Hendaye, fifteen kilometers from the city of San Sebastian. Some brought their furniture, some had suitcases, many had nothing. They were bankers, artists, businessmen, aristocrats; men, women and children of all ages, their faces drained of blood by fear.[1]

The Spanish frontier *Guardias* did not know what to do; these people were not tourists, nor did they have work visas, so on what grounds could they come in? While the *Guardias* discussed between themselves what category the people fit into, they waited, pleading, crying, glancing behind them, relieved to see no Nazis yet, but squeezed breathless by the near certainty that soon they would.

Their Sergeant listened to the *Guardias* describing the Jewish refugees. "I will have to consult about this. Return to your posts." In his office he searched through the rulebook for a precedent but found nothing comparable.

The Captain walked toward the gates. More and more refugees were arriving.

In Madrid the Sub-Secretary General of Immigration listened to the Captain's description of the attempted exodus.

Ramón Serrano Suñer was just leaving to go to the *Real Club de Puerta de Hierro* for lunch. Walking with him toward his car the Sub-Secretary General presented the problem. Changing his plans, Serrano Suñer told his chauffeur to take him to El Pardo.

"At least five hundred, Paco, with more arriving every minute . . ."

In San Sebastian Captain Tomás Figueroa answered his telephone and heard, "I am the aide to his Excellency *El Generalísimo*. His Excellency wishes to speak with you."

"Captain Figueroa? I am General Franco."

Hearing the voice that he knew from the radio the Captain instinctively got to his feet. "At your orders, *mi General!*"

"I authorize you to facilitate the immediate entry into Spain of any civilian persons wishing to come in. Do the paperwork within Spain. Bring them inside our borders without delay. Raise the barrier immediately."

Sí, mi General . . ." He hesitated. *Mi General?* Some are without passports or money to sustain themselves."

"Admit them. House them in the garrison. Treat them as guests of the Spanish Government. When they are inside inquire what their hopes are: to remain or to continue on to Palestine . . ."

When he had hung up Serrano Suñer observed, "We are going to have to answer to the *Führer* for this."

"Better the *Führer* than God."[2]

Von Stohrer's Mercedes-Benz, flying the swastika pennon on its right front fender, careened through the streets of Madrid, using its horn as a siren, clearing the way of horse-drawn wagons, pedestrians and occasional cars. Behind von Stohrer followed another Mercedes containing the usual four Gestapo agents who backed up those in von Stohrer's car. Reaching the edge of Madrid the vehicles picked up still greater speed, raising a cloud of dust on the dirt road as they raced toward El Pardo.

The aide, perturbed, reported, "Excellency. The German Ambassador is at the gate. He has no appointment. . ."

Franco said, "I will receive him."

Von Stohrer strode into *El Caudillo*'s office, his face lacking its usual ingratiating smile.

Franco scowled at the German. "I am pleased that you are here because I was about to summon you. I will not tolerate the censorship of the American Ambassador's mail. He has formally registered a complaint. And rightfully so. You have put me in a position in which I must apologize for an act allegedly committed by Spaniards and which, despite my apology, could be used to develop a reason for some action against Spain. I don't know how you evaluate the United States of America, but I look upon her as a major world power with whom I require good relations. Any damage by you to Spain's relations with North America is unpardonable. If you cannot control your overzealous Gestapo I assure you that I can and will."

Von Stohrer was shaken at seeing *El Caudillo* display anger. Forgetting his mission of complaint he rediscovered his ingratiating smile. "Excellency, I give you my word that I know nothing of this, but I apologize and will immediately investigate and put an end to abuse of the privileges we enjoy."

The German Ambassador stood twelve inches taller than Franco and he represented the greatest military power in the world. But the shorter man, who ruled a broken, starving country, dominated the other. "Very well," he allowed. "Now, what was it you wanted?"

Wary of further provoking *El Caudillo*'s anger, Von Stohrer underplayed. "It was nothing important, some French citizens who have been fleeing into Spain at San Sebastian . . . political enemies of the Third Reich . . . " Seeing impatience on Franco's face, von Stohrer spluttered, "I apologize for intruding. I will take it up with Don Ramón . . ." He was backing out as Franco's *mirada* followed him to the door.

The incredibly quick fall of France and her request for an armistice caused universal belief that England would soon surrender, that she could not fight alone. But Prime Minister Churchill, in the House of Commons, stated his inflexible resolve to continue the war until victory was achieved:

"Let us therefore brace ourselves to our duties, and so bear ourselves that, if the British Empire and its Commonwealth last for a thousand years, men will say '. . . this was their finest hour.'"[3]

Dressing, at last, for his first private interview with General Franco, Sir Samuel listened to the English-language news broadcast from Radio

Gibraltar. It was June 22nd and he heard details surrounding the negotiations for France's surrender to Germany, which had begun the day before. The atmosphere of the event was heavy with vindictiveness. The French surrender had been staged, taking place in Compiegne, the woods where the Kaiser's representative surrendered to the French in 1918.

With the loss of the French fleet and its bases at Marseilles, Bizert and Casablanca, only Gibraltar stood, preventing the Mediterranean from being closed at its mouth by the Germans, thus cutting England off from easy access to India, China and her Pacific Empire. Overnight Spain's strategic position had soared in importance. Now more than ever it was vital that she be kept out of the German camp. If, with Spain's help, Hitler could take Gibraltar, he could easily close the Mediterranean, then he would cross to North Africa and dominate the continent. With bases in North and South Africa the U-boats would threaten the Atlantic highway and England, unable to supply herself, would be lost.

At this solemn hour in the life of the Empire, Hoare remembered Admiral Phillips saying, "Your mission is military, not diplomatic."[4]

Sir Samuel reviewed his strategy: first, psychological poise, an air of indifference to the fall of France insofar as it effects England's future. He would assure *El Caudillo* that England would win the war without question. But without question.

Hoare had needed to be in Spain very little time to understand that the best offer he could make would be economic aid. Spain lacked food, transport, clothes, everything. Unfortunately, England could barely supply her own needs and he was not authorized to offer a solitary thing. So, he would have to lie, grandly offering to arrange for the British Empire to provide all that Spain lacked to prevent her from turning to Hitler. It was a double play, the second advantage being that such an offer would be excellent propaganda as a sign of England's strength. Sir Samuel was pleased with the economic tactic for it boiled down to: Germany's price to supply Spain was Spain's entry into the war, whereas England's price was that Spain *avoid* the war.

And who knows? Maybe some supplying could actually be arranged. The main thing was to gain time, to stall Spain's joining the Axis for as long as possible until America could be brought into the conflict.

Driving to the Palace of El Pardo Sir Samuel observed the war damage around University City. The area had been devastated. He saw a woman dressed in black driving a cart of foodstuffs drawn by a donkey; her children in rags tagged along, barefoot.

They passed a man who wore a yoke with two large buckets attached to either end, walking to Madrid. It had to be Madrid because there was nothing between the city and that point. Hoare asked his chauffeur, "What could possibly be in those buckets to make it worth his working like a beast for the entire day?"

The chauffeur was a long-time Embassy employee, a Spaniard. "Your Excellency, with little steady work, little food, and no money around, his time is not valuable. He will be content if tonight he can feel ten or fifteen pesetas in his pocket."

They had not passed one automobile between Madrid and the town of El Pardo. Only there did he see a few official cars. Petrol was so short that the few privately owned cars that existed in Madrid were rarely used. Even trucks to transport food were largely replaced by animal-drawn carts and wagons. He regretted that he could not offer to supply petroleum. That would be a high card. But the *Caudillo* would see through the lie, he would know that Great Britain herself was dependant on America for her petroleum. He would have to remain with foodstuffs. That would probably be enough.

Being led through El Pardo it occurred to Sir Samuel that it was tiny compared to the Royal Palace, and he thought it rare for a dictator not to be gaudy.[5] He would have been further surprised if he knew that the Francos had closed off half of the palace because it was larger than they required, as well as an expense to keep heated.[6]

El Caudillo was awaiting him, standing in the center of his office. He offered his hand and with the help of the Barón de las Torres he and Sir Samuel exchanged amenities. Then Franco gestured toward a chair.

Sir Samuel found himself looking past Francisco Franco at photos of Adolf Hitler, Benito Mussolini and Pope Pius XII. He supposed that the photos on display like that were another appeasement tactic.

Franco was waiting for him to state his business. Sir Samuel had hoped to begin with light conversation, but clearly that was not going to be possible. Very well. But before making the economic offer Hoare thought he would let Franco wait.

"I was surprised and confused by your Excellency's change of policy from 'neutral' to 'nonbelligerent' and had been hoping that your Excellency would explain what this new 'nonbelligerancy' actually means."

Franco understood enough English to get the gist but he always allowed the Barón de las Torres to make the translation, giving himself more time to prepare his answer.[7] As the Barón asked the question in Spanish Franco listened without expression, continuing to look at Hoare as if it were the British Ambassador speaking. Then he replied, "What it does *not* mean is any departure from our policy of keeping out of the war."[8]

"I am relieved and gratified."

"Spain has no enthusiasm for an Axis victory, and remains neutral in the struggle between the western powers."

"I am interested in your Excellency's use of the word 'neutral.'" He glanced at the photos behind the *Generalísimo*. "It is readily observable that German agents operate in Spain with complete freedom."

Franco nodded, "Not only with freedom, with our help."

"You *admit* that?"

"Mr. Ambassador, apart from the fact that it would be indelicate at this time to refuse the *Führer* this minor courtesy, German military intelligence has been operating in Spain without interruption since before 1915. They are superbly organized and they provide my own police with extensive information related to subversive activities here. They have, in fact, warned us of seven separate assassination plots against my person, which, as you can see, we were able to thwart."

Rattled by the unexpected, Hoare pursued his point. "The Gestapo has observers all along the Spanish coast monitoring Allied shipping and reporting to their Naval attachés here, who in turn report to the U-boats, to the great detriment of Allied ships. Is that neutrality?"

"Have you ever been advised of any British espionage agents being arrested or detained by Spanish police?"

Sir Samuel stiffened in his chair. "I do not know of the presence in Spain of any British agents."

"If you would find it useful I will provide you with the names, addresses and passport numbers of one hundred and twenty British espionage agents operating in Madrid, ninety-seven in Algeciras, and others in Cádiz, Tarifa, Barcelona and Seville. None has declared himself to Spanish authorities as being a foreign agent. Yet none has been arrested. That is neutrality."

Flustered, Hoare said, "But the heavily pro-Axis press . . . surely your Excellency cannot call that a sign of neutrality."

"Would it serve England to have an angry Germany occupy Spain?"

Hoare thought, *Obviously there is more to him than meets the eyes, or how ever could this young officer of Jewish origin, little family influence and unimpressive personality have risen to the highest post in this state?*[9]

"But your pro-German speeches, combined with the pro-German press . . . your Excellency must surely understand that when Germany has lost the war these will have severely compromised you as pro-Axis. Your words have been obnoxious to British ears."

"If they were not obnoxious to British ears they would not be effective on German ears." Sweetly smiling, Franco recited, "'Words and feathers the wind will waft away.' And finally, I will have to be judged by my actions."[10]

Sir Samuel decided he had better get to his point. "His Majesty's Government would like your Excellency to know that they are sympathetic to Spain's economic plight and stand ready to give substantial aid."

Saving the condition for last he waited for the Barón de las Torres to make the translation.

Before Sir Samuel could continue Franco replied, "You and your Government are very kind. I am grateful. But I assure you Spain needs nothing from the British Empire. Nothing. Everything we require can be obtained from North Africa."[11]

Then *El Caudillo* leaned toward his guest and in an avuncular tone advised, "Why don't you end the war now? You can never win it. All that you will accomplish if the war is allowed to continue is the destruction of European civilization. And the longer it continues, the weaker both sides become, the more vulnerable you'll make all of Europe toward the increasing Communist threat."[12]

An hour later at the British Embassy Hoare spluttered, "The man is unmanageable. He has absolutely no idea of the moral and material strength of the British Empire. Nor, it would seem, of his own people's poverty. You would not believe his unshakable complacency and self-confidence. Not only did he deny the need for aid but then he offered his advice on how to run the British Empire!"

Not being the type of diplomat who adapts easily to the country to which he is accredited, on the contrary, being a man who becomes more English every day he is away from home, Sir Samuel had a low tolerance for foreign foods and customs, even when he was the foreigner, and after a while in Madrid, whose atmosphere he found "disturbing," he yearned to hear English spoken by Englishmen and to have lunch and dinner at civilized hours. Thus, he undertook the discomforts of travel by car and journeyed to Seville, then Jeréz and through the *Zona Militar*, which caused him anxiety, for it was there that the heavy guns of Tarifa commanded the Straits of Gibraltar.[13]

Arriving at La Linea he was delivered from Spanish soil as his car passed into the territory of Gibraltar via the strip of neutral ground that joins the Rock to Spain's mainland and the mountain, which is called "The Queen of Spain's chair." As soon as he had reached the coast he had heard the explosions coming from Gibraltar and if he had not known better he would have imagined, as some tourists did, that the Rock was being bombed. In fact, the civil colony was in the process of being transformed into a military fortress, and as a result of the fall of France it was a race against time.

Teams of British mining engineers were at work twenty-four hours a day, hollowing the Rock, making room for a garrison of twenty thousand men in barracks with hospitals, arsenals, warehouses, a radio station and water-purifying system, which would make the garrison independent of the mainland.

Six thousand Spaniards walked or rode bicycles onto Gibraltar daily to work in the tunnels. The hundreds of tons of stone being scooped out were dropped over the western end of the Rock as fill to support a one-thousand-yard airstrip the RAF required and that could only be provided by extending some six hundred yards of runway over the water. Until now the infrequent civilian air traffic at Gibraltar had made do with a three-hundred-yard emergency landing strip in the center of a racetrack. It was hoped that working at top speed, day and night, the broad, long airstrip would be made ready by 1942.

Sir Samuel enjoyed inspecting the work, going down into the tunnels, then climbing the outside of the Rock and examining the deeply carved gallery, which housed eight quick-firing anti-aircraft guns.

His visit to Gibraltar gave him a refill of hope and belief in British strength and resourcefulness. He also refilled his whiskey supply and treated himself to a suitcase full of British biscuits, butter, marmalade and other foods not available in Madrid. Then, refurbished by this breath of fresh British air, he returned to Spain.

CHAPTER FOUR

A T FIRST IT WAS A MASSIVE CLOUD OF DUST. NOW FROM WITHIN IT BLACK SWASTIKAS BEGAN EMERGING ON THE HEAVY TANKS OF THE *WEHRMACHT*, GRAY TANKS WITH OPEN TURRETS IN WHICH A SOLDIER stood, visible from his chest up to his helmet on which another swastika was displayed. Ahead of him bobbed the tank's long and powerful cannon.

German troops had arrived at the Spanish frontier at Irún in the Pyrenees, the mountain range between France and Spain. It was just after nine A.M. on the 27th of June, 1940.

The *Guardia Civil* at the frontier handed the binoculars to his partner. The other looked and the ruddiness drained from his face. "*Han llegado!* They have arrived."

The first *guardia* rushed into the customs shack and telephoned his superior, "*Mi Capitán, han llegado!*" The Captain telephoned to the Minister of War in Madrid.

The bad news traveled throughout Irún to nearby San Sebastian. "*Han llegado, las tropas Alemanes! The German troops have arrived.*"

Church bells called the people to mass and hundreds hurried to the church, for sanctuary, and to pray that the Germans would not come into Spain. They were mostly women, old men and children—so many of the nation's male young having recently been killed in the Civil War.

Hearing the news the few young men who had returned did not go to church to pray; they stayed home and honed edges on bayonets they had carried in their war.

An elderly woman who lived alone in a one-room hut, her face so wrinkled that it seemed always to be crying, went to the gas stove and poured the last of her olive oil into a pot and waited for it to boil. She wore the only dress she owned and it was black. First the militiamen, then the war had taken every person she loved. When her husband and three sons had gone to fight "the reds" her fourth and youngest son had stayed behind to work their small farm and support her. One night he found that his dinner had not been prepared. His mother said, "I don't cook for a coward." And he went to join his father and brothers. When the war was over there was no one to come home to her. But at least there was peace. Let anyone try to take that and she would fight him with boiling oil, with a kitchen knife, and he would have to kill to make her stop.

The two customs officers waited in the front of the spindly wooden roadblock, lowered as always, and stared across the border at the terrain of the French border town of Hendaye. The tanks were interspersed with open trucks carrying black-helmeted soldiers sitting at attention, their rifles held in front of them. On hundreds of trucks, thousands of men could be seen, rigid, the only movement being in the motion of the trucks and the furling of the flags each flew, large swastikas, black on a scarlet field. And between the trucks and the tanks was the heavy field artillery, and the end of it all was still not visible.

The first tank was half a kilometer away when, from behind, motorcycles appeared and took the lead, falling into formation four-abreast. They were followed by another four, and then by an open-topped General Staff car, with eight more motorcycles behind the Army's commanding officer.

The *guardias* stood at attention in front of the wooden barrier, staring at this force, which it was their duty to stop.

The tanks began fanning off to the left and to the right. All vehicles were drawing up into a waiting formation. The end of the on-coming column could not yet be seen and still they were arriving, men and machines. Through noon, past dusk and into the night the drone of heavy engines continued, bringing still more to where already ten divisions, one hundred and twenty thousand men and the greatest firepower ever known, a blackness of swastikas and the *Wehrmacht*'s boots, drew to a halt, massed at terrified Spain's doorstep.

At the Palace of El Pardo General Franco dined with his wife, his daughter and his aide. He had ordered *Radio Nacionál de España* to make no mention of the arrival of the Germans. His wife and daughter knew nothing of it and throughout the meal Franco spoke animatedly of plans he had for building a series of dams in order to increase hydroelectric power, and he asked his daughter about her studies that day.

Later, alone with his wife, he said, "Carmen, the Germans have arrived."

Carmen Polo looked at her husband in his pajamas, slippers and robe, on his bed, studying one of a stack of reports that he always brought from his office. In 1928, when he was thirty-six, he founded the General Military Academy at Saragossa and wrote a list of Ten Commandments for the aspiring officers. His fifth commandment was: "Never grumble, and do not tolerate the grumbles of others." He was never hot, or cold, or tired, even when certainly he had to be hot, or cold, or tired. And she had never known him to show anger. She supposed that when you have spent half of your life in the desert, in its extremes of heat and cold, with sand in your mouth and your eyes, when you have seen your friends fall dead around you, when you have had to sign death warrants for thousands of men, when you have had to look into a prisoner's eyes and say, "Execute him," . . . when one's emotions have been subjected to all those things then perhaps understanding occurs before anger.

She had first seen him as *Commandante*, Major Franco. She and the other girls in Oviedo who waited for him to ride by on his horse every day after lunch thought he was the most glamorous man in the world. His bravery in the Riff wars was known throughout Spain. The stories had begun forming his legend when he first went into battle as a Lieutenant. He believed that, "How a man leads is how he will be followed," and he had ridden at the head of his troops on a white horse, deliberately white, and as they charged the enemy he stood upright in his stirrups. When fighting on foot he walked toward the enemy, his head held high, defying the bullets as a *torero* contemns the bull. "God gave me life and only God can take it away." During four years, through hundreds of battles in which tens of thousands died, in which he rose to the rank of Major, he was never touched. His Moorish soldiers followed him with blind devotion, believing him to be a man with *baraca:* touched by God.

Then he had been wounded in the stomach. Standing in his stirrups, searching ahead through his binoculars, a bullet entered his body on one side and went out the other. The battle had been a particularly bloody one, and there were more casualties than hospital beds and trucks to transport the wounded, so the doctors walked among them, leaving the hopeless, taking those whom they believed they might save.

Looking at the young Major a doctor said, "There is nothing that can be done for him."

Franco called out, "No! I am not going to die."

"I'm sorry," the doctor said continuing on.

Standing beside Franco, weeping, was his Moor *asistente*, a combination servant and aide that all officers in Morocco had.

"Give me your rifle," Franco said. When it was in his hands he cocked it, pointed it at the doctor and ordered, "Halt!"

The doctor halted and stared at him.

"Send me to the hospital or I'll shoot you."

Upon arrival at the hospital, after further examination, it was learned that Major Franco was indeed with *baraca*, for though he appeared to be gravely wounded it was not in fact fatal because though the bullet had struck at exactly the point where the liver is, it had not touched it. Such was his *baraca* that precisely as the bullet penetrated the abdominal wall he must have inhaled, raising his liver, and the bullet passed through his body without touching a vital organ.

Because of his wound he was removed from active duty and sent to Oviedo to command the garrison there; but he had no intention of staying on in executive work and pleaded with the War Department to let him return to Africa, where the fighting and the promotions were.

Carmen Polo's parents thought that he was a poor choice of husband. Nor could she have imagined that he would be as devoted a husband and father as he was, because during their courtship he had not spoken of a longing for a home and a family, but of his greatest ambition: ". . . that Spain become as great again as she was of old." When he recovered and was about to return to active duty, she said, "You might be killed." To which the young Major replied, "If you fear dying then the Army is a poor choice of professions."

General Millán Astray, founder of the Spanish Foreign Legion, said, "He is the greatest military strategist of the century." When he was age thirty-three the War Department, noting that "Colonel Franco is a positive national asset," elevated him to the rank of General, the youngest in European history, equaled only by Napoleon Bonaparte.

It was not surprising then that after the Army had risen against the Republic, the military chiefs, eight generals and two staff colonels, voted him to be their leader and conduct the war. By the age of forty-six he had commanded the winning side in the Spanish Civil War, and now at forty-seven he was trying to rebuild his country with little more to work with than faith.

"Paco? What are you going to do about the Germans?"

"Anything except let them in. I'll promise that we'll enter the war at the first possible moment, and I'll keep finding reasons why that moment has not yet come. By flattering them, saying whatever I must to avoid angering them." He paused as if hearing his own statements. Then, looking at his wife he said, "When I was a person I never told a lie in my life."

Carmen Polo was accustomed to her husband's feeling that he was not an individual functioning according to his personal standards, responsible only to himself.

To play the cards he was playing had to be revolting to his pride, yet he tolerated the intolerable, accepted the unacceptable—anything to save Spain.

Feeling his wife watching him Franco looked over at her and seeing the list of movies from which he or she selected what they would watch every Thursday and Sunday after dinner he asked, "What's good this week?"

"*Gone With the Wind.*"

"That I have to see. A romantic, glamorous civil war."

Franco sat at his desk, biting a pencil, pondering what he should do to illustrate that he was not quaking with fear over the threat implicit in the presence of all that war power mounted at his border. Falling over backwards before Hitler's might would be as perilous as angering him.

And the line between the two was fine.

He telephoned to his Minister of Foreign Affairs. "Juan, advise our Consul General in Belgium that the children of King Leopold are invited to occupy the Palace of La Granja as guests of the Spanish State for as long as the war lasts."

That was good, he thought, a mild pass before the wild bull.

Calling Beigbeder back, he said, "Also, tell the British Ambassador that we agree to the proposed commercial agreement with England and Portugal with exchanges of wheat through the Sterling area. He may begin with thirty-four ships of wheat."

He hung up. A slightly bolder pass. But a good one. What else . . . ?

After lunch Franco told his wife, "I am going to paint a self-portrait," and he went into his dressing room to change clothes.

He enjoyed shooting and fishing; played tennis and golf for exercise—the latter with two balls, scoring the better shot; he never took a siesta and painting was something relaxing he could do after lunch before going back to the office at five o'clock.

Franco had set up his easel in the bathroom. His wife drew a chair nearby to watch him work. When he came out of his dressing room he was wearing the uniform that was his as Commander in Chief of the Navy. Standing before the mirror he began sketching his head, shoulders and torso.

She thought of his place of birth, the naval town El Ferrol; and the Franco family's four-generation tradition of service in the navy. At the age of twelve Francisco attended the Naval Preparatory Academy, planning to enter the Naval Academy in 1907. However, because of the loss of nearly every ship in the Spanish Armada during the Spanish American War in 1898 the government, having little need for more officers until they had more ships, canceled the 1907 examinations. There was no prospect that they would soon be resumed, so Francisco Franco entered the Infantry Academy at Toledo.

His wife recognized that his childhood ambition lingered strongly enough in his heart so that even after thirty years as a soldier he chose to portray himself as an Admiral.

Von Stohrer's car stopped outside the Ministry of the Interior. Blue-shirted Falange youths, upon seeing the German Ambassador's car, snapped to attention, their right arms rigid in salute. Surrounded by his Gestapo he strode upstairs to the Minister's office. The guards left him at the waiting room where Serrano Suñer's own bodyguards, six powerful Falangists, were seated. They greeted the Germans amiably, offering them cigarettes that were refused with arrogant disdain for such undisciplined conduct as smoking on duty. If the Spaniards took offense at being looked down upon in their own country, for their own customs, they did not reveal it.

The German envoy settled his huge frame into a soft chair beside Serrano Suñer's desk and moaned. "Why did he have to authorize the British Consul to open a British Institute in Madrid?"

Serrano Suñer sighed, "A British Institute when soon there will be no Britain."

"And worst of all, categorically impossible for me to explain to Ribbentrop . . . why, at this delicate moment, why does he authorize the opening of . . ." he extracted a newspaper clipping from his briefcase and read, "Instituto Arias Montano, a scholarly organization devoted to the study of Hebrew, Sephardic and near-Eastern cultures.'"

"When soon there will be no Jews."

"A good joke, but Ribbentrop has no sense of humor. And the *Führer* less." He held out both hands as in a plea. "Inexplicable. Jews he invites to come in. His German friends, no."

"What Jews?"

It was not Nazi policy to acknowledge their plans for Jews. "I refer to that assortment of misfit refugees who were given asylum in Spain."

"I'm not familiar with it," Serrano Suñer lied. And seeing von Stohrer's face he was relieved that he seemed to believe him. Though he and his brother-in-law yearned for a Catholic Spain, that dream did not forbid the worship of other beliefs—a dogma of Catholicism being that all human beings are children of God—and Spain was four hundred and fifty years past the Inquisition. His joke about the extinction of Jews stuck in his throat as he smiled at this man who was Spain's principal contact with Nazi Germany.

"And how do I reply to a cable from von Ribbentrop asking me, if the *Caudillo* needs wheat, why does he not ask Germany to provide it? To say nothing of Spain's invitation to King Leopold's children. The *Führer* is bewildered. He does not make war against children, but wouldn't the *Caudillo* be showing more friendship if he let *us* worry about the people we defeat?" He smiled bitterly, "I am amused by the belief among the English that 'von Stohrer can do anything he likes with the obstinate and obdurate *Caudillo*.' It serves me that they think so, but the fact is that the damned fellow seems to make a point of doing exactly the opposite of what I suggest he should do."

Sir Samuel Hoare allowed himself to hope that Franco was not going to buckle under to Hitler. Only four days had passed since the German arrival at the frontier, but at least they had not been immediately welcomed in as had been feared. He wrote to Halifax: "Already the Germans and Spaniards are fraternizing on the frontier, though I am doing my utmost to stop it. It looks as if the Germans' game is to create a friendly atmosphere before they make their demands. When the demands come, it is difficult to see how they can be resisted. The will to resist is there, but not the power." [1]

Franco received a message in cipher brought to him by General Vigón. It was from his most valued informant within the Third Reich:

"*On July 16 Hitler signed a Directive which is prefaced as follows:*

Since England despite her militarily hopeless situation still shows no sign of willingness to come to terms I have decided to prepare a landing operation against England, and if necessary to carry it out.

'The aim of this operation is to eliminate the English homeland as a base for the carrying on of the war against Germany, and if it should become necessary, to occupy it completely.'

"*Consequently, preparations for Operation Sea Lion, the invasion of England from across the Channel, were begun by Keitel in the name of the* Führer. *The date of Sea Lion will be named by Hitler depending largely on the outcome of Operation Eagle, the all-out air offensive against England, which will begin after August 5th. It is hoped that Sea Lion will be possible by mid-September.*

"The alternate in the unlikely case of the failure of Sea Lion is an attack against Gibraltar for the purpose of closing the Mediterranean to the British navy. This attack would be launched from the Spanish coast. It is code-named Operation Felix.

"An attack on Gibraltar, to which a great deal of study has been given in Germany, could be made only with the help of Spain. If England is to be driven out of Gibraltar, that could be accomplished only by an attack from the landside. It has been determined categorically that Gibraltar could not be conquered from the sea and air. The attack can be made successfully from the Spanish coast alone."

At the Palace of El Pardo, alone with his wife after dinner, Franco said, "The British are blockading our petroleum shipments from America because of an article in the *New York Times* saying that we have been re-exporting American petrol to Germany."[2]

As though reading her mind he explained, "Truth or fiction does not count. What matters is that the article was then published in the London press with the result that now American ships en route here with fuel will be turned back by the Royal Navy. The British politicians fell for a story by our enemy's propagandists."

Seeing her husband deep in thought, biting a wooden pencil, knowing there was not a thing she could do to help, she was astonished to hear herself saying, "Paco, don't chip your teeth."[3]

He put down the pencil. "Between the 'Government in Exile' and the Comintern the Americans are being trained to misunderstand Spaniards. And we're not easy to understand under the best conditions."

CHAPTER FIVE

Von Stohrer deciphered the coded cable.

MADRID, MOST URGENT BERLIN, AUGUST 2, 1940
TOP SECRET

PLEASE COME TO BERLIN, PREFERABLY BY THE END
OF THIS WEEK. FOR YOUR PERSONAL AND STRICTLY
CONFIDENTIAL INFORMATION. WHAT WE WANT TO
ACHIEVE NOW IS SPAIN'S EARLY ENTRY INTO THE WAR.

    I INTEND, CIRCUMSTANCES PERMITTING, TO VISIT
THE SPANISH GOVERNMENT AT AN EARLY DATE IN
ORDER, IF OPPORTUNITY PRESENTS ITSELF, TO MAKE
FINAL ARRANGEMENTS.

    PLEASE DO NOT MENTION ANYWHERE OUR
INTENTIONS OR THE POSSIBILITY OF MY VISIT.

RIBBENTROP[1]

Fending off the August heat, his feet in the swimming pool of *Club Real de Puerta de Hierro,* Serrano Suñer's thoughts were penetrated by a murmuring throughout the area.

Looking up he was surprised to see the von Stohrers arriving. The brevity of their stay in Berlin suggested that their visit had not been a pleasure trip or to escape Spain's warm climate.

The von Stohrers' extraordinary height and good looks, alone, would have attracted attention, but their manner of dress added impact: he in a white linen suit, carrying his briefcase, she neck to ankles in a near-transparent white cape over a swimming suit that was clearly brief.

Spanish women did not appear in the American and European bathing costumes of the day, some of which were made of two separate pieces, permitting bare waist to be seen. They were against the law. Spanish women wore bathing suits with skirts to the knee, referred to as "Jantzens" no matter who the actual manufacturers were. And Spanish men were required by law to wear tops over their almost knee-length swimming trunks.

This was not a lack of fashion sense, nor prudishness, but part of an effort by the Franco government to return Spain to her traditional ways and morals, to support the institutions that the Republicans had permitted the Anarchists and Communists to attack and nearly destroy: the family, church, love of country; and to turn Spain away from the morally disruptive currents that had been encouraged: pornography, divorce, civil marriage and adultery. Upon taking power the Franco government had even had to restore Spain's traditional flag and national anthem, which the Republicans had changed.

Thus, Baroness von Stohrer's beachwear was much discussed in Madrid, as was her taste for sun-bathing in the nude, which became known the previous August when on the beach at San Sebastian, a municipal policeman wrapped the Baroness in a blanket and carried her off to the police station despite her threat that she was the Ambassadress from Berlin and the *Führer* himself would punish such insolence.

To prevent another such incident, and to accommodate the tastes of the foreign diplomats who moved their embassies from Madrid to San Sebastian when Franco vacationed there in August, the Spanish Government established a section of the San Sebastian beach—the section most distant from town—for the exclusive use of the *Cuerpo Diplomatico*, the Diplomatic Corps, who there, in a series of tents provided for them, could dress or undress in any manner and use the beach as if they were at home. The area was forbidden to Spaniards. Afterward, the people of San Sebastian joked that the letters *C.D.* on the license plates of diplomats' cars did not stand for *Cuerpo Diplomatico*, but *Cuerpos Desnudos*, Nude Bodies.[2]

Ramón Serrano Suñer greeted the von Stohrers, kissing the hand of *La Embajadora* as she was called, in the Spanish custom of giving over the husband's title to his wife, as in the way that Carmen Polo was spoken of as *La Generalísima.*

Von Stohrer got Serrano Suñer aside. "Don Ramón, I have just returned from Berlin." His voice was urgent. "Our troops did not lose their way and arrive at your border by accident. The *Führer* wants to be invited to enter Spain. England will fall within days, weeks at most. The time to prove friendship to the Third Reich is now." Von Stohrer lowered his voice and spoke urgently, "Look, Don Ramón, frankly Spain's entry is valuable to us even in addition to military action against Gibraltar. The psychological value will be enormous. The effect of the declaration of war against England by Spain will be very strong in England and also on the entire world. England's prestige will suffer a great blow while, upon success of the military operation, ours will be greatly increased."[3] He paused, "Don Ramón, it is still possible to have the *Führer*'s friendship. I repeat: the *Führer* would like to enter Spain and for Spain to enter the war. There are now twenty divisions at your frontier, nearly two hundred and fifty thousand men with the most modern arms. They are a small fraction of our forces while Spain's entire army today is only some three hundred and forty thousand men. How can you hesitate? I remind you that the great names of history: the *Führer*, Frederich the Great, Napoleon—belonged to men of action. The prudent negotiators are not remembered. They and their names were ground into oblivion by the boots of the men of action."

On August 13th after weather delays Operation Eagle began. Flying conditions were poor, but impatient to start, Goering sent one of his three air fleets across the Channel from France. German losses were severe: forty-five *Luftwaffe* were downed against twenty-three RAF.

On August 15th Goering sent all three of his air fleets. The massive raid was a failure. The clumsy Stuka dive-bombers were no match for England's new Spitfires. Seventy-five *Luftwaffe* fell, against thirty-four RAF.

On August 23rd the RAF bombed Berlin for the first time. There was little damage but the Berliners were astonished. Hitler had assured them that this could not happen.

Rome, August 25, 1940

Dear Franco,

Ever since the outbreak of the war I have been constantly of the opinion that "your" Spain, the Spain of the Falangist Revolution could not remain neutral but would change to non-belligerency and finally to intervention.

Should that not happen, Spain would alienate herself from European history, especially the history of the future which the two victorious Axis powers will determine.

I should like to say to you, dear Franco, that I, with these my objective considerations, do not wish to hasten you in the least in the decision that you have to make, for I am sure that in your decisions you will, as always, be inspired by the defense of the fundamental interests of your people and I am just as certain that you will not let this opportunity go by of giving Spain her vital African space.

There is no doubt that after France, Great Britain will be beaten. The British regime exists only on one single element: the lie.

I certainly do not need to tell you that you, in your aspirations can count on the full solidarity of fascist Italy.

I beg you, dear Franco, to accept my most cordial and comradely greetings.

Mussolini [4]

Carmencita asked, "*Papá,* it's the same Rock that it was last month, with the same strategic position, no?"

They were in the Yellow Room having coffee after dinner. Franco believed that the greatest gift a parent could make to a child was to instill the love of country, as his mother had done for him. After the war, one of his early projects was to urge all schools to emphasize the teaching of Spanish history; her discovery of the New World; the giving of her language and culture to so many of its countries. He believed that a child's Spanish heritage was a richness above and beyond anything material, and that their understanding of it would restore the sense of dignity that centuries of bad government and military losses had taken from them.

Children were taught about their own country first, then about others; about the meaning of the Spanish flag, whose gold represents the riches that had been hers, and whose red, the blood spilled in countless wars.

He was pleased by his daughter's interest in Spain's role in the world. "Gibraltar has the same strategic *position* but what has changed is its strategic *value*. Hitler's plan was to soften England from the air with bombings of all the coastal defenses, their arsenals, railroads and power plants, until they were so weakened and defenseless that he could then send troops across the English Channel from France in small landing craft to physically invade England. But what has happened is not what Hitler planned. The bombing is not succeeding. To his surprise the RAF is shooting down many of the German bombers and chasing the others away before they can do the damage that must be done if the landings are to be possible. Unless she can be softened from the air to the point of near-collapse then the invasion will be too risky because England has strong coastal defense weapons, she has the very strong Royal Navy and the RAF, plus the Channel as a natural defense because of its treacherous currents.

"So, as the invasion of England becomes more dubious every day, Hitler will begin an alternative plan, his only alternative: it is called Operation Felix, the taking of Gibraltar in order to cut England off from her Empire. If he controlled Gibraltar and also the Suez Canal he would control the two doors to the Mediterranean, and he could close it to British ships. If England could not obtain supplies from her Empire except by traveling the very much longer routes, which the U-boats would make hazardous, then Hitler might well be able to force her to negotiate a peace, which is another way of saying to surrender. Therefore, though Gibraltar is the same Rock, its importance to the *Führer* is more urgent today than it was six months ago.

"That is where we come in. Hitler's only approach to Gibraltar is from our southern coast. He is counting on us to allow his troops to pass through Spain in order to make that attack."

"Are you going to let them do that, *Papá?*"

"That's the appropriate question, child. You will find the answer one day in the history books."

Later, alone with his wife, Franco read her a copy of a speech that Hitler had made the day before, on September 4th at the *Sportpalast* in Berlin.

"When the British Air Force drops two or three thousand kilogram bombs, then we will, in one night, drop one hundred and fifty thousand, two hundred and thirty thousand, four hundred thousand kilograms!

"When they declare that they will increase the attacks on our cities, then we will raze their cities to the ground. We will stop the handiwork of these air pirates, so help us God."

Franco peered over his reading glasses at his wife, "A curious man to seek the help of God."

"But things are getting more serious, aren't they, Paco?"

CHAPTER SIX

ADOLF HITLER, HOLDING A REPLICA OF THE ROCK OF GIBRALTAR IN BOTH HANDS, STRODE ACROSS HIS OFFICE CHANTING, "GIBRALTAR . . . GIBRALTAR . . . GIBRALTAR . . . THE MOST STRATEGIC ROCK IN THE world . . . the most valuable rock in the world."

He was in the chamber with his naval chief, Grand Admiral Raeder and his chief of land forces, General Jodl. He faced them. "Fact: it is now essential that we take Gibraltar. Inevitability: we will take Gibraltar." He gazed at the scale model of the Rock. "Put this in my hands—give me Gibraltar . . . and I will give you the world. Give me Gibraltar and I will give you North Africa. Give me North Africa and I will give you Central and South Africa. With all the wealth of Africa I will give you India and China, South America and North America. Give me this rock and I will give you the world."

Putting down the Rock, removing his wristwatch and letting it dangle before their eyes, he said, "Operation Felix must be of such precision as this. And, I want it orchestrated into such fearsome efficiency that the world will be absolutely convinced that resistance is impossible . . . impossible. Resistance to Germany's desires and requirements is impossible! Anywhere! By anyone!

"The gods of war continue to prefer our camp. I have just been informed of the discovery by our occupying forces in France of a mountain formation in the French Jura, which is similar to the Rock of Gibraltar. This is not coincidence, it is Providence. Admiral Canaris has again proven himself the Grand Master of Espionage and provided us with minutely detailed blueprints of the fortress and the airfield. Using these plans I want that mountain formation in the French Jura made iden-tical to the Rock of Gibraltar. Identical in size, identical in armaments, identical in the number of men defending it, identical in approach. Then our assault troops can train for the attack under perfect conditions. They will practice and practice until they will be able to take the real Rock with their eyes closed.

"The Admiral has also provided us with meter by meter descriptions of the terrain, roads, bridges and all obstacles between Irún and Algeciras. Thus, five days before the invasion date our troops now on the frontier will enter Spain and move south to Algeciras and La Linea, from which the invasion will be launched.

"I have no doubts the invasion will work out. Gibraltar is weak, almost defenseless. But I want more than victory. Gibraltar's collapse and surrender must be dramatic. A horrifyingly overwhelming defeat for the world to see: the Ultimate Invasion by the Invincible Third Reich. Thus, the absolute necessity for clockwork precision, everything anticipated, everything planned to the most minute detail, then practiced, practiced, practiced."

When it was possible to speak, General Jodl said, "My *Führer*, the concept of Operation Felix is predicated on the use of Spanish territory as well as with Spanish cooperation. If we are given free entry we can reach the southern coast in the allotted five days. But, my *Führer*, without per-mission to cross those mountains, to pass through that terrain in winter would be impossible. Admiral Canaris' splendid information also refers to reports filed from there by the Condor Legion, describing the weather as the worst in Europe. There exist only two points of entrance into Spain, of which only one is a passable road that is in terrible postwar condition. The terrain apart from the road is untraversable without Franco's permis-sion. If we encountered even weak resistance it would be a catastrophe."

Hitler glared at Jodl. "The Third Reich does not suffer catastrophes! It *causes* them!" He stood up. "Do not worry about our 'non-belligerent' friend the *Caudillo*. He will join us when I tell him it is time to do so because I am the Master of Europe and he will obey orders."

It was dusk, the September air was gentle and the donkey and his rider seemed unhurried as they ambled toward the gates of El Pardo. The rider smiled at the two *Guardias Civiles* who stepped through the door in the gates to ask him his business. "Will you kindly inform his Excellency *El Caudillo* that Ignacio Moreno de Talavera, a humble monk who has traveled from Toledo, would be most grateful for an audience."

"You ask the impossible. *El Caudillo* does not receive visitors without appointments."

"In God's world all things are possible. I am certain that He would smile upon you if you have the kindness in your heart to telephone to the palace and learn if perhaps my painstaking journey from Toledo might not have been in vain."

Indeed, the sergeant had taken note of the pallid skin, the moisture on the silver hair that protruded from under the monk's hat.

Seated in the office of *El Caudillo* "the monk" said, "Eagle is failing. Hitler has authorized another massive air raid on September 15th, to punish London and destroy the RAF. The air raids have been hard on the English nerves, and he is hoping for this one to cause mass hysteria, but I see little chance for success. The RAF seems to know where the bombers will strike and each time has been there waiting for them.

"Hitler knows that he cannot undertake a landing without air supremacy, that it would be extremely hazardous and that if it failed the first time it could not be attempted again, because while England now fears the loaded pistol of invasion, after a failure she would know that Germany holds only an empty one.

"I anticipate, therefore, that Sea Lion will soon be shelved. Then all emphasis will be on Felix. I repeat, Excellency, *all emphasis!* Hitler will stop at nothing to take Gibraltar. Already he has authorized unlimited funds and manpower for a full-scale replica of the Rock in the French Jura, to be used in a training program."

"Is there a date for Felix?"

"Not yet, Excellency. Raeder and Jodl are still studying it. But Hitler will be pushing them. He is impatient and Gibraltar is now an obsession with him." He paused, selecting the right words. "Excellency, a word of warning: Ribbentrop and others close to Hitler are infuriated by Spain's seeming ingratitude and they speak of Spanish treachery. The Gestapo has reported that on more than one occasion the British Ambassador here in Madrid, Hoare, has been in possession of documents and information that he could have of obtained only from the Spanish Foreign Ministry, and at a high level. As a result, Hitler is being urged by his inner circle to treat Spain as an enemy and to invade her immediately."

"Beigbeder," Franco said. "Since separating from his wife he has been seeing a Miss Butler."

Serrano Suñer nodded. "I have seen them together myself. She is a teacher at the school for English children."

"Martínez-Campos' investigation proves that she is also a British intelligence officer reporting directly to Hoare."

Serrano Suñer absorbed what, to him, was the best possible news. "Then Beigbeder must go."

"Yes. Though not quite yet."

"But he's dangerous."

"Not if we don't tell him anything we don't want the English to know. Meanwhile, there are a few 'messages' I would like to have Miss Butler carry for *us*." Franco was well aware of his brother-in-law's ambition to be the Foreign Minister. "Patience, Ramón. Poor Juan has made a bad mistake and he will have plenty of time to regret it." Franco's face mellowed as he remembered Beigbeder as an especially capable and valuable officer in Africa. Snapping himself out of it he said, "I want you to go to Berlin. You must make it clear that there has been an unfortunate accident that we have discovered and are correcting, but that at no time did it have anything to do with governmental policy.

"The fact is that our communications with the Reich are not adequate. I want you personally to know the men who make the decisions: the *Führer*, Goering, Goebbels, Ribbentrop, Jodl, Raeder, Himmler. They are the ones running the war . . ."

"And inevitably the world."

El Caudillo feared that his brother-in-law's zeal for Germany, which had its advantages up to a point, could on the other hand blind him to the realities. "Ramón, what would you say if I were to tell you that contrary to winning our war for us, Germany tried to prolong it?"

"I would ask you why they would do that? And why you believe they did?"

Franco went to his desk and returned with a six-page typewritten report. He showed his brother-in-law a notation at the top: *Muy Reservado:* top secret.

Then he turned to the last page and showed the date and signature: Berlin, 17 November 1938, Chief of the High Command, Military Attaché, General Roca de Togares. Franco explained, "During the war I sent Roca de Togares to Berlin ostensibly as a military liaison. In fact he functioned for me principally and effectively in espionage. Take this report with you and read it thoroughly tonight. But for now just read what I have underlined."

> *General Richthofen was here to see Marshall Goering for the purpose of asking for reinforcements for the Condor Legion in order to end the war in Spain.*
>
> *It appears that the result of this conversation with the Marshall was entirely negative. He said that Germany was very disillusioned by Spain's attitude after having helped us so much.*
>
> *Germany considers herself defrauded by Spain, seeing that on the first occasion that we have had to demonstrate our gratitude, we have declared our neutrality, showing the world that Spain does not show solidarity with German policy, and is as much as giving France a guarantee of her future neutrality.*
>
> *From the Führer's point of view the continuation of the war in Spain, or at least the prolonging of it, offers Germany the security that during this period of time French troops cannot pass over Spanish soil to Africa and interrupts communication between France and French Morocco.'*[1]

Serrano Suñer was as stunned as his brother-in-law had intended him to be. He murmured, "Dragging the war on . . . letting more Spaniards be killed . . ."

"When I received this report I understood why supplies had become slow in arriving. I had been pursuing the war very carefully, trying to lose as few Spaniards as possible, to destroy as little of our cities as was possible. From that day on I escalated the pace and ended it in seven months.

"If Hitler had had his way, if we had not ended the war eighteen months ago, if he could have kept us still militarily dependant upon him he would not be waiting on our frontier as he is now, he would not have to ask permission to enter. He would already have Gibraltar and Portugal and be well into Africa. We need not be paranoids to assume that once in Spain he would not merely pass through but would leave enough of his troops here to dominate us, and that once into Africa he would give us his 'protection' in Ceuta, Melilla and Tangier. Spain would be a property of the Third Reich."

"Why didn't you tell me this before?"

"It wasn't your business until today."

"Paco, I am not only your brother-in-law, I am your Minister."

Franco gestured to the cumbersome stacks of papers on his desk. "My dear brother-in-law and Minister, can you see any reason why you and the other Ministers would want to read all of these reports that come in by the kilo every day? I give each of you only what pertains directly to you. I had forgotten about this document until I began thinking of how to bring you to a more realistic outlook toward the Germans.

"I have further unpleasant information." He handed him another paper. "This is from von Stohrer to von Ribbentrop.

"Re: Ramón Serrano Suñer.

Undoubtedly the most outstanding person in the present Cabinet but he is a fanatic who inclines toward mysticism, and whose actions it will be difficult to predict. Although, or perhaps precisely because he always emphasizes his great sympathy with Germany in his meetings with me and tries to prove it by example, I am inclined to believe, as I always have, that he is no friend of ours. He is Jesuit trained and has strong church leanings."

Stunned, Serrano Suñer looked up from the paper.

"Look, Ramón . . . it is easy to be dazzled by the Führer and the Duce. The von Stohrers ride on all that glamor. But let us not be blinded. Categorically, Germany and Italy are not our friends, and that is perfectly proper. Nations are not friends except for as long as it serves those nations' interests.

"When the Germans and Italians were here we enjoyed the Italians, we made fun of them for putting on hairnets before going to sleep; you can

76

laugh at people you like. We never made fun of the Germans. There was never anything amusing about them. And then, after the war, many Italian soldiers remained in Spain, marrying Spanish girls. Few Germans stayed."

He went to his desk and returned with a sheaf of handwritten pages. "The Germans will quickly bring the conversation to center on Spain's entry into the war. I have written our position on every related subject, as well as itemizing our economic and military needs that are deliberately inflated, and our territorial aspirations that are absurd.

"Your job is to make friends with the Germans without giving them anything, while at the same time asking for so much aid and such broad territorial concessions as to make Spain's entry into the war appear to be an enormously costly and less desirable enterprise for Germany."

"And I am to make friends in that manner, eh?"

Franco nodded.

Serrano Suñer studied the notes, and in the days that followed *El Caudillo* drilled him, questioning him, surprising and offending him as the Germans would. When Serrano became tired Franco urged him on, working with him long into the nights. "When I went into battle I was always prepared, I never left anything to improvisation."

The Germans, too, were preparing for the visit of the Spanish Minister. Von Stohrer wrote a letter to von Ribbentrop:

Madrid, September 6, 1940

Dear Herr Reichminister,

    I take the liberty of sending you another memorandum with material for the visit of the Spanish Minister of the Interior, Serrano Suñer. In the memorandum are again assembled the essential considerations which I took the liberty of presenting in person and of supplementing through my "G. A." of Aug 8 and my letter of Aug 27.
    Heil Hitler!

Stohrer

The enclosures were voluminous and labeled "Top Secret". It began:

TRIP TO GERMANY OF SERRANO SUÑER, THE SPANISH MINISTER OF THE INTERIOR.

(Double surname, pronounced: Serrano Sunjer; given name is Ramón—Raimund

I

The trip has been arranged in order to discuss with a leading responsible Spanish statesman the question of Spain's possible entry into the war (which the Spanish Government itself proposed, see memorandum, enclosure 1.)

A. According to Spain's own statement, the conditions for Spain's entry into the war are of a political and military—economic nature, namely:

    1) Assurances as to the political territorial aspirations of Spain (these appear in the Spanish memorandum, enclosure 1)

    2) Military and other (i.e. economic) aid by Germany.

B. Our demands in return for satisfying the Spanish aspirations and desires; the following should be considered:

Von Stohrer here listed seven manners of economic repayment Germany could extract in the form of raw materials, notably wolfram, the mineral required for making tungsten, which is essential in the hardening of steel for machine tools and armor-piercing projectiles. Also, transfer to Germany of French and English financial interests in Spanish companies; and territorial concessions Spain could make to Germany.

II

In enclosure 6 there is material for conversations with Sr. Serrano Suñer regarding questions of foreign policy, economic problems, and questions of domestic policy. The suggestions have purposely been kept very critical.

III

Serrano Suñer is today the most influential and important Spanish statesman, the confidant and brother-in-law of Franco. Negotiations and conversations in the fields discussed above can therefore at present be conducted only with him with any prospect of success.

His political activity, however, makes him a controversial figure in Spain and there is strong opposition to him.

In his utmost heart, Serrano Suñer who is a strict, not to say intolerant Catholic, may still have certain reservations with regard to the Third Reich.

Enclosure 8 gives information regarding the person of Serrano Suñer.

IV

The strong opposition mentioned, which exists in large parts of Spain and particularly in Army circles against Serrano Suñer, since he is being made responsible for the (currently) very unsatisfactory situation in Spain, requires that certain precautions be taken on our side. It might be desirable in public utterances connected with the Minister's visit (speeches, press articles, etc) which are naturally being forwarded to Spain, besides the customary courtesies for Sr. Serrano Suñer always to give prominence to the achievements of the Generalissimo and Chief of State and of the Spanish Army and also to mention the Falange.

It might also be mentioned incidentally in addresses that the visit of Sr. Serrano Suñer was taking place at his request.

The names and personal data of the persons accompanying Serrano Suñer on his journey are given in enclosure.[9]

Stohrer[2]

In Berlin, teams of economists and military supply personnel had studied Spain's stated needs, tried to analyze her true needs and were preparing a report for von Ribbentrop and the *Führer*.

Berlin, September 16, 1940

BRIEF FOR THE CONVERSATION WITH SUÑER REGARDING SPANISH REQUESTS FOR DELIVERIES

1) Military material

Requests for the amounts are too high. The individual items requested cannot be evaluated until it is known for what military actions the weapons are to be used. In general the Oberkommando der Wehrmacht is of the opinion that support by complete German military units would be more effective than deliveries of weapons to Spain.

2) Economic Deliveries

All amounts requested by the Spaniards seem to be greatly exaggerated and should be checked.

a) 6–7000 tons of bread grain . . . . Can be delivered

b) 4000 tons gasoline

100,000 tons diesel oil

200,000 tons kerosene

40,000 tons lubricating oil

We need more exact data as to time of delivery and minimum quantities

Absolutely needed; it will be possible to deliver these

c) 200,000 tons coal . . . . Can be delivered

d) 625,000 tons nitrogen fertilizer . . . . Can be delivered by postponing important German needs.

e) 100,000–150,000 tons scrap

100,000 tons paper pulp

48,000 tons cellulose . . . . .Can be delivered

f) 35,000 tons Manganese ore

25,000 tons crude rubber

100,000 tons cotton

25,000 tons manila, hemp and jute

30,000 tons peanut seeds . . . . Can be delivered[3]

80

Bidding farewell to his brother-in-law, Franco said, "You will have no official reason to meet with Goering but make a point of paying a social call on him. He is too important for us to allow him to feel slighted or overlooked."

Franco summed up the strategy, "In your meeting with the *Führer* and von Ribbentrop you must be as though made of quicksilver. You must not say 'no' to anything and you must not say 'yes' to anything. You are there to discuss, not to reach agreements. You can say nothing that will commit us to enter the war. Only *El Caudillo* can make that statement. Hide behind me. I am the door you can always leave open.

"Lean heavily on the device of convincing them of the danger of Spain becoming an insupportable burden on Germany if we should enter the war—cutting us off from Allied aid—before Germany has successfully invaded and occupied England."

"What if that happens while I'm there?"

"If it does, then weep for England but rejoice for Spain, because in that event Germany will not need to pass through here to Gibraltar. She will own the Rock and her troops will ride there aboard the ships of the Royal Navy."

CHAPTER SEVEN

S MILING AT VON STOHRER WAS COMING MORE EASILY NOW. FEELING DECEIVED AND BETRAYED BY THE NEGATIVE COMMENTS MADE ABOUT HIM, WHEN FIRST THEY HAD BOARDED THE TRAIN IN MADRID, SERRANO had found it difficult even to look at the Nazi, but after a few hours the pretense at friendship became satisfying. And observing the German continuing his own act of close friendship and affection, Serrano Suñer was impressed with how well he played his role.

At the Spanish-French border, Irún-Hendaye, where the narrow-gauge French tracks met the wider-gauge Spanish tracks, they changed trains, leaving the antiquated Spanish cars and boarding the luxurious special train sent by von Ribbentrop.

It was a slow trip by rail, but flying was impractical because Franco had felt it advisable to send along a large party of economists, military strategists and various technical experts who, other than the interpreter Antonio Tóvar, were not necessary in as much as all economic and military subjects had been prepared by *El Caudillo*. Therefore their function was purely as window-dressing to impress the Nazis with their number.

They stopped in Paris, sad, deserted. Nobody strolled the once-so-strollable boulevards. Through a window of their car as they rode to dinner Serrano Suñer noted that only occasionally a man or woman could be seen moving along a street, timidly. Storm troopers were on every corner, swastikas everywhere.

For the first time, he began thinking of what it might be like to be occupied by another power.

Von Stohrer commented, "How tranquil the streets are."

82

Serrano found it incredible that the German did not see them as abandoned, and he silently disdained their motorcycle escort as pompous, pretentious and gratuitous.

"Historians will see the *Führer* as a humanitarian. He has ordered that our troops conduct themselves as liberators, not conquerors. He has forbidden our soldiers from acting in France the way the French behaved in the Rhineland in 1918. He has ordered that anyone found looting will be shot on the spot."

After three days of travel they arrived at Berlin's Anhalter Banhof. As the train stopped in the station von Stohrer emerged from his compartment wearing a heavy, fur-lined cape.

Von Ribbentrop and a large entourage were on the platform awaiting Serrano Suñer, and he was introduced to several Ministers, Generals and major personalities of the Third Reich. Most of them, like von Stohrer, were large, but towering above them all was the red-headed Chief of Protocol Baron von Doernberg, standing four inches taller than von Stohrer's six feet, six inches.

Shaking hands, von Ribbentrop said, "I am so pleased by this opportunity to get to know your Excellency personally. Our mutual friend Count Ciano has already told me so much about you that I feel we are not strangers."

"I share that feeling with your Excellency. And I am grateful for such a cordial reception."

"Lamentably, the reception that Berlin can give our distinguished guest is only a wartime gesture owing to the danger of air raids. I hope, however, that your Excellency will also visit Berlin in peacetime in the near future, when it will be possible for us to afford quite a different reception."[1]

Outside the station there was an honor guard to be reviewed by the visiting Minister from Spain. He performed side by side with von Ribbentrop. At the end of the honor guard were groups of spectators, with children waving small Spanish flags. As one whose work included the preparation of similar demonstrations he understood that there is a distinct protocol, that these displays of enthusiasm are organized, props such as the small flags are provided, with even the degree of fervor and the number of people moderated to be exactly appropriate for the occasion.

They set off on a tour of the city, riding in open-topped cars. Despite his Madrid winter clothes he was underdressed compared to the Germans' heavy woolen and leather fur-lined and rubberized coats. Finally they were at the hotel Adlon. Then, within one hour they were arriving at the Ministry of Foreign Affairs for the first conference.

Von Ribbentrop's office was opulent, but neither comfortable nor personal, designed it seemed, solely to impress visitors with the extent of German power. Maps on the walls showed German-dominated countries, their national flags mounted beneath the swastikas. Suspended from the ceiling at one end of the room were squadrons of airplanes in flying formation. On a table that ran the length of the room, some thirty feet, were miniature German tanks, hundreds of them in formation. Behind them were miniatures of troop transport vehicles, each containing toy soldiers, and behind them hundreds of pieces of heavy field artillery, machine gunners and antitank weapons and their crews: an exact replica of a *Wehrmacht* division.

Ribbentrop seated himself behind his desk. "When will Spain enter the war?"

The Spaniard recoiled. But, without losing a beat, as if he had not been startled by the rude abruptness he replied, "My country has always stood in support of our friends, wishing always to help in our common cause. But we are less than a year and a half past a civil war due to which Spain has had to suffer great economic difficulties. These are expressed particularly in the lack of grain, gasoline and war materials . . . "

Ribbentrop cut him off. "What's your price? What do you need?"

Serrano Suñer's blood heated with fury as it can in a Spaniard whose dignity has been offended. Under any condition other than his country's salvation, he would have walked out. Instead, he smiled.

Then his face became somber. "*Herr Reichsausseminister*, we are now six hundred thousand tons under our minimum annual requirement of grain. That figure could be reduced to four hundred thousand tons by imports from abroad and from French Morocco, but the latter figure is the absolute minimum. We have petroleum reserves for less than one month and need fifty-six thousand tons of petroleum per month. We need rubber, cotton, nitrates and transportation equipment . . ." He then detailed how many thousand tons of each was essential before Spain could possibly enter another war.

"Excessive!"

"*¡Ojalá!*" Would that it were!

"Especially the petroleum. Fifty-six thousand tons of gasoline a month is an absurd amount unless every Spaniard is driving around in a Mercedes-Benz, for in the present military situation no large-scale troop movements are necessary in Spain." [2]

"At the moment, *Herr Reichsaussenminister*. But there is always the possibility of an English attack on our northern coast from the Atlantic side. Further, no one knows yet how the very strong French army in Morocco is going to act. It is quite possible that it will place itself at the disposal of England or General de Gaulle.[3] Our present supplies of gasoline for motor vehicles can last for one hundred and fifteen days, our aviation fuel is only enough for two hundred and fifty days and our stocks of lubricating oils are even lower."

Von Ribbentrop sneered. "You can rest assured that no aggressive actions against Spanish territory are probable thanks to the presence of a few groups of dive-bombers. As soon as German dive-bombers appear on the scene all the ships within a radius of three hundred kilometers would have to withdraw. But it is not only the gasoline figures that seem high, they all do."[4]

"It is possible that our economists have erred, *Herr Reichsaussenminister*. Perhaps a German petroleum expert could be sent to Spain? Also an expert from the ministry of food."

Von Ribbentrop shrugged, "This is a lot of talk about nothing considering that the 'end phase of the war' in which Spain will participate will be short. Spain will be provided with what she actually needs.

"As for military support the *Führer* personally will communicate everything necessary during tomorrow's conference. Thus, we are left with the need to work out economic accords: debt repayments, German participation in French- and English-owned businesses on Spanish territory, etc."

"None of those will be a problem," assured Serrano Suñer, smiling, "except perhaps the 'etc.'"

Von Ribbentrop looked at him coldly, then stood up and went to a wall map of Africa. Using a pointer he traced a large zone of German interest that included all of central Africa. "The Third Reich requires bases in two parts of French Morocco: the seaport Agadir, here in the southwest zone, and Mogador, this other seaport here in the western zone. We will also require bases for our *unterseebooten:* undersea boats, i.e., U-boats, on Rio de Oro and on the island of Fernando Po . . ."

"I must decline any concession on Fernando Po for historical reasons. Spanish public opinion would not stand for it."

Staring at him for a moment, von Ribbentrop then lectured, "Spanish public opinion, like German public opinion, is the opinion of the Chief of State." He stared at him again, then added, "The *Führer* feels that it is also necessary that Spain cedes one of the Canary Islands for a German base."

Until now Serrano Suñer had simply been role-playing, but this last demand genuinely stunned him. "But that is impossible . . . the Canary Islands are as much a part of the Spanish National territory as are Madrid and Burgos."

"Never the less, common necessity calls for this."

"I will be forced to interrupt these conversations and return to my country unless your Excellency withdraws the petition for one of the Canary Islands."

"The cession of one of the Canary Islands is entirely in Spanish interest. Germany, Italy and Spain, as a family of three, will have to direct the destinies of Europe and Africa jointly. What we will have won jointly in Europe and Africa obviously we will have to defend jointly if necessary. You must understand, my new and dear friend, that you and Spain are isolated, with old-fashioned ways. There is a new and modern world on this side of the Pyrenees, and modern technology with which you are obviously not familiar. Owing to the increasing speed of airplanes America is moving closer and closer to this European-African area. In ten years from now, in 1950, say, the distance from Africa to America will possibly be no greater than today the distance from Germany to England across the North Sea." He gazed blandly at Serrano Suñer, "Thus the need for a base in the Atlantic, thus the need for a Canary Island. I trust that General Franco will see this our way."

"I cannot even transmit such a message to El Caudillo."

"You can and you will. In fact, a fast plane is at your disposal for the purpose of transporting your courier with messages to and from El Caudillo."[5] Obviously pleased with himself, Ribbentrop explained, "There will be no problem of delays over issues that 'can only be decided by El Caudillo,' we are not new to our business." He pointed to the table of toy solders and vehicles. "That is one Wehrmacht division. I bring to your attention that we have two hundred and fifty of those."

With such an offensive man the only defense was to be offensive. Serrano Suñer smiled at his host. "I hope you don't have to dust them all yourself." Ignoring the German's outrage he added, "Your Excellency must understand that you need not threaten a friend such as Spain. You have only to tell us what you wish and we will do it to the limit of our capabilities. I must stress the contribution Spain has already made in her Civil War. If we had not risen successfully against the Popular Front Government then today strategic Spain, whose help you want, would be in the hands of Soviet Russia."

"You are quite right. Both of our countries can well be content with ourselves: Spain has won the Civil War, Germany the Battle of Flanders which will influence the development of Europe in the future just as decisively as in ancient times the Battle of Cannae."[6]

Serrano Suñer decided that he had let the German dominate the conversation long enough. "Herr Reichsaussenminister, in entering the war Spain wants to conform entirely to the general plan of Germany . . ."

"Of course."

". . . and above all to avoid the possibility of becoming a burden to Germany. I wish to stress El Caudillo's strong desire not to enter precipitately and possibly divert Germany from her main objective."[7]

Von Ribbentrop raised an eyebrow. "How might that happen?"

"The British blockade. Relations with England become more difficult every day. They block our imports of foodstuffs and make gasoline deliveries a nightmare to accomplish. And, all this while we are still a neutral nation, eh? But the moment Spain declares war against England then Germany will have the responsibility of both supplying all of Spain's needs and transporting them to her through that blockade. It could become a major undertaking."

Not allowing von Ribbentrop to reply, he continued, "Let us turn to the heart of the matter: Spain is awaiting with great impatience and enthusiasm the possibility of an operation against Gibraltar . . ."

Von Ribbentrop smiled.

Standing up, placing both hands on von Ribbentrop's desk and leaning toward him sincerely, Serrano Suñer said, "*Herr Reichsaussenminister*, be assured that if not for our economic difficulties we would have entered the war long ago. And that even despite these difficulties we are now eager to join the fight in proportion to the support that can be given us in augmenting our inadequate supplies."

Serrano Suñer's face suddenly took on a ludicrous smile, then a self-rebuking shrug. "Here I am, telling you of our enthusiasm for joining the great conflict, but on the other hand I want you to know that we in Spain will fully understand if at this moment Germany might have no interest in the Spanish problems since you are thoroughly occupied elsewhere in your fight against England, to say nothing of the occupation of most of Europe."

"No, no . . . we are interested."

"We would also understand if, possibly due to the Italians, the operations against the other gateway to the Mediterranean, the Suez Canal, were to be given priority for the time being."

"I assure you, *Sr. Ministro*, Germany is desirous of Spain's entry into the war."

"*Bueno*, then let me preface my remarks by stating the obvious: any nation that has just suffered three years of civil war would look terribly on its leaders if they were led into another war without being assured of appropriate rewards."

"Spain will be supplied all that she lacks."

"Thank you. But, as they say, 'Man does not live on bread alone.' I fear that the *note verbale* delivered by our Embassy here in Berlin, regarding Spain's wishes regarding Gibraltar and Morocco, must have been presented in an unfortunate way because we have had no answer from you.

Therefore, let me try to present our position more clearly. Regarding Morocco, my government appeals to Germany's sense of justice in making it possible for Spain to have all of French Morocco in her hands. Morocco belongs to Spain's *lebensraum* just as Austria, Czechoslovakia and Poland were a part of yours.

"From the economic standpoint, Morocco is an area that compensates for certain of Spain's deficiencies, and whose phosphates could provide the necessary fertilizers for our agriculture.

"From the political standpoint, Morocco is the historical and natural objective of Spanish expansion. The present division into the Tangier Zone, the French Zone, and the Spanish Zone, was something entirely unnatural, forced upon us, as you surely know, by the French at the Algeciras Conference. Whereas for Spain, Morocco was a natural objective of expansion, the French expansion to Morocco had an aggressive character, to say the least. However, thanks to the *Führer* the French will no longer be able to perpetrate such injustices, and the past can be corrected.

"Morocco must become a Spanish Protectorate as one unit. Its population is notoriously unable politically and administratively to govern itself and therefore some European country must exercise general supervision. Among all European countries Spain alone is appropriate, both by geography and by tradition.

"Even from the standpoint of security it is essential for Spain to acquire all of Morocco and eliminate the danger that exists today along our uncomfortably vulnerable three-hundred-kilometer border with French Morocco. Spain has quite enough to do with her two European borders and definitely wants to make the Moroccan border absolutely secure by shifting it to the Sahara.

"Moreover, *Herr Reichsaussenminister*, *El Caudillo* strongly feels that the region of Oran should be ceded to Spain, since the population there is Spanish. And finally, we wish to lay claim to a small border rectification south of the Spanish colony, Rio de Oro, as far as Bahia del Galgo . . ."

Handing over a map illustrating Spain's territorial claims, Serrano Suñer said, "I'm sure the *Führer* will be pleased with a conversation I had with the Portuguese Ambassador in Madrid."

"Oh?"

"Yes. Portugal was very much concerned about Germany's advance in France as far as Hendaye. But I explained to the Portuguese Ambassador that if Portuguese policy were no longer subject to English influence, then every reason for fearing Germany would disappear."

Von Ribbentrop nodded. "And what was the Portuguese Ambassador's reply?"

"The Portuguese attitude has improved. However, she has not believed in German victory as we have and so her policy is vacillating. This is a situation that causes us great concern; we share a twelve-hundred-kilometer border with Portugal, which at times has been synonymous with sharing a border with England."

"That is why the *Führer* does not approve of Spain's friendship with Portugal. There is always the danger of the British landing in Portugal and crossing into Spain as Wellington did against Napoleon. This is most important. England is simply a colony of the United States. Portugal must break with England or she too will be a colony of the United States and a dangerous bridgehead."

"Actually, *Herr Reichsaussenminister* Portugal has no right to exist. If one looks at a map of Europe one cannot avoid the realization that geographically speaking, she simply has no reason to exist as an independent state; she has nothing more than a moral and political justification for independence as a result of her eight-hundred-year history. *El Caudillo* recognizes this, but he remembers her good attitude during our Civil War. Also, it would be difficult for Spain to absorb seven million weeping Portuguese, so she continues to enjoy independence. But we must definitely require her to align herself with Spain in her political attitude, and we will do so."

"Very well," said von Ribbentrop. "Let me say that from the German standpoint, we feel great satisfaction over the fact of Spain's revising her former attitude, and now being willing, in principle, to enter the war."

"Eager."

"Better. I assume that *El Caudillo*'s letter to the *Führer* contains approximately what your Excellency has just told me?"

"No, *Herr Reichsaussenminister*, the letter to the *Führer* contains only the statement that Spain will do everything in her power to intervene effectively in the struggle, and that we are anxious now, following sporadic feelers, to formally make contact with the German statesmen by sending to Germany the Minister of the Interior as a special representative of Spain and of *El Caudillo*."

Von Ribbentrop hesitated. "Well, no matter. Without wanting to anticipate the *Führer*, I can nonetheless even now communicate Germany's basic position. The reason why the Spanish *note verbale* concerning claims in Morocco and Gibraltar has not yet been answered is that the question is so important that we have been subjecting it to close study here. Through our Embassy in Madrid and through Admiral Canaris we have made inquiries that have led us to obtain an exact picture of the situation. It is good that the answer can now be made in the course of personal contact with a Cabinet member. Somehow, notes of reply and written expositions usually contribute less to the solution of problems than personal contacts and acts.

"The *Führer* and the *Duce* stood at the side of Spain during her Civil War. Today, we are happy that we gave help at that time, for it is precisely in the southwest of Europe that we need a new Spain. Franco's victory caused rejoicing here in Germany. And we understood that owing to the need for reconstruction, Spain could hardly enter our war the first day.

"However, things have changed considerably since the beginning. We have destroyed France, and as you so astutely anticipate, I can assure you that the *Führer* intends that in the future that country will play no role that could in any way lead to new conflicts. France is finished in Europe's politics.

"We are involved in a decisive battle against England, as is Italy with her attack against Egypt the day before yesterday. England will finally be defeated. The only question is: how long will that take? The *Führer* recently said that he will do everything possible to end the war quickly but that he is also prepared for a long war if necessary. Personally, I feel the war will be short. Victory by Germany and Italy is now absolutely certain. All the English can do is battle on longer than is useful or intelligent.

Things are worse in England every day. Soon there will be nothing left of London but rubble and ashes. Truly patriotic Englishmen should hope for an early German invasion before their country is totally destroyed.

"The British have two possibilities: either give up the war now, or take off with their government to Canada in which case we will of course occupy the British Isles. For practical purposes the war is already decided . . ."

How many times, Serrano Suñer wondered, *has he assured me the war is won? Three, four times in one breath?*

". . . Whether England will succeed in drawing America into her war actively is extremely doubtful. The Americans want simply to play the role of an heir to the British Empire. Therefore, projecting forward: following the victory, which is not at all in doubt . . ."

Again.

". . . Germany, Italy and Spain have the major task of reorganizing Europe and Africa. I am happy that in addition to Italy and Germany another great nation will participate in the reorganization of these areas, for through her entry into the war Spain will be able to play the important postwar role appropriate to her." Ribbentrop paused, then, "At the same time, I wish to stress, *Sr. Ministro,* that Spain's entry into the war will take place entirely of her own free will, on condition that the necessary military and economic assistance are accorded to her. Spain must not feel any sense of debt or pressure from Germany."

Glancing at the miniature *Wehrmacht* division, of which there were twenty real ones at Spain's frontier, Serrano Suñer thought, *Pressure? My dear friend and Herr Reichsaussenminister, why would I possibly feel pressure?* He said, "What Spain feels is friendship, *Herr Reichsaussenminister,* and all of Spain, from her leader to her most humble worker, is desirous of entering the war at Germany's side. We have the will; we need only the materials and then we will have both the will and the way."

A luncheon was given in honor of the Spanish Minister, and he and his party had the opportunity to meet more ministers and figures of importance in the Third Reich. The ambiance was friendly, though Serrano Suñer found the conversation to be brilliantly boring. He could hardly believe the lack of sophistication, boorish table manners, and language that often surpassed vulgarity. These were not statesmen or career diplomats, for the most part, but crass politicians who had backed a winner and risen to power and rank.

Appraising von Ribbentrop, the Spaniard thought that though he was of a higher level than the others, better educated, had a good build and wore well-cut, expensive clothing, he was not the least bit distinguished or elegant, for the same reason that he didn't appear humane or even intelligent: he was all affectations.

Ribbentrop interrupted the amiable atmosphere. "*Don* Ramón . . ."

Don Ramón? Serrano Suñer thought, *Suddenly we like each other so well that we are now at first names.*

". . . you who are such a trusted friend of the Third Reich should know that the *Führer* is displeased by Spain's equivocal foreign policy. The *Führer* considers it gross ingratitude. He is outraged by the *Caudillo* harboring a Foreign Minister who is in the service of England."

There was silence.

Serrano Suñer thought, *Couldn't we have handled this at the office? Lunch simply is not the time for ungentlemanly thrusts. On the other hand, these are not gentlemen.* Seeing Heinrich Himmler waiting for the answer he realized that it was not a question that could have been handled at the office, that in fact it had been planned to be asked and answered in front of the Gestapo chief.

He had practiced saying "Joachim" and could pronounce it perfectly, with much more ease than *Reichsaussenminister,* but he replied, "*Herr Reichsaussenminister,* Colonel Beigbeder and I disagree on almost everything, but I can absolutely assure you that he is a Spanish patriot in the service of no nation other than Spain. It is a fact, however, that we have recently uncovered and corrected a security problem at the Foreign Ministry, which we traced to British Intelligence agents. But Minister Beigbeder's loyalty is categorically unquestionable."

Himmler nodded slightly.

Impressed by the directness of admitting a security problem and naming what had been worrying them, von Ribbentrop said, "Then we have been misinformed. I am pleased. So, then, satisfied now of Minister

Beigbeder's loyalty to Spain we come to the question of Spain's loyalty to the Third Reich. I warn you here and now that in the matter of Spain's foreign policy, a lack of clarity, repeat, a lack of crystal-clear clarity, might one day cause the *Führer* to decide to occupy the Iberian Peninsula as a security measure due to its strategic value to the Allies." He stared at Serrano Suñer, awaiting his reply.

"I hope with all my heart that such a day never comes, because I can assure your Excellency that there are few Spaniards who would not prefer to be dead than to see their country occupied. *El Caudillo* himself would be unable to stop them from rising against any force that might seek to occupy them. The women as well as the men would kill, with pitchforks, burning oil, with any weapon they might utilize. We are fanatics."

Serrano Suñer noted that whenever von Ribbentrop disliked what was said, he ignored it. "I insist that as a courtesy to me you advise *El Caudillo* of Germany's need for a base on one of the Canary Islands. That is not asking so much, considering that you are looking for all of French Morocco to fall to you as a result of Germany's victory over France."

"Spain is quite prepared to conquer French Morocco with her own blood. I have explained that it is a message I cannot communicate, but as you insist, and as you consider it a courtesy, I will try."

"Let me ask you one last question regarding Spain's entry. Precisely when do you believe that will be possible?"

"That is something that only *El Caudillo* can say. I have come to Berlin with authorization to discuss only those problems within the framework of the *note verbale* and our requirements on food and other materials."

"Then you will write a letter to *El Caudillo* regarding the time of Spain's entry, raising the Canary Islands question as well and send it to him by courier on our fast plane."

"With pleasure, *Herr Reichsaussenminister*. And purely of my own speculation I would venture that with military, economic and territorial problems resolved, Spain could enter the war immediately. Or, as mentioned earlier, when the *Führer* has successfully landed in England."

"England is beaten. She is on her knees. It is now simply a matter of days, a few weeks at most . . ."

As von Ribbentrop continued guaranteeing him of the imminent fall of the British Empire and the invasion of England, Serrano Suñer thought, *Weren't we supposed to be attending the Führer's cocktail party in London, yesterday? September 15th?*

". . . and I would bring to your attention that it is customary to divide the spoils of war with proven friends, not those who wait to see which way the wind will blow."

"But *Herr Reichsaussenminister,* at the risk of repeating myself, I assure you that *El Caudillo* is being a friend in the best sense, and at great sacrifice, by preventing Spain from entering the war before you successfully occupy England."

Heinrich Himmler was looking at him over his pince-nez. "Please repeat yourself for my benefit, *Sr. Ministro.* My one-track policeman's mentality cannot grasp this line of thinking."

"With pleasure, *Herr Reichsführer. El Caudillo* knows, as we all know, that Germany has won the war, that it is only a matter of time until the British accept that fact. By remaining outside of the war Spain does not help her postwar position when it is time to divide the spoils. But still *El Caudillo,* as a friend of Germany, waits because on the day that Spain enters the war at the side of Germany and Italy we will instantly lose all trade with the Allies; all food and vital materials will be cut off from America and Canada. And even if we could arrange for supplies from elsewhere, Argentina, for example, those shipments would never reach us because the Royal Navy would enforce the strictest blockade. They did it recently, with gasoline, just on the false rumor that we were re-exporting to Germany. If we join the war a moment too soon the *Führer* could find himself committed to feed twenty-three million Spaniards. A most insupportable burden. Take that from one who sees our Government unable to accomplish it even without blockades.

"How much worse for Spain, yet better for Germany if we wait until England surrenders and you gain our strategic advantage with no burden." He shrugged, "If there were doubt of this being imminent it would be a different story, but as we all know, it can only be a case of weeks at most. No?"

"She is on her knees. She is beaten and just doesn't know enough to surrender."

The women offered to him were ravishing.

Ribbentrop explained, "A business luncheon of all men is possible, but to dine also in that atmosphere is not civilized. I therefore invited my niece Ilke and three of her friends to joins us."

They were Gestapo women. Four of a team of sixteen, which had taken two years to find, screen and train. They had to be beautiful, cultured, preferably aristocrats with known names, and finally they had to be fanatically devoted to National Socialism so that nothing they might be required to do to please a man, no matter how repugnant, would stop them from extracting the information that he might give them intentionally or otherwise.

They were well paid, provided with appropriate wardrobes, cars, servants and suitable apartments, which were "sound stages" with concealed motion-picture cameras and microphones in every room, anywhere that an indiscreet word might drop, or failing that, a photograph of a man dining with a strange and beautiful woman, even fully clothed, could be embarrassing and thus useful.

The women had been trained by psychologists in ways of causing men to volunteer information; by professional prostitutes; and finally by an SS officer who taught them how to kill with makeshift weapons: such as a sharpened wooden pencil stabbed upwards under a man's chin.

It would have flattered Serrano Suñer's ego if he had known who they were and that they were brought into situations only of the highest political or military interest. But what he *did* understand was that he could have any one, or all four of them, if he wished. He noted that apart from their beauty they incorporated among them each basic type of woman, appealing to every taste; they were a pleasure to converse with as they were accomplished linguists, speaking Spanish with only an appealing trace of German accent.

He was thoroughly charmed throughout dinner. But immediately after dessert he excused himself, rather than sit in a bar drinking with his hosts, which they urged, surely as a prelude to slipping off with one of the girls.

He thought of Beigbeder, whom he planned to succeed. No. It was all too good and too menacing.

Awakening early in the morning and getting out of bed he noted how much colder it was in Berlin in September than in Madrid. *Especially when you are going to meet Adolf Hitler for the first time.*

Dressed in the plain black uniform of the Falange, calculated to be ideologically pleasing to the *Führer*, he went downstairs where von Ribbentrop and von Doernberg were awaiting him, again in an open-topped touring car, with motorcycle police in front and behind. As they sped through Berlin, attracting salutes from storm troopers and *"Heils"* along the way, seeing the hundreds of swastikas flying, Serrano Suñer, who had left Spain with a sense of importance: a man going off on a diplomatic mission with Adolf Hitler, now saw his visit in a different perspective, as he knew was intended: *He is the sovereign of nearly an entire continent, the master of a powerful and triumphant nation. I'm just a Minister of a proud but spent country.*

Helmeted SS troops in black uniforms with white belting stood at both sides of the entrance to the Chancellery, a bronze door situated between two massive columns above which the traditional golden eagle of Germany now clutched the Third Reich's garlanded swastika in its claws.

Inside, more SS troops guarded the door. The building was L-shaped, had a yellowish-brown exterior, with dignity and dimension appropriate for housing the office of the Chief of State.

Passing the threshold of a large door they were facing a long hallway lined with floor-to-ceiling windows some twenty feet in height. Flanked by von Ribbentrop and von Doernberg, Serrano Suñer walked toward a doorway below a portico supported by two gigantic Doric columns, beside each of which were two immense statues of nude athletes. Passing through the portico they entered into another long corridor.

Suddenly everything changed. The walls and floor were a spectacle of various colored marble polished to such brilliance that they seemed to glow from within. The ceiling, paneled in gold and white with a perfect system of indirect lighting, combined with the floor to make the whole thing so beautiful as to be fatuous.

Looking down the length of the corridor, Serrano Suñer had the feeling that perhaps they had left the car too soon. On the other hand, he reasoned to himself, it wasn't necessary to walk the entire length because keeping up with the strides of his two companions caused him to be sliding there.[8]

To the right was the entrance to a huge receiving room where Serrano Suñer and von Ribbentrop waited while von Doernberg passed through to the *Führer's* office. A moment later he reappeared, beckoning them in.

Adolf Hitler was standing ten feet inside the room. He wore black trousers and the gray jacket of the uniform of the National Socialist party, bearing the spread-winged golden eagle insignia of the Third Reich on its left sleeve. He was smiling.

The *Führer* was not underframed. His office was the length of a grand ballroom and fully fifty feet in width.

At the near-end where he stood was a sitting area of couches and comfortable chairs. The decoration was so overladen that the Spanish Minister had the feeling that the Nazi oligarchy shared a superb sense of bad taste and a distinct leaning toward nouveau riche.

Hitler, having that morning discarded Operation Sea Lion as an impossible task, was more than ever interested in meeting with the Spanish Minister. He was desperate for Gibraltar.

Shaking hands, Serrano Suñer said, "I bring your Excellency a message from *El Caudillo* of his gratitude, high esteem and the guarantee of his loyalty of yesterday, of today and for always."

"It is kind of you to come to see me," Hitler said taking the Spaniard's elbow and guiding him to a heavily tufted and tasseled couch.

"Now then, I understand that you would like six-hundred thousand tons of wheat. Would you care to have a cup of coffee with it?[9] Or perhaps a nice hot chocolate?" He smiled warmly, "Don't worry about provisions. Friends of the Third Reich want for nothing.

"What is vital," Hitler continued, "is that we share the same political theories. We European countries can maintain ourselves against the American continent only if we too conduct a continental policy, and make Africa an absolutely integral part of the eastern hemisphere. The bloc of North and South America must be confronted by the European-African bloc."

"*Führer*, what European could not greatly admire and thoroughly agree with that?"

"The German interests are, first, to render the northern area free from blockade; second, to create security toward the east, for danger always threatens from the east, and Germany is filling a very useful role as the eastern bulwark for Europe. Third, Germany needs to be assured of a great colonial area, which is not required to be an area for settlement—of which we possess enough on the European continent—but purely a matter of colonies for raw materials."

Seeing the direction in which he was headed, Serrano Suñer referred to ". . . Spain's just claims in Africa, our *lebensraum*. . ."

Hitler said, "I reluctantly concede your point." Again he smiled and, Serrano thought, with sincerity reflecting in his blue eyes.

"The *Führer* is generous as well as kind to me. Thank you."

Hitler laughed lightly, "The *Führer* is not so generous because I make this important concession on the condition that Germany receives a most favorable trade agreement for the raw materials of that region."

"But of course, *Führer*. I would like, if I may, to give notice of one additional Spanish territorial claim against France at the Pyrenees border. This does not involve extensive territorial demands but merely rectification of the border, which, since it was set by France, runs entirely to Spain's disadvantage."

"Of course," Hitler sighed. "How familiar I am with borders set by France when she had the power and abused it so that now we must have war to rectify her misdoings." Then he commented offhandedly, "Eventually Spain as a European nation must be part of Europe's unity and its systems. Spain's geographical situation offers her the opportunity to make an important contribution in the Europeanization of Gibraltar and Africa, and one day she must play her role."

"And the sooner the better, *Führer*. But for the moment we are simply incapable of making war. We are barely surviving in peace."

Hitler studied the Spaniard's face. "One way or another we must take Gibraltar." Again he stared into Serrano Suñer's eyes. Then, "Very well, if you cannot be actively helpful at the moment, and since Germany does not need Spain's help militarily, it will be enough for us to be permitted to pass through your territory to attack Gibraltar."

Franco had anticipated this and had prepared his brother-in-law. Serrano Suñer's face took on a tragic expression, and when he spoke his tone of voice was pathetic. "*Führer*, as a German patriot you can understand how a Spanish patriot would feel if he were to play this ignominious role; to render himself with such little dignity as to stand meekly by while a powerful force crosses through our land. Surely you would not ask this of the *Generalísimo*.

"I am desirous of entering the war, *Führer*. *El Caudillo* is desirous of entering the war. Re-arm us, organize us well so that we can make an early intervention as your active ally. But *Führer*, do not ask us to stand in silence, our arms folded, helpless, humiliated, as you pass across our country.

"This you *could* do, you have the power. But with our consent, no. With our protest. And there would be resistance." He looked into Hitler's eyes, "You would win, *Führer*. I am certain you would crush us. But before the eyes of the entire world you would play the role of hangman to one of the two nations remaining on this earth who are truly your friends . . ."[10]

Hitler had been looking into Serrano's eyes. Now he looked down, staring at his clasped hands. His shoulders fell. There was a silence.

Serrano thought, *It worked. But for today. Eventually it will come back again to "Despite everything, we must take Gibraltar."*

Looking up, Hitler said, "But one way or another we must have Gibraltar. Germany is in a decisive struggle against England. Continentally, the struggle is already decided. A British landing on the continent of Europe can only be characterized as a chimera. The single military possibility still existing would be an attempt by England to alienate the French colonies in North Africa from the Pétain government and use them as a new position for the continuation of the war. We, therefore, are faced with the necessity of getting there first and annulling England's last remaining military possibility. Of course, to do this we must begin at the beginning: Gibraltar."

"*El Caudillo* has given long and profound thought to the taking of Gibraltar . . ." Serrano Suñer replied, and following instructions he made a request that he knew Germany was not able to fulfill. "Our military strategists estimate that we would require a substantial amount of 380 mm: 15 inch guns for the coastal barrage."

"No, no, no, no. No! All wrong." Hitler said. "Wrong. Very wrong. A long-barreled canon requires maintenance after firing two hundred rounds of shells, each of which contains only from seventy to seventy-five kilograms of explosives, whereas a squadron of my *Sturzkampf-flugzeuge*, thirty-six machines in use thrice daily, can drop one hundred and twenty bombs of one thousand kilograms each, a total of one hundred and twenty thousand tons of explosives. I can set your mind at rest that if a group of *Sturzkampfflugzeuge* and a group of heavy pursuit planes are made available for the conquest of Gibraltar, then within eight days no enemy ships would dare to venture within three hundred and fifty kilometers of those Spanish waters, for while it is true that heavy bombs could perhaps not destroy a ship, a direct hit would render it incapable of battle and require several months for repairs. I can assure you that at the mere sight of my *Sturzkampfflugzeuge* the Royal Navy will flee from Gibraltar." He looked at Serrano Suñer in triumph. "And without the British navy to contend with there is no need for heavy artillery."

Hitler nodded, confirming that he agreed with what he had said. "I will speak to the *Caudillo* about this strategy. And don't worry, Germany will do everything in her immense power to help Spain in every way possible, every way, every way. Perhaps it would be an excellent idea for the *Caudillo* and I to meet. I will be in Paris on October 22nd to see Laval and to arrange a meeting with Pétain. I will put Pétain on the 24th and meet with the *Caudillo* on the 23rd. I will train to Biarritz and meet the *Caudillo* on the frontier at Hendaye at two o'clock on the 23rd of October. I will already have taken lunch . . . my customs are not the same as you Spaniards. But I will be delighted if the *Caudillo* will dine with me aboard my train after our meeting. And he will be delighted too. My cuisine is superb. My dinners are always perfect. I personally follow a vegetarian diet, and since the war began, a spartan one at that, nothing more than the most ordinary German soldier has to eat. But I do not impose this idealism on my guests . . ."

Serrano Suñer had listened to the performance, which had begun with a military discourse far over his head. Then, without taking a breath, he had casually suggested a meeting with *El Caudillo*, and in the same breath named the precise time, place and date and ended with a soliloquy on eating habits. But most significant: he had lied. Serrano Suñer knew that the Stukas had been taken out of action against England in August, fully a month ago, because they were ineffective against the British Spitfires. Certainly the *Führer* did not imagine they would fare any better against the Royal Navy and those same Spitfires over Gibraltar. If he were truly confidant, why would he lie?

Hitler was motioning to follow him to the other part of the office, to his desk. Serrano Suñer noticed that whenever possible he avoided the use of interpreters, preferring a gesture if it would work, treating him more personally.

The desk was a spectacle. Some sixteen feet long and eight feet wide, it was covered with relief maps and charts and slide rulers. Hitler put on a pair of glasses and began measuring relative distances from Irún to Algeciras by road, train and air, as if he didn't have a hundred crack drafts-men who could quickly tell him anything he wanted to know.

"Look at this," he said, displaying a box of compasses. His face glowed with infantile delight.

An aide entered and whispered something to Hitler, who nodded. Taking Serrano Suñer by the arm he led him back to the sofas where a photographer was setting up a camera. "I thought you'd like to have a photograph of our meeting . . . . a little memento." He gestured for the interpreters to sit in, and removing his glasses, he looked at Serrano Suñer in a "listening" manner while the picture was taken.

Despite Hitler's warmth and lack of pressure the highly volatile nature was clear, and Serrano Suñer was certain that *El Caudillo* had selected the right strategy, that with a man like this, a mixture of mon-strous genius, the petty bourgeois, sentimental, hard, fanatical, childish and maniacal—to have categorically said no to any of his desires, let alone demands, would have caused him to develop an irresistible urge to violate Spain's neutrality.

Dropped off at his hotel by von Ribbentrop, the Spanish Minister knew that he should not have been surprised to encounter Ilke in the lobby with two other "girl-friends", gorgeous, and so cordial that following a meeting with Adolf Hitler he would have welcomed a drink and such companionship. But even without knowing they were *Gestapo* he knew for sure that they were not Spanish patriots. Excusing himself from the girls he went upstairs to write a report. It would be taken to Madrid in the special plane the following day in the hands of a Spanish courier. In the same plane would be a German courier with a letter to *El Caudillo* from the *Führer*.

That afternoon, Hitler wrote to Mussolini.

The Chancellery
Berlin   September 17, 1940

Duce,

I am convinced that it can be important to make it possible for Spain to enter the war. In this regard the Spanish Government has approached Germany with a number of military and economic requests.

The military requests can be filled very easily, for they involve in the main only the detachment of some artillery and a number of special troops.

The economic requests are more difficult. My Foreign Minister will report the details to you, Duce. The German harvest can be called a good average harvest. The potato, turnip, and cabbage crop will probably be very good; perhaps it will even set a record. In these circumstances and considering the fact that we still have reserves available, I believe I would be justified in giving the Spanish Government the needed help . . .

"Excellency," the aide said, "Sr. Reed Rosas is calling by telephone."

The voice, which Franco recognized with its mixture of German and South American accent, said, "Operation Sea Lion was shelved this morning. The alternative plan, Operation Felix, is now going forward as quickly as possible. No date is set as yet . . ."

When Franco had hung up the telephone the aide returned with a cablegram:

THE FUHRER HAS INVITED YOU TO MEET WITH HIM
ON OCTOBER 23, AT 1400 HOURS AT THE RAILROAD
STATION AT HENDAYE.

RAMON

Hitler was closing in.

At seven o'clock that afternoon *El Caudillo* was notified that the Minister of Foreign Affairs wished to see him on an urgent matter.

"Excellency," Beigbeder explained, "I have just received a cable in cipher from Eduardo Propper y Callejón, who is presently our Counselor in Vichy. We have a serious Jewish problem. Propper informed me that the Sephardic Jews are being persecuted like all other French Jews. Several of them have gone to our Consular office seeking asylum on grounds of Spanish ancestry."

The Sephardim, Jews of Spain and Portugal, had not seen Spain since Ferdinand and Isabella had expelled them in 1492 after giving them the opportunity to remain by becoming true Catholics.

In 1927, as a Colonel in Morocco, observing the Arabs persecuting the descendants of those Jews who had immigrated there four centuries earlier, Franco had written to the dictator of Spain, General Primo de Rivera, seeking and receiving permission to protect them with Spanish troops. Nine years later, in 1936, at the beginning of the Spanish Civil War, the Moroccan Jewish community demonstrated its gratitude by coming to Franco's aid with strong financial backing.

When Primo de Rivera had granted permission to protect the Sephardim he also advised Franco that the Jews could return to Spain, worshiping as they chose, by becoming Spanish citizens again.

With legal precedent why would it not be an appropriate and defensible gesture now? Defensible? What would it matter to Hitler if there were legal pretenses or not? Angered, he could take revenge on the whole Spanish nation. This was not like a few thousand refugees at the border whom Spain could reasonably claim not knowing were Jews. Giving passports to the Sephardim left no way to pretend ignorance of protecting Hitler's victims.

Franco stood up. "We'll talk again tomorrow."

Carmencita's friends Maruja and Margarita Orfila and Maria Dolores Collantes were spending a few days at El Pardo and so dinner conversation was mostly Franco-the-father chatting with them about their day. After dinner the girls went off to their rooms and Franco, *El Caudillo*, told his wife about his day.

"In Poland they are experimenting with 'killing centers' at a concentration camp, Auschwitz, where they've built immense gas chambers . . ."

"But Paco, you have the power to save some of those people? Why are you hesitating?"

"When I was a person," he said, "I wouldn't have hesitated." He looked into his wife's unfathoming eyes. "Carmen, this power that was put in my hands, it was not so that I could gratify myself performing noble deeds. God chose my sword to be used for the good of Spain. And I have sworn to give my life protecting Spaniards.

"This Hitler has taken it upon himself to exterminate an entire race. I used to believe that he would win the war. But now, no. God will not support such a person. Yet, Hitler is still capable of revenge, such as bombing our cities to hurt and kill as many Spaniards as he wishes, to punish us. It would seem that human beings would not be capable of such acts. But human beings killed Jesus Christ. When you understand that a species could commit an act like that, then nothing is impossible.

"I remember when I was fifteen, standing in front of the statue of Carlos V in Toledo and reading the inscription on a stone plaque: QUE VENCIA O MORRIR. That thought stayed with me as a soldier, I would win or die. When I became a Captain that changed. It was my responsibility to plan the battles. Depending on what I did, well or badly, not only *I* might die but a company of a hundred men with me. As a Major the number rose to a battalion of a thousand. As a Colonel, a regiment of several thousand men went into the battles that I planned and ordered.

As a General and later Chief of Staff it continued increasing. During the war it was around a million men.

"Today the number is twenty-three million. The way I wage this war with Hitler—if I lose it a whole nation dies or goes into slavery."

"But you believe that God won't support him."

"God has mysterious ways. For an evil man the *Führer* has come very far without being stopped."

"He will be stopped."

Franco looked at her with affection. "Can you give me a date on that, Carmelita?" He walked toward the chapel beside their bedroom, the chapel where King Alfonso XII had died, and he prayed for help in making the right decision.

In the morning Franco told Beigbeder, "Advise Propper that he is authorized under Spanish law to issue passports to all Sephardic Jews."[11]

"One question, Excellency. This will become known to non-Sephardic Jews throughout France because all Jews are being moved into ghetto areas of each city. Surely the non-Sephardic Jews will try for the same protection in order to escape from France. How will we know if they truly are Sephardim or not?"

"They are *all* Sephardim! We are saving human beings. Instruct Propper to be most discreet and to beg the Jews to exercise all discretion possible for our sake, as well as their own, because the moment this maneuver is known to the Nazis they will spirit those people away to places from which they will not be able to walk into our Consulates and ask for passports."

On September 19th the aide said, "Excellency, the German *Chargé d'Affaires*, in Ambassador von Stohrer's absence, Herr Heberlein, wishes to deliver a letter which the *Führer* has sent by special plane."

"He may pass by here immediately. Ask when he will arrive and then call the Barón de las Torres to be here at that time, but to wait in the library and avoid being seen by the *Chargé*."

Herr Heberlein arrived within an hour and handed over the envelope. "Excellency, it was anticipated that you would be eager to learn the contents and I was instructed by *Reichsaussenminister* von Ribbentrop to offer my services to your Excellency to translate from the German."

"A letter from the *Führer* is something to which I always wish to give my undivided attention. At the moment there are some matters that I must attend to first." He stood up. "I will try to send my reply with courier Figueras on September 22nd."

As the door closed Franco was slitting open the envelope. The letterhead was engraved with the emblem of the Third Reich. The only word that Franco recognized was *Caudillo*. He opened the door to the library and gave the letter to the Barón de las Torres, who translated aloud.

The Chancellery
Berlin   *September 18, 1940*
Dear Caudillo,

> *Minister of Interior Serrano Suñer has brought me your letter, and I cordially return your greetings and the friendship they express. We have entered into an exchange of ideas regarding the problems that at the moment affect not only Europe but probably the entire world. The suggested conferences as well as those that have just taken place and those still going on with your Minister Serrano Suñer prompt me, my dear Caudillo, to describe my thoughts to you on these problems in a few points. The opinions of my General Staff are entirely the same as those set down here.*

> 1. *The war will decide the future of Europe. There is not a country in Europe that can avoid its political and economic effects. The end of the war will also decide Spain's future, perhaps for centuries. But even today Spain is suffering, though she is still not a participant in the war. The virtual blockade imposed on Spain by England will not be loosened as long as England herself is not conquered, but will only become more severe. In the face of this, any measures for economic assistance can only be of an emergency and temporary nature. But the mere expulsion of the English from the Mediterranean will convert it into an inland sea withdrawn from English interference and again open for commerce. This alone would provide a radical solution to Spain's supply problem. And this aim can and will be attained rapidly and with certainty through Spain's entry into the war.*

2. *Spain's entry into the war on the side of the Axis powers must begin with the expulsion of the English fleet from Gibraltar and immediately thereafter the seizure of the fortified Rock.*

   This operation must and can be successfully carried through within a few days, if high-grade well-tried, modern means of attack and attack troops are employed. Germany is willing to provide them under Spanish command in the quantities needed.

3. *Once Gibraltar is in Spanish possession the western Mediterranean is eliminated as a base of operations for the English fleet. Aside from the threat from isolated British submarines, then possible only to a limited extent, a sure connection will have been brought about between Spain and North Africa. The Spanish Mediterranean coast itself will then no longer be endangered.*

4. *Aside from the blockade, which for all practical purposes has already been imposed on Spain, England will then have only the possibility of operating against the Atlantic coast of Spain. Defense of this coast by heavy batteries could only be assured—and even then only to a limited extent—if quantities were used that neither Germany nor anyone else can make available.*

   The best—in fact, the only—sure protection consists in placing dive bomber units in the vicinity of the coast . . ."

He went on for pages of military tactics, strategies and enticements, finally concluding:

"These, dear Caudillo, are, briefly stated, the ideas concerning the decisive character of a Spanish participation in a conflict whose outcome will in any case decide the future of Spain for a long time to come . . .

Please accept, my dear Caudillo, my most cordial regards.

In comradely affection,

Adolf Hitler [12]

[See Appendix IV for complete text.]

Franco took note how carefully Hitler broached the matter of protecting the Canary Islands, and unlike von Ribbentrop did not—as a report from Ramón Serrano Suñer had informed him—make an outright demand for the cession of one of the islands to Germany.

El Pardo, September 22, 1940

My *dear* Führer,

I received your letter in which you stated to me your view and those of your General Staff in connection with the problems with respect to Spain that are arising from the war, views that with the exception of small details match my thoughts and plans and those of my General Staff.

I must thank you for the cordial reception that you and your people prepared for my Envoy, Minister Serrano Suñer, who reported to me about your conversation and about your esteemed ideas, which satisfy our wishes, and with which we believe ourselves to be in complete agreement as you will see from the content of this letter . . .

Franco replied with a multi-page discourse, agreeing with much, tactfully disagreeing with what he would not cede to Hitler. [See Appendix V for complete text.]

Returning to Berlin from Rome, where he had spent several days with Mussolini and his son-in-law and Minister of Foreign Affairs Count Galeazzo Ciano, von Ribbentrop met again in his office at the German Foreign Ministry with Serrano Suñer. "I bring your Excellency warm greetings from Count Ciano. Both he and the *Duce* asked me to say that they hope to welcome you in Rome on your return trip."

Thanking him, Serrano Suñer got to business, "I have had communication with *El Caudillo*. Your Excellency will be interested in learning that the British Ambassador had a demarche with our Foreign Minister, Beigbeder. Hoare intimated that England would be prepared to see to it that after the war French Morocco would be ceded to Spain."

"After the war?" Von Ribbentrop laughed. "After the war, when they are stripped of everything they ever owned and Germany occupies the British Isles? What a perfect example of how little the English take into consideration their former allies." Could there be any action more typically English than this?"

Von Ribbentrop asked, "Did *El Caudillo* reply to the *Führer's* request for the cessions of one of the Canary Islands?"

"As I told you, I could not transmit such a message, although I did later say I would try. But the fact is that within the limits of my authority to negotiate I was not in a position to communicate the request officially to the *Generalísimo*, being strictly confined within the bounds of my mission: namely to negotiate within the framework laid down by the Spanish note regarding Spanish claims and needs . . ."

Von Ribbentrop smoothed his forehead and looked as if he were being dizzied trying to understand the Spaniard's answer.

". . . however, I did manage to bring this request to the attention of my brother-in-law . . ."

"Ahhh . . ."

". . . but not officially. Purely for his information, and unofficially. Officially he's not aware of the request."

"But he knows of the request?"

"Unofficially."

"Ahhh. And did he make a reply?" He rushed to add, "Even if only unofficially?"

"In a manner . . . yes. You see, Excellency, Spain has already made so many defense preparations in the Canary Islands that she can now defend them herself quite adequately. Therefore, the unofficial reaction of my brother-in-law could be called quite negative."

"With all due respect to the bravery of the Spanish soldiers, a fact that is well known to us, I must point out that present wars are won by those who have the best technical equipment and who, if possible, have prepared materially for the struggle for decades."

"I, myself, personally, thoroughly agree with your Excellency, but in military matters you and I are laymen. *El Generalísimo* strongly feels that bravery is worth tons of equipment."

"Do you have an official or an unofficial reply to our request for Spanish Guinea and Fernando Po?"

"As I told the *Reichsaussenminister* last week, for national reasons it is impossible to cede islands that belong to Spain historically and constitute a part of Spain."

"What you are saying is that the request has been rejected."

"Yes, officially the reply is in the negative."

"And the matter of Morocco, can you give me a precise answer regarding what Germany can count on for herself in Morocco and the bases?"

"Distinctly. Spain agrees to satisfy, in individual negotiations, Germany's economic interests in Morocco. However, as to the enclaves you have requested, *El Generalísimo* was distressed—in a friendly way—at the request for bases in Morocco.

"The value of Moroccan territory for Spain would be extraordinarily decreased by the cession of such bases. However, I personally am sympathetic to Germany's needs, so may I suggest that if Germany held the Portuguese island of Madeira and San Luis de Senegal as defense bases, just as good a system could be established as one with the Canary Islands and the bases of Mogador and Agadir."

"What you are saying is that the reply is negative."

"One could say that."

"Negative, negative, negative!!!" Von Ribbentrop could not remain seated and he paced the floor trying to control his anger.

Finally, seating himself again, he said, "We will discuss the economic issues and debt consolidation. Germany wants all English- and French-owned business on Spanish territory to be transferred to her. In return she will consequently credit them to the Spanish debts. In some cases the companies are one hundred percent French-owned, and of these Germany wishes only fifty-one percent, leaving the remaining forty-nine percent for Spain. This majority and minority ownership could vary with each company. But in principal, the shares transferred to Germany will be credited to the Civil War debts. In this transaction Spain would gain the following three advantages. 1. Instead of a purely French-owned company, Spain herself would own a large part of such a company. 2. A debt reduction in the amount of the credit for the German shares in the company would result. And 3. Instead of a French company a mixed German-Spanish management would then continue the operation.

"In fact there is a fourth advantage to Spain. Revenge. As for example in the case of the Rio Tinto matter, which was an 'economic Gibraltar' forced upon you in a moment of economic and political weakness. Losing one of the world's greatest mining companies is an outrage and a humiliation that Spain need no longer suffer.

"At such time as Spain wishes to unfurl her flag and gain back lost ground in the name of her honor, she will have to claim ownership rights in the Rio Tinto Company of which she was robbed . . ."

CHAPTER EIGHT

RAMÓN SERRANO SUÑER BURST INTO LAUGHTER WHEN ALEJANDRO ENTERED THE DINING ROOM OF THE PALACE OF EL PARDO WITH A PLATTER OF DUCK IN ORANGE SAUCE. HE UNDERSTOOD THAT THIS was more elaborate food than usually served and he appreciated that his sister-in-law had ordered it to celebrate his return home, which reflected *El Caudillo*'s approval of his mission to Berlin, but he explained, "Because of the food scarcity in Germany all the big shots—Goering, Goebbels, Ribbentrop—go out of their way to demonstrate the pursuit of the spartan life by serving wild game, which is plentiful. In five consecutive official dinners the food was exclusively and monotonously wild duck.

"The spartanism is in canyonesque contrast to the ostentation in which they live and work. Goering's home is a palace in the center of Berlin, surrounded by a private park with acres and acres of woods. His idea of a birthday trinket for his wife was a private railway car. If any Spanish Minister had the audacity to live like those Germans he'd be devoured by scandal within hours. Goering is the most materialistic man I have ever seen in my life. He has the most magnificent clothes and jewelry and actually wears medals with business suits. He practices the protocol of a king: he never awaits a visitor; only when everyone is assembled does he enter. Even Hitler was waiting for me.

"He has a passion for push-button efficiency. He pushes a button and a movie screen comes out of the ceiling; another button and the movie starts, with the MGM lion roaring at you."

Smiling broadly he paused. "I am not exaggerating as I tell you that I was having tea with the Goerings when into the salon walked a lion. I do not mean a 'social lion.' I am speaking of a genuine, immense, yellowish-tan cat from Africa with a large fur collar exactly like the MGM lion's. He walked up to the coffee-table and sat down beside me. Goering put a biscuit in his mouth, so I had the opportunity to see that this lion had not suffered preventative dentistry. Then, to my utter distress he put his mammoth head on my lap to demonstrate a distinctly one-way street of affection."

Serrano Suñer paused and was serious. "But despite all his silliness, Goering is the shrewdest, cleverest of them all. He took me into his basement and showed me the most expensive set of miniature railroad trains I have ever seen, and surely the most complex. Nothing was lacking: bridges, tunnels, stations, garages, lakes, rivers, switching posts. After working them he told me, 'I am not retarded. I do enjoy playing with these trains, but this is a precise model of all the secondary railway lines in Germany and a useful toy because while I play with them I am studying how to use them in the unlikely, but always possible event of the destruction of our principal railway lines.'

"While I was in Berlin von Ribbentrop went to Rome to see Mussolini to deliver a letter from the *Führer*. He traveled in a private train belonging to the Ministry of Foreign Affairs, bringing with him all the logical advisors as well as several secretaries, his barber, his doctor, a masseur and a gymnastics teacher." He looked at his brother-in-law. "Excellency, why aren't you that generous with us?"

Carmencita asked, "Uncle Ramón, what is the *Führer* like?"

"Very real, very factual, also very theatrical. He is the character of all characters. When he speaks he has a habit of repeating himself, for emphasis, I suppose. At one point I had trouble keeping myself from laughing. He was telling me about his air force, referring repeatedly to the planes that I have only heard called Stukas but which he referred to by their formal name, *Sturzkampfflugzeuge*, each and every one of at least ten times he mentioned them, as if he were an airplane salesman trying to merchandise the trademark.

"Goebbels is also impressive. He has a foot deformed from polio, but he is so extraordinarily persuasive and astute when you speak to him that he gives the feeling that he could convince anyone of anything he wishes."

Franco commented, "He has convinced most of Europe that resistance to Germany is impossible."

Serrano Suñer continued, "Himmler was a surprise. Heinrich Himmler, the fearsome head of the SS and Gestapo has the timid manner of a schoolmaster."

"And Ribbentrop?" Franco asked.

"A bullying, detestable boor. No sense of humor. A salesman who has one message and keeps hammering it home to you: 'England is beaten. England is on her knees.' There is no five-minute period one can spend with him without being thus assured. In the middle of our second meeting there was an air raid, so we went downstairs to his private bomb shelter. As the RAF's bombs were exploding above us he was saying, 'England is on her knees, beaten.' You can imagine how I yearned to ask, 'Then why are we sitting in this bomb shelter?'"

He continued, "And there they are with the world's worst climate and they decline to have tops on their cars. Everywhere we went it was in open touring cars. Both Tóvar and I got the grippe the day we arrived and they kept airing us out, half-freezing us to death. Finally, one day, driving to the Ministry in the rain, I said to Tóvar, 'These guys are going to kill us with these open cars.' I did not allow for the possibility that the driver spoke Spanish. He stopped the car, saluted and asked, 'Perhaps your Excellency would like to sit up front beside me where there is more protection?'

"There were a few fairly hectic moments due to the German translator, Gross, who spoke deficient Spanish. He must have learned it in South America in some commercial business, and was incapable of translating nuances. Fortunately, Tóvar's German is so good that we were able to correct things that could have been dangerously offensive . . ."

Following dinner they had coffee in the Yellow Room. The aide returned to his office, Carmecita had said goodnight, the Polo sisters chatted, and Serrano Suñer sat apart with *El Caudillo*. "I can joke about them, and one can only dislike them, but their power is undeniable. When the *Führer* invited me to make the tour of German fortifications in France and Belgium, no doubt it was to cause me to be sitting here right now telling you that I am impressed. But they were impressive! The

Führer told me that Operation Sea Lion was just waiting a break in the winter, then at Dunkirk I was shown the landing craft prepared for it."

Franco said, "Sea Lion was postponed indefinitely by the *Führer* on the morning of the seventeenth, the day of your first meeting with him."

Serrano frowned. "It was already postponed when he told me about it?" Franco nodded. "Well, I sure fell for it." Serrano reflected, "But one thing is fact: the intensity of their interest in Spain's entry. In my first interview with Ribbentrop he would not even reply when I spoke of Morocco. A week later, during my final meeting in his office, we stood in front of a wall map and with all the largesse in the world, sweeping his arms across all of North Africa he as much as said, 'Help yourself.' His message was: no price is too high for Spanish cooperation. They are going to press hard to bring us in."

Franco said nothing.

"I refrained from mentioning at dinner that when I made my social visit to Goering he asked me, 'Well, what's happening?' Very carefully I told him we were preparing, trying to get ready to enter, that our desire was great. He cut me off. 'Look, Mr. Minister. You are very clever, very sharp, very bright and you do your things well. But I am a frank person and I'm going to tell you something. If I were Hitler, Spain would today be militarily occupied by us. I think there has been too much talk, too many words. This is the hour to act. If I were Hitler we would be in Spain right now. Germany needs Spain's geography, we need to occupy her, and that's that. If I were the head of the Third Reich it would be done.'"

On October 17th the Official Bulletin, published in the daily news-papers, stated:

> Excmo. Col. Juan Beigbeder has ceased to
> be Minister of Foreign Affairs. Excmo. D.
> Ramón Serrano Suñer has ceased to be
> Minister of the Interior and will assume
> the office of Minister of Foreign Affairs.

Minutes before Beigbeder read it in the newspaper, a black-leather-clad motorcyclist from the Palace of El Pardo brought him a letter from *El Caudillo* thanking him for his good and faithful service. Among gov-ernment insiders the motorcyclist was known as "the angel of death."

Franco chose always to avoid the use of time and emotion in personally telling a Minister of his dismissal, of needing to reject an appeal against what had been carefully studied and was final. He followed the same procedure in not personally telling the other man of his gain. Even his brother-in-law would learn of it in the newspapers.

Sir Samuel Hoare was distressed at having lost such a valuable source of information. He was equally disheartened by the selection of Serrano Suñer, making it clear that Franco was leaning toward the Germans rather than to him.

Hoare knew that Lord Lothian, the British Ambassador to the United States, happened to be in Lisbon that day, and he contacted him to learn if there was any chance that the U.S.A. might provide Spain with petroleum products, which England could not. Gasoline and high-octane aviation fuel added to the food would make a package that could compete with the Germans. Lord Lothian replied in a letter:

> There is no doubt that the interest of the U.S.A. and especially of Roosevelt, in Spain, Gibraltar and West Africa is rapidly growing.
>
> The trouble of course is that the U.S.A. is still officially neutral and will remain so until there is an overt act affecting their virtual national interests and until their rearmament has progressed much further—and that will not be until 1942. They will not declare war until they have an effective weapon in their hands. Therefore, at present they have to rely upon us, supplying us with munitions and money lavishly to do the work that they ought to do themselves.
>
> The President, with the consent of His Majesty's Government, has arranged to send a Red Cross Food Ship to Spain, with food to be distributed by the American Red Cross, as the U.S. Minister in Madrid agreed that today was the psychological date to make Spain realize that neutrality meant food and that war spelt starvation. This will probably be followed by others on the same terms.

Sir Samuel, having now been in Spain for several months, did not approve of the threat factor, which always worked in reverse with the Spaniards. But he was pleased in general. With the Americans willing to supply aid, they could surely be convinced to supply it in its most useful form, and he would have his petroleum/food package to which Spain could not fail to respond.

On October 20th the Chief of Spanish Intelligence, General Martínez-Campos, *Duque de la Torre*, went to Hendaye to check out the site of the meeting between Franco and Hitler. It was a routine procedure, but as he crossed the border at Irún what he encountered was not at all routine. He returned to Madrid and reported that the *Gestapo* had arrived at Hendaye on the 16th, one week before the meeting with Hitler and they had cleared the town of every man, woman and child. Hendaye was a ghost town, completely without French population. There were only *Gestapo* and *Wehrmacht*.

Hitler called Admiral Canaris, the Chief of his Military Intelligence, the *Abwehr*, who had many years of experience in Spain and maintained a large number of agents there. "I'm going to be meeting with the *Caudillo*. What can you tell me about him that I should know?"

"*Mein Führer*, he is a little man in physical stature and in his thinking. The *Führer* will encounter no difficulty. Spain will be even easier than France."

Franco pondered Hitler's possible actions when in the course of their meeting he would eventually realize that he was not getting his way. The obvious was physical invasion of Spain, but Hitler knew that would be too expensive and slow. Their meeting was to take place aboard the *Führer*'s train near which there were almost a quarter of a million German soldiers and armor. How much simpler than war, to give a signal for his train to roll back into German-occupied France with Francisco Franco aboard as a hostage for Spain's entry.

On October 21, 1940, the day before he was to leave for Hendaye, Franco wrote a letter designating a triumvirate to replace him in the event that he did not return: General Vigón, General Varela and the Minister of Justice Don Esteban Bilbao y Eguia.

I emphatically instruct that in the event that I am not able to return to Spain, that Spain's independence of the war shall be maintained despite any threats or acts against my person or well-being.

    Viva España. Arriba España.

Francisco Franco[2]

At dinner Carmencita and Maruja were animated about Sunday's movie. There were two good possibilities, "Wuthering Heights" with Laurence Olivier, or "Three Smart Girls" with Deanna Durbin.

"What do you think, *Papá?*"

"You and Maruja decide. "I'm not a man who likes taking responsibility."

Before retiring, Franco and his wife went into their chapel and prayed.

In the bedroom she looked at him, thinking that he was the man with whom she prayed and said the rosary every night . . . but in the morning he would leave to meet with Adolf Hitler.

He would come back. She was not being deliberately brave, as she had needed to be during the years when he went off to war in Africa and as a soldier he had believed "It is my duty to die." Now, as the Chief of State it was his duty to survive. She reasoned, God had chosen Francisco Franco to save Spain, so it was unlikely that He would have brought him safely through all of the battles in the Riff, then victorious after three years of civil war, only to be lost in a kidnapping to Adolf Hitler, an atheist.

When they had said goodnight he reached across the short distance between their beds and patted her hand. She appreciated what he was telling her. She understood that as he never made promises he was not certain he could fulfill, he would not say, "Don't worry, I'll be back."

After reading for a while he turned off his light and within minutes she heard him breathing rhythmically. She looked toward him in the darkness admiring his talent for restoring himself. And rarely had he needed to be rested as much as in the days to come.

CHAPTER NINE

THE TRUMPETERS OF THE MOORISH GUARD PROCLAIMED THE DEPARTURE OF THE CHIEF OF STATE; THE INFANTRY STOOD AT PRESENT ARMS, THE GATES OPENED AT 13:00 HOURS AND A CARAVAN OF eight automobiles moved out of the grounds of the Palace of El Pardo.

The "pilot" car, a Ford convertible, was driven by a corporal of the *Guardia Civil*. In a second, a Buick, were two aides. The third, a Hudson, contained the Chief of the *Casa Civil*, Don Julio Muñoz Aguilar, the Marqués de Salinas. In the fourth car, a Dodge, rode an escort of four guards wearing the red beret of the Carlists and the blue shirt of the Falange. Franco rode in the fifth car, a bullet-proofed Chrysler, accompanied by the Chief of his Military Household, General Moscardó, the hero of the battle of the Alcázar. A pennon bearing Franco's coat of arms flew from its right front fender. The Chief of State's car was distinguished from all others by the fact that it had no license plates. In their place was the red and gold flag of Spain.

In the sixth car, an Hispano Suiza, was a second escort of four more guards. The seventh, a Chrysler, carried the Second Chief of Franco's Military Household, General Uzquiano.

The eighth car, a bulletproofed Cadillac, a *coche de respeto*, empty except for the driver, was for the use of the Chief of State in the event of any problem that would cause him to need to change cars.

The last car, a Plymouth station wagon, carried two mechanics and a supply of spare parts.[1]

Doña Carmen watched the gates of the Palace close behind her husband's caravan. She telephoned to her sisters, Isabel and Zita, Ramón's wife, and a few intimate friends to come to the Palace and have tea, as she often did. She did not tell them it was anything special. The cars she sent brought them to the large chapel of the Palace, adjacent to the main building where she was waiting.

Lola Collantes, entering the chapel observed the Francos' priest, José Maria Boulart, praying with *la Generalísima*. She joined in prayer with the few others there who had in common the quality of discretion. No one asked their friend, or sister, Carmen what they were praying for. People close to the Franco family understood that there were things that they could not be told. If they had not understood that, they would not have been there.[4]

Carmencita and Maruja were looking at shoes in a shop on *Calle Argensola* when they heard a woman saying, " . . . he's on his way to Hendaye with *el Generalísimo* to meet Adolf Hitler tomorrow . . ." A moment later, recognizing Franco's daughter, the woman said, "Carmencita, I didn't see you." Then, understanding that Carmencita did not know her, whereas Franco's only child was easily identifiable, she explained, "My husband is one of the drivers with your father."

When the two girls were in the car and being driven back to the Palace, Maruja said, "I didn't realize that your father was going to meet Adolf Hitler tomorrow."

"Nor I."

"He didn't mention a word of it at dinner."

"That's how he is. *Mamá* says that when he was young he was very talkative, but that as soon as he became Chief of State he changed. For a lot of reasons. In this case it's security. That woman was indiscreet."

Maruja was remembering the dinner conversation and then kissing goodnight, not goodbye.[5]

Led by motorcycles the caravan set out on the highway to France, which would bring them through Burgos and Vitoria to San Sebastian, where they would spend the night at Franco's summer home, the Palace of Ayete. They would arrive at around eight P.M., have dinner at Ayete and in the morning ride by train the short distance to Hendaye, the French border town just south of Biarritz.

Security was strict: newspapers were not permitted to mention the trip; pairs of *Guardias Civiles* and municipal police, who had not been told who would be passing, were positioned in every town along the route, and at close intervals in populated areas. When they passed through towns the motorcycle escort dropped back and surrounded the car of the Chief of State.

They had been on the road for about an hour when they approached a large billboard advertising *Restaurante Alcázar de Toledo*, showing a picture of the famous fort. Franco touched General Moscardó firmly on the arm. The General nodded in appreciation.

In 1936, then a Colonel, Moscardó and his troops in Toledo had sealed themselves into the Alcázar and the great fort was under heavy siege by the Republicans. The small band resisted. Then the Republicans captured Moscardó's teenage son, Luis. They telephoned to the fort. "Moscardó, we have your son. Surrender or he will die."

"Let me speak with him."

"*Papá?* They say they will kill me unless you surrender."

"Then make your peace with God, my son, say "*Viva España*" and die like a patriot. The Alcázar will never surrender."

Other such sacrifices had been made by the Nationalists in their "Crusade to Save Spain." The Spanish Foreign Legion that Franco had helped found functioned on the principal of comradeship and the oath never to abandon a wounded comrade no matter what the danger might be, to come running instantly at the cry of "*¡A mi la Legion!*" In Africa Franco had seen a soldier lay dying in a ward full of wounded legionnaires like himself. Delirious from pain the man cried out "*¡A mi la Legion!*" and at the call his comrades, bleeding, maimed, trailing their mutilated limbs behind them, left their mattresses and heedless of nurses or doctors, gathered around the dying man and stayed with him until the end.[2]

In the car with Moscardó, Franco's eyes felt a reminder of the tears that had fallen from them as he had watched it. And again he resolved, *I cannot allow my people to be forced into another war.*[3]

122

On the morning of the 23rd, Franco and his party had breakfast in the dining room of the Palace of Ayete. Also present were Ramón Serrano Suñer, the Barón de las Torres, who would interpret, Antonio Tóvar, who often worked with the Barón, and General Espinosa de los Monteros, the new Spanish Ambassador to Berlin.

The rendezvous with Hitler was to take place at two P.M. in the railroad station at Hendaye at the edge of town. The train ride from San Sebastian to Hendaye was estimated to take forty-five minutes, allowing for delays because of the postwar condition of the tracks. But *El Caudillo* elected to leave early and wait outside Hendaye in order to be certain of arriving at exactly two o'clock.

At noon they boarded a train borrowed from the Ministry of Public Works. The Franco party required only an engine and two parlor cars, but again because of the post-war condition of the railroad they had been provided a train consisting of five cars in order to weight down Franco's parlor car and keep it on the tracks.

The train had in prewar days been luxurious but after three years of transporting troops and supplies, without normal maintenance during that time, it was not its former self.

Boarding, Serrano Suñer looked around the car. There were holes in the ceiling through which he could see the sky. Sitting down beside his brother-in-law he said, "*Paco, con este trenecito tan viejo y malito*, with this miserable little old train, we're lucky it's not raining or we'd arrive to meet the *Führer* in wet clothes."[6]

"When he sees this, he'll believe we're poor."

The train coughed, a violent jolt, and came to a halt. It began moving. A few minutes later it stopped. Ten minutes passed before it started up again. Within five minutes they came to a halt. The condition of the tracks had not been exaggerated. By one o'clock it became clear that they were going to be late.

In an effort to ease the tension in the parlor car General Moscardó said, "I have known his Excellency for many years and I have never known him to be late. Before the war he and *Doña* Carmen and I were going to a wedding outside of Madrid. When we got to the station we discovered that his plumed hat was not with us in the car. But his Excellency had allowed so much extra time that it was possible to return to the house, get the hat and catch the train with ease. He has never been late. He wasn't even late in arriving to rescue us at the Alcázar—and he had to fight his way there."

Franco asked, "Don't you love my choice of whom to start with?"[7]

Adolf Hitler was strolling up and down the station platform with von Ribbentrop. It was a quarter of three and he was enjoying the palm trees and the sunny day but he commented, "These lazy Latins and their precious siesta. They've probably had to stop the train while the *Caudillo* rests." Then he said, "Under no conditions can we give the Spaniards anything in writing concerning transfers of territory from the French colonial possessions. With these talkative Latins the French would hear about it tomorrow."[8]

Francisco Franco positioned himself in the doorway of the train as it entered the station and began slowing. He wore boots, breeches and the uniform of Captain General with an overseas cap. Around his waist he wore a General's red sash with golden tassels.

In the station swastika flags had been placed at every ten feet, creating a background of red, white and black cloth. The platform was lined with a red carpet and an honor guard of the *Wehrmacht* rigidly at attention.

Franco saw Hitler and von Ribbentrop awaiting him. The *Führer* was dressed in a gray military uniform with boots, breeches and a peaked cap. With him were his entire High Command, whom Franco recognized from photos, some of them soldiers he respected: Marshal Keitel; von Brachitsch. It was a few minutes past three P.M. when the train stopped. Franco raised his hand in greeting as his eyes met those of Hitler, who was walking toward him, also smiling.

When Hitler and von Ribbentrop had reached the doorway of his train *El Caudillo* stepped down and clasped the *Führer's* hand in both of his own.[9]

A military band played the Spanish national anthem, *La Marcha Real*. Both Chiefs of State stood at attention, facing the standard bearers who held the Spanish and German flags side by side while next the band played *Deutschland Über Alles*.

The two dictators turned toward the honor guard, whose bayoneted rifles were held at salute arms, and with Hitler at his right Franco reviewed the troops. Behind them followed their translators and Foreign Ministers.

Hitler's private train, the "Erica," was composed of fifteen cars. After the engine the first and last cars of the train contained anti-aircraft batteries and crews.

Stopping to look at one, Franco's face indicated appreciation and Hitler boasted, "Those four-barreled anti-aircraft guns are effective to a height of 1,500 to 2,000 meters. Recently Field Marshal Goering's train was attacked by a British plane, which they shot down with little effort. I made a gift to the *Duce* of two of these cars for his train. It takes months to prepare them. I will have some put in the works for you, *Caudillo*. As in the case of the *Duce* I will sleep better knowing that you are safe." They walked on. "Everything is directed toward maximum security, efficiency and also comfort. I have radio-operated teletype machines, we have showers and baths . . . and this is my work coach." He gestured for Franco to precede him.

Franco boarded the train. He was followed by Hitler, then by Serrano Suñer, von Ribbentrop, then the Barón de las Torres and the German interpreter Gross. Entrance was forbidden to all others. Antonio Tóvar was not allowed to work with the Barón de las Torres because Hitler had only one interpreter present, his other, Paul Schmidt, not being able to speak Spanish. Ambassador von Stohrer, his Spanish counterpart General Espinosa de los Monteros, and all others waited outside on the platform.

The heavily curtained parlor car had been prepared with seats for six at a rectangular table. Hitler was at the head with Franco on his right; Serrano Suñer at his left. Von Ribbentrop sat to Franco's right and the two interpreters filled the two places between the Foreign Ministers. The other head of the table was not occupied.

Franco began, "*Führer*, I cannot express too strongly the satisfaction that I experience upon meeting you today for the first time and having the opportunity to reiterate the profound gratitude that I and every Spaniard feel for you and for the help so generously lent to Spain at a time when we were very much in need of a strong and true friend as you and the Third Reich turned out to be."

"*Caudillo*, I too arrive at this place and at this moment with the greatest sense of pleasure upon seeing you personally for the first time in my life, you whose shield was the first in Europe to suffer the blows of Communism. Not I, nor anyone can extol with too much fervor the great achievement of the Spanish people whom I personally know to have confronted Communism under the orders of your Excellency. Nor can I stress too strongly the importance I attach to this meeting between both Heads of State at this critical moment of the war in Europe, the war that France has just lost so decidedly."

He paused and the cordial mask which had covered his face now changed to one of a serious nature. "*Caudillo*, I like to have all the key points and nerve centers that could be of interest to my enemies well foreseen and carefully tied up before I go into action. For that reason this conversation with your Excellency is of great interest to me because I also like to know where my friends stand, and that I can count on them."

"*Führer*, Spain has at every moment felt as one with the Axis. In the Civil War the soldiers of the three countries fought together, side by side, and a profound and everlasting unity has risen among them. In that same manner Spain most happily finds herself closely attached to Germany, bonded together by their history of friendship."

"I am gratified, *Caudillo*. Then let me begin by saying that there are various ways in which Spain is called upon to play a very important role that she can accomplish by paying attention to German political interests. This is a once-in-a-lifetime opportunity that if let pass through your fingers will never occur again. Never. Never. Never."

Franco, hands folded on his lap, looked into Hitler's excited eyes, waiting.

"*Caudillo*, I am especially interested and concerned over Gibraltar, Morocco and the Canary Islands. Gibraltar is a question of honor for the

Spanish people, who must return and reintegrate into the Motherland this piece of ground that is still in the hands of foreigners after four centuries, and that by its strategic situation in the straits could be a point of great support for the Third Reich." He leaned toward Franco, enumerating on his fingers. "With Spain now in Tangier, in addition to Melilla and Ceuta as she has been for centuries, and if she had Gibraltar, which she should have had for centuries, then we could effectively close the straits, thus eliminating Allied navigation of the Mediterranean."

Franco was listening with obvious interest. Hitler moved into point number two. "Now we come to Morocco. Soon my Panzer units will drive the British out of Africa. Spain by its history, by having been in Morocco long before anyone else, is now called upon to remain there and in possession of all of French Morocco and Oran, and naturally with Spain in the war at the side of the Axis she is guaranteed dominion of those desirable territories.

"Finally, regarding the Canary Islands, I am convinced that the United States will not enter the war. They have little interest in a large-scale conflict. However, the English—even though at the moment I have them in a most precarious position—the English fleet could in a given stroke, a deaththroe, seize the Canary Islands. This would be a blow against our submarine warfare now operating so effectively in the Atlantic. Thus, we must protect the Canary Islands from the British."

Having made his three points Hitler sat back in his chair, prepared to be agreed with.

There was silence as Franco was thoughtful for a moment. "The *Führer* is correct that Gibraltar is a piece of Spanish territory that for too many years has been in the hands of others. And, *Führer*, may I comment on how well you understand Spanish pride to know what an embarrassment this Gibraltar situation continues to be. However, *Führer*, you must also understand that what appears easy for you to accomplish with the might of the German army, taking the offensive against Gibraltar— despite the fact that it is not well fortified or heavily manned—puts, for a people who have just passed through a civil war, an excessive sacrifice at this time when she has not yet closed the wounds that she has suffered. Though Gibraltar is a bone in the throat of every Spaniard, its return would be small compensation for the ravages and difficulties that Spain would suffer by going to war against England at this time."

Hitler's face lit-up with a shrewd smile. "Don't worry about it *Caudillo*. My *Wehrmacht* has been training near here on the most extraordinary equal of Gibraltar, the size of the Rock itself. I refer to our elite units, which captured the Eben Emael Fort of Liege, our magnificent *Sturm Abteilung Koch*. They are equipped with special armor-destroying guns—called *Scharten*, or in simple language *Bunkerknacker*, pillbox-crackers. They have been practicing for weeks, perfection has been reached. Success is inevitable! On January 10th, with twenty divisions having passed through Spain, they will go on to Gibraltar, on to Gibraltar, on to Gibraltar . . . taking the Rock in a single blow—under Spanish command, of course, as I stated in my letter—and on that day, *Caudillo*, I pledge that I will personally hand Gibraltar back to Spain."

He confided, "Its assault is code-named Operation Felix and I assure you it will be a joy to behold, a precision instrument, flawless, irresistible—Gibraltar will fall within hours and immediately be returned to Spain, her rightful owner."

While speaking, Hitler had failed to see the enthusiasm he had expected. Now he watched wide-eyed as Franco's right hand, raised slightly in the air, index finger extended, moved slowly, negatively from left to right.

"*Führer*, it is inconsistent with Spanish pride to accept the return of her rightful property as a gift from the hands of a more powerful nation and friend. Gibraltar must be taken by Spaniards alone." As if thinking aloud, "Of course our soldiers will need to be extensively trained in such an operation and provided with special arms and equipment. We will have to study the time period required for the training . . ."

Hitler stared at him, struck wordless.

". . . and essential to the operation would be a most substantial number of 380 mm guns . . ."

Re-animated Hitler interrupted, "I explained to your esteemed brother-in-law . . ." and he looked to his left for Serrano Suñer's confirmation, "that it is much more efficient to disperse the British Navy from Gibraltar with a squadron of my *Sturzkampfflugzeuge* . . ."

Franco listened attentively as Hitler ran through his tour de force on the firepower of his *Sturzkampfflugzeuge* versus 380 mm guns.

"I quite agree, *Führer*, as regards dispersing the Royal Navy from Gibraltar, as well as for the protection of our lengthy and vulnerable coastlines, that the Royal Navy will surely attack if Spain attacks Gibraltar. And please believe my profound respect for your methods, which smashed the Maginot Line in ten minutes, but I must refer your attention to the special conditions of the Rock that I pointed out in my letter. Though there is some exposed artillery that might be destroyed by the *Bunkerknackers*, the Rock has points of resistance that can withstand even the strongest action from the air. This—despite the fact that the British have carved the Rock nearly hollow, removing hundreds of tons of stone—still is so dense as to be, at these crucial points of resistance, invulnerable to anything short of the most powerful artillery, accurately and relentlessly played against them."

Seeing that Hitler was still not convinced, Franco asked, "*Führer*, have you ever been on the Rock of Gibraltar?"

Hitler could only shake his head.

"Then you must take my word on this, *Führer*, for I have been there many times, and one must see it to believe it. This is a problem to be studied most carefully.

"As for your Panzer units driving the British from Morocco: yes, and no. To the edge of the great desert, very possibly. But Central Africa would be protected by the desert belt, in the same way that an island is protected by an open sea. As an old African campaigner I am quite certain of that."

As the translator conveyed Franco's military lecture, Hitler's face reddened. "*Caudillo* . . . I can guarantee . . . the efficiency, the domination, and the mastery of German military forces over any in the world. The might of history's greatest military machine is irresistible. In the past thirteen months my armies have restored to the Fatherland all of those parts of Germany that were so easily given away at Versailles. We have invaded Poland, Denmark, Norway, Belgium, Luxembourg, the Netherlands, France. Nothing, no one can stand up to us.

"Perhaps you are not fully aware of the strength of your friend and ally. I am reorganizing my armies and by March I will have a total of 230 divisions, of which 186 are assault divisions, the rest consisting of defense and occupation troops. Of the 186 assault divisions 20 are armored, equipped with German matériel, while four additional armored brigades possess captured matériel in part. In addition I have 12 motorized divisions. And, *Caudillo*, let me not stop with my land forces, let us go to the sea, to under the sea. At this moment German factories are producing 10 U-boats every month. In spring it will rise to 17. In July to 25; after that up to 34 per month.

"*Caudillo*, Germany is ready to face any eventuality." He glared into Franco's eyes. "I am the master of Europe and as I have presently 230 divisions at my disposal there is no choice but to obey me."

Franco, face tranquil, turned to the Barón de las Torres and asked that the translation be repeated.

Forced to wait while his threat was repeated Hitler then leaned toward Franco, his forehead moist, eyes blazing, "It is a question of very little time . . . very little time . . . before the annihilation of England. I have the invasion prepared to the most minute detail. With the first break in the weather Operation Sea Lion will go forward . . ."

Franco's eyes remained on Hitler but both he and Serrano Suñer recognized the lie.

". . . England is beaten. Beaten." Hitler raised his right hand and pointed to the floor, "England is on her knees!"

"Perhaps she is simply praying."

Hitler slammed his fists on the table and stood up. "There is obviously no point in continuing this conversation."

Unlike all other Chiefs of State, Prime Ministers and ranking diplomats who had immediately buckled at first sight of Hitler's wrath, Franco looked at him without expression.

Serrano Suñer was thinking, "*El Caudillo* has just lost his anti-aircraft *trenecito*.

Speaking quietly but caustically to von Ribbentrop, Hitler said, "I have dealt with Molotov, with Mussolini, with Chamberlain, with Laval, Pétain . . . I will deal with this little *Caudillo*."

Hitler sat down. "Your Excellency, does it not strike you that the Spanish Empire, that at one point ruled the world, can again rise to world power, that the spoils of war that I have offered, and still offer, will make the name Francisco Franco go down in history and live forever in the hearts and pride of your countrymen?"

"Of course, *Führer*. And I greatly appreciate the offers you have made for after the war in case of Spain entering it. I refer to your kind promise to give us French Morocco and Oran . . ." He paused, allowing Hitler to smile graciously. ". . .but I believe that in order to offer things it is first necessary to have them in hand, and the fact is that as of this moment the Axis does not have them."

Hitler remained in his seat, both hands gripping the sides of his chair. As if not noticing, Franco continued, analytically. "It is a fact that Spain has not been given justice in Morocco. The problem of Morocco is vital to Spain and I don't intend to abandon the situation, which by right and history correspond. But, since it has been—as the Algeciras Conference proved—a problem that stirs up the passions and the intervention of all other countries, even the most distant, I believe that it must not be taken lightly, but on the contrary, without abandoning any rights which exist, we must examine the problem dispassionately.

"*Führer*, you should also bear well in mind the strength it requires, from a Spain still not recovered from a civil war, to maintain the active army we have in that zone at this moment and that serves Germany by forcing the French to keep an equal number, thus inactivating them for duty in zones where DeGaulle would yearn to have them in use against you."

Hitler made no indication of agreeing or disagreeing.

Franco continued. "Finally, with regard to the Canary Islands, I recognize that the military installations we maintain there might not be sufficient to defend them in the event of the Royal Navy's trying to seize them. Nor are our armaments in that zone of nearly enough strength to be useful despite the fact that we have transferred the best guns available from less threatened areas . . ."

"*Caudillo, Caudillo, Caudillo*, when you enter we will immediately send from Germany the batteries of coastal weapons of the highest caliber, plus engineers to mount them and to train your men in their use. The Canary Islands will be defended impregnably."

Franco knew that along with the engineers would come other "required personnel," that once he opened the door there would be a heavy German presence and he would as much as have ceded an island to Germany.

"*Führer*, in this case I agree with your theory regarding the more effective firepower of your esteemed dive-bombers. I would be comforted by the presence in Las Palmas of dive-bombers and long-range fighters, and even horizontal bombers. And I repeat my view, in my letter, that a very substantial amount of bombs and petrol and spare parts must be in Las Palmas long before the presence of the actual planes can be known, which should only be in the event of a sighted invasion force of Royal Navy vessels. The surprise element is essential in order to avoid heavy Spitfire support, which has proven inconvenient to the Stukas over England.

"Returning to Gibraltar and the closing of the straits, *Führer*, if I want to catch a thief who is in a room that has two doors, it would not be useful to close one door without closing the other. Closing the straits would be useless without closing the Suez Canal. *Duce*'s troops in Egypt could do that. With that door closed it would make sense to close the other and bring the usefulness of the Mediterranean to an end for the Allies."

"The Mediterranean must first be closed at Gibraltar."

"Why?"

"Strategic necessity."

"I don't see that necessity."

"You are wrong."

Franco looked at Hitler with just a flicker of surprise. "*Führer*, I am a professional soldier. A military strategist of long experience."

Hitler clenched his fists, opening them violently, flinging his fingers outwards. Again he clenched them closed and flung them open. "*Caudillo*, I am not exactly without military experience or success." His voice was rising to a shout as his body rose in his chair. "I have conquered more than half a continent."

Nodding, Franco observed, "The perfect illustration of the difference between Spain's condition today and Germany's condition when she set off to war. When the great army of the Third Reich went to war it did so after years of preparation militarily and economically. Spain's Civil War was caused by a condition of chaos, rampant anarchy, national poverty, an army that had been deliberately stripped of its strength by the reds in power. Now, after a three-year internal conflict we stand depleted to the point of starvation . . ."

Hitler yawned openly.

". . . we have no wheat, no petrol, no trucks, no shoes on the feet of most Spaniards. A hungry nation thrust into war can only fight its imprudent leaders.

"Spain has no gold reserves. None. Most of Spain's gold, the fourth largest supply in the world, was stolen by the reds and sent to Soviet Russia to pay for arms. Thanks to your invaluable help, *Führer* we were able to drive them out of Spain. But the economic damage has been done. In October of 1936 they removed from the Treasury 7,800 boxes of gold bars and loaded them aboard four Soviet steamers bound for Odessa. I am told that when the shipment arrived Stalin gave a banquet and announced, 'The Spanish will never see their gold again, just as one cannot see one's own ears.'

"As a result, in order to buy fertilizer from abroad, I had to appeal by radio to my countrymen for their wedding bands, a crucifix, anything made of gold that we could use for foreign purchasing. You will be fascinated *Führer* by the response. There came one day to my headquarters a quiet woman from Arroyomolinos de Montánchez, a poor little village hidden away in the province of Cáceres. She was accompanied by three others, carrying in a basket, carefully wrapped in paper, all the bits of gold that could be found in the village, in each tiny packet a name, all the rings and wedding jewelry of the village; holiday earrings handed down from mother to daughter, medals time-worn, small pins, the gold chains and crosses of girls more well-to-do.

"From villages throughout Spain a mountain of personal odds and ends poured into my headquarters from citizens who saw our Nationalist movement as the defense of their fireside, of the family, of the Faith; freedom from Marxist tyranny in their work. And we could make a beginning. But just a beginning . . ."

Hitler approached the Spanish pride. "Spain is in desperate need of food. The Allies allow you to import a certain amount but not enough, always subject to their Certificates of Navigation through their blockade, which is tantamount to a gun at your head. They control the shipments at a rate calculated to keep you in starvation and thus docile to their demands. It is intolerable. *Caudillo!* I offer you freedom from Britain's humiliating, insulting restrictions on Spain's dignity and sovereignty. Join me, *Caudillo*, join me and let them be damned with their 'navicerts.'"

Looking warmly at Hitler, Franco confessed, "Spain must mark time and often look kindly toward things of which she thoroughly disapproves."[10]

Hitler's fury at Franco turned against the British. "They have always acted badly. In 1937 and 1938 I sent Herr von Ribbentrop to London to negotiate and they were impossible, immovable, like their damned Rock of Gibraltar. Your Rock of Gibraltar."

Franco knew of Ribbentrop's threats to Churchill. "In political dealings with the English one should not try to gallop, *Führer*. Churchill would never have imposed himself over the moderate conservatives if your distinguished Foreign Minister had trotted along in the British way."

Von Ribbentrop clasped his hands together in his lap but said nothing.

Hitler said, "You spoke earlier of gratitude for the help that Germany gave to Spain during your war. *Caudillo*, it was expensive to be such a good friend. There is still a debt of 374 million Reichmarks. It must be paid in some way."

Franco looked at the German leader with hurt and disillusion in his large, brown eyes. "*Führer*, you are confusing idealism with materialism. When Spain arrives at the moment when she can enter the war, then she will do so with pleasure because of her spiritual alliance with the Axis, and with yourself in particular. Not because of a minor amount of money."[11]

Hitler struck the table with his fists. He stood up, holding onto it, leaning toward Franco, and bellowed, "The moment has come for Spain when she must finally make a decision! She can no longer be indifferent to the reality of the events nor to the fact of the German troops that now find themselves at her border." His eyes narrowing, Hitler stared at Franco long and hard. "I have twenty divisions at your frontier, *Caudillo*. And they are disposed to enter Spain. They are equipped with the most modern war matériel, they are on the move, they have tasted victory after victory and they hunger for more. They have traversed Europe, swept through France . . ."

"Without encountering an enemy," Franco said softly. "You did not lose one soldier in Belgium."

Holding the table Hitler stared disbelieving at this tranquil *Caudillo*. "Did you not hear what I just said? Did you not hear me? I just told you that I have all those units at your frontier. Ready to fight. Eager to fight! They can enter Spain tomorrow."

It was Hitler's reliable threat-tactic. It had cowed all of Europe's statesman who had come to bargain with Hitler. But Franco had ridden into too many battles to be frightened by words. He replied, "And on that same day we will begin guerrilla warfare." His voice was neither threatening nor conciliatory, simply stating facts. "I cannot oppose you as a military power. I have no food, no matériel with which to confront you. But I know my people and they will not tolerate being occupied. They would rise up against you and even I, their victorious Chief who was touched by the Grace of God, could not stop them.

"We Spaniards have always practiced a hospitality toward strangers, the poorest of us offering to any traveler some bread and a chair in which to sleep by the fire. But let that same traveler try to break into and take over the Spaniard's humble home and, *Führer*, he will kill him.

"Bear it well in mind that the attempt of anyone to invade Spain will bring us to guerrilla warfare, and in *that* Spain has always come out triumphant. Why did Napoleon pass thus the guerrilla warfare? And you know how powerful Napoleon was. Take note *Führer*, that the word *guerrilla* was born of the Spanish language. As you do not know our language let me explain that *guerra* means war, *guerrilla* is the diminutive, little skirmishes. We invented guerrilla warfare. And Spain never loses in guerrilla warfare, never."

Hitler paced the length of the car, then sat down. "Tomorrow I have a meeting with Marshal Pétain and Mr. Laval at Montoire-sur-le-Loir, and I must know Spain's attitude before that meeting in order to know how I will work with France in regard to her African claims."

"I fail to see that Spain's attitude has anything to do with your conversation with a vanquished France, at whose expense you have just made attractive offers to me. Unless of course those offers were no more than bait for a possible entry of Spain into the war, and that you don't truly mean them. Clearly Germany's attitude with the government of a beaten France is not excessively harsh. Not often does one see a conqueror waltzing with the conquered."

"I have a reason. Somebody, France or England, will have to pay the cost of the war. The blood that has been sacrificed cannot be compensated for, since the dead cannot rise again and the cripples will not be healed. But, material and territorial payments can and will be made.

"I met with Laval yesterday and he stated that in his opinion France's declaration of war against Germany was the greatest crime ever committed in the course of French history. He said that the war had not been popular in France; that the people did not know why they should fight and that in fact, the two million prisoners of war from a country that has proven it can fight is proof that its people did not want war.

"He said that even before the war he personally had been an advocate of French-German cooperation—which I know to be true—and that he could therefore pursue the same political policy again now without restraint. He assured me that he and Pétain understand that France must bear any hardships that Germany chooses to impose, and that sincere and unreserved cooperation with Germany is France's only salvation.

"I suggested the possibility that the war costs might not be charged to a country that had not wanted the war, as France had not, forced in by England. I pointed out that it is up to France to cooperate in defeating England in order to create her own possibilities of compensation for territorial losses; if, with France's aid, Germany could win the war faster, then I would be disposed to giving France easier peace terms in return and let England pay the bill for the whole war.

"Therefore, it is my plan to have Pétain convince the French people to actively come into the war with Germany against England."

"*Führer*, forgive me for being blunt, but this is pure delusion. The French will never ally themselves with Germany to fight the British. I guarantee that."

"You guarantee it?" Hitler screamed, "You guarantee it? Well . . . what I guarantee to you is that before I go to Montoire tomorrow to interview Pétain I want to know a definite attitude on the part of Spain." He rapped the table with his knuckles. "*Caudillo*, I call upon you to sign a protocol here and now for Spain to declare war on Great Britain on January 3, 1941. That will give my troops ample time to reach your southern coast, where Operation Felix will be launched on January 10th as scheduled."

"But why else am I here? I am eager to make such a treaty. But I ask you to understand that it can only be possible if Germany is willing and able to provide the food and matériel which Spain requires, as well as agreement on territorial claims."

"*Caudillo*, you don't understand . . ."

"Yes, yes, I understand perfectly and I am sympathetic with your predicament. Quite possibly it is you who do not understand: you are asking me to sign a protocol giving assurance of what you need, while you are unable to commit to paper the Moroccan territory that you might need in your negotiations with Pétain."

Hitler stared at him like a magician whose rabbit fell out of his sleeve before he could take it from the hat.

"And, regarding Spain's eventual entry, it is of course on the urgent condition that Spain, for her internal reasons, will decide the moment of attack. January 10th is a date that must be carefully studied. Spain has just suffered a long and terrible civil war that has left her with a million dead. . ."

Hitler turned to von Ribbentrop. "I can't stand it, I can't stand it, I can't stand it. I won't stand it."

". . . she simply can't be carried off into a war just because it suits your purpose and because you desire it, *Führer*."

While making the translation, Gross was afraid to look at Hitler.

". . . Spain's attitude of loyalty and gratitude and of friendship remains unchanged. Lamentably, her physical condition has changed as little.

Our immediate needs are one million tons of wheat, 300,000 tons of root vegetables . . ."

Hitler rose to his feet slowly, heavily. They had come full circle and he had lost the strength to continue. "*Caudillo*, it is twenty minutes before seven and perhaps we should rest before dinner. Our Ministers can have further discussions."

Franco stood up. "I look forward to the pleasure of dining with you."

CHAPTER TEN

"**H**OW DARE HE?" HITLER RAGED. "HOW DARE HE? HOW DARE HE? CHEAT! LIAR! INGRATE! HE OWES US EVERYTHING BUT NOW HE WON'T JOIN IN WITH US. A MILLION TONS OF WHEAT HE NEEDS? A million tons of wheat? Ohhh . . . I'll bake him a bread that will choke his dear little starving Spaniards." He mimicked Franco's high-pitched voice, 'Spanish pride cannot tolerate being given Gibraltar by a powerful friend.'" Hitler turned to von Ribbentrop. "You heard that with your own ears, I'm not hallucinating that I just had a meeting with a crazy man. Spanish pride! How will their pride tolerate being bombed out of existence?"

Hitler strode the length of his work coach. Reaching the end he punched the door with the heel of his fist, turned and strode toward the other end. Stopping in mid-car where his Foreign Minister was standing he reasoned, "I am the Master of Europe. I went to his rescue. I won his Civil War for him and when I mention payment of debts he makes me feel like a Jew . . . a Jew!!! Haggling over mankind's most precious possessions.[1] Generalissimo? Hah! In Germany that man would never rise higher than a sergeant . . .[2] He must have become leader of Spain by accident . . .[3] Arghhhh!!!"

Hitler crumpled onto a sofa, resting. Then, turning to von Ribbentrop again, he appealed, "Where does he think he would be if not for me? Does he think it was the intervention of the Mother of God that won his war? Doesn't he know that it was the bombs of the German squadrons that rained from the heavens that decided the issue?"[4]

Prudently, Ribbentrop dared not even agree with the *Führer*.

Hitler was meditative for several minutes, then suddenly bellowed, "Why was I not warned of this man? Why was I not warned? What manner of man is this? I talked and talked and talked, and when I asked him for a simple yes or no, what did I get? 'This will have to be carefully studied.' I threatened. I cajoled. Useless. Nothing would make him commit himself." Hitler smirked, "I promise you that if I met him in an elevator and I asked, 'Up, or down?' he would tell me, 'This has to be studied.'"

Relieved to see Hitler's fury lessening, Ribbentrop ventured, "He's a coward, a weakling."

"Neither a coward nor a weakling. I despise him, but . . ." Hitler was shaking his head slowly, ". . . he is very strong. There are few strong men, Joachim. The *Duce* is not strong. I am strong. The *Caudillo* is strong. That is a man to have on your side in a war.

"Why was I not properly prepared? I took the precaution of asking Canaris for a briefing. And what did the illustrious chief of German Intelligence say? 'A little man in both stature and thinking.' Hah!" Hitler was quivering with rage. "Communicate my fury to Admiral Canaris."

He fell silent, then hollowly he said, "We have reached the end with this Franco. It is useless." He whirled around. "But with or without the *Caudillo* Germany will take Gibraltar. And . . ." he smiled vindictively, "we will occupy Spain most thoroughly."

Serrano Suñer, with the Barón de las Torres and the Spanish Ambassador to Berlin, General Espinosa de los Monteros, boarded the German Foreign Ministry train in which von Ribbentrop was awaiting them at seven o'clock, an hour before their scheduled dinner, and they quickly agreed on a joint statement for the press concerning the meeting.

"Don Ramón," von Ribbentrop sighed, "this has not been a good day. But we can still save matters. Let's you and I put the pieces together. You have the draft of an acceptable protocol. Ask the *Caudillo* to sign it. Surely you can understand the dilemma. The *Führer* came here in good faith, as a friend, to learn if Spanish claims in Morocco are compatible with French hopes. I can categorically offer you whatever French properties you wish in Morocco, to the extent that France can be indemnified from British colonial possessions, which we will seize. Spain will have the rewards of victory for very little involvement."[5]

Serrano Suñer hardly concealed his anger. "The offer of French Morocco was, at best, intangible, considering that you have not occupied French Morocco, and indeed there is a powerful French force there, loyal to de Gaulle, not Pétain. Now you offer a protocol saying that Spain will receive the French Moroccan zones only if they can be replaced by the British possessions, which you have also not yet won. In this new circumstance it must be considered as doubly doubtful that Spain will receive anything at all. I am sorry, but El Caudillo would need an extraordinary oratorical power to explain such 'rewards of victory' to the Spanish people." [6]

Von Ribbentrop's manner returned to normally officious. "You are making a grave mistake. People do not anger the Führer. See that you have the draft back here at eight o'clock tomorrow morning with the typewritten and signed protocol. Be punctual. I will have no time to waste: instead of leaving here with the Führer after dinner tonight I am staying over to wait for this. As a result I will have to rush to an airport in the morning in order to be with the Führer when he meets with Pétain at Montoire. I will expect you at eight sharp. Good evening."

The Spanish Minister of Foreign Affairs and his colleagues, carrying flashlights in the blackout, walked along the platform toward their own train.

General Espinosa de los Monteros, understanding the affront Serrano Suñer had borne in silence, said, "Your Excellency must surely have urgent business in Madrid that prevents you from meeting tomorrow with the German minister. I would happily deliver the protocol or a message in your stead."

All members of the retinue of El Caudillo and those of the Führer were in dress uniforms. Non-military men wore black tie; with matching moods on both sides.

Seating El Caudillo to his right the Führer looked plaintively at the waiters, young SS men in white uniforms, pouring champagne. "When I was in France yesterday I made a point of ordering the finest wines, anticipating that we'd be celebrating an historic occasion."

The SS men were serving the first course, caviar and blinis. Hitler said, "I hope that your Excellency enjoys caviar, despite its place of origin."

Franco smiled, "I tend to be forgiving of Bolsheviks when they are voiceless fish who cannot spread the ideology."

"*Caudillo*, people wonder why we are fanatics against Bolshevism. They don't understand that it is because we Germans have lived through the same thing as you in Spain suffered in 1936."

"Then certainly, *Führer*, you must understand the grave error it would be for me to lead my people into an unpopular war. Unpopular wars make unpopular leaders. The Communists are just waiting for something like that to exploit. The Comintern has thrown unlimited financing in support of the single act of overthrowing our present regime. They are not concerned with social objectives or subtleties of Marxian dialectics. They just want to get me out. And if they do, poor Spain. Nor could a Communist Spain be an advantage to the Axis."

Hitler looked at Franco and nodded. It was inarguable.

Franco continued, "I never had the ambition to be a dictator, but events caused it to happen. It is not a popular role. Half the people want a monarchy, the other half want democracy. Our beloved King Alfonso XIII, after reigning for twenty-three years, finally accepted the fact that the monarchy was not viable in Spain's condition in 1930 and so he put himself into voluntary exile to make way for the Second Republic, which promptly failed and brought us within two or three weeks of a 'people's revolution' and a Communist takeover. Yet, there are Spaniards who hope that I will make way for another republic, while others hope for me to restore the monarchy.

"At the right time Spain can have any type of government the people wish, but for a society living in a permanent state of latent civil war dictatorship is the only containing dam that can control the waters. I love my country and I understand her people and I will lead them to a period of stability and economic recovery until they will be invulnerable to the Communists."

Hitler's face was covered with pleasure. "*Caudillo*. And I have never been interested in appearing as a great military leader. That's why I don't have any rank in the Army and I wear no insignia whatsoever even

though I am the supreme commander.[7] In my heart I am an architect."
He made a face. "Not a housepainter or a paperhanger as the Allies'
propaganda calls me. My ambition was to be an architect and I sold
paintings to support myself while I was studying.[8] But like you, circumstances called me to serve my country. Others have forced me to be a military leader. I would have been happy if the war had ended in June or July,
for no gain through war is in any proportion to the sacrifices imposed by
the conflict. As the leader of my people, what interests me is assuring the
cultural and social advances of the German nation."[9]

Franco raised a glass of wine; "I drink to the day in the very near
future when Spain will be able to attach herself more than emotionally
to Germany. I lament that I must say 'the future' rather than 'today.'
However, I have been pondering the astute things that you put forth
this afternoon, and I believe that I am inadvertently serving you best
by holding back Spain's entry at the moment. *Führer*, are you exactly
correct on your calculations as to how fast the Panzer divisions could
move through Spain? I don't know how familiar you are personally with
the territory but there is range after range of mountains with treacherous passes, and only two roads by which to enter, both of which are in
appalling condition. If Operation Felix is planned for January 10th I
must tell you that the January weather in that area in Spain is the worst
in Europe, with snow and ice on the heights, and such heavy rain in the
valleys that even tracked vehicles would bog down on the best stretch
of road. There are times, as it was proven by Napoleon, when even the
most powerful forces and the finest materials are subordinate to the
weather.

"As for railroad transport, I would not have been so rude as to be late
in arriving today if the tracks were not in such bad condition. They are
single line for long stretches, and as you know they are a wider gauge
than French or German tracks." He shrugged with humor, "But what
matter how bad the tracks are when we have little rolling stock to lend
you for troop transport? You will note that rolling stock is on our list of
priority requirements, second only to matériel for it to carry."

The main course was served.

"I hope you enjoy duckling with orange sauce."

"*Führer*, I enjoy it immensely. In truth I am devoted to all food. I enjoy gourmet cooking but I also find happiness with simple food such as I had all of my life as a soldier."

"But you don't smoke?"

"No."

"Nor I. The evil of tobacco is something that I incessantly lecture against to my 'family.' I have a standing offer of a gold watch for any of them who gives it up."

Franco observed that his host was not eating duck, that he had been served a plate of vegetables. Hitler said, "The elephant is the strongest animal. He also cannot eat meat."

The dinner proceeded amiably. Serrano Suñer even found ways to be pleasant to von Ribbentrop. Franco's earnestness and his expression of facts that Hitler knew to be true gave the *Führer* a glimmer of hope. As dinner finished he said, "I am more than ever convinced that this is an historic day and one that can end as we both hoped it would: in an alliance for immediate action against the bourgeois, leftist British."

Franco and Hitler returned to the work coach with their Foreign Ministers and interpreters, and at ten-thirty P.M. began an unscheduled conference.

"*Caudillo*, I assure you that Spain will have as much help as she needs, as much in provisions as in armaments. Let us resolve this to our mutual satisfaction by signing a protocol in which Spain commits to enter the war when it is estimated possible that she can, but in the reasonable future."

"*Führer*, I am not the King of Utopia, merely *Caudillo* of a starving, broken Spain. My country simply is not prepared to enter any war whose scope cannot be measured and from which her people could gain nothing."

"Nothing? *Caudillo*! A hundred thousand tons of wheat that I have in Portugal and that I offer to deliver to you today is not 'nothing.'"

"Spain needs one million tons. *Führer*, at this moment there are hundreds of thousands of workers in the Asturias, Bilbao and Barcelona who are so weakened by hunger that they cannot raise themselves in order to work."

"Germany will give you everything you need when you declare war."

"When Spain has everything she needs then she will declare war."

Hitler was shaking his head. Just shaking his head back and forth, staring at the oriental carpet. "It could be so quick. In through Spain. We take Gibraltar. Into North Africa. The Mediterranean closed. Great Britain sues for peace. I am already the Master of Europe. Just a little more and it will all be over." He pleaded with Franco. "Hardly a shot need be fired. Not one Spaniard could get hurt."

"*Führer*, war offers few opportunities to practice nonviolence."

"Perhaps. But then we would have peace at last, peace protected by the Thousand Year Third Reich."

Franco said, "Let us not be so unreflecting as to think in terms of eternal peace since we have seen that it lasts approximately twenty years."

"*Caudillo* . . . *Caudillo* . . . you think you are being prudent, but you are standing back from an opportunity that will never again occur . . . the war will end and Spain will be left a starving nation . . . your people will never forgive you, never. You are making a tragic error, *Caudillo*."

"*Führer*, I can only do what I believe best. When I arrive at my final hour I will leave without fear of history. They will have plenty of time to examine and weigh my actions."

Hitler had been rubbing his shoe with his forefinger. He turned to von Ribbentrop. "I've had enough. Since nothing will do, we'll handle things ourselves in Montoire."

He stood up quickly, and without looking directly at anyone in particular, said "Goodbye," and left the train.

Franco, with Serrano Suñer and the Barón de las Torres, returned to his own train. Within minutes General Espinosa de los Monteros entered. "Excellency, the *Führer* would like to bid you farewell on the station platform."

El Caudillo was relieved to have a better ending to the meeting.

The *Führer* and *El Caudillo* exchanged handshakes on the station platform. The press was permitted to photograph them together, for which both leaders presented facades of good will.

At 12:55 A.M. Franco boarded his train again. Hitler stood on the platform to see him off. Wishing to be especially courteous, Franco did not go into the parlor car to wave goodbye through a window, but remained standing on the landing above the stairs, with the door open, facing Hitler. The Chief of the Spanish State raised his right arm in salute to the Chief of the German State. At that moment the train started up with a violent lurch, throwing Franco off balance, pitching him forward. As he was falling, an arm from behind caught him. It was General Moscardó, whose physical strength and quick reflexes averted the fall, and the train continued rolling back into the safety of Spain.

What Serrano Suñer had just seen climaxed the emotionally exhausting day. Sitting alone, he thought, *The important things occur in a second, as in a second we are born and in a second we die. Without Moscardó it would have been a tragedy. At the angle Paco was falling he would have struck the platform head first and so violently that he surely would have been killed. This broken down train almost changed the history of the world. If Paco had been killed the power would fall to the army and every one of the Generals wants to enter the war. They're young, they're soldiers. And they would have changed his policy and entered the war and the Germans would be in Cádiz tomorrow.*[10]

The Barón de las Torres observed *El Caudillo* sitting by himself. A nobleman and a career diplomat, he decided to write down his impressions.

> *The Generalísimo has taken out of this meeting an impression of Hitler, distinctly different to that which he had imagined that gentleman to be, so that he must almost believe that he had met a different person, and he is very disappointed.*
>
> *My impression as a Spaniard could not be better, because knowing the Germans and their methods, and having in mind the power which they have today, entirely dominating Europe, the attitude of El Caudillo could not have been more virile, nor more patriotic, nor more realistic, because he maintained himself before the pressures of the Führer and has passed over, with the most dignity, the bad way and methods and the simple bad manners which the Führer displayed upon not seeing his desires satisfied.*[11]

Arriving at his home in San Sebastian at 2:30 A.M. Franco telephoned to the Palace of El Pardo and asked the aide on duty, "Has the *Señora* retired?"

146

"No, Excellency . . ." A Lieutenant Colonel, he could not conceal his excitement at hearing the Chief of State's voice, ". . . I was advised by her Excellency that she would remain awake all night in the event that your Excellency might call."

Sitting up in bed Carmen Polo stiffened as she heard the ring of the telephone on the night table between her bed and her husband's. Then she heard, "*Carmelita*, I will be home tomorrow."

El Caudillo returned to the salon where his party was awaiting him, and speaking principally to Serrano Suñer and the Barón de las Torres, he said, "The Supplementary Protocol which we left with poor Espinosa de los Monteros will, as intended, be unacceptable. The Germans will not ratify the phrase in paragraph five: 'in the French Zone of Morocco, which is later to belong to Spain.' We gained a little time. But very soon we will have to sign something so we had better have it ready in a form we can live with."

They sat down at the dining table and read the German draft Protocol. "We will adjust the offending paragraph five but not so much that it will be fully acceptable . . ."

SECRET PROTOCOL
Hendaye, October 23, 1940

1. *The exchange of views between the Führer of the German Reich and the Chief of the Spanish State. . .[See Appendix 6.]*

The key departure from the Germans' version was that Spain's entry would be by "common agreement," a compromise between "When Germany considers it necessary" and "Spain will decide the moment of attack." Franco was satisfied that by retaining an equal vote he had made the compromise necessary to show good will, but had merely promised to have another talk.

Carmen Polo was kneeling in the chapel of the Palace. It was late afternoon and she had been there most of the day, in gratitude, as she had been there the whole of the day before in appeal. So engrossed in prayer was she that she did not hear the Moor Guards' trumpeters heralding the return of the Chief of State, nor did she see her husband enter the chapel. She was not aware of his presence until he was kneeling beside her.

They prayed together. When he had finished he did not move. Looking at the altar, the crucifix, and the candles, smelling the incense, he imagined the sound of an organ, the Latin singing, the beauty of a religious ceremony. Alone with his wife, in the silence of the chapel, he thought, *How far removed from the cannibalism, the barbarism, the gigantic destruction of war, and the misery it leaves behind.*[14]

CHAPTER ELEVEN

THE PHOTOGRAPHS FIRST APPEARED IN THE GERMAN AND SPANISH PRESS, SHOWING THE TWO DICTATORS SMILING AT EACH OTHER UPON FRANCO'S ARRIVAL AT HENDAYE; WALKING SIDE BY SIDE WITH FRANCO making the Fascist salute, then exchanging warm good-bys on the station's platform. In Spain the headlines were: FRANCO Y HITLER. In Germany they were: HITLER UND FRANCO.

In London the press front-paged the photos and lashed out against the open display of friendship between "an alleged neutral and the monster that is dropping tons of bombs on English homes every night."

Political columnists and cartoonists plunged into the issue, portraying Franco as a smiling, miniature Hitler, opening the door of Spain to the also smiling *Führer*, who is looking beyond Franco at the Rock of Gibraltar.

In the House of Commons the Hendaye meeting was denounced as final proof that Franco was about to join Hitler in open warfare against England.

It was Friday afternoon and Ramón Serrano Suñer, now the Spanish Foreign Minister, fatigued from pressure and long hours while taking over a new Ministry, was looking forward to resting. The hunting season had just begun and he was going to spend Saturday and Sunday at a partridge shoot at a private preserve between Madrid and Toledo. He enjoyed the atmosphere, the people, and especially that it was away from the city and the telephones.

His secretary entered the office. "Excellency, the German Ambassador is on his way upstairs."

"But he has no appointment."

"He is in the elevator, Excellency."

Von Stohrer was shown into the Minister's office. "Don Ramón. Herr von Ribbentrop has just cabled that the *Führer* wishes to see you most urgently at Berchtesgaden. Because of the *Führer's* other commitments only November 18th could be considered. In order to be at the Berghof on the morning of the 18th we will have to leave Madrid on the 15th. Herr von Ribbentrop will send a parlor car to the Spanish border for you.[1] May I cable that you will go?"

"One week is very short notice. I will have to let you know."

"But the *Führer* wishes . . ."

"I am not a minister of the *Führer*. I am a minister of *El Caudillo*. I have work to do here for this government. I will let you know as soon as I can."

Serrano Suñer went immediately to the Palace of El Pardo and Franco convened the High Command.

"How many times do we dare say no?" General Varela asked. "If we could think of some plausible reason why you can't go, yet without provoking the *Führer's* anger . . ."

Serrano Suñer agreed. "If I do not go to meet the Germans in Berchtesgaden I fear that we might encounter them here in Vitoria."

Sir Samuel Hoare was advised by Lord Halifax that because of the controversy over the Franco-Hitler meeting, and the fear by the Minister of Economic Warfare, Hugh Dalton, that food sent to Franco's Spain would either be stockpiled for use in the war against England, or be re-exported directly to Germany, the British Government was therefore canceling all existing trade agreements with Spain.

This was distinctly not the sort of occasion Sir Samuel would have chosen to present himself to the new Foreign Minister, especially because of Serrano Suñer's well-known leaning toward the Germans, and also his grudge against the English because of the deaths of his brothers during the Civil War. Sir Samuel had tried to find information to the contrary and though he claimed that the Serrano Suñer brothers had not been turned away, he knew it was probable because British policy gave asylum in their Embassies to no one but British subjects.

Serrano Suñer greeted Sir Samuel with brittle courtesy, but as the Englishman delivered his country's message to Spain, he paled and could pose no longer. "Are you telling me that shiploads of wheat, which my country has been anxiously awaiting, will not be delivered because London does not approve of the press reports of General Franco's meeting with Adolf Hitler?"

"I regret to say that is the case."

"When Neville Chamberlain visited Hitler did they frown at each other for the photographers? Hardly. I have seen the British newspapers and they have fanned this meeting into a major political fire. But are your leaders so gullible as to be swayed by what they read?"

"Sir, in democratic process the government responds to the will of the people."

"No, sir. They respond to the will to be voted back into office, with no thought or concern that millions of Spaniards will starve at that expense. In parts of Spain the poor are filling their stomachs by eating grass, roots and leaves from trees."

When Hoare made no answer Serrano Suñer looked at him with distaste. "I don't recall a clause in our signed treaty that limits General Franco's political or social meetings. England's honor and integrity are obviously in as short supply as her heart." Suddenly, further alarmed, he asked, "And the shiploads of citrus fruits with which we have paid for this wheat will be returned to us, having rotted by the time it reaches Spain again."

Hoare was silent.

"And the navicerts for the 150,000 tons of corn and the 100,000 tons of meat we were able to buy in Canada; will they be issued? Or will the ships carrying that food be blockaded until the food rots?"

Hoare was afraid to admit that the Certificates of Navigation that would allow those ships past the British Navy blockade would not be issued. Nor could he lie to this man who already understood. "Your Excellency, it is a natural result of the reports of General Franco's rendezvous with Hitler. The apparent friendship would hardly rest well with people who suffer nightly air raids from the Germans. It is normal human reaction."

"It is inhuman reaction. And worse, it is not reaction, but a strategy calculated to bend Spain to England's will. And not a clever strategy. You are forcing us to turn to Germany."

"Sir, I disagree with my government's action. I believe that this 'strategy,' if you will, is not in Great Britain's best interests and I intend to do everything I can to reverse it. And though I understand that it is also in our best interests that your press continues to pacify the Germans lest they march into Spain, still, if there could be a small change, if your press could from time to time show England's true wartime condition, then I could use that evidence of good will to beg our Minister of Information to urge a change in the attitude of the British press. For example, if the Spanish press were to note the superiority of the RAF over the *Luftwaffe*; increased war production . . ."

"You must excuse me for being abrupt," Serrano Suñer said, rising to his feet. "I acknowledge receipt of your government's message. And on your next return from Gibraltar with your automobile filled with English delicacies, as you pass through Madrid if you see a Spaniard fall to the ground from hunger, do stop and tell him that the RAF is more powerful than the *Luftwaffe*. I am certain that he and millions like him will be simply fascinated."

Outside, Sir Samuel sank gratefully into the refuge of his car. As he passed through the streets of Madrid he looked at the people and saw that indeed they were famished; he could see it on their faces. Though he did not see anyone topple over he had heard of that happening, and he felt a genuine regret for his government's useless action and a resolve to try to correct it quickly.

El Caudillo summoned von Stohrer to El Pardo and told him, "When you arrive at Berchtesgaden I would like you to convey my dismay to the *Führer* that no sooner had I agreed to align myself with the Axis, than I was astonished to learn of Italy's ill-timed attack on Greece. The *Duce* proves that he is a politician and not a military strategist and I feel little temptation to align my country with such irresponsibility."

"Excellency," von Stohrer replied urgently, "I assure you that the *Duce* acted entirely on his own, without the *Führer's* knowledge. The *Duce* wanted revenge against the *Führer* for German action in Rumania and France without first consulting him. He did this to pay the *Führer* back in kind, to 'show him' as it were, with a fait accompli. I believe it was also so the *Führer* would not be able to order the action not to be taken, as he did once before, which of course did not please the *Duce*."

"Worse!" Franco was genuinely amazed. "It was bad enough when I thought the *Duce* had misrepresented his strength to the *Führer* and they had agreed on a bad idea. Inform the *Führer* of my grave misgivings on entering into a collaboration whose leaders act on ego and in competition with each other. I do not intend to have Spaniards go to war with emotionally motivated partners."

CHAPTER TWELVE

O N THE 18TH OF NOVEMBER 1940 RAMÓN SERRANO SUÑER ARRIVED AT BERCHTESGADEN, A QUIET TOWN IN THE SOUTHEAST OF BAVARIA, WHOSE SERENITY AND BEAUTY HITLER HAD CHOSEN AS THE SETTING for his fortified mountain chalet, the Berghof. Looking through the train windows at the snow-covered Alps, Serrano Suñer dreaded the German open-topped cars almost as much as meeting again with Adolf Hitler.

Von Ribbentrop, waiting on the station platform with an entourage that included two generals, escorted him to the Hotel Berchtesgadener Hof. Because the *Führer* normally stayed up very late and did not rise until noon, the morning was free so Ribbentrop invited "Don Ramón" on a sightseeing tour and lunch at his shooting lodge in Fuschl.

The car was, blessedly, closed and at ten in the morning they set off over icy roads at terrible speeds. It was the Spanish Minister's first time in the Alps and it was at least an opportunity to see Salzburg and a marvelous stretch between Bavaria and Austria. En route to von Ribbentrop's shooting lodge they met up with a fleet of cars in which there was an Italian delegation, among them Count Ciano. Only when they were well on the way did Serrano Suñer learn that Fuschl was 60 kilometers distant, and that after lunch they would have to return over the same 60 kilometers of treacherous roads. It seemed to him to be such an absurd misuse of time as to be either stupid, or a strategy to deliver him to Hitler in a condition of emotional and physical exhaustion.

Serrano studied the lunch of spaghetti and crepes for which they had traveled sixty kilometers, most of the time in fear for his life. He wondered if perhaps being delivered to Hitler weakened from hunger was also a part of the German strategy. And he amused himself by anticipating his return to El Pardo and reporting, ". . . Herr von Ribbentrop, his finesse consistent and unwavering, treated the Italian Foreign Minister to the novelty of a nice bowl of spaghetti."

During the meal von Ribbentrop's conversation faithfully reminded his guests: "England is beaten!" this time supporting the declaration with "England has only two hopes: Russia and the United States. She can forget about Russia, with whom we have a treaty. As for the United States her fleet is thoroughly occupied in the Pacific and will continue to be so, a fundamental reason for including Japan in our Tripartite Pact. Secondly, America's armament will take years. Finally, it is doubtful if England can bring America into the conflict. The Americans want merely to play the role of heir to the British Empire."

Perhaps boredom is the fourth element of his strategy, Serrano Suñer mused.

He liked Count Ciano, whom he knew well, but there was little opportunity to speak with him as no sooner had they finished the ridiculous lunch than they were speeding the 60 kilometers back to Berchtesgaden.

Awaiting them at the outskirts of town were open-topped half-tracks, military vehicles having wheels in front and caterpillar tracks behind, and they changed into them to ride up the steep and icy road to the Berghof. As they arrived von Ribbentrop said, "The *Führer* is waiting for us in the Tea House. The *Führer* walks there every afternoon after lunch. It is a twenty-minute walk."

The building was silo-shaped and caused Serrano Suñer to think nostalgically of the Moor watchtowers along Spain's southern coast. Inside at last von Ribbentrop led the way to a large round room with picture windows providing a view of the towers of Salzburg and the Ach River.

Without preamble Hitler said, "I have called you here according to our agreement at Hendaye to fix the soonest possible date for Spain's participation in the war. It is absolutely necessary to attack Gibraltar and haste is vital, for psychological reasons. As the *Caudillo* understands, the Italians committed a grave error in beginning a war against Greece without anticipating weather conditions that have made their strongest arm, the air force, useless.[1] Their ground forces are floundering embarrassingly and they have made the Axis look, for the first time, to be a force that can be resisted. An immediate and resounding victory is necessary to counteract this damage."

Serrano Suñer said, "Excellency, may I remind you that the agreement reached and detailed in the secret protocol is that Spain would enter the war at a time to be mutually agreed upon."

"I have had enough double-talk. The *Duce* agrees that this is the time. And I agree that this is the time. Now the *Caudillo* must agree and we will be mutually agreed." He waved his hand, dismissing any reply. "The hour has come for Spain to play her role in the writing of world history. And history will not wait for *El Caudillo!*"

"*Führer*, upon receiving your invitation to visit you here I was completely ignorant of what you wished to discuss. Thus, I come unprepared, without the judgment of my government, so what I say can only represent my personal thought and comment . . ."[2]

Hitler now understood Franco well enough to know that his representative would not arrive at Berchtesgaden without thorough preparation. "Don't worry about your 'personal thought and comment' because I did not summon you here to listen to your 'personal thought and comment.' I sent for you to hear *my* personal thought and comment; and not to 'discuss' anything, but to tell you clearly what Spain will now do—however," and he leaned back on the divan with an elaborate sigh, "as a matter of politesse I will impatiently listen to your personal thought and comment, all of which is anticipated and useless. But go ahead."

Caught between fear and fury Serrano Suñer replied, "Thank you, *Führer*. I simply want to explain that if Spain contributes to the closing of the Straits of Gibraltar the British will close the Atlantic to us. They have already demonstrated this. Merely on the press reports of your Excellency's meeting with *El Caudillo* the British government canceled our economic accord and the Royal Navy blockaded large shipments of corn and meat that we had bought in Canada. Further, a Red Cross ship from the United States, carrying 30,000 tons of wheat from President Roosevelt was ordered to turn around and return to America without delivering its cargo . . ."

Hitler crossed his legs with visible impatience, from left to right, and then right to left, twice, as if to amuse himself with a dance.[3]

". . . Now again we are expecting most desperately needed shipments from the United States, but if anything should occur to cause the Allies to question our neutrality those shipments will cease instantly."

Hitler snapped, "What do they provide for? How much? And when due?"

Startled by the change of pace, Serrano Suñer retorted, "Cereal. 400,000 tons. Within two months." He added, "I hope within two months. Half of my work is a daily battle with the British Ambassador in Madrid, a despicable man whose own colleagues refer to him as 'having descended from a long line of maiden aunts.' He has the power to speed or slow the issue of navicerts. The British continue to permit merely a trickle of food and petroleum to pass through their navy's blockade. Yet, without those deliveries Spanish life would be paralyzed."

"Do you know something?" Hitler asked.

"Tell me, *Führer*."

"You bore me. I cannot stand the tedium of the economic difficulties with which you constantly defend yourselves against my wishes. Do you seriously believe that your condition will better itself by staying out of the war?[4] Entering the war is your only salvation. At that moment your condition will better itself immediately and dramatically. Does not the distinguished foreign minister see that?"

"Yes, *Führer*, provided the war would end quickly. But if President Roosevelt decides to join the war then I think . . ."

Hitler thrust his arms skyward and gazed towards heaven. "What I pray for myself is you will *stop* thinking, stop questioning my judgment. It is such a waste of time and energy. Everything has been thought of. If Spain intervenes immediately according to my instructions, we will quickly isolate Great Britain, forcing her to surrender, and then there will be no war for President Roosenfeld to join!"

"*Führer*, another problem is that Allied propaganda keeps assuring the Spanish people that if Spain stays out of the war then food shipments from Canada, Argentina and the United States will be facilitated by the Royal Navy. And this rests well on the ears of a nation of hungry people who are tired of war."

"It does not rest well on my ears, which are hungry for war and tired of talking. Do not believe Allied propaganda. On the contrary, they will seek every opportunity to blockade shipments—making war, thereby, on women and children—pressuring you more and more, hoping to create unrest among your people and topple the Franco regime because it is not in their democratic image. I assure you they will fulfill none of their promises."

"On the subject of promises, *Führer*, a friendly complaint: *El Caudillo* is disappointed that Germany is not sending foods or materials of war, not even those that we contracted and paid for in advance by the building of a Heinkel airplane factory in Seville, and that we need for our defenses."[5]

Hitler got to his feet, leaned towards Serrano Suñer and shouted, "My friendly answer to your friendly complaint is that Spain is not at war. Germany is at war and needs every last kilo of materials. We have no surpluses of wheat for people claiming to be friends but who sit on the fence waiting to see which way will be the most comfortable to fall." He sat down. "However, when Spain enters the war then she will be proportioned all of the materials she needs, as was done for you during your Civil War, and as was done for the Italians since the first day they declared themselves at war. It is that simple."[6]

"*Führer*, perhaps we should make a protocol as to exactly what Spain needs and would receive upon declaring war on England?"

"Perhaps. . ." Hitler glared, "perhaps the Spanish *caballero* must take my word and not insult me by insisting on an itemized and written document.[7] And why would you need it in writing? Are you planning to take me to court?"

Satisfied that he had intimidated his guest, Hitler explained, "We are presently waiting for a period of good weather in order to launch an air raid of four thousand bombers, four thousand machines relentlessly pounding England senseless in wave after wave of bombs. This period of waiting must be used advantageously. I have concluded that in these moments the most urgent, the most useful and desirable action is to attack England decisively in the Mediterranean. I have irrevocably, unequivocally, categorically, decided to attack Gibraltar. Everything is prepared in the most minute detail. Nothing remains except to begin. And we will begin. I am not asking you, I am telling you."

Serrano Suñer dared not reply.

Hitler stared at him hard, and for a full minute. Then, "Of the many divisions that make up the German army there are presently one hundred and eighty-six divisions that find themselves inactive. I did not build the greatest war machine in the history of the world merely to have a large personal bodyguard. I have idle soldiers and I am disposed to utilize them where it is necessary and valuable." He leaned toward Serrano Suñer, "As to Spain's needs, Germany is generous with her friends, whereas she annihilates her enemies. If that sounds like a threat, then let me assure you that it *is* a threat. And the issue of Spain's friendship is most seriously in question. I have chosen to look away from the detestable because it suits me at the moment, but I find the *Caudillo* a very strange friend . . . very, very strange. I have received, with disbelief, the outrageous, provocative news that Spanish passports are being issued to Jews who have never seen Spain, nor have their ancestors in precisely 448 years." His voice was rising. "Suddenly French are Spanish. And from Poland suddenly Poles are Spaniards. And in Denmark and the Netherlands . . . overnight my enemies have Spanish passports and are able to leave my jurisdiction." He made a fist with his left hand and began punching it lightly, rapidly into his right palm. "I find the *Caudillo* a very strange friend. I look away from treachery because it serves me to do so, but there are limits to everything and we have been very patient with our elusive little friend . . . perhaps too patient, much too patient . . ." He stared for a long while into Serrano Suñer's eyes and the Spaniard had no doubt that this was not showmanship. "There are men under my command, men more passionate than I, men of less patience than I, who have suggested retaliation, urged it, swift and harsh . . . but I am an egotist who keeps hoping that he has not been unwise in considering the *Caudillo* a friend . . . so I wait . . . but for how long?"

There was a terrible silence. When Hitler had rested he asked, "What is the shortest possible period of time Spain needs to prepare herself?"

"*Führer*, sincerely I am not qualified to say, being neither a military man nor an economist."

"Then send your men who are qualified to Berlin for conferences with my people." He stood up and paced around the area. "November is half gone. That leaves us December, a full month to prepare. We can still meet the January 10th date of Operation Felix. It is good for our German soldiers to fight in winter. They are accustomed to cold and will find it easiest to fight on Spanish soil in December and January. Besides, in March or April they will need to be available for other tasks."[8] He stopped walking. "Everything has been said. I wish to hear no more. We will adjourn and have tea."

"Yes, *Führer*." Serrano Suñer rose to his feet. Gingerly, he asked, "May I broach an entirely different subject of importance?"

Hitler gave it a moment's thought then nodded.

"*Führer*, surely British Intelligence is aware of my visit here. Spain needs this time to stockpile all the foreign provisions possible before they are cut off again as a result of Spanish action not to Allied liking. It would be a catastrophe if they were to blockade what is now en route. To avoid that, perhaps it could become known that my visit here was solely to petition Germany for cereal and wheat? That would also serve as excellent propaganda with the Spanish people, further demonstrating Germany's strength by her ability to send supplies to Spain."

Hitler turned to Ribbentrop. "Have Goebbels handle this. Quote: The Spanish Foreign Minister met with the *Führer* to request cereal. The request was summarily refused. End quote." He turned to Serrano Suñer. "Germany will demonstrate her strength without outside advice. In the meanwhile, the British will be pleased by that announcement. They might even be moved to issue you another navicert."

Then Serrano Suñer found himself outside again walking with Hitler back to the Berghof, another twenty minutes in the snow. He noticed that Hitler did not seem to like it any more than he did.

Finally inside the Berghof they entered a salon that opened onto a continuation of the room with a large fireplace and picture windows, a walled-in winter garden with a panoramic view of the Alps. Waiting there were Generals Jodl and Keitel, Count Ciano and von Stohrer.

SS men in white uniforms served coffee, tea and hot chocolate with whipped cream. Hitler had apple-peel tea then went to a table on which there was a relief map of Spain including Gibraltar and the Bay of Algeciras. An SS man brought him a chair and he sat down while the others stood around him. "Look," he said, to Serrano Suñer, "let me show you how brilliantly and minutely in detail we have Felix worked out." He pointed to the Pyrenees, to a mass of miniature tanks, trucks and soldiers representing the real ones on Spain's border.

"On the 3rd of January Spain will historically make her declaration of war against England. The *Wehrmacht* will have begun its descent through this pass . . ." He looked into Serrano Suñer's eyes. "Incidentally, this key bridge at Hendaye is in bad repair. Have construction crews begin on that immediately." Turning back to the map, he continued, ". . . then moving southward along the coast they will arrive at Algeciras . . ."

The Spaniard listened to Hitler describing the attack, the landings, the occupation. Everyone was listening. And from Keitel and Jodl, even from von Ribbentrop, whenever their eyes met there were smiles of camaraderie. And that was frightening. Above the detailia of Hitler's plan and the man's obsession to take Gibraltar, the most chilling part was his certainty, and that of his colleagues, that to pass through Spain was a fait accompli.

CHAPTER THIRTEEN

BERLIN   MADRID, NOVEMBER 28, 1940
TOP SECRET

FOR THE HEAD OF THE OFFICE OR HIS REPRESENTA-
TIVE; TO BE DECIPHERED BY HIM PERSONALLY. TOP
SECRET. REPLY BY COURIER OR SECRET CODE.

THE SPANISH FOREIGN MINISTER JUST TOLD ME
THAT THE GENERALISSIMO HAS AGREED TO THE
STARTING OF THE PREPARATIONS WHICH WERE
CONTEMPLATED.

A DETAILED TELEGRAPHIC REPORT WITH OUR
RECOMMENDATIONS, THAT IS, WISHES OF FRANCO
ARE TO FOLLOW.

STOHRER[1]

BERLIN   MADRID, NOVEMBER 29, 1940
TOP SECRET

FOR THE FOREIGN MINISTER PERSONALLY.
WITH REFERENCE TO MY TELEGRAM NO. 4074 OF
NOVEMBER 28.

FOR YESTERDAY'S DISCUSSION OF FRANCO'S POSITION
ON THE QUESTIONS DISCUSSED AT BERCHTESGADEN
THE SPANISH FOREIGN MINISTER HAS MADE WRITTEN

NOTES WHICH HE READ TO ME. THE PASSAGES
BELOW WHICH ARE IN QUOTATION MARKS ARE
GIVEN VERBATIM.

1) "IT IS AGREED THAT THE PREPARATIONS FOR
   SPAIN'S ENTRY INTO THE WAR ARE TO BE SPEEDED
   UP AS MUCH AS POSSIBLE.
2) "THE TIME REQUIRED FOR THIS, HOWEVER,
   CANNOT TODAY BE DEFINITELY DETERMINED
   BECAUSE . . ."

And again there were three pages of the strategy of delay, "Yes, but"
and "Yes, if." [See Appendix 7 for complete text.]

Hitler glared at von Ribbentrop. "Stop looking so pleased with yourself. I do not see a date of entry agreed to. But, in fairness to you and to
von Stohrer I can see that at least now the hook has been taken. Now we
need an expert slippery-fish catcher to pin down the *Caudillo*."

"*Mein Führer*, I will personally go to Madrid."

"No . . . my dear Joachim, though you are my most valued Minister,
you are no match for the *Caudillo*. No, this is a special job for a special
man . . ." He began pacing the length of his office at the Chancellery,
von Ribbentrop walking slightly behind. "We are so close, after such
effort . . . this is so urgent that we dare not fail. But who can we send?
Who? Who?"

After mentally thumbing through and discarding his top people,
one remained: Admiral Wilhelm Canaris. He was the man who could do
it. More so than Goebbels, or Goering or Himmler. If anyone was a
match for the elusive *Caudillo*, if anyone could pin Franco down it would
be this man: feared by some, hated by some, mysterious to all and
respected by all. Apart from all else, if a meticulous man like Canaris
could think of Franco as "a little man," then possibly he understood the
key to him.

Wilhelm Canaris was a born spy: intelligent, silent, a man with an
instinct for covering his tracks; with an enormous sense of fantasy, he was
fascinated by the sea and exotic places. He was an adventurer, a romantic,

a cynic. He was curious, nervous, restless, yet patient. As a child the toy he had enjoyed most was invisible ink. He was a good listener, cultivated, and he could make friends at any level; he was a grand master in the art of treating people as they needed to be treated. Consequently, as his results had proven consistently, no door was locked to him.[3]

He had become one of the most powerful men in the Third Reich. Working with unlimited funds to accomplish Germany's ends as head of Secret Intelligence, Military Sabotage and Counterespionage since 1935 he had developed a worldwide military intelligence system so efficient and reliable as to win battles with information as Goebbels had won battles with propaganda. He operated a chain of elegant salons in every major city of the world where high ranking military and political figures were entertained by fabulous women of social standing who were *Abwehr* agents, voluntarily or under pressure. He spent millions to maintain these women, and the information they produced was invaluable.

Fluent in Spanish from his long missions in South America as a young naval officer during World War I, Canaris first appeared in Madrid in 1916 under command of the German Naval Attaché, Captain von Krohn, and built up a force of coast watchers to report activities of British and French ships. He developed so many influential Spanish friends that he was later sent from Germany on commercial business, to arrange for the manufacture in Spain of German submarines and torpedoes forbidden to her by the Versailles Treaty but which the German Naval officers and scientists would not abandon.

Hitler sent for General Alfred Jodl, Chief of the *Wehrmacht* Operations Staff of the OKW. "Jodl, we will soon have some action. Prepare yourself so that immediately after Canaris cables Franco's agreement to our January 10th target date, you will go to Madrid to make arrangements for the necessary military operations as the officer enjoying my special confidence.

"And, for precaution against being recognized by British Intelligence, Admiral Canaris suggests that you travel in civilian clothes with a Ministerial passport under a fictitious name."

MADRID   BERLIN, DECEMBER 4, 1940
FOR THE AMBASSADOR PERSONALLY

I REQUEST YOU TO TELL THE SPANISH FOREIGN
MINISTER ON MY BEHALF THAT THE FUHRER HAS
LEARNED WITH SATISFACTION OF THE GENERALIS-
SIMO'S DECISION.
  THE FUHRER HAS DIRECTED ADMIRAL CANARIS
TO GO TO MADRID AS SOON AS POSSIBLE TO DISCUSS
MORE ABOUT THE PREPARATIONS AND ABOUT THE
EXECUTION OF THE ACTION. CANARIS WILL ARRIVE
IN MADRID ON SUNDAY.
             RIBBENTROP[4]

Franco received the news with gravity. If Canaris were being sent it meant that his strategy had been too convincing; that instead of discouraging Hitler with impossible conditions, he had excited him into believing that now Spain would enter. And Hitler would be all the more angered when he learned that no date would be set.

"Ramón, advise von Stohrer that I will be pleased to receive the distinguished emissary of the *Führer* on the day that he arrives, Sunday. You might obliquely point out that I have canceled plans to be at a shoot this weekend in order to extend this courtesy.

"Also, you can tell von Stohrer that regarding his request several months ago for refueling rights for German tankers in remote bays along our coast, we have finally been able to solve the problems that delayed our ability to grant this, and are now happy to make these facilities available."[5]

It was a relatively small bone to throw, which would surely please Hitler and help Spain to delay such greater commitments as Canaris was being sent to extract.

Von Stohrer was having a lovely day. Having sent off the good news about the long sought-after fueling rights, he then telephoned Serrano Suñer. "Don Ramón, I have a most pleasant mission to perform on behalf of the *Führer*, the delivery of a gift for *El Caudillo*'s forty-eighth birthday. May I come by after lunch?"

At five o'clock that afternoon the sentries and the two mounted Moorish guards in front of the gates of the Palace of El Pardo displayed proof of their discipline by failing to gawk at the sight of the largest and strangest-looking automobile they had ever seen. Ambassador von Stohrer was at the wheel of a gigantic, open-topped six-wheeled Mercedes-Benz. At his side was one of his bodyguards. The back seat was not occupied; behind that where normal automobiles end, this one continued, providing seats for three of von Stohrer's bodyguards, faced backwards so they could observe the rear.

Franco went down to the courtyard of the palace and inspected the vehicle while von Stohrer explained, "It is for reviewing troops and for parades. The *Führer* designed it personally." He gave Franco a letter from Hitler.

The Chancellery   *December 4, 1940*
My *dear* Caudillo,

I greet you with deep affection today on the occasion of your 48th birthday and I hope with all my heart that you will enjoy many more happy, healthy and peaceful birthdays in the years to come.

Please do me the favor of accepting this gift from your friend, who, upon ordering an identical automobile for himself, thought how appropriate that you, I and the Duce should share this in common as we share so many other more important ideals.

Therefore I have taken the liberty of ordering and sending you this car, one of three in the world, in which I hope you will be comfortable and safe while reviewing your fine Spanish troops. Greatest attention has been given to the armoring of the body of the car and the glass which you will notice reaches higher than the height of one's head while standing.

Your friend in the peace soon to be won,

Adolf Hitler

Von Stohrer showed *El Caudillo* a support in the back seat, not visible from the outside, by which he, like the *Führer*, could stand while the car was moving without fear of being jolted off balance. "The leather and woodworking are, of course, the finest in the world," von Stohrer said. "And, Excellency, there are no ashtrays, by design . . ."

The important question: What was the gift saying? Was Hitler telling him, "I am confidant of your loyalty," or did he feel the need to strengthen their relations with gestures of friendship?

When von Stohrer had gone, Franco sent for his wife and daughter. Amused, he asked, "What am I going to do with this thing?" For, unlike Hitler, he did not review miles and miles of troops. When annually there was a parade in Madrid to celebrate the Victory, Franco stood in one place and reviewed the troops as *they* passed in parade.

At lunch the following day Franco said to his daughter, "Julio Muñoz Aguilar told me that you are shooting so well that you could become one of the best guns in Spain."

The Chief of the *Casa Civil* had been teaching Carmencita to shoot partridge and pheasant. Franco was pleased that his teenage daughter was becoming proficient in one of his two favorite sports, the other being fishing. "After lunch today you can come with me in the Jeep and try for a dove."

It was the nicest way he could show that he was proud of her, the hunting of doves being far more difficult than partridge and pheasant because the former fly higher and faster and unlike the latter they do not run in flocks and cannot be directed toward the hunters by beaters. It is necessary to chase them cross-country on horseback or in a Jeep. Franco, a cavalry officer, could easily do it on horseback but the Jeep was better because his valet, Juanito, who served as his loader, could be there with him.

Excited about hunting with her father Carmencita asked her mother to come with them.

"I'd love to, but that's too many people for the Jeep." Then her face took on that expression that says, "Idea!" "Paco, why not use the *Führer*'s gift?"

The Mercedes-Benz left the courtyard of the palace, bearing *El Caudillo*, Carmencita and Juanito in the back seat, an aide at the wheel, and the First Lady of Spain in one of the rear seats designed for Hitler's storm troopers.

Searching the sky for almost ten minutes, finally *El Generalísimo* said, "There to the left . . ." and the driver, spotting the bird, gunned the engine and turned into the field in pursuit. Franco and Carmencita stood, their guns ready. A few yards into the field the car's forward motion began diminishing. Quickly, they had no forward motion at all; what they had was downward motion as the 6,500 pound Mercedes sank into the rain-softened terrain.

The Francos got out of the car and stared at the great machine, all six wheels engulfed in mud up to the running boards.

Doña Carmen said, "Paco, I'm sorry. It was a bad idea."

"Don't apologize. Fortunately, during our war I conducted troop movements less impulsively. Let's get the Jeep."

Characteristically doing the unexpected, Admiral Canaris arrived in Madrid on December 7, 1940, one day earlier than scheduled. He went directly to the German Embassy.

Von Stohrer was excited to meet, eager to spend time with this man who though often in Spain rarely appeared at the Embassy, always keeping out of sight, protecting his movements from becoming known by all the espionage people in Madrid. Referred to, behind his back, as "The White Admiral" and "Father Christmas" he had been Mata Hari's lover and it was believed it was he who planted the code on her person that caused her to be arrested and executed by the French.[6] Such icy ruthlessness contributed to the awe that surrounded Canaris, and rightfully so, for he thought nothing of utilizing anything or anyone to accomplish his purpose.

Von Stohrer suggested dinner.

"Thank you, no. I will see the *Generalísimo* this afternoon and then leave Madrid."

"But the appointment is tomorrow."

"You will please telephone and change it."

Von Stohrer hesitated, wondering if he dared ask Admiral Canaris to reconsider if it was prudent to call for an appointment that *El Caudillo* might refuse. The Chief of the *Abwehr* held such high rank that he was privileged to call the *Führer* directly, so maybe he didn't understand. On the other hand, von Stohrer was aware of this man's custom of never staying anywhere too long, not even to see the results of his work.

Admiral Canaris was looking at him with controlled impatience. Von Stohrer asked, "At what hour shall I say we would like to see him?"

"Whenever he wishes. But I will be seeing him alone. The famous Spanish pride will react better to having its arm twisted in private."

It was impressive that Canaris understood what so few of the Berliners did: how to handle Spaniards, who simply were not like other people. He was all the more intrigued by the *Führer*'s chief spy and the method he would use to convince Franco to enter the war.

Von Stohrer called the Minister of Foreign Affairs and asked that the appointment be changed. Serrano Suñer called back ten minutes later to say that *El Caudillo* would receive the Admiral at seven-thirty that afternoon. Relieved, and further impressed by the clout of this superspy, von Stohrer asked Canaris how he might be of service during the next two hours.

"Thank you. I would appreciate a glass of cold water and a room in which I can sit undisturbed."

General Franco was standing in the center of his office, almost at attention, his facial expression impenetrable.

"Your Excellency," Canaris said, bowing stiffly. The aide closed the door. Hearing it click, Canaris looked toward the sound and confirmed that the door was indeed shut. He turned again to Franco.

A splendid smile now covered *El Caudillo*'s face and his large brown eyes were bright and warm. He walked toward the Admiral, shook his right hand and with his left briskly patted his shoulder.

General Vigón had been standing in the background. "Juan," Canaris said, "*¿como estás?*" and the two men exchanged a more typical *abrazo*, a sort of bear hug with simultaneous pounding of each other's shoulder.

Wilhelm Canaris was a small man with a head that appeared to be too large for his body, his face very white-skinned, and his hair slightly thinned and silver. He wore no tinted glasses to conceal his blue eyes, as "Reed Rosas" had needed to do. He was, of course, "Reed Rosas," "Don Ignacio de Talavera, the humble monk who had traveled by mule from Toledo." He was "Kika." He was Juan Guillermo . . .

The Chief of German Military Intelligence had become a traitor to the Third Reich because he was a profound German patriot. He had supported Hitler faithfully until he began to see that Hitler had Germany on a course to certain destruction.

Canaris had first met Francisco Franco in the palace of King Alfonso XIII in the 1920's when Franco was known as "the King's favorite General." While operating his spy network during the Moroccan wars he was able to offer and produce valuable help to Franco and other Spanish generals.

At the beginning of the Spanish Civil War, praising Franco as a soldier, he had urged Adolf Hitler to support the Nationalist side in its effort to oust Communist forces.

By chance he had early made friends with the man who would become Chief of State, as well as with Generals Vigón, Kindelan, Varela, Martínez Campos and others who later, as Franco's elite, never forgot his help. When Hitler had sent him to Spain a year earlier, in 1939, to survey secretly the possibilities of taking Gibraltar, he went straight to General Vigón, explaining why he was there and what he needed, and the Spaniards spared him a lot of work by giving him the information, as well as providing him with the uniform of a Spanish army officer, identity papers and "full help" of the Spanish secret service in moving comfortably around Spain, gathering whatever he wanted. Also with the aide of the government he developed a network of 367 *Abwehr* agents throughout Spain that functioned with such efficiency that he had on various occasions served Franco's police with information on subversive elements that they might not have obtained themselves, including, as mentioned earlier, assassination plots against *El Caudillo*.

Admiral Canaris said, "I pray that you are able to withstand Herr Hitler's pressures . . ."

Franco had earlier noted that Canaris had stopped referring to Hitler as the *Führer*, and he understood that it was because he no longer considered him to be his leader.

". . . I urge your Excellency to avoid being forced into a war that Germany cannot possibly win. Hitler crosses back and forth between genius and madness, and month by month the time on the side of madness seems to be increasing. He justifies any act he wishes to commit by explaining to us, 'I am superior to any other human being. I am the first and only mortal to have emerged into a super human state. My nature is now more God-like than human. Therefore, as the first of the new race of supermen I am bound by none of the conventions of human morality. I stand above the law. My only superior is God Almighty.'"

Franco said, "I hope he retains his modesty."

"Excellency, frankly I worry he is trying to appear humble when he suggests that he has a superior. He makes military decisions contrary to the urgings of his greatest strategists, simply on the grounds of his baseless instinct. Confronted with a realistic argument he has answers like 'My genius and my willpower will conquer any enemy.' He says, 'I must name my own person in all modesty: irreplaceable. Neither a military man nor a civilian could replace me.' Little by little he has made puppets of his best advisors because they are afraid to disagree with him. If one does, either he shows mad fury or he feigns a heart attack.

"We are long past any defensible *lebensraum*, yet on the basis of intelligence that he requests from me I know that he wants all of Africa, Russia . . . he wants the world. He'll tell Jodl and Rader, 'We will take the Suez Canal and Gibraltar and seal the Mediterranean and cut Britain off from India. India will be useful to us.'

"He looks upon the whole world as his private real-estate development and he doesn't want any partners or shareholders. He had a disastrous meeting with Molotov on November 12th. When he heard Molotov's demands he twice walked out on him, saying, 'I have to leave now, there is going to be an air raid.' And that night he refused to attend the banquet at the Russian Embassy."

General Vigón asked, "What are the chances of his trying to invade us?"

"He knows that it would be difficult and costly and it might not even succeed. But! Provoked, he is capable of maniacal actions. And the more things go badly for him the crazier he becomes. He questions Spain's friendship. But he does not want to learn for certain that she is not his friend. Therefore he remains susceptible to the treatment you have been giving him . . . I hope. I can read his mail, listen to his telephone, but I cannot read his mind—worse, neither can he.

"Time is your best friend. The longer your Excellency can resist his pressures the less they will become. Roosevelt is eager to get into the war. With the election behind him it is simply a matter of time. He has already begun with supplies to England. Under the guise of a 'Defense effort' America is preparing for war. Their army of only a hundred and fifty thousand soldiers a few months ago, armed with useless rifles from the first World War, will soon number millions. American industry has converted to an all-out effort toward building arms and in another year she will have the men and the machines to fight. But, he is still confined to the Democratic Party's platform of not sending troops to fight on foreign shores unless America is attacked, so he will have to provoke that attack. Hitler is making every effort to avoid any provocation with America. He's given orders to the U-boats to avoid involvement with American shipping, virtually to the extent of even-if-fired-upon." Canaris shrugged, "In this instance he's rational, prudent, aware of another power.

"But my guess is that somehow Roosevelt will encounter a provocation to declare war on the Axis, and that will be the end of my country. The Axis simply cannot survive against the American economy and production, together with the British and their incredible resolve. We bomb England to splinters but she does not bend.

"Hopefully, Hitler will suddenly die. I am trying to arrange it. So are a number of the highest ranking military who, like myself, pray that without Hitler we could negotiate a peace that would not again leave Germany decimated. Many people he trusts are trying to finish him. There have been several well-planned attempts on his life, but he's been incredibly lucky, each time leaving a given place earlier than scheduled and missing the bomb explosion that would have destroyed him. He now enjoys these escapes. They contribute to his belief that he is more God-like than human.

"But his luck could change. There is also a very high level group with a plan to kidnap him and turn him over to the Allies."

When it was time to leave, Admiral Canaris said, "I will report to *Herr* Hitler that Spain's very real necessities make it impossible for your Excellency to name the date, and I could not 'pin you down.' And I will convey your Excellency's most cordial greetings."

That evening after dinner, his hands clasped behind his head on the pillow, staring at the ceiling, Franco said, "Carmelita . . . the *Führer* has decided that he is superior to any other human, that he is the first and only mortal who has emerged into a superhuman state . . . he is the first of a new generation of supermen, bound by none of the conventions of human morality . . ."

She began laughing.

Franco had known that his wife's devout Catholic mind would find Hitler's statements so ludicrous as to be funny. Hitler was, indeed, funny. Except that after the first smile he was not the least bit funny.

Remembering something that he knew would interest her, he said, "Regarding the Jewish refugees we've been admitting, there's a rather touching situation: of those who really are Sephardim many, despite living in France, Poland, Rumania, Greece . . . for sixteen generations, many of them speak Spanish; not our modern Castilian but the ancient Spanish of the 1400's. And one of them arrived here carrying the key to his ancestors' home in Toledo. The family had been passing it down from generation to generation for over four hundred years."

Taking a stack of papers from his night table he began reading.

"Paco? Is it true that Ramón wants to be the Chief of State?"

He looked up. "Why would you ask that? Have I retired?"

"I know that he's been asking you to appoint his friends as Ministers, so that in effect he would be running the Government, and that Berlin supports the idea."

"I have not followed his suggestions. Nor Berlin's."

"Then it's true?"

"I am certain that tears would not appear in the eyes of the *Führer* if I should fall from power, and it is also true that Ramón is ambitious. I have no doubt that in his opinion he could lead Spain more effectively than I. His problem is that I do not agree. If he were to replace me, the Falange would be running Spain and that would be intolerable to the Army, intolerable to the Church, intolerable to Traditionalists, and the Carlists . . . to all factions. We would have another civil war within months.

"Our traditional problem with government is, as the saying goes, 'In Spain every man is a political party unto himself,' and Ramón personifies that. Look, Carmelita, I melded all of the factions under one roof, The National movement. And this 'one-party system' is devoted to reverte-brating the country, of pulling together, and most distinctly not to lose time or momentum because of individuals' desires for power, or the espousal of political philosophy. Our one philosophy is: 'Everything for Spain.' And Ramón knows this. He understands that in this land of heroes and martyrs, what we need today is producers. But, when in order to end friction between the Requetes and the Falangists, as a symbol of unity I took the red beret of the one and put it with the blue shirt of the other, making it a new uniform for both, and I personally wore that uni-form when I addressed the National Council of the Falange and called for unity . . . who is it who continues bickering with the Requetes and refuses to wear their red beret? Ramón! A member of the government. Apart from the fact that he should set an example, he is defying me. I told him, 'Ramón, we will never accomplish our recovery if we remain splintered. You are too political. Do as I do, stay out of politics. This is not the moment in time for ideologies. The country is in need of gov-erning, not politicking. We had that in '36 and the results indicated an imperative need to try another road.' "

"Do you think he has enough followers?"

"To force me out? On the contrary. The Army alone would put him down immediately. He has few supporters, only the old-line Falangists. But it would never come to that. Whatever else he is, he is a patriot; he would not deliberately cause another conflict here."

Franco's eyes became merry. "What Ramón would like is for me to appoint him President of the Government and to stand in the back-ground commanding the armed forces in his support. But have no fears for Spain on that score, Carmelita, I have no intention of becoming the Queen Mother."[7]

174

BERLIN   MADRID, DECEMBER 8, 1940
DO NOT DECIPHER.
FOR THE FUHRER ONLY.
REPEAT. DO NOT DECIPHER.

ON THE EVENING OF DECEMBER 7TH I MOST FORCE-
FULLY SET FORTH TO GENERAL FRANCO THE NECESSITY
OF SPAIN'S PROMPT ENTRY INTO THE WAR. FRANCO
REPLIED THAT SPAIN COULD NOT ENTER THE WAR ON
THE DEADLINE DEMANDED BECAUSE SHE IS NOT PRE-
PARED. THE DIFFICULTIES ARE NOT SO MUCH MILITARY
AS ECONOMIC. FOOD AND ALL OTHER NECESSITIES OF
LIFE ARE LACKING. THE DELIVERIES OF FOODSTUFFS BY
GERMANY DID NOT AID VERY MUCH BECAUSE THE
LACK OF PETROLEUM CAUSES TRANSPORT CONDITIONS
WHICH MADE DISTRIBUTION IMPOSSIBLE.

I REPEATEDLY AND URGENTLY ASKED GENERAL
FRANCO IF HE WAS PREPARED TO ACCEPT A NEW
DEADLINE OR COULD SUGGEST AN EXACT TIME LIMIT
FOR LATER. GENERAL FRANCO REPLIED THAT HE
COULD NOT FIX SUCH A DEADLINE SINCE IT DEPENDED
UPON THE FURTHER ECONOMIC DEVELOPMENT OF
SPAIN, WHICH COULD NOT BE PERCEIVED TODAY, AS
WELL AS ON THE FUTURE DEVELOPMENT OF THE WAR
AGAINST ENGLAND. GENERAL FRANCO MADE IT
CLEAR THAT SPAIN COULD ENTER THE WAR ONLY
WHEN ENGLAND WAS ABOUT READY TO COLLAPSE.

IN CONCLUSION, GENERAL FRANCO EMPHASIZED
THAT HIS REFUSAL TOOK THE INTERESTS OF BOTH
SIDES INTO ACCOUNT. IT IS TO BE FEARED THAT,
AFTER THE CONQUEST OF GIBRALTAR, SPAIN WOULD
PROVE A HEAVY BURDEN FOR THE AXIS POWERS.

HE ASKED THAT THE PREPARATIONS BE CONTINUED
AS BEFORE WITH THE NECESSARY CAMOUFLAGE.

HEIL HITLER.

CANARIS[8]

Hitler clutched the cable. "I can't believe it. He got away. He got off the hook. I can't believe it!" Hitler handed the cable back to von Ribbentrop. "So, now that I have earmarked coastal batteries for the defense of the Canaries and the Peninsula, now his problem is not military. Now the problem is economic. And now that we have sent him wheat, the wheat is useless because he has no gasoline to make home deliveries to each and every Spaniard." He glared at von Ribbentrop. "But you are happy about this."

"Happy? *Führer*? Why should I possibly be happy?"

"Yes, yes, yes. Very happy. Because Canaris did not succeed where you and von Stohrer have failed. In your heart you are leaping with joy. Only I . . . only I care first and foremost for the success of the Third Reich."

Dismissing him, Hitler sent for Keitel. "Stop delivery of the coastal defense batteries for the Canaries and the Iberian Peninsula . . . those Spaniards . . . those Spaniards . . . that Spaniard is hopeless . . ."

MADRID,   BERLIN, DECEMBER 8, 1940
MOST URGENT
TOP SECRET
FOR THE AMBASSADOR PERSONALLY

THE RESULTS OF ADMIRAL CANARIS' DISCUSSIONS
WITH GENERAL FRANCO ARE IN FLAGRANT CONTRA-
DICTION TO THE HENDAYE DISCUSSIONS AND ALSO
IN CONTRADICTION TO GENERAL FRANCO'S POSITION
REPORTED BY YOU RECENTLY REGARDING THE RESULTS
OF THE DISCUSSIONS WHICH WE HAD HERE WITH SER-
RANO SUNER DURING HIS LAST VISIT IN GERMANY.
    THE FOREIGN MINISTER REQUESTS YOU TO
EXPLAIN IN DETAIL BY TELEGRAM HOW YOU ACCOUNT
FOR THIS SITUATION AND WHAT, ACCORDING TO
YOUR OBSERVATIONS, LIES AT THE BOTTOM OF IT.
    THE FOREIGN MINISTER REQUESTS YOU TO
REFRAIN FOR THE TIME BEING FROM AGAIN
APPROACHING SPANISH STATESMEN.

GAUS[9]

PART TWO

CHAPTER FOURTEEN

W INSTON CHURCHILL REQUESTED A MEETING WITH SPAIN'S AMBASSADOR TO LONDON, THE DUKE OF ALBA. THEY WERE COUSINS. THE PRIME MINISTER WAS INVITED TO LUNCH AT THE SPANISH Embassy on December 9, 1940.

The Duke of Alba, Jacobo Stuart Fitz James y Falco, Europe's most titled man, nineteen times a Grandee of Spain and also a Scottish nobleman, was a student of politics and diplomacy, immensely wealthy, a sportsman, and had been President of El Prado Museum in Madrid at the age of twenty-two. His taste in clothes was classic, but with a touch of adventure, being the first man to wear a burgundy velvet dinner jacket. He always dressed for dinner even when dining alone, and in Madrid, where no one but the servants dined before ten-thirty, he sat down at the dinner table at nine-thirty whether the guests had arrived or not, no matter who they were, and he was in bed every night at eleven-thirty.

An extraordinarily able Ambassador, he was also "very Spanish." During the Civil War, upon hearing Spain attacked in the House of Commons, he had protested by leaving the chamber, whereupon Winston Churchill had stood up and said, "I must apologize for my cousin," a statement that Alba neither liked nor forgot.

At one o'clock sharp the Prime Minister was at the entrance to the Spanish Ministry. He was accompanied by Lord Lloyd, Britain's Colonial Secretary; Lord Crof, Parliamentary Undersecretary for Foreign Affairs; Col. Moore-Brabizon, Transportation Minister, and Mr. R. A. Butler, Undersecretary for Foreign Affairs. Present with the Duke of Alba was the Embassy's Counselor, the Marqués de Santa Cruz.

Since the Civil War the Prime Minister and the Ambassador had not seen each other socially until this luncheon, and now Churchill made a distinct effort to smooth over any ill feelings that might remain. "You know, Jimmy, at the beginning of the Spanish Civil War I was a supporter of yours, for had I been a Spaniard either the reds would have killed me or without hesitation I would have served on Franco's side. I detest Communism as much as you do. Later, seeing the intervention of Germany and Italy, as a good English patriot I thought that a Franco victory would not be in my country's interests, and for that reason I even started writing against you. Later still, I became convinced that I had been mistaken and tried to show it in my speeches in the House. I have been pained, to be sure, that my words were not published in the Spanish press."

"Winston, I too am pained by that," Alba replied, "but there is so little in the British press that is favorable toward Spain that no doubt our journalists have fallen out of the habit of looking for it."

"So much for the past, Jimmy. As far as we are concerned, we wish to have the best and most friendly relations with you, and if these change you may be sure that it will not be our fault."

When Churchill felt the moment was right, he leaned toward his cousin, "What do you think, Jimmy? Will Franco be able to resist German pressures?" [1]

"He's trying. But you know the very real problems we have."

"To be sure. And I am ready to help keep Spain supplied. There will be no repetition of the blunder of cutting her off. I will personally intervene wherever necessary to see that she is kept supplied, with the only condition being that you promise not to re-export foodstuffs and materials to the Axis powers."

"Re-export!" Frustrated, Alba explained, "Spain is dying of starvation. Despite the British Embassy in Madrid and the many British Intelligence agents throughout Spain, you here in London truly do not grasp the difference between wartime England's austerity, which means standing in ration lines to receive little food, and present-day Spain, where there are no ration lines because there is no food at all."

The meal was being served by Alba's butler Williams, who was known as *El Largo* because of his height, assisted by a waiter whom Alba addressed as "Adolfo."

Churchill reacted elaborately, "Adolfo? Adolfo? You will have to change your name."[2]

It caused the desired and needed laugh.

With his business completed, the Prime Minister addressed his attentions to the splendid lunch. "This chef of yours is everything I've heard he is."

"He is my great luxury. He is so talented and imaginative that he makes wartime austerity hardly noticeable."

The Duke of Alba employed a Frenchman, Alfonse Diot, who was said to be among the best in the world. Alba provided the French cuisine as a tool of his ambassadorial work. As a Spanish patriot he might have wished to serve Spanish foods and certain Spanish wines that he knew to be excellent, but he was not there on a mission to promote Spanish trade; the Embassy was intended to make friends and to influence them politically, so when luncheon was finished and he offered Churchill a cigar and cognac they would have labels the Prime Minister would recognize and enjoy before he had even tasted them.[4]

Savoring the last morsel of dessert, Churchill joked, "We must see much more of each other, my dear cousin, to make up for lost lunches, as it were . . ."[5]

Churchill wrote to Roosevelt:

> *The situation in Spain is worsening and the people are not far from starvation. Suggest that you offer food, but on a month by month basis, which manner should help cause them to keep out of the war . . .*

"My *Führer*," Admiral Raeder warned, "in forty-eight hours it will be too late to mobilize 'Operation Felix' for January 10th."

"I know, I know, oh how I know. There is just one little problem . . . a stubborn little man in Madrid who is stopping the progress of the most powerful war machine in the world." He paced the room, his agitation increasing. "What I really should do is let him try to stop us . . . let him try. I should let the *Wehrmacht* continue its march . . ."

Admiral Raeder cleared his throat.

"I know," Hitler chided, "Jodl and Keitel say it can't be done. 'Too risky. Too expensive.'" He demanded, "Are they soldiers or bookkeepers? Are we conquerors or salesmen trying to outbid the English? Did we get where we are by such caution? If the Spanish are so weak from hunger how can they be effective fighters?" He brightened, "Perhaps there is an alternative. Perhaps we don't need the *Caudillo* at all with his precious passageway . . ."

The Commander in Chief of Germany's airborne forces, General Kurt Student, arrived within minutes of being summoned urgently.

Hitler said, "Fact: Germany wants Gibraltar. Problem: Spain is unwilling to name a date for entry into the war. Assignment: Give me a plan for taking Gibraltar with a massive invasion by parachute and gliders. Warning: Do not remind me that you have already studied it and told me that it cannot be done. I have an excellent memory. Study it again and find a solution."

The Chancellery
Berlin   *December 31, 1940*

My dear Duce,

    When I consider the general situation, I come to the following conclusions:

    The war in the west has actually been decided. The overwhelming of England requires a powerful, final thrust.

    Spain . . . has for the time being refused to cooperate with the Axis Powers.

    I fear that Franco is committing here the greatest mistake of his life. His idea that he can obtain grain and other raw materials from the democracies, in thanks for his aloofness, is in my opinion unrealistic naiveté.

I regret this, for we had made all the preparations for crossing the Spanish border on January 10th and attacking Gibraltar at the beginning of February. In my opinion the attack would have led to success in relatively short time. From the moment in which the Strait of Gibraltar was in our hands the danger of any kind of untoward behavior on the part of French North and West Africa would have been eliminated.

For this reason I am very sad about this decision of Franco's which does not take account of the help which we—you, Duce, and I—once gave him in his hour of need.

I have only a faint hope left that possibly at the last minute he will become aware of the catastrophic nature of his own actions and he will after all—even though late—find his way to the camp of the front whose victory will also decide his own fate.

Now, please accept my most cordial wishes for success in the coming year—the year of final victory. That is the best wish that I myself can express at the turning point of this historical time.

In loyal comradeship, yours,

Adolf Hitler [6]

Benito Mussolini, accompanied by Count Ciano, sat in the main salon of the Berghof. Hitler picked up a pillow from a couch and pressed it against his stomach, which was aching him terribly because of an advanced condition of meteorism, which caused him to be taking from one hundred and twenty to one hundred and fifty anti-gas pills a week, and which was aggravated by his vegetarianism and by disagreeable subject matter, as at the moment.[7]

"*Duce*, do you realize that today, January 19th, we would have crossed into Spain, be headed toward Gibraltar, then we could have had twenty divisions penetrating Africa thereby sending the British and the French fleeing, like another Dunkirk. And we would have had all that if not for that miserable ingrate and his miserable nation of starving people." Hitler lowered himself onto a couch and stared up at Mussolini. "*Duce*," his voice had dropped to a whimper, "*Duce*, he has sold out to the enemy for some loaves of bread. Can you believe that the history of the world is being changed because of that . . . that baker!"

He stood up and began walking again. "Franco has no integrity. Not a shred. And he is a complete slave to the Catholic Church.[8] How did he ever come to be a leader? He's not even smart enough to be a follower." He stopped walking. "We are asking him to take part in history and he is counting up how many loaves of bread he wants." Hitler groaned. "And adding plenty of yeast, you can be sure. The amount rises every week despite the fact that the Allies are pouring food all over Spain. Soon the Spaniards will be so fat that they won't be able to fight."

Count Ciano, who as Italy's Foreign Minister had endured many a disagreeable session with the Germans, was thinking, *If Spain falls away from us I would imagine that the fault rests in great part with the Germans and their uncouth manners in dealing with Latins, including the Spanish, who, probably because of their very qualities, are the most difficult to deal with.*[9]

Not seeing the reaction he wanted on Ciano's face, Hitler recounted, "He asked for transport planes in '36 so I sent him transport planes in '36. The Russians went into Spain and he started losing, so I went into Spain and he started winning. Isn't that true? I'm not a dumbhead with an ossified brain hallucinating that I sent the Condor Legion to Spain with bombs and bombs and more bombs? Am I? Now the Third Reich would like a favor in return and after interminable negotiations I am finally informed that Spain is willing to play her historic role in this war under the following conditions. Listen clearly." He read aloud from a report: "One: 'Germany is to deliver for the coming year 400,000 to 700,000 tons of grain.' Two: 'Germany is to deliver fuel.' Three: 'Germany is to deliver the equipment the Army lacks.' Four: Germany is to supply artillery, airplanes, as well as special weapons and special troops for the conquest of Gibraltar.' Five: 'Germany is to turn over to Spain all of Morocco and, besides that, Oran, and is to help her get a border revision west of Rio de Oro.'"

Hitler paused for theatrical effect. "I will now read to you what Franco offers for all of this. Quote: 'Spain is to promise to Germany, in return, her friendship.' End quote."

He stared from Mussolini to Ciano. "What manner of man is this?"

Mussolini consoled, "*Führer*, in '36 Franco asked us for 'twelve planes to win the war in a matter of days'. Those twelve planes became more than a thousand planes, six thousand dead Italian soldiers and fourteen billion lira, which we have never heard him say he would like to repay."

Hitler flung open the fingers of both hands. "Be careful, be careful, be very, very careful. I warn you, do not raise the subject of repayment of debts; he will make you feel like Shylock." Hitler put a finger to his lips, indicating silence. "Shhhhh. A word to the wise. Don't ask him."

Mussolini said, "*Führer*, your prestige seems to be the best hope we have. Why don't you meet with him again and try?"

"Negative! Flatly, simply, categorically, no! No, no, no, no. I would sooner have four teeth removed one by one and slowly. Without gas." He shuddered. "I have taken on the British Empire. But negotiate with Franco once more? Never."

Bombastically Mussolini pronounced, "Then it's up to me." He told Ciano, "Write to Serrano Suñer suggesting a meeting between the *Caudillo* and the *Duce* next month." Speaking again to Hitler, he continued, "I will talk to him. Franco's Spain will be unable to stand away from the great fight. He'll listen to me. He respects me. We're both Latins; I know how to speak to him."

Ciano observed, "To us has fallen the lot of causing the return of the Spanish prodigal child." [10]

Reanimated, Hitler ordered von Ribbentrop, "Get started on a campaign of ultimatums and threats to wear him down so that by the time the *Duce* meets with him he'll be grateful to follow the advice of a powerful friend."

MADRID   BERLIN, JANUARY 19, 1941
MOST URGENT

THE FUHRER SENDS PRE-EMPTORY INSTRUCTIONS
THAT YOU NAIL DOWN THE CAUDILLO TO A STRICT
PROMISE OF A DEFINITE DATE OF ENTRY IN THE VERY
NEAR FUTURE.

                                          RIBBENTROP

BERLIN   MADRID, JANUARY 20, 1941
FOR THE FOREIGN MINISTER

HAD IMMEDIATE AND LENGTHY INTERVIEW WITH THE
CAUDILLO THIS AFTERNOON, STATING THAT THIS IS
THE TIME FOR SPAIN TO SOUND THE HISTORICAL
HOUR, AND THAT SPAIN MUST MAKE A DECISION
IMMEDIATELY. MEETING LASTED ONE HOUR AND
THIRTY MINUTES. THE CAUDILLO ASKED FOR TIME
TO CONSULT WITH HIS CABINET. HE SAYS THAT FEB-
RUARY IS NO TIME TO START A CAMPAIGN IN SPAIN.

STOHRER

MADRID   BERLIN, JANUARY 21, 1941
MOST URGENT

YOU ARE FORBIDDEN TO TAKE NO FOR AN ANSWER.
GO BACK TO FRANCO AND READ WORD FOR WORD
A STRONGLY DRAFTED MESSAGE WHICH I WILL SEND
YOU IMMEDIATELY. REPEAT! YOU ARE FORBIDDEN TO
TAKE NO FOR AN ANSWER.

RIBBENTROP

BERLIN   MADRID, JANUARY 22, 1941
MOST URGENT
FOR THE FOREIGN MINISTER

HAVE RECEIVED YOUR EXCELLENCY'S STRONGLY
WORDED MESSAGE FOR GENERAL FRANCO. AFTER
MUCH DELIBERATION I FEEL IMPELLED TO ASK YOUR
EXCELLENCY TO ALLOW ME TO SOFTEN CERTAIN
STATEMENTS, MOST ESPECIALLY THE THREAT AT THE

END. MY LONG EXPERIENCE IN SPAIN HAS PROVEN
THAT SPANISH DIGNITY WILL REACT ADVERSELY TO
STATEMENTS THAT COULD BE MADE TO CONVEY THE
SAME MEANING BUT IN A MANNER THAT THE SPANISH
PRIDE CAN ACCEPT. HEIL HITLER.

STOHRER

MADRID   BERLIN, JANUARY 22, 1941
MOST URGENT

THE FUHRER AND I ARE SICK TO DEATH OF THE
SPANISH PRIDE. YOU ARE ORDERED TO FOLLOW
INSTRUCTIONS. SEE FRANCO IN PERSON AND READ
THE MESSAGE EXACTLY AS IT WAS SENT TO YOU
AND IN FULL.

RIBBENTROP

On January 23rd, the German Ambassador's car passed through the gates of the Palace of El Pardo and von Stohrer raised himself heavily from his cushions. As a career diplomat he was angered to be put in this situation that was cavalier and would only result in damaging the good relations that he and his wife had developed with the Francos. One doesn't make friends with Spaniards overnight. The trouble with von Ribbentrop was he had experience only with the Italians, who have their arms around your shoulders in eternal friendship within minutes of meeting them. The Spaniards are slow, cautious. But, when a friendship is formed it has foundation and it lasts. And a diplomat having a friend-ship with a Chief of State is invaluable. True, he had not been able to persuade the *Caudillo* to enter the war, but at least he had been able to gain an audience whenever necessary, even on short notice. Samuel Hoare had been in Madrid for a year and a half and had succeeded in obtaining only two private meetings with the *Caudillo*.

Franco was standing in the center of his office, awaiting the German Ambassador. Ramón Serrano Suñer was also present.

Von Stohrer stalled by reading the letterhead and the date, January 21, 1941, then:

1. *Without the help of the Führer and the Duce there would not today be any Nationalist Spain or any Caudillo.*

2. *The English, French and Americans have one aim: the destruction of Franco and Nationalist Spain. The democracies will couple every aid with political extortion weakening Franco's regime. It is our conviction that for technical reasons alone (lack of tonnage, etc.) the shipment of significant quantities of grain across the ocean is out of the question. England herself is already unable to provide for her own needs and is on the road to hunger.*

3. *The existence of Nationalist Spain and Franco and the great future of Spain are therefore indissolubly bound up with the fate of the Axis and the Powers allied in the Tripartite Pact. Only Germany is in a position to give Spain any real effective aid in her food situation.*

4. *The war for the Axis is today already won. The closing of the Mediterranean by the capture of Gibraltar would contribute toward an early end of the war and also open up for Spain the road to Africa with its possibilities. For the Axis, however, this action would be of strategic value only if it can be carried out in the next few weeks. Otherwise it will be too late for it because of our other military operations.*

5. *The Führer and the Reich Government are deeply disturbed by the equivocal and vacillating attitude of Spain. This attitude is completely incomprehensible to them both in view of the help that they gave Franco in the Spanish Civil War and in view of the crystal clear political interest of Spain in an alignment with Germany and her allies.*

6. *The Reich Government is taking this step in order to prevent Spain at the last minute from taking a road that, it is firmly convinced, can end only in a catastrophe for Spain.*

   Unless the Caudillo decides immediately to join the war of the Axis Powers, the Reich Government cannot but foresee the end of Nationalist Spain.

Ribbentrop[11]

As a soldier Franco would hardly have reacted with anger to an enemy attack; so he was not angered by this offensive letter, understanding what it was calculated to accomplish. However, he decided that in the case of these Germans, who did anger easily, or conveniently, anger would be the appropriate response.

BERLIN   JANUARY 23, 1941

MOST URGENT—TOP SECRET—

FOR THE FOREIGN MINISTER

IN ACCORDANCE WITH INSTRUCTIONS I HAVE JUST DELIVERED TO FRANCO IN THE PRESENCE OF THE FOREIGN MINISTER THE MESSAGE OF THE REICH GOVERNMENT. A DETAILED REPORT FOLLOWS BY SPECIAL AIR COURIER.

STOHRER[12]

Deutsche Botschaft In Spanien   *January 23, 1941*
His Excellency Herr Reich Minister von Ribbentrop
Ministry of Foreign Affairs
Berlin
Secret for Officer in Charge.
For the Foreign Minister Personally

After I had read aloud the message from the Reich Government, Franco declared that these communications were of extreme gravity and contained untruths. When I immediately protested against this Franco very heatedly asserted that he had never taken a vacillating position and that his policy was unswervingly on the Axis side, from gratitude and as a man of honor. He had never lost sight of entry into the war. This entry would come; his feeling of responsibility for his country because of the catastrophic economic condition had hitherto not made possible an actual entry into the war.

When I replied that from a military standpoint the war would be virtually waged by us alone and that we were willing additionally to give Spain economic aid, Franco stated that it wasn't the military aspect of

the question that caused him any concern; Spain would bear the necessary
hardships of war, without faltering. In an economic sense, however, we
still failed to realize the true situation of Spain. In a lengthy discourse the
Generalissimo then listed all of the long-familiar aspects characterizing his
country's economic weakness and distress; in so doing he went into special
details about the transport problem; he also stated that on the basis of
information he had gathered he doubted whether the French rail and road
network would permit the delivery of sufficient economic aid over and
above the necessary war material for the campaign against Gibraltar.

I disputed this, stating that the Führer had promised to give Spain
economic support and also to see to it that this aid could be furnished.
What better employment, I said, was there for the huge vehicle park of
our armies, at present not engaged in operations, plus the enormous
booty of motor trucks captured in occupied regions, etc.

Franco seemed chiefly to be stung by the reproach of a vacillating policy, because he reverted to this again and again as being an unwarranted
accusation. From the beginning of the war, he said, he had pursued a policy friendly to Germany. Even today he personally took care of all sorts of
details—mentioning a few—in order to promote our interests, despite
occasional heavy pressure from our adversaries, and right now, in the face
of the current food shortage, he had yet to deviate one millimeter from his
Germanophile course; nor had he made any political concessions.

Again and again I tried to steer the discussion back to the essential
points. I emphasized especially how important for Spain was the time
element, the need to make a prompt decision, and the importance of our
promises of military and economic support.

In particular I impressed upon the Caudillo that we wished only the
best for him; that we did not propose to lead the country down the road
to disaster; that it was to our own interest to see Spain emerge strengthened from this conflict, etc.

I also stated repeatedly that, subject to the familiar requirements,
we were ready to alleviate the country's most acute distress by advance
deliveries of supplies.

To this point Franco replied that he had immediately asked the
Council of Defense to study this question, with instructions to make an
immediate survey of the fundamentals that Spain needed urgently.

At this point the Foreign Minister spoke for the first time, saying that during his conferences in Germany he had from the beginning insisted that Spain would need economic assistance even before entering the war, a fact which had become still more clear lately with the rapid deterioration of the situation. We too, therefore, by declining this request so far, were co-responsible for the fact that Spain was so little ready for war.

When the conference, because of Franco's many digressions into details and non-essentials, threatened to drift off more and more from the point of the matter, I repeatedly reverted to the core of the question and called for a prompt decision and resolve, again emphasizing that Spain would have to act in the immediate future, otherwise her action would have no value.

On my taking leave Franco promised to give me an answer as soon as possible, with the renewed assurance that he would continue as in the past to work toward making Spain quickly ready for war.

These exchanges, lasting an hour and a quarter, revealed even more clearly Franco's irresolution, and disclosed the difference—which Franco on one occasion had himself mentioned—between him and the Foreign Minister, who seems more willing to take the decisive step, once we have delivered the most urgent advance supplies.

Most obediently,
Stohrer [13]

MADRID
MOST URGENT
SPECIAL TRAIN, JANUARY 24, 1941 11:05 PM
FROM THE SPECIAL TRAIN RECEIVED BERLIN
JANUARY 24-11:40PM
FROM THE FOREIGN MINISTRY SENT JANUARY 24-12:00
MIDNIGHT
FOR THE AMBASSADOR PERSONALLY

HAVE READ YOUR REPORT. IMMEDIATELY ON RECEIPT
OF THIS PLEASE ARRANGE A NEW APPOINTMENT
WITH FRANCO AND DECLARE TO HIM IN THE NAME OF
THE REICH GOVERNMENT (PREAMBLE AND VERBATIM)
THE FOLLOWING:

(1) ONLY SPAIN'S IMMEDIATE ENTRY INTO THE
WAR IS OF STRATEGIC VALUE TO THE AXIS AND ONLY
BY SUCH A PROMPT ENTRY INTO THE WAR CAN
GENERAL FRANCO STILL RENDER THE AXIS A USEFUL
SERVICE IN RETURN. A LATER ENTRY INTO THE WAR
WOULD BE OF ONLY MINOR SIGNIFICANCE IN VIEW OF
THE POWERFUL MILITARY OPERATIONS CARRIED OUT
BY THE AXIS IN THE COURSE OF THIS YEAR, AND
WOULD SCARCELY CONTRIBUTE ANYTHING TO THE
ULTIMATE VICTORY OF THE AXIS.

(2) SPAIN'S BAD ECONOMIC SITUATION, IN THE
OPINION OF THE REICH GOVERNMENT, SHOULD NOT
ONLY BE NO OBSTACLE TO SPAIN'S IMMEDIATE ENTRY
INTO THE WAR BUT SHOULD BE THE MOTIVE FOR IT.
BECAUSE: ENGLAND WILL NOT AND CANNOT HELP
SPAIN ECONOMICALLY IN ANY CASE. ONLY GERMANY
CAN DO THIS.

(3) IF SPAIN ENTRUSTS TO THE AXIS THE DETERM-
INATION OF THE DATE FOR SPAIN'S ENTRY INTO THE
WAR, GERMANY, AS A PRELIMINARY SERVICE, IS
READY TO MAKE AVAILABLE TO SPAIN BEFORE ENTRY
INTO THE WAR THE ONE HUNDRED THOUSAND TONS
OF GRAIN STORED IN PORTUGAL AND TO SUPPLY
FURTHER AID SHIPMENTS OUT OF GERMAN RESERVE
STOCKS AFTER ENTRY INTO THE WAR. TRANSPORTA-
TION DOES NOT PRESENT ANY INSURMOUNTABLE
PROBLEMS.

(4) IF GENERAL FRANCO NEVERTHELESS DOES NOT
ENTER THE WAR AT THIS TIME, THIS CAN ONLY BE
ASCRIBED TO THE FACT THAT HE HAS DOUBTS ABOUT
THE ULTIMATE AXIS VICTORY, AS REVEALED ALSO IN
HIS REMARKS TO ADMIRAL CANARIS. SERRANO SUNER
IS WRONG IN SAYING THAT BECAUSE GERMANY HAD
FURNISHED NO ECONOMIC ASSISTANCE SHE WAS

CO-RESPONSIBLE FOR THE FACT THAT SPAIN STILL
WAS NOT IN THE WAR. GERMANY HAS DECLARED
HERSELF READY TO SUPPLY ECONOMIC AID IN
ADVANCE IF SPAIN WOULD FIX A DEFINITE DATE FOR
ENTERING THE WAR. THIS, HOWEVER, WAS DECLINED
BY SPAIN. GERMANY MUST THEREFORE REJECT THIS
ACCUSATION.

(5) GERMANY ASKS GENERAL FRANCO ONCE MORE
FOR A FINAL, CLEAR ANSWER.

RIBBENTROP[14]

BERLIN   MADRID, JANUARY 27, 1941
MOST URGENT

GENERAL FRANCO SAYS THAT HE IS SYMPATHETIC
TO OUR PROBLEM OF NEEDING GIBRALTAR.

HE ASSURES ME THAT HIS DESIRE TO ENTER THE
WAR IS GREAT AND URGENT, BUT HIS ABILITY TO DO
SO IS NON-EXISTENT.

HE SAYS THAT HE CAN ONLY REPLY THAT HIS FINAL
AND CLEAR ANSWER IS "AS SOON AS POSSIBLE." HE
SAYS THAT HE SUSPECTS THAT THE GRAVITY OF
SPAIN'S PLIGHT IS IN QUESTION AND THUS SUGGESTS
THAT GERMANY SEND A TEAM OF ECONOMIC EXPERTS
TO SPAIN TO SEE FOR THEMSELVES, AS HE HAS LONG
BEEN URGING.

GENERAL FRANCO SUGGESTS THAT FIELD MAR-
SHAL KEITEL BE SENT AS PERSON HIGH IN MILITARY
WHO ENJOYS THE FUHRER'S CONFIDANCE.

STOHRER

MADRID   BERLIN, JANUARY 28, 1941
MOST URGENT
TOP SECRET

I REQUEST AN ENTIRELY PRECISE STATEMENT
WHETHER YOU HAVE READ WORD FOR WORD TO GEN-
ERAL FRANCO THE TWO MESSAGES OF THE REICH
GOVERNMENT.

I REGRET THAT IN THE CONVERSATION YOU HAVE
GIVEN GENERAL FRANCO THE OPPORTUNITY TO
DIVERT YOUR DEMARCHE FROM ITS PURPOSE AND TO
SHOVE OFF ON GERMANY, SO TO SPEAK, A FURTHER
INITIATIVE. BOTH MESSAGES WERE INTENDED BY US
TO MAKE UNMISTAKABLY CLEAR TO FRANCO THAT
ONLY AN IMMEDIATE ENTRY IN THE WAR BY SPAIN
HAD ANY STRATEGIC VALUE FOR US AND TO GET
FROM HIM A CLEAR YES OR NO WHETHER HE WAS
PREPARED TO ENTER THE WAR IMMEDIATELY.

INSTEAD OF THIS YOUR CONVERSATION WITH HIM
HAS HAD THE EFFECT THAT HE HAS COME TO US
WITH THE REQUEST TO SEND TO SPAIN ECONOMIC
EXPERTS AND IN ADDITION A MILITARY FIGURE LIKE
FIELD MARSHAL KEITEL.

IN THAT WAY FRANCO AND SERRANO SUÑER HAVE
ATTEMPTED TO GAIN THE POSITION THAT OBVIOUSLY
THEY WANT—NAMELY, TO BE ABLE TO SAY, IN REPLY
TO A STATEMENT OF THE REICH GOVERNMENT, THAT
SPAIN HAS NOT KEPT THE SPIRIT OF HER AGREEMENTS
WITH US, THAT GERMANY HERSELF HAD FAILED TO
FULFILL THE NECESSARY CONDITIONS FOR ENTRY IN
THE WAR.

I REQUEST YOU THEREFORE TO STATE PRECISELY
WHETHER GENERAL FRANCO UNDERSTOOD UNMIS-
TAKABLY FROM WHAT YOU SAID THAT WE EXPECTED
AN IMMEDIATE ENTRY BY SPAIN INTO THE WAR, AND

THAT ONLY SUCH ENTRY INTO THE WAR HAD STRATE-
GIC VALUE FOR US, AND THAT HE NEVERTHELESS HAD
REJECTED PLAINLY AND DEFINITELY IMMEDIATE ENTRY
INTO THE WAR.

RIBBENTROP [15]

BERLIN   MADRID, JANUARY 29, 1941
URGENT
TOP SECRET

AS INSTRUCTED I HAVE READ BOTH MESSAGES
EXACTLY WORD FOR WORD TO FRANCO.

FROM THE MESSAGES WHICH I DELIVERED MOST
EXACTLY, AND FROM MY STRESSING THIS POINT
REPEATEDLY, FRANCO MUST HAVE RECOGNIZED
UNMISTAKABLY THAT WE EXPECTED AN IMMEDIATE
ENTRY INTO THE WAR BY SPAIN, AND THAT ONLY
SUCH AN ENTRY HAD STRATEGIC VALUE FOR US.

IN REPLY TO THE QUESTION WHETHER HE WAS
READY FOR IMMEDIATE ENTRY INTO THE WAR,
FRANCO HAS BROUGHT FORWARD SO MANY REASONS
AND OBJECTIONS AGAINST HIS IMMEDIATE ENTRY
INTO THE WAR, THAT ONE CAN REGARD THIS AS A
REJECTION OF IMMEDIATE ENTRY INTO THE WAR.

HOWEVER, WHETHER THE REPLY GIVEN BY FRANCO
MEANS A CLEAR AND FINAL REJECTION MAY DEPEND
PRIMARILY ON THE QUESTION OF WHAT IS UNDER-
STOOD BY IMMEDIATE ENTRY INTO THE WAR—THAT
IS, WHAT IS THE LATEST DATE ENVISAGED BY US FOR
SPAIN'S ENTRY INTO THE WAR?

STOHRER [16]

MADRID   BERLIN, JANUARY 30, 1941

HOW COULD YOU LET HIM WRIGGLE OUT OF GIVING A
STRAIGHT ANSWER TO A STRAIGHT QUESTION?

RIBBENTROP[16]

BERLIN   MADRID, JANUARY 31, 1941
URGENT

IN DEFENSE OF MY CONDUCT OF THIS MATTER I HAVE
FOLLOWED INSTRUCTIONS FAITHFULLY AND UTILIZED
A LIFETIME OF TACT AND PERSUASIVE EFFORT AND
ABILITY. BUT I SIMPLY CANNOT OFFER YOUR EXCEL-
LENCY A DECISION THAT ONLY FRANCO CAN MAKE
AND THAT OBVIOUSLY HE WILL NOT MAKE UNTIL HE
IS READY. HEIL HITLER.

STOHRER[17]

"Forget it," Hitler said to von Ribbentrop, handing back the cables.
"Leave it to the *Duce*. And put those in your pocket. I can't stand the
sight of them."

Serrano Suñer showed *El Caudillo* the letter from Count Ciano suggesting a Mussolini-Franco meeting at Bordighera, a town on the Italian
coast near Genoa.

"To reach Bordighera we must pass through occupied France. A danger we'd like to avoid. Also, a visit to Italy would anger the Allies. Invite
the *Duce* on a State visit to Spain."

The following afternoon on entering Franco's office Serrano Suñer
saw his brother-in-law seated at his desk, visible only through the space

separating two large piles of papers. Franco looked up from sketches of a "gasogeno," a device that when attached to the rear of an automobile, injected air into the carburetor causing a substantial saving of gasoline, though also causing the car to travel more slowly.

Sitting down beside his brother-in-law's desk, he said, "Regarding the *Duce* and a State visit to Spain," he shook his head negatively.

Franco took off his reading glasses.

"After much probing by me as to why, and after much hemming and hawing by the Italian Ambassador, I finally got the fact: the *Duce* is jealous of the *Führer*. You went to see the *Führer* and so the *Duce* strongly urges that you go to see him. I explained the substantial difference between meeting just outside our own border and traversing occupied France to arrive in Italy. The Italian Ambassador explained that because of Italy's military reverses things have not been going too well politically for the *Duce*, and that when you went to visit Hitler, recently the more glamorous member of the Axis Powers, it created an uproar among the people around the *Duce*."

"These passionate Latins."

"Therefore, in order to be effective with his people the meeting must occur on Italian soil, making it clear that you are going to him, as you went to Hitler."

Franco designated the same triumvirate to succeed him, with the same instructions in the event that he could not return.

Hitler could not accept the idea of himself, Ribbentrop and finally Canaris failing to sway Franco, and he could not stand the concept that it was now necessary for Mussolini to try to accomplish what the Third Reich had failed. He could not resist one final, ten-page letter of appeal. [See Appendix 8 for complete text.]

The letter contained nothing that had not been said or written to Franco a dozen times before except the forecast:

"If you, *Caudillo*, were successful in your struggle against the elements of destruction in Spain, then it was only for the reason that
the attitude of Germany and Italy forced your Democratic opponents to move with caution. But never, *Caudillo*, will you be forgiven for that victory."

After the Barón de las Torres had read it to him Franco summoned
von Stohrer. "I agree with much of what the *Führer* says, Eberhardt, but
I have my questions about some. Perhaps it is the fault of the translation.
In any event, when I get back from Italy I will reply."

Hans Lazar sat at his table at the Ritz Bar, his expression smugger
than usual. Stirring his gin fizz, he merchandised the day's news item. "*El
Caudillo* is going to meet with the *Duce* next week. In Italy."

"Franco leaving the country? How do you interpret that?"

Lazar shrugged. "Franco has the power to close the Mediterranean at
its mouth; Mussolini, at the Suez Canal."

"That means Spain is joining the Axis."

"But keep it quiet," Lazar ordered.

"Hans, I would never repeat a word . . ."

Within twelve hours the unannounced meeting between the two
leaders was common knowledge in Madrid and making its way to the rest
of Spain, to Gibraltar, Lisbon and ultimately London, Washington,
wherever newspapers were published.

Sir Samuel concluded that a meeting between Franco and Mussolini
was ominous. Franco had paid a heavy price in lost food as a result of his
meeting with Hitler. Would he risk that again unless he expected not to
be needing Allied supplies any longer?

Hoare was thinking of three shiploads of food scheduled to pass
through the British blockade the following day. What if that food is

allowed to reach a belligerent Spain? England would find herself feeding the Axis. He sent a message to delay the navicerts.

Leaving Spain at the frontier town of El Perthus, Franco's caravan of twelve automobiles was met by groups of *Wehrmacht* motorcyclists that would stay with them in relays throughout the trip across occupied France. Additionally, Marshal Pétain provided one infantry division, twelve thousand soldiers posted along the route.

Swastikas and German storm troopers were everywhere, and the timidity of the French people was clear even from the window of a moving car. In the towns, cities and even countryside Franco and Serrano Suñer could see all the signs of an occupied country, and even though the French had historically been little friend to Spain and her distinct enemy during the Civil War, still the sight of a once grand country now so humbled produced a feeling of compassion.

In Arles, when they stopped for lunch, they learned that Genoa had been bombed the night before.

They crossed into Italy at twilight and Mussolini was waiting for them at Bordighera. He had brought with him a company of the 2nd Regiment of Sardinia Grenadiers and a section of the 89th Artillery Regiment. Several thousand civilians cheered: "*Duce . . . Caudillo . . . Duce . . .*" and the two leaders reviewed the troops for the benefit of the press photographers and the cheering crowd.

Later, in private, at the magnificent villa Regina Margherita, which he placed at their disposal, Mussolini looked defeated. Even while he had been performing for the public the spirit had been missing from his strut. Now, inside the villa he seemed shriveled, his lantern-jaw slack. Wishing to cheer him up, Serrano Suñer said, "*Duce*, you should be proud of this display of warmth your people offer you even in these bad times."

Notoriously susceptible to flattery, Mussolini would accept praise even where it was not due, but now he shook his head, "Don't you believe it. They hate me." Then, with simplicity, he added, "Look, dear Serrano, in the end that's not important. These are bad hours for Italy. If tomorrow things go well my people will like me again. But these things don't count in politics. We're pros."

The following morning they met to talk near Ventimiglia, in a villa on the Ligurian Sea. Speaking at first in generalities about the war, eventually Mussolini asked, "And you, *Caudillo?* When can we expect Spain's entry into our glorious and historic effort?" His melancholy voice conveyed that he did not think it glorious at all.

"My people are tired and hungry, *Duce.* I shall do only what will serve them best."

"I understand . . ." Mussolini said, his voice slow and heavy. "I well know the responsibility in making the decision to enter an entire country into war."

"*Duce,*" Franco asked, "if you could get out of the war, would you do it?"

"You bet your life I would." From his throat there emitted a sound that was not a laugh, not a sob—a sound of futility. "But I can't. You cannot get out of a war, you know. After you enter there is only winning or losing. And you must be prepared to go the distance . . . the unknown distance . . ."

"That's what I have been telling the *Führer.*"

"The *Führer* is a fanatic."

During lunch Mussolini continued, "He's a fanatic. At the moment of waging war on Norway he wrote to me saying that the dice were tossed, that his soldiers were going to initiate the occupation of that country contrary to the advice of his strategists, that above the cold, solid reasons they gave he put his infallible instinct." Mussolini exclaimed, with his broad smile, "He is an audacious man." He was silent for a moment, his face somber. "On the other hand, I find Stalin very astute. He, far above the Allies, is the enemy to be feared . . ."

CHAPTER FIFTEEN

Rome, February 22, 1941

Führer,

I have transmitted to you the text of the Bordighera conversation. I shall give you my personal impressions, Führer, when I shall once again have the pleasure of welcoming you to Italy.

I reiterate to you my opinion that Spain today is in no position to embark on any sort of belligerent action. She is starved, has no arms and strong factions in the country (a pro-English bourgeoisie and nobility) are hostile to us; and in addition she is now being subjected to natural disasters. I believe we shall be able to draw her over to our side, but not just now.

Yours,

Mussolini[1]

Von Ribbentrop cabled Stohrer to drop the issue of Spain's entry, to be reserved, and to continue propaganda to counteract British propaganda.[2]

On March 6th, having been informed that the Spanish Ambassador in Berlin, General Espinosa de los Monteros, had arrived at Berchtesgaden and was on his way to the Berghof to deliver a letter from the *Caudillo*, Hitler prepared for the experience by fortifying himself with a heavy dosage of anti-gas pills.

The interpreter, Gross, was there to read Franco's letter in German. It was almost as long as Hitler's, and equally detailed and repetitive. [See Appendix 9.]

This time he arrived outside the gates of the Palace of El Pardo, riding an admirable black horse and wearing the stiff-brimmed, black, flat-crowned hat that originated in Córdoba and was worn traditionally by Spanish horsemen. His black mustache contrasted sharply with his pale skin. He wore a black cape furled tightly around his slender body; his boots were well polished. With the air of the Spanish nobleman he bid the guards good evening and said, "My name is Juan Guillermo . . ."

In *El Caudillo*'s office Admiral Canaris was grave. "Excellency, Hitler has decided to go to war against Russia. He has kept this top, top secret under the code-name Barbarosa."

Franco was pensive. "I receive this news with pleasure. German might will finally be directed toward what will serve Europe best, the defeat of Communism." Then he asked, "How do you think the United States will react?"

"Roosevelt will support Russia. He and Churchill apparently see a difference between German totalitarianism and Russian totalitarianism. In their telephone conversations their affectionate code-name for Stalin is 'Uncle Joe.'"

Franco was disheartened. "If only America would stay out of it and let the Communists and the Nazis exhaust each other. In my judgment Germany cannot beat Russia, even with the most powerful armed force; she has no valid ally: Italy is now a liability, Vichy France is an uncertainty and Japan is on the other side of the world. On the other hand, Russia, unaided, could not beat Germany. They would simply wear each other down. Such a war would make Hitler unpopular in his country and he could be removed, leaving Germany to stand as a natural bulwark against Communism in Europe."

"I also have very bad news, Excellency, for Spain. Hitler has given up all hope of your cooperation and now is thinking in terms of invading Spain."

Franco did not visibly react.

"You are not surprised?"

"According to my religious faith, miracles do occur, but infrequently. I am amazed we have been able to stall for these ten months."

The spy nodded and continued, "At first Hitler explored taking Gibraltar without passing through Spain, by a landing of gliders and parachute troops, but General Student has convinced him it would fail disastrously, that the only access to Gibraltar is from Spain's coast. Thus, the new plan is Operation Isabella, a still highly secret contingency plan for the invasion of Spain over the Pyrenees in the event that the British take advantage of Germany's forthcoming involvement in Russia and try to seize Tangier, Portugal, or herself land in Spain."

"Do you know the date for Barbarosa?"

"No. But it will have to be launched soon, no later than next month because of the Russian weather."

On April 7th Hitler attacked Yugoslavia, Belgrade was bombed virtually out of existence and in just ten days the remnants of her Army surrendered.

Lazar didn't need to invent rumors. The facts were more terrifying than his best fiction. "The *Führer* called it Operation Punishment because the Yugoslavs angered him." Lazar filled in the details. "He invited them to join the Axis. He did not want war with Yugoslavia, he just wanted to pass through her territory to Greece to help Mussolini. But the Yugoslavs played games with him."

Taking no chance that anyone would miss the threat he pointed out, "Spain is in exactly the same position. The *Führer* merely wants to pass through to attack Gibraltar. I hope Franco doesn't anger him. I shudder to think of an Operation Punishment against Spain . . . razing Madrid . . ."

On April 28th 1941, Ambassador Espinosa de Los Monteros arrived at the Chancellery, summoned by Hitler, who told him, "I am concerned about the present English propaganda that speaks of the transit of German troops across Spanish territory: the construction of airfields for the *Luftwaffe*, and other false reports. I hope the *Caudillo* is on his guard.

This propaganda can only be for the purpose of building a pretext for some operation against Spain or Spanish Morocco.

"I cannot escape the impression that the English intend to establish themselves on Spanish territory. I am also convinced that the British will do everything possible to replace the *Caudillo* with a leftist government that would be more amenable to their wishes.

"Warn the *Caudillo*. You may also convey my deep regret, my very deep regret, that the operation against Gibraltar could not have been launched as planned in January or February. Point out that if it had, Gibraltar would be taken today; German troops would be in Morocco and the situation of the English in the Mediterranean would be impossible, whereas today it is no longer such an easy matter to take Gibraltar as it would have been in February because the English have been working feverishly, fortifying the Rock, which is evident from the countless shiploads of cement which have arrived at Gibraltar.

"Warn the *Caudillo* to take great care with the English or he will find himself looking for political asylum in Germany."[4]

Franco continued painting as Serrano Suñer read him Los Monteros' report on his interview with Hitler, ending, "'And with that the *Führer* quite coldly bid me 'Good day.' Signed, Espinosa de Los Monteros." He looked at his brother-in-law for a reaction.

Franco stopped painting, stepped back a bit and, still looking at his self-portrait, asked, "What do you think of the mouth?"

By the beginning of May those few Neutrals remaining in Europe began to make their peace with Germany: Turkey accepted a nonaggression treaty; Sweden allowed the transit of German troops across her territory; on May 14 Marshal Pétain broadcast to France calling for full collaboration with Germany.

That same day Hitler announced that the war would be over in 1941.[3]

Carmen Polo was distressed, "Paco, is it a fact that the American Embassy is closing and returning its people to the United States?"

"No. Ambassador Weddell has simply ordered the return to the States of Embassy personnel who have children."

"That's almost as bad, no?"

"It does not demonstrate American optimism."

Three million German soldiers waited, positioned across the 930-mile Russian front extending from the Baltic to the Black Sea. It was June 22, 1941. The signal for Barbarosa came at 3:15 A.M. Flame and smoke raged from German tanks and artillery and from the *Luftwaffe* in such volume as to brighten the sky so greatly that no one noticed when the sun rose.

Franco addressed his High Command. "I feel moved to go to Germany's aid in this single aspect of war only, and send a division to the Russian front. In order to clearly separate Spain from 'belligerency' we will call these men volunteers and they will wear clothing that is distinctly not the uniform of the Spanish army."

"Excellency," said General Vigón, "our involvement against Russia could cause us to be considered an enemy of the Allies."

"It is my position," Franco said, "that we take that risk in order to fight Communism."

BERLIN   MADRID JUNE 22, 1941
FOR THE MINISTER OF FOREIGN AFFAIRS

EL CAUDILLO SENDS HIS COMPLIMENTS TO THE
FUHRER, HIS DELIGHT THAT THE FUHRER HAS
TURNED HIS ATTENTION TO THE FUNDAMENTAL
FIGHT AGAINST COMMUNISM AND HE OFFERS A DIVI-
SION OF SPANISH SOLDIERS TO FIGHT ON THE RUSS-
IAN FRONT "IN MEMORY OF GERMANY'S FRATERNAL

ASSISTANCE DURING THE CIVIL WAR AGAINST THE
SAME ENEMY." THEY WILL BE CALLED THE BLUE DIVI-
SION, DUE TO A UNIFORM OF A BLUE SHIRT, UNDER
COMMAND OF GENERAL MUÑOZ GRANDES. THEY
WILL NUMBER 18,000 MEN.

STOHRER

Adolf Hitler sighed, "That *Caudillo!* Even when he sends help he
sends it in disguise."

Fifty thousand young Falangists standing in the Plaza del Oriente
looked up to the balcony from where Serrano Suñer's emotionally
charged voice called out, "Russia is to blame for our Civil War . . .

"Russia is to blame for the deaths of one million Spaniards who died
in that war by the aggression of Communist Soviet Russia . . .

"Russia is to blame for the burning of our churches, the slaughter
without reason or mercy of thirteen bishops, of 5,225 priests, of 2,669
monks of 112 nuns . . ."[5]

"Russia is to blame for the death of our beloved founder José
Antonio . . .

"At last a powerful force has turned on hated Communism to put a
stop to it. This is not the hour for speeches but for action . . . on to
Moscow . . . on to Moscow . . . ON TO MOSCOW!!!"

In Rome the Pope supported the German fight against Bolshevism as
". . . high-minded gallantry in defense of Christian culture . . ."

In London, Winston Churchill, who had previously stated, "If Hitler
invaded Hell I would make at least a favorable mention of the Devil in
the House of Commons," now made a stirring radio broadcast:

"We are resolved to destroy Hitler and every vestige of the Nazi
regime. From this nothing will turn us—nothing. We will never parlay,
we will never negotiate with Hitler or any of his gang. I pledge that
Great Britain will give the utmost help to the Russians. We shall also
appeal to all of our friends and allies in every part of the world to take

the same course and pursue it, as we shall, faithfully and steadfastly to the end."

And President Roosevelt stated: "Giving assistance to Communism will benefit American security. Hitler must be stopped even if it means giving aid to another totalitarian country."

At lunch Carmencita asked, "*Papá*, if the democracies are people who want freedom, then how is it possible for them to make friends with the Communists?"

Always slow and careful about answering questions, *El Caudillo* did not answer this question at all.

Later, alone with his wife, he pursued it coldly. "Stalin, the arch-criminal, the arch-totalitarian is now the ally of democracy. Stalin recently murdered twelve thousand Polish officers. The Allies know that. They also know that since 1922 he has murdered some thirty million of his own people. That is the entire population of Spain plus seven million more. If England and America would only stay out of it entirely. Let the two fight it out. I agree: hate the madman. But don't support the Devil against him."

Searching for justification of what he and his wife considered incredible, he said, "Roosevelt is far away, America is in her own world and though he should know better I can understand if he doesn't. But Churchill . . . impossible! One of the best descriptions I have ever read about Communism since I began studying it in 1920 was made by Winston Churchill. I know it by memory:

" '*It is not only a creed, it is a plan of campaign. A Communist is not only the holder of certain opinions, he is the pledged adept of a well-thought-out means of enforcing them. The anatomy of discontent and revolution has been studied in every phase and aspect, and a veritable drill book prepared in a scientific spirit of sabotaging all existing institutions. No faith need be kept with non-Communists. Every act of good will, or tolerance or consolation or mercy or magnanimity on the part of governments or statesmen is to be utilized for their own ruin. Then, when the time is ripe, and the moment opportune, every form of lethal*

violence, from revolt to private assassination, must be used without stint
or compunction. The citadel will be stormed under the banners of liberty
and democracy, and once the apparatus of power is in the hands of the
Brotherhood, all opposition, all contrary opinion must be extinguished
by death. Democracy is but a tool to be used and afterwards broken.'"[10]

Pained by what he had just recited, Franco asked his wife, "How can
the man who understands that support Soviet Russia?"

President Roosevelt released forty million dollars in frozen Soviet
assets. And, on July 7, 1941, American forces arrived in Iceland to replace
British troops then occupying the island, releasing them for service where
the fighting was.

On July 17, 1941, Franco made his annual address to the National
Council of the Falange, marking the fifth anniversary of the Spanish
Generals' uprising. With the entire Madrid Diplomatic Corps present he
made a tribute to the power and skill of the German armies:
  ". . . the soldiers of the New Order who are winning the victory over
Bolshevism, which Europe and Christianity had been so long awaiting.
  "And if the tides of battle should change, if the barbarous Russian
Communists should succeed in invading Germany, then not just one division but one million Spanish soldiers would rush to the defense of Berlin."
  Franco referred for the first time in public to the British policy of
delaying the navicerts and consequently killing Spaniards by slow starvation, denouncing it as ". . . Great Britain's inhuman blockade which
overrides international law, makes a farce of the freedom of the seas and
inflicts intolerable suffering on its victims. Relations with England
become more difficult every day and it is conceivable that this could easily bring about a situation no longer compatible with Spain's honor and
her instinct to defend herself."
  He spoke of democracy in general as being "outmoded, decadent,"
concluding: "For the United States to enter the war would serve only to
prolong it, and in the process the noncombatant nations would be put to
great hardships . . ."

The Allied press ran the speech boldly and overnight American business concerns in Spain began withdrawing. Physicians sent to Spain by the Rockefeller Foundation to introduce a new typhus vaccine were recalled. The United States announced that no more Red Cross ships bearing flour, milk and drugs would be sent to Spain.

Anthony Eden denounced Franco in the House of Commons:

"His Majesty's Government have now noted that General Franco has displayed complete misunderstanding not only of the general war situation, but also of British economic policy toward Spain.

"If economic arrangements are to succeed, there must be good will on both sides and General Franco's speech showed little evidence of such good will. His statements make it appear that he does not desire further economic assistance from this country. If that is so, His Majesty's Government will be unable to proceed with their plans and their further policy will depend on the acts and attitude of the Spanish Government."[6]

The Duke of Alba met with Eden and rebutted coldly, "I cannot imagine any Spaniard reacting with anything short of anger toward anyone who would support Russia. I must stress the fearsome dangers for Europe of a Russian victory . . ."[7]

Eden replied, "My dear Jimmy, first of all the Soviets are now Nationalists, not Internationalists. Besides, after the war they will be so broken financially and materially that they'll be incapable of exerting pressure beyond their own borders. But even if they should you can rest assured that if necessary Great Britain will fight the Russians with American aid."[8]

Alba had listened to the British Secretary for Foreign Affairs call Russia "Nationalist" despite the fact that the Comintern derived its name from Communist International and was operating in every country of the world. Such naiveté, or ignorance, or will-to-disbelieve, was simply amazing, unanswerable and painfully frustrating.

Serrano Suñer was alarmed by a letter from the German Ambassador, dated July 30, 1941.

Deutsche Botschaft in Spanien

My distinguished Señor Minister and dear friend,

Permit me to transmit to your Excellency the following information which I have just received from Berlin.

"From a source worthy of credibility has arrived the news that there recently took place in the Embassy of the United States of America in Mexico, a meeting of high-ranking Spanish reds under the command of Miaja. The theme was the intervention of Spanish reds in the projected occupation of the Canary Islands by the United States. The United States has declared themselves disposed to recognize the red Spanish troops' right of belligerency and to transport them in American ships for the expedition planned against the Canary Islands."

I believe that Berlin has marked interest that this attitude of the United States be publicized most amply.

If your Excellency does not see this negatively, I would be truly grateful to you for the diffusion of the same to the press.

Accept once again, my distinguished Señor Minister and dear friend, the expression of my highest regard and personal esteem.

Eberhardt von Stohrer[9]

Carmen Polo saw that her husband was preoccupied with some problem. It was just after lunch and they were having coffee in the Yellow Room. Carmencita was with them so Doña Carmen did not ask her husband what was wrong, yet sensing her unease he said, "It's just a small matter with the Government in Exile."

Carmencita asked, "What is a 'Government in Exile?'"

"It is a contradiction in terms," her father said. "In 1939, when the leaders of the Republican Government, Juan Negrín, Largo Caballero and the others, saw that they were going to lose the war, they began to prepare to leave Spain to go into exile in Moscow, London, Paris, New York and Mexico City.

"When the war had begun they shipped all of Spain's gold reserves to Russia, and a bit to France, to buy arms. Later, seeing the end near they stripped the Treasury of everything valuable that remained, largely silver and ancient treasures of the Crown—its value has been estimated at three thousand million pesetas. They also used the Assault Guards to drill open privately held safe-deposit boxes in Madrid's banks and took jewels, money, everything of value they encountered. This was accomplished by a decree stating that in order to finance the war the Government of the Second Republic could legally confiscate personal property of all 'Fascists,' as enemies of the Government. Presumably they judged that anyone having money or jewels was automatically a Fascist.

"Then they put all the money, jewels and treasure on a ship, the Vita, and sent it to Veracruz, in Mexico. The exiles in Mexico City had a meeting that they called a session of the Parliament, and following Parliamentary procedure they voted themselves to be officially known as 'The Spanish Government in Exile.' Then they voted themselves into various offices of the Spanish Government, allotted themselves salaries and made various laws required as a result of the inconvenience of the sudden change of locale: among those being that the temporary capital of Spain and its seat of government would be Mexico City."

Carmencita was laughing.

Her father nodded. "It is ridiculous seeming, but it is nevertheless true. Then, after voting themselves to be the Spanish government they presented this matter to the Mexican government which officially recognized the Spanish Government in Exile as the official government of Spain, and extended full diplomatic courtesies and help."

Though she was staring at him, disbelieving, Carmencita knew that her father was serious.

"It is a fact," he assured her. "Today I am not recognized by the Mexican government as the Chief of State of Spain. All of the Great Powers recognize us as the official Spanish Government. Only Russia and her satellites, of which Mexico is one, *do* not recognize us.

"Since then, having a substantial treasury, as well as a 'Government' lacking only a people and a country to govern, they set about to re-acquire Spain, to get rid of me to clear the way for their return. Their method is to work toward influencing the governments of the United States and England and other powers against the existing government of Spain, to cause them to exert economic power and cause

211

us to step down. They do this with propaganda to turn public opinion against us.

"But have no fear. I do not intend for those particular exiles to return to Spain except under arrest." He gestured to indicate that he was finished.

"It sounds like a movie," she said, going to her own room.

Alone now with his wife and not wishing to alarm her with the details Franco changed the subject. "I'll paint my nose now," and went into their bathroom where the easel was standing, supporting his self-portrait.

As he worked he spoke over his shoulder. "Carmelita, do you think me egotistical because I'm painting my own picture?"

"No. I assumed you were doing it because your own face is the easiest thing for you to paint because you know it best."

"Precisely," he replied, and satisfied that she was not nervous he began closing in on this new problem.

Until then the Government in Exile had been a nuisance, an inconvenience at times, but now they had become a threat. The United States, still not in the war but openly preparing for "defense," was certainly looking at the Canary Islands, the Balaerics and the Azores as important Atlantic Ocean bases. What more convenient way for the United States to take the Canaries than to ". . . recognize the red Spanish troops' right to belligerency . . . ' to aid them with a few transport ships in a fight to recover their homeland, and to receive in return vital bases—without going to war?

There were some two hundred thousand Spaniards in exile: around two thousand in Russia, twenty or twenty-five thousand in South America, principally Argentina and Mexico, ten thousand in French Morocco, and around one hundred and fifty thousand in France, under German jurisdiction. Though this kept the majority of them away from Allied purposes, with Hitler now thinking of invading Spain, if it had not occurred to him to employ the exiles in France, also for the alleged "fight to recover their homeland," this memorandum of the meeting in Mexico City could well give him ideas.

The exiles would serve any master against Franco's Spain. The question was: which side would use the enemies of Franco's Spain's first? Or might they both?

CHAPTER SIXTEEN

ITLER GLOATED OVER A MAP. "IN SEVERAL WEEKS WE SHALL BE IN MOSCOW . . ." IT WAS SEPTEMBER 5, 1941; HE WAS AT HIS FIELD HEAD-QUARTERS WOLFSSCHANZE, WOLF'S LAIR, IN A FOREST SEVERAL miles from Rastenburg, East Prussia. Surrounded by his Generals he put his finger on Moscow. ". . . I will raze that damned city and construct in its place an artificial lake with indirect lighting. The name *Moscow* will disappear forever."

On the last day of September, Typhoon, the code-name for the attack on Moscow, was launched by sixty-nine German divisions. The Russians were caught completely off guard by the major offensive at that time of year.

By October 2nd Hitler was so certain of success that he left the front and went to Berlin to make a speech at the Sportpalast. "The enemy is beaten. They will never rise again . . ." And as his thousands of listeners screamed themselves hoarse, Hitler also screamed himself hoarse itemizing the statistics of victory:

"Two million, five-hundred thousand prisoners . . .

"Twenty-two thousand artillery pieces destroyed or captured . . .

"Eighteen thousand tanks destroyed or captured . . .

"Fourteen thousand, five-hundred planes destroyed . . .

"Our glorious armies have in only two days of attack already penetrated one thousand kilometers more toward the heart of the enemy . . ."

Winston Churchill telephoned to the Duke of Alba and asked that they meet privately, with only their top aides present, for a discussion that he wanted to keep off the record.

The Duke of Alba invited him to lunch in the Ambassador's private living quarters at the Spanish Embassy in order to eliminate protocol and with it the need for a stenographer to make notes.

Since the Prime Minister and the Ambassador had broken the ice the year before, the Prime Minister had made a point of lunching or dining with his cousin once every few weeks for both political and gastronomical advantage. But when the Spanish Ambassador received the list of who would be present at this particular luncheon he showed it to his friend and Counselor, the Marqués de Santa Cruz, who shared his surprise and curiosity that for an off-the-record chat the Prime Minister was bringing along Anthony Eden, R. A. Butler, the Undersecretary for Foreign Affairs, and Sir Samuel Hoare.

Promptly at one o'clock on October 2, 1941, the British group arrived and were escorted to the Ambassador's quarters. Having a before-luncheon glass of port, Churchill asked, "And how is Alfonse today?"

"He is always especially in form when he knows he'll be cooking for you. He admires you tremendously."

"Not as much as I admire him."[1]

When they were in the small dining room Churchill quickly got to his mission. "Jimmy, when England wins the war—and there is no doubt that she will—France will owe her everything and she will owe nothing to France. Thus, England will be in a position to exert strong and decisive pressure to satisfy Spain's just claims in North Africa. With England's help Spain could become the greatest power in the Mediterranean."[2]

Alba asked, "And Gibraltar?"

"Yes. We will seriously discuss returning Gibraltar."[3]

"What are you asking of us, Winston?"

"Only that Spain does not allow the Germans to pass through her territory. The Germans must not be allowed to attack Gibraltar from the Spanish coast."

Alba traveled to Madrid to personally convey the offer to *El Caudillo*.

Franco said, "It will amuse you to know that now both protagonists have offered us the Moroccan territories that neither possesses." Then, "As to the 'Gibraltar question' lamentably there is no question at all. It is completely clear: if Germany wins, England will not have Gibraltar to discuss. And if England wins the war she most surely will not return Gibraltar to our national territory.

"Spain cannot and will not make any formal agreements with either side. We are less interested in our claims in Africa, and Gibraltar, than we are in keeping this peninsula free of invasion by anyone.

"But assure Mr. Churchill that my principal work is keeping Germany out of Spain. For the moment the *Führer* is occupied in Russia, but he is still maintaining those twenty divisions at our frontier. Please mention this to Mr. Churchill and remind him of it at every opportunity. We know that our enemies make a point of keeping him informed on what we say, so let us make a point of keeping him in a position to judge us by what we *do*. Obviously Anthony Eden was so upset by my my recent words that he overlooked the more significant fact that Germany still has not been allowed to enter Spain and take Gibraltar."

Lazar had taken over a restaurant for the occasion, invited close to a hundred Spanish journalists and their wives, and with the help of his Embassy's food supply the meal was "a banquet," as one journalist shouted, leading the others in grateful applause.

Standing, Lazar said, "A banquet would be appropriate, for in a matter of weeks Spain's problems will be over. The limitless wheat of the Ukraine will be aboard German freight trains speeding to the aid of Spain!" Raising both hands for silence, he promised, "Our great armies are racing so quickly through Russia that in two, perhaps three weeks at most Spain will no longer be reliant upon the Allies' good will. Spain will be independent . . . needing nobody . . ."

"It feels good to be rich," Franco said.

"Are we?" Carmen Polo asked.

"Immensely," said the Chief of State. "As you know, we already have Gibraltar and North Africa as gifts from both the Allies and the Axis. Now, soon the *Führer* is going to give us all the wheat in the Ukraine and the petroleum of the Caucasus."

"But he could do it, no?"

"If he had it."

"The *Wehrmacht* is moving quickly through Russia."

"So, too, the Russian winter is moving quickly onto the *Wehrmacht*."

November 7, 1941: President Roosevelt instructs the new Office of Lend Lease to give immediate aid to Russia in the amount of one billion dollars.

December 7, 1941: Japanese planes attack Pearl Harbor, Hawaii, the International Settlement at Shanghai, Thailand and Hong Kong.

December 8, 1941: The United States of America declares war on Japan. Hitler is elated: "We cannot lose. Now we have a partner who has never been defeated in three thousand years."

December 11, 1941: The United States of America declares war on Germany and Italy.

Outside of Moscow the temperature stood at minus forty-two degrees Fahrenheit. One million, two hundred and fifty thousand German troops were fighting in waist-deep snow, icicles hanging from their eyelashes and nostrils. Water froze within the boilers of locomotives; machine guns would not fire; trenches and foxholes could not be dug in earth that was hard as stone; the German Mark IV tanks, slowed by mud from October rains, now in January were frozen into the solid ground as if they had been set in concrete. They fought also against one hundred divisions of Soviets hardened to their own weather. Hitler's massive blitzkrieg was stopped dead.

General Franco did not take the traditional Spanish siesta. Instead of snoozing after lunch he relaxed by painting. This was in "el monte del Pardo" the hills surrounding his Palace of El Pardo.(Courtesy of the Duchess of Franco)

While rising in rank, leading the Spanish troops in Morocco, Franco impressed his troops with his bravery by riding into battle at their lead on a white horse that would attract gunfire. This picture was taken in later years as Chief of the Spanish State. (Courtesy of the Duchess of Franco)

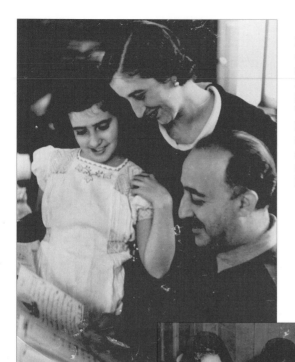

Left: General Franco, his wife Doña Carmen Polo and daughter Carmen (now the Duchess of Franco), after the Spanish Civil War, looking at "Carmencita's" homework. For security reasons she could not attend conventional school outside the grounds of El Pardo. Courtesy of the Duchess of Franco.

At top left, Doña Carmen Polo (wife), top center, Carmen Franco Polo (daughter) and General Franco at a baptism. The children: Carmen Martínez-Bordiú Franco (left) and her younger sister Mariola (right). Courtesy the Duchess of Franco.

Self-portrait of General Franco in his Admiral's uniform. The navy was his family tradition, but when it was time for him to attend the Naval Academy the Spanish-American War had destroyed the Spanish navy, thus not needing more officers the Academy was closed and young Francisco Franco became a soldier who went on to win the Spanish Civil War and govern Spain for thirty-nine years as El Generalísimo. But in his heart he was always a naval officer. Courtesy the Duchess of Franco.

Carmen Franco with her father. Walking to his horse, son José Cristóbal Martínez-Bordiú Franco. Courtesy the Duchess of Franco.

President Dwight Eisenhower, visiting Spain in 1952 exchanges *un abrazo* with General Franco. Ike was the first American President to visit Spain and did so because of first-hand knowledge that Spain had been a friend to the Allies during World War II. Photograph by Jaime Pato, used with authorization by Gráfica Agencia EFE.

One of three bullet-proof Mercedes-Benz made for Franco, Mussolini and Hitler. Gift of the latter.

Hitler greeting Franco at the French-Spanish border railroad station Hendaye-Irún as Franco arrived for their historic, and only, meeting. TimePix.

In Hitler's "work car" of his private railroad train during their meeting at Hendaye. The picture was posed, eliminating their respective Foreign Ministers and interpreters. Dever/Black Star/TimePix.

Above and below:
On the station platform
at Hendaye-Irún, posed for
the world press, orchestrated
by Hitler for propaganda
to demonstrate solidarity
between Germany and
Spain, a condition he was
soon to learn was only in
his mind and hopes.
(Both: Timepix)

Franco bidding farewell to Hitler. El Generalísimo nearly lost his life a moment later as the train began to move. TimePix.

More propaganda. Hitler and Franco in the traditional reviewing of Hitler's troops at Hendaye. PixInc./TimePix.

Franco was the subject of nine *Time* magazine covers. The one to the left demonstrates the precarious role he played during World War II, walking a tightrope between the two sharp swords of Nazi Germany and the Allies, both wanting him to enter the war on their side. © 1946 Time Inc.

The *Time* magazine cover at right shows Hitler in 1931 in the pose that struck terror in the hearts of all the Chiefs of State and Prime Ministers with whom he negotiated. When they hesitated to grant his wish Hitler showed threatening rage and all buckled. Only Franco did not. © 1931 Time Inc.

PART THREE

CHAPTER SEVENTEEN

PRESIDENT FRANKLIN DELANO ROOSEVELT SPOKE ACROSS HIS DESK IN THE OVAL OFFICE, TO CARLTON J. H. HAYES, PROFESSOR OF HISTORY AT COLUMBIA UNIVERSITY, WHOM HE HAD JUST APPOINTED AS HIS new Ambassador to Madrid. It was March 19, 1942. "Spain's neutrality is urgent to pending Allied plans. Perhaps we are too late diplomatically. Quite possibly, despite our best endeavors, General Franco will join Hitler. In that case the whole peninsula—Portugal as well as Spain—will be overrun by the Nazi armies; Gibraltar will be doomed . . ."

The President explained that if German troops were allowed to pass through Spain to Gibraltar they would swarm over North Africa with no real opposition. In fact, the Arab world with its vast oil resources would happily join the Third Reich, united by their hatred of the Jews. If Hitler were to gain control of two continents, the whole of Europe and Africa, the Allies could well despair for the war.

"It is our urgent business to prevent that," Roosevelt said. "Spain's neutrality is of such immense importance that if you see a crisis that you yourself cannot avert, I personally would be willing to meet with General Franco in the Canary Islands or elsewhere outside of Spain." [1]

Ambassador Hayes had planned to travel by ship in order to bring with him his red four-door Buick convertible as well as household effects for the Embassy such as linens, crystal and silver, which the government did not provide, but there was such a strong feeling in the State Department that Germany might invade Spain at any moment and his stay would be brief that he and his family took a minimum of luggage and left

New York's La Guardia Airport aboard a Pan American Clipper, beginning the thirty-six hour journey to Madrid.

Hayes was received promptly by *El Caudillo*, who, following the formal ceremony, invited him, with Serrano Suñer and the Barón de las Torres to an adjoining room for the traditional few minutes of conversation with the newly received Ambassador.

Observing Franco as he spoke, Hayes thought, *This is not the General Franco of the caricatures in our press. He was neither so short, nor so stout and he did not "strut."* As Franco laughed, easily, naturally, Hayes thought, *Hitler could not do that, and Mussolini wouldn't, except in private.*[2]

Franco listened to Hayes describe American resources of men and materials, the scale and speed of preparations under way to wage war in Europe as well as the Far East. But Hayes feared that Franco thought he was telling fairy tales.

"The Fortress of Europe," Franco said, "which German arms have built, is impregnable. All efforts of the British and the French proved vain. France is defeated and the British Empire is spent. Even if America could now train and equip large armies you could not repeat your feat of 1917 and 1918 and transport them across the Atlantic because of the increased effectiveness of German submarines. And even if you should get through the masses of submarines there would be no place for you to land as there was in France during the first World War. I believe America should concentrate its strength in the Pacific against Japan and accept the presence of the Axis in Europe."

"Excellency, can you contemplate with equanimity for Spain the lasting preponderance, all over the continent, of Nazi Germany with its fanatical radicalism and anti-Christian paganism?"

"It is not a pleasant prospect for me or for Spain, but I trust that it will not materialize. I believe that Germany would make concessions if America would, and a kind of 'balance of power' could be re-established in Europe. Be assured that Spain does not wish an Axis victory, but it most ardently wishes the defeat of Russia. Our nonbelligerency means that we are not neutral in the struggle against Communism in any way and specifically in the war between Russia and Germany. But we are neutral, we take no part in the conflict between the Axis and the western powers. Spain has no hostility toward the United States."

"I remind your Excellency of the tyranny and the vaulting ambition of Nazi Germany and of its steady succession of broken pledges and forceful aggressions. Excellency, it was not Russia that attacked Germany, but Germany that attacked Russia. I cannot accept the possibility of attempting to compromise with Germany or to aid it against one victim of its aggression while professing sympathy for the others."

Franco said, "The danger for Europe, and for Spain, is not so much in Nazi Germany but in Russian Communism."[3]

They spoke for an unprecedented fifty minutes. When Hayes left the meeting he hoped he had convinced Franco of the enormous and ever-growing war power of the United States, but he feared that Franco's respect for German military strength was not much diminished by the entry of the United States into the war. And while Franco had been courteous in attitude and speech, Serrano Suñer had remained mute and appeared dubious, even cynical. Hayes felt that at heart Serrano Suñer was distinctly pro Axis.[4]

Franco's approval of Hayes was immediately noticeable. Madrid's newspapers carried front-page photos of the new Ambassador and *El Caudillo*, along with detailed accounts of the ceremony and their speeches in full.

Adolf Hitler was disconcerted. Why suddenly a new American Ambassador to Madrid? And obviously chosen with care: a Catholic; a professor specializing in Spanish history. He studied the maps on his desk and concluded that the Allies planned a landing in French or Spanish Morocco . . . perhaps on the Iberian Peninsula as well. He ordered General von Runstedt to draw a new and highly detailed plan for the invasion of Spain, replacing Operation Isabella.

"It is called Operation Ilona, Excellency." Wearing the uniform of a Colonel in the Spanish army, even to the detail of the pencil-line mustache popular with the Spanish military, Admiral Canaris told Franco everything he knew about the new plan for invasion. "If the Allies make any effort to gain control of the peninsula, or if they even appear to be making such an effort, that will trigger the action, a German counter-offensive across the Pyrenees. Bilbao, Vitoria and Pamplona will be taken in the first wave. In the second phase the circle will widen from Santander to Saragossa . . ."

Franco told Serrano Suñer, "Take the von Stohrers to Jeréz. Ask the Domecqs to invite them to the wineries, organize a fiesta in their honor; a bullfight; anything that will keep them in the south for at least one week. And arrange 'problems of communication' in order to keep them as out of touch with their Embassy as possible."

In the north, on the only two roads over which it was possible to pass into Spain there suddenly appeared massive concrete fortifications and roadblocks. Spain did not lack sand and cement, and hundreds of tons of concrete were poured as if overnight. To the sides of the roads the engineers used dynamite to create vast craters as tank traps. Everywhere that vehicles and men on foot might pass, obstacles were placed to make passage impossible. Franco and his Ministers had mobilized the Army Engineers in an operation without name but in direct reply to Ilona.

They divided the Pyrenean area into five defensive regions. The key frontier bridge that spans the Bidesoa River that links Spanish Irún to French Hendaye, in bad condition, was weakened still further and mined with enough explosives to blow it out of existence in sixty seconds. Teams of men rotated duty twenty-four hours a day to protect the mines from being defused, or to detonate the charges when ordered.

Five dams were prepared to be opened wide enough so that within hours their waters could flood the region, making it as marshy and boggy as later in the year the winter weather would do naturally. Farmhouses became arsenals for the implements of guerrilla warfare: knives, guns, hatchets, gasoline, dynamite—anything that could kill a soldier and destroy his vehicles.

Finally, the Army's rosters were studied for men who came from the north and then one hundred and twenty thousand of them were transferred and stationed as close to their homes as possible: a fundamental of guerrilla warfare being the intimate knowledge of one's terrain.

BERLIN   MADRID, JULY 15, 1941
MOST URGENT

... THE MEN WERE ON GUARD, THE BRIDGES MINED AND
THE CEMENT DRYING WHEN I RETURNED TO MADRID.

STOHRER

"I knew it. No, I didn't know it. I should have known it. Yes, I should
have known it from the beginning. Lies, evasions . . ." Then Hitler's
anger faded into despondency. Operation Ilona had been conceived
requiring the cooperation of the Spaniards or at least their acquiescence
and the use of their airfields.

"Well, it's easier to wage war when you know who your enemy is."
Hitler's mind began turning over an idea. "Problem: Franco. Solution:
Franco must go. Another civil war in Spain. I will succeed where the
Comintern failed."

He knew there were forty thousand Spaniards working in German
factories, and one hundred and fifty thousand exiles in France. With
them as a nucleus . . .

Franco had said that being a dictator was unpopular, that none of the
factions liked him. Hitler sent for Walter Schellenberg, head of civilian
Foreign Intelligence, and instructed him to find out who of those high in
the military and of prominence in Spain might be well disposed to help
toward a change in government.

General Vigón reported to Franco that Germany had suddenly begun
reinforcing its Third Air Force around Bayonne right at Spain's doorstep.
And in addition to the twenty divisions still at Irún-Hendaye, more
Wehrmacht divisions were arriving in an area south of Bordeaux.

Excellency.

*Enclosed is the treaty which last July Eden assured me would never be
signed.*

Alba

Attached to the note was a copy of Great Britain's Treaty of Alliance with the Union of Soviet Socialist Republics.

Franco looked at the word "Republics." How chilling the way the Soviets knew how to use the right word in the wrong way. They had done it so effectively during the Spanish Civil War when the Comintern recruited, supplied and trained the International Brigades and named them after heroic figures in their countries of origin: the Abraham Lincoln and George Washington Battalions from the United States; the Garibaldi Battalion from Italy and similar symbols of patriotism from throughout the world. Public sympathy was immediately with them in the Comintern's theme to make Spain "the grave of European Fascism,"[4] In the minds of their countrymen how could such idealists as soldiers fighting under the names of Lincoln, Washington and Garibaldi be battling anything but evil?

In a separate note Alba reported:

> General Dwight Eisenhower, who arrived in London in June, is rumored to be the choice of Churchill and Roosevelt to be the Commander in Chief of the North African Theater of Operations.
>
> Recently, he and General Mark Clark, Commanding General of the U.S. Fifth Army, have been lunching with Churchill every Tuesday.

Sir Samuel took Hayes aside at a dinner early in July. "Look here, on the 17th Franco is going to make his annual speech to the National Council of the Falange—or as Americans would say, 'the big shots of the Falange.' Last year it was so obnoxious that I felt that Ambassador Weddell and the Allied diplomats who attended the meeting should have ostentatiously withdrawn during the speech in protest. I advise you to absent yourself from the whole affair to avoid any similar embarrassment."

Ambassador Hayes had taken a crash course in disliking Ambassador Hoare. "Thank you for your advice, but I have been accredited to General Franco, and if he chooses to say things I don't like at a ceremonial meeting to which the entire Diplomatic Corps is summoned then the mere gesture of absenting oneself would rejoice the Axis, and be for General Franco only the petty discharge of a pop gun."[8]

Hayes recognized the prime need for full and loyal Anglo-American cooperation for forwarding their joint war effort and the American staff invariably put their cards face up on the table for the British. But he felt that Sir Samuel was intent upon playing a lone hand and was seldom frank with the Americans about his dealings with London and with the Spanish Foreign Office. His usual practice was to obtain information that the Americans had, while withholding his from them, on the assumption, surmised Hayes, that it was more blessed to receive than to give.[5]

He felt that Hoare was not only a diplomatist in Spain, but a politician in England.[6]

The British Ambassador further irritated the American by seldom, if ever, speaking of "The United Nations", but habitually of "Great Britain and its Allies" and acting accordingly, bringing Hayes to conclude that as a kind of reconstructed Tory, Hoare still regarded Americans as rebellious subjects of George III.[7]

It was Hayes' first look at an assemblage of the entire Madrid Diplomatic Corps. On July 17, 1942, the Axis delegations were in a ground-floor box in a large chamber of the Palace of the Senate, and the Allies were in a box on the balcony, with neutrals scattered between them.

Hayes' Counselor, Willard Beaulac, pointed out von Stohrer and various other Axis diplomats. Then, gesturing toward the Japanese Minister, Suma, he whispered, "He affects being a connoisseur of Spanish art, which amuses the Spaniards no end because as soon as he opens his mouth it's clear that he knows nothing, and they have been selling him their worst pictures at fantastic prices."

A voice rang out, "His Excellency, the Chief of the Spanish State."

The American Ambassador could not understand much Spanish but reading von Stohrer's face was easy. When Franco had begun to speak von Stohrer's countenance had been pleasantly anticipatory, like a man preparing to see a play that he had heard and enjoyed before. But quickly the German's face began showing disappointment, then disbelief, and finally restrained anger.

"What is he saying?" Hayes asked Beaulac.

"He's distinctly less pro-Axis than last year . . ." Beaulac listened for a moment to catch a sentence, then translated, "'. . . and one million Spanish soldiers will stand ready to fight Communism at our borders in the Pyrenees . . .'" He explained, "Last year it was 'in defense of Berlin'" Again he listened, then, "'. . . the form of government suitable to one country is not necessarily the right form of government for another country . . .'"[9] Beaulac was exuberant. "Last year he denounced 'outworn democracy.'"

Carmen Polo had been reading until she sensed her husband taking his attention from the papers he was studying. He was looking ahead, his face expressionless. She said, "What El Caudillo is thinking even Francisco Franco doesn't know." As her words penetrated his thoughts he turned to his wife. "That's what people say about you," she explained.

"I was thinking that Ramón must leave the Government." She showed no reaction to the fate of her brother-in-law. "As is often the case with 'court favorites' he has developed too many enemies. The Army is against him because he is the leader of the Falange and the Falange is offensive to the Army; the Falange is against him because he has not used his influence with me to gain them the power they want. People are jealous and resentful of him."

Franco said, "In those circumstances, for him to be without enemies would be like trying to walk through a river without getting wet. However, it doesn't help that it is not his fault. During these years of unification and revertebration we cannot stand dissension.

"Also, with the Allies-Axis balance of power equalizing it will serve us to have a Foreign Minister less identified with the Axis. I'm sorry. He has been of great service to me and to Spain."

The war was going badly for the British at Singapore; in Africa; wherever they met the German troops they succumbed easily. It went as badly for the Americans in the southwest Pacific, where the Japanese overwhelmed them bloodily at Luzon, Guam, Wake, Bataan, and Corregidor.

In August a joint English and American attack was launched against Dieppe and was hurled back into the sea by the Germans.

Goebbels broadcast by shortwave radio, and in every European language, ". . . the English hoped the Americans could help them. Now we wonder who the Americans hope will help them. There have been nothing but Allied defeats . . . all Allied efforts have failed . . . the Fortress of Europe built by German arms is impregnable . . ."

There was little that Allied propagandists could suggest to the contrary.

CHAPTER EIGHTEEN

W INSTON CHURCHILL, WEARING A DARK BLUE ZIP-UP JUMPSUIT, MET WITH SIR SAMUEL HOARE IN HIS BASEMENT OFFICE AT NUMBER 10 DOWNING STREET. "PRESIDENT ROOSEVELT AND I, with our combined Chiefs of Staff, have decided that the first major Allied offensive will be the invasion of French North Africa. Code-named Operation Torch it will be military history's most spectacular and daring amphibious enterprise.

"A simultaneous landing at Casablanca is in consideration, but strong tides and autumn storms could make large-scale landings there precarious. Consequently, use of the Atlantic coast is not certain.

"Gibraltar is now the key. All naval, air and landing forces will assemble there before staging the assault.

"Some among us say that by using Gibraltar as our main air and naval base we are putting our heads in a guillotine: once in the strait, Franco's heavy guns in the hills of Tarifa could put the harbor out of action in a few hours and the airdrome in as many minutes." He picked up a memo from his desk. "General Marshall says, 'The combined air forces, other than carrier-borne and a few transports and heavy bombers, must be funneled through the single restricted field of Gibraltar, which could be put out of action in less than half an hour. There is no choice but to accept this hazard.'

"I feel that a note must be struck now of irrevocable decision and superhuman energy to execute it.[1] With the war going steadily in favor of the Axis both in Europe and the Pacific, and now after the failure at Dieppe, our war effort desperately requires resounding success from our first major offensive against the enemy. We dare not fail once more. How can you tell a soldier to get up and fight again if he really believes the enemy is invincible? It is no exaggeration to say that on the success of Torch rests the outcome of World War II, the survival of the Empire, and indeed Christian civilization. And the success of Torch is dependant upon General Franco remaining neutral.

"Torch will be a heavy operation, too large to be physically camouflaged. There will be a crisis period of days, perhaps a week, whilst the expedition is assembling, when 1,000 airplanes on the airfield at Gibraltar, 310 ships of the United States Navy, 240 British warships, plus more than 500,000 men will be in plain sight of the Spanish mainland.[2]

"Some of the accumulated ships will surely spill over into Spanish waters in the Bay of Algeciras, and we have to hope that General Franco will not exercise his legal right to fire upon them. If he should, he would destroy them. And we must pray that he will not mobilize his 150,000 man garrison in Tangier to aid the soldiers of Vichy France. If he should he would impede or even prevent the landing. We can assure him that neither the Spanish mainland nor Spanish Morocco will be touched. But why should he believe us? And we cannot tell him what we *do* plan.

"Our second problem is that with a tremendous concentration of spies in Tangier, Berlin will learn about it the moment the first machinery arrives."

Hoare ventured, "The strait is lined with a chain of radio and infrared stations reporting to Berlin the movement of every Allied ship and plane—everything. Whenever I go to Gibraltar the news of that minor event is broadcast in Germany within minutes of my crossing the Spanish frontier. But even if Torch were smaller and could be concealed within the Rock itself, secrecy would be impossible because of the six thousand Spaniards who work there and return every evening to Spain."

"Precisely. So, when the Germans learn of activity in the area they are going to wonder where it intends to strike. They must not learn of our target and have time to fortify its defenses.

"For this purpose we are establishing a special department of misinformation at Whitehall. Its sole work will be the diffusion of false information and misleading rumors. We will flood Europe, especially the peninsula, and Africa, with tendentious evidence directed to create the impression that the offensive is planned against Italy and the eastern Mediterranean. Distinctly not Africa.

"While you are here in London do not go near Eisenhower's headquarters; do not be seen with any American military personnel or it will be a clear indication that the offensive involves Spain. Everything you will need to know will be explained to you by our British liaison officer to General Eisenhower."

Churchill wrote to Roosevelt:

> *All depends on secrecy. Secrecy can only be maintained by deception. When your troops start for Torch everyone except the secret circles should believe they are going to Suez or Basra, thus explaining tropical kits. The Canadian Army here will be fitted for Arctic service. Thus, we shall be able to keep the enemy in doubt until the last minute.*[3]

A sign-painter was lettering "Department of Cultural Development" on a door to an office at Whitehall. Inside, three British espionage officers worked at psychologically camouflaging Operation Torch. Under their command was a team that would seem unlikely for a military operation, for it included make-up artists and scenic designers.

Deception has three elements. One: visual. This would include the hundreds of plywood dummy tanks now under construction, and dummy guns and artillery pieces that would be shipped where the Allies wanted the enemy to believe the true fighting force was going. Seen from above by German reconnaissance planes they would be convincing. Two: fake signals. Misleading documents and radio messages that are intended to be overheard and deciphered. Three: double agents: German Intelligence agents captured in England and "turned around" so that they would transmit reports prepared by British Intelligence.

The officers heading the deception team would devote themselves largely to the spreading of false information that an Allied invasion would be launched against Sardinia and Sicily and the eastern Mediterranean, and that Malta was receiving a major military build-up.

Before making their decisions on precisely what false information they would disseminate, they had made an "enemy appreciation" of the situation to learn how it would look through German eyes, because even the most plausible information would not be accepted as fact unless it fit with the enemy's previously held intelligence picture. German Intelligence could accept Sardinia, Sicily and Malta as Allied targets.

Supreme Allied Headquarters had produced maps and plans and schedules to serve as the "secret plans for Operation Figaro," the alleged Italian landings. They appeared authentic in every way. And, because the enemy would put the greatest stock in what they believed their agents had obtained illicitly, these documents would be planted where *Abwehr* agents could discover and transmit them to Berlin.

They also wished to "deliver" the documents into German hands. For this they needed a volunteer for a virtual suicide mission, a man with either such strong belief in the Allied cause or such hatred for the Nazis that he would accept a mission to be deliberately captured by the Germans while ostensibly carrying to the British Embassy in Tangier plans for Operation Figaro.

With the help of Army Intelligence they found him. He was a corporal who had survived Dunkirk. Fleeing the Germans he ran into a cul-de-sac and slid, as on oil, to the ground. He found himself among some twenty children, women and elderly men whose bodies were floating in a lagoon of their own blood. They had been sprayed so heavily with machine gun fire that one child was cut in half across the torso, others dismembered. The sight of butchered civilians had turned a normal British youth into an urgent anti-Nazi.

But one "courier" was not enough. What if something went wrong, what if fate played like a Charlie Chaplin comedy and he "couldn't get arrested," failed to fall into the enemy's hands? They needed at least two. The other should be washed up onto the shore, dead of drowning, the papers he was carrying to the Allied command in a waterproof pouch strapped to his body beneath his clothing. Either the Germans would find him or the Spanish police could be expected to cooperate and turn him over to them and they'd discover the false orders indicating an attack on Sardinia. At the right moment they would find a young man in a British hospital who had died of double pneumonia. His flooded lungs would resemble those of a victim of drowning. Once prepared with the papers and a proper uniform his body would be dumped into the Mediterranean, close to where they wanted him to be found.

The winds were heavy as the young paratrooper carrying plans for Operation Figaro jumped from the British airplane into the darkness over Spanish Morocco. As had been calculated his parachute was blown toward French Morocco and within minutes he landed safely, and as advantageously as anyone at Whitehall would have dared hope: directly in the center of a village where his descent was observed by the police. Seeing that he was not carrying an assault weapon they did not fire upon him, and he was brought to Gestapo headquarters.

With scorn for Allied incompetence the Germans accepted his story of being blown off course while trying to reach Tangier. The captured documents had been written in a code the British knew the Germans had broken, and the Gestapo easily deciphered them. Then they interrogated him. He had no information. He had been given a package and been told to deliver it. The Gestapo satisfied themselves that as a corporal, logically he would know little. They passed the information immediately to Heinrich Himmler. From Himmler it went to Intelligence, and in turn to Adolf Hitler.

Though it was hoped there was no breach of security at such a crucial place as Lt. General Eisenhower's U.S. Army Headquarters in London still, because of the reality of espionage, plans for Figaro were left "carelessly" in what was assumed to be the most secure offices. Sure enough, a cleaning woman who swept floors and emptied wastebaskets left Eisenhower's headquarters at Norfolk House in Grosvenor Square at five P.M. and went to a small apartment in the West End. From the clothes closet she withdrew a small suitcase. Before unlocking it she checked the threading she had left. It was not broken. She traveled with it across London by bus and checked into a commercial hotel near the

Thames. From the suitcase she removed a radio transmitter, an *Afu*, designed in Berlin especially for the *Abwehr's* field agents. Rapidly she sent off the message: "Operation Figaro . . . Allied attack on Sardinia and Sicily . . . no date yet." She shut off the transmitter, repacked it and hurried from the hotel before British counterespionage agents in a radiotracking van could catch and follow her radio beam to the hotel.

The information was received in the *Abwehr's* listening post in the underground bunkers at Wohldorf, just outside of Hamburg, and forwarded to Berlin.

Soon *Abwehr* agents in London, Africa and Madrid had sent in reports on Figaro, basically the same material but with an added detail or two, appropriate to the sources from which it was obtained. Cannily, from the Spanish Embassy in London there was no information on Figaro—as the Allies would not inform a neutral about their war plans, but from there the *Abwehr* agent forwarded the message: "The Duke of Alba has been informed that there will be an Allied military build-up at Gibraltar but that Spain need not be alarmed." In Berlin it was added to the other reports. It fit perfectly. Gibraltar would logically be the assembly point for fueling and supply before driving on toward Sardinia and Sicily.

"The world's largest mousetrap," Hitler gloated, tracing his finger along the coastlines bordering the Mediterranean. Placing the index finger of one hand at the Suez Canal and the other at Gibraltar he looked elatedly at Raeder and Jodl. "We'll let them get deeply inside, then seal off both ends and capture the whole force." He looked toward heaven, "What I pray for myself is that they send the entire Royal Navy for Figaro." Returning his attention to the map on his desk, again he traced the coastlines of the "Inland Sea": France, Italy, Yugoslavia, Albania, Greece, Turkey, Egypt, Tunisia and Algeria. He skipped over the small area from Alexandria to Palestine that the British controlled. "We'll blockade that with U-boats. Then, with control of every meter of land, every port where they might refuel and supply themselves, we'll starve them out." He chuckled, "Raeder, how long will it take for the great Royal Navy to run out of water, fuel and food, and be bobbing about like so many toys in my bathtub, anxious to surrender and be fed?"

"My *Führer*, little time, but . . ." he placed a finger on the map at Spanish Morocco on one side of the straits then moved his finger along the lengthy coast of Spain, where the British fleet might find refuge afforded by a friendly, neutral nation.

"Yes, yes, I know." Quelling his frustration he said, "Well, if we should find ourselves betrayed by Franco and we cannot capture 'Figaro' and utilize those ships ourselves, at least we can be waiting to bomb them to infinity." He stared at the Spanish coastline, almost disbelieving that it was not yet his. The frustration hardened to determination. "We will increase pressure on the *Caudillo*."

Hans Lazar's imperative instructions directly from Goebbels were to create such fear of the Allies that Franco would invite the German army onto Spanish territory for Spain's own protection. He did not need to spend five minutes or seconds pondering how to approach this. In 1936, to half of Spain, the name of Prime Minister Negrín spelled blood, death and Communist takeover.

At the Ritz Bar, the German press attaché's great talent was kissed by Lady Luck with the rare visit of one of Madrid's best-known couples. He was a Spanish *Marqués*, she an Italian who owned a dozen important titles, but her title most interesting to Lazar was: the biggest gossip in Madrid.

"The Allies are going to invade Spain," he confided. "Soon. Worst of all, they are going to install a government headed by Negrín." [4]

They reacted with the terror Lazar had expected.

"The British are incredibly stupid." He shook his head in a show of amazement. "An Englishwoman, 'Caldwell,' posing as a tourist took a room here at the Ritz and the first thing she did was ring the British Ambassador, telling his secretary that 'Miss Currier was calling.'" Lazar made a face, "Presumably her idea of an unbreakable code-name for courier. Hoare took the call immediately. 'Oh, Ambassador Hoare, I've come with plans for the gardening of your Sussex Estate.' Hoare made an appointment with her for that afternoon. Then, she went to the hairdresser," Lazar rolled his eyes, "stupidly leaving in the room, tucked beneath her clothes, the plans for an invasion of Spain, the new government of Negrín, everything. Naturally, the Gestapo photographed and was reading it before she returned and could take the plans over to Hoare."

They listened with interest to the background story, but the man was a Spaniard and the thought of a return to the 1936 Government terrified him. "Negrín . . ."

"Yes," Lazar twisted the knife, "the Commies are going to have Madrid again."

She was one of Madrid's most prominent and active hostesses; A Countess, a Grandee, wealthy, and her guests this evening included, as usual, Ministers of the Government, Generals and ranking diplomats. Hans Lazar's curious charm as well as his endless supply of fascinating secrets had brought him where his job as Press Attaché could not, even though he held the higher rank of Counselor. Knowing that the seating by diplomatic protocol would put him far from his hostess during dinner, Lazar got her aside during cocktails.

"I'm telling you this as a friend in order to give you time to evacuate your family from Madrid," he said, speaking very discreetly. "Churchill had a secret luncheon last week at Downing Street with Negrín. The next day Negrín was received by the King at Buckingham Palace. This confirms that the Allies definitely plan to have him head the Government they put in here . . ."

He could see her become weak. Her husband had lived under Negrín's Republican Government in Madrid, had escaped with his life and joined Franco's forces in the north. "It's not illogical," Lazar reasoned. "After all, the Allies are supporting Stalin and it was the Comintern that made Negrín the Popular Front's Prime Minister . . ." Lazar paused, then gestured with his head toward two members of the present Franco cabinet. "You would be well advised to use all of your influence with people who might make Franco see the logic of joining the Axis and getting Germany in here to save him and the country . . ."

As the news of the King of England, George VI, personally receiving the exiled Negrín spread through the party, it fused with early rumors and Lazar's logical reasoning as to why the Allies would invade Spain.

"Of course! They saw what happened to them at Dieppe. It was another Dunkirk! They now know for sure that the *Führer*'s Fortress of Europe is impregnable. Their only hope is to invade a weakened country like Spain, which cannot resist them. From here they could launch attacks on land against German positions in France . . ."

By the time the evening was over Lazar was delighted to tell the hostess, "I'm sorry to have ruined your party."

"Ruined my party? My dear! There are things more important than dinner parties. Thank you, Hans. I am going to do everything I can."[5]

The Official Bulletin published in the morning newspaper stated:

Excmo. Sr. Don Ramón Serrano Suñer has ceased to be
Minister of Foreign Affairs.

Excmo. Lt. General Don Francisco Gómez-Jordana y Sousa, Count of Jordana, is appointed Minister of Foreign Affairs.

BERLIN   MADRID, SEPTEMBER 3, 1942
URGENT

NEW FOREIGN MINISTER, COUNT JORDANA IS NOTORI-
OUSLY PRO ALLIES.

                                              STOHRER

Hitler was outraged. The *Caudillo* was completely out of hand and seemed to have forgotten where the power lay. Spain needed to be awakened, rudely, and taught a lesson for her accumulating list of flirtations with the Allies. He sent for Admiral Doenitz, who commanded the fleet of U-boats.

On September 25th Ambassador Hayes was called to the British Embassy to receive a top-secret communication from Washington via the British code, which was considered safer than the American diplomatic code that was believed to have been broken by the *Abwehr*. The British code was known in Madrid only to Ambassador Hoare and Mr. Yencken. The deciphered message read:

The combined Chiefs of Staff together with myself and Prime Minister Churchill plan an early invasion and occupation of French North Africa as a start to removing Italy from the war. General Franco can be told nothing other than that Spain is not involved. General Franco's neutrality is urgent to the success of this important offensive. My best personal wishes to you.

Franklin D. Roosevelt

The swords between which Spain stood were now sharper and more terrifying.

Winston Churchill, still in bed after a late night's work, a breakfast tray in front of him, surrounded by stacks of papers and several telephones, received Sir Samuel Hoare and told him, "You are going back to Spain to see to its end the most vital mission of your career. I cannot over emphasize the urgency that General Franco be convinced to remain neutral if Torch is to succeed. And it must succeed or Christian civilization may disappear beneath the heel of Nazi tyranny. Work hard, work well, work unceasingly, for you are walking with destiny."

In the waters off Martinique two of Admiral Doenitz' U-boats waited below the surface, their periscopes scanning the horizon for a ship coming from Argentina. Laden with a full cargo of wheat, carrying an all Spanish crew and mostly Spanish passengers, the Spanish ship *Monte Gorbea* had almost returned to her home base.

Their prey sighted, down below the surface slid the two U-boats. Then invisible destruction was hurtling toward the *Monte Gorbea*. The torpedoes struck fore and aft, breaking the ship in two. A second salvo passed overhead because she sank so rapidly to the bottom.[6]

Count Jordana, the new Foreign Minister, had sent for Hayes. Normally mild-mannered, now he was unwilling to conceal his agitation. Holding clippings from American newspapers, he read, "'Rupture Relations With Spain,' 'Spaniards Building U-Boats for Nazis,' 'Spain Leases Bases To Italy.'" The Foreign Minister searched Hayes' face for some sign. "This is sinister. *El Caudillo* and I interpret this propaganda against us as the start of a program to justify an invasion of Spain or Spanish territory."[7]

Hayes was as distressed as Count Jordana. With the North African invasion so dependant upon Spanish good will and confidence, with Spain's power to destroy the Allies' plan soon to reach its highest point, these false stories in the American press were akin to being shot at by one's own troops. "Excellency, I can assure you that whatever plans my government may have there is absolutely no thought of aggression against Spain or Spanish territory."

Pleased but not satisfied, Jordana asked, "Then where does all this come from? With major war events occurring throughout the world how can you explain newspapers preoccupying themselves with 'Rupture Relations With Spain' if not directed by your government's propaganda machinery?" He appealed to Hayes, "And how thoroughly unjust! We have just lost a Spanish ship carrying Spanish people and desperately needed wheat, sunk by Germany as punishment for our attitude which they consider pro Allies. And your newspapers accuse us of being pro Axis! How could this be unless they are guided by American policy?"

"Excellency, I can only guess that the source of these stories that I know to be untrue, is American Communists and 'fellow travelers' who take their cue, as usual, from Moscow; and second, the 'Spanish Government in Exile.'"[8]

Jordana sat down behind his desk. "'Spanish Government in Exile'! Are you telling me that a man who edits a metropolitan newspaper would consider those people even faintly credible?"

"Forgive me, Excellency, but those exiles have money, they're educated men, the same people whom those editors and newspapers supported during the Civil War. They supported the Republican side then and they remain sympathetic to them today. In the United States, Alvarez del Vayo has been especially effective with leftist publications like the New York Nation and P.M. that are antagonistic to Communism's enemy, General Franco. At the same time del Vayo does well with the Hearst papers and other major press on the grounds of their antagonism for dictators and totalitarian aggressors—curiously excepting Josef Stalin. Yes, Excellency, lamentably they would find them entirely credible."

Jordana was saddened, not understanding, not at all. A graduate of the Spanish Military Academy the year Franco was born he had served his country for more than forty years, and he knew only that in 1936 the Republican Government, taking orders from Moscow, had been deliberately failing to function, paving the way for revolution by not ordering police to check the spreading anarchy, and that Spain would have been lost to Communism if the Army had not been successful in its uprising, the date of which had not been set until the Generals learned that Soviet ships had landed in Spanish harbors with munitions and arms for the revolution the Comintern had planned and organized.

Sympathetic to this Spanish patriot,[9] Hayes said, "Excellency, in America there is a colossal ignorance of Spain. What more graphic proof of this than the fact that American Intelligence personnel in Spain have been ordered to obtain information only from Communist sources."[10] Jordana's face expressed his curiosity. "Sir, I would have to give you a bit of background to explain this."

"I would be most grateful."

Hayes said, "Americans think of the Spanish Civil War as a struggle between fascism and democracy, as those terms are understood in the United States. They do not know it for what it was: the rescue of Spain from becoming a satellite of Soviet Russia."

Minutes before, Count Jordana had felt lost in his own office, finding intolerable the combination of power and ignorance of historical fact that this man represented, and Spain's need to curry favor with that power. Now he felt a great deal better and said, "It was most aptly explained by Dr. Gregorio Marañón, who supported the Republic: 'If one were to ask one hundred people, regardless of whether they are Spaniards or not, why they were fighting against one another, few based their reason on the true purpose of the struggle: 'I defended the Republic because I am pro-Communist, or I sympathized with the Nationalists because I am anti-Communist.' Yet that was the crux of the question.'"

Hayes said, "In 1931 the news that Spain would become a Republic was popularly welcomed, for we Americans are predisposed to regard with special favor the adoption of the republican form of government by any nation. It should produce abroad—we like to believe—the same workable type of liberal democracy as we have at home. Thus, news of the army uprising in 1936 was a surprise and a shock. And when General Franco was reported to be receiving military aid from Nazi Germany and Fascist Italy, most people in the United Nations concluded that Franco and his Nationalists must be fascists and therefore 'bad,' while the Republicans being democratic were therefore 'good.' The fact that Republican forces here were not peace-loving democratic liberals, but Communists and Anarchist contingents, was not known. Nor was it recognized that the Spanish Republicans were receiving extensive help from the Russian dictatorship and International Communism before the Nationalist side began receiving military aid from Germany and Italy."

"If you know that . . . why don't these journalists know it?"

"I am an historian by profession, sir. Unfortunately, though there were correspondents from all news services and important newspapers covering both sides of the war, dispatches from the Republican side usually agreed better with what most Americans believed and wanted to read and were therefore displayed more prominently and bulked larger than dispatches from the Nationalist side. And to make matters worse, on the Republican side the Comintern's professional publicists gave every aid to war correspondents, while correspondents on the Nationalist side had difficulty getting their news through because of inadequate facilities and little effort made by the Franco staff to create them."

"General Franco is a soldier, our leader, not a publicist," said Jordana. "*El Caudillo* does not feel the need for public relations. He is prepared to be judged, finally, by God and by history."

"I would agree with him, providing everyone were playing by the same rules. But, with the Comintern ceaselessly working at discrediting him, I respectfully submit that today *El Caudillo* might prefer that he had been a bit of a 'publicist' as well as a soldier."

Returning to the Embassy, Hayes was furious with those segments of the American press who were provoking anti-Spanish opinion. He wished he could shed the reserve of the academician and diplomat and send off nasty "Letters to the Editors." He would write,

> *Irresponsible fools! Whose side are you on? The Nazis? Can't you see the danger of frightening Spain into the war on the side of the Axis? Look at your maps. Spain owns or controls every foot of territory on both sides of the straits. Thus she easily dominates the mouth of the Mediterranean, which we are desperate to keep available to us.*
>
> *And though Spain doesn't own the Rock, she even controls that because the British built their base on the land side of the Rock, facing Algeciras and staring straight into the muzzles of all those heavy guns at Tarifa that could blast it to hell with little effort.*
>
> *And finally, the next time you call for "rupturing relations with Spain" will you please note that your President has sent me here to accomplish exactly the reverse? As the Commander in Chief of our Armed Forces his opinion is that it's urgent to have a neutral Spain standing between German forces in France and Allied forces soon to be landing in North Africa. If we force Spain over to the Axis, the Wehrmacht will be welcomed down to southern Spain to attack our flank . . ."*

He stopped. It wasn't amusing. He fervently believed in American democracy with the good and the bad of it, but at that moment he wondered how it had survived all these years. More urgently, what could he do to keep the American public from tampering with things it knows nothing about, and possibly causing the deaths of their own sons coming over here to fight?

El Caudillo told his wife, "I do not understand the American or the democratic mentality. Today Ambassador Hayes categorically guaranteed Jordana that those inflammatory stories were not directed by his government; that they resulted from freedom of the press. Need I say that

I do not believe in freedom of the press under the best conditions! But in wartime? How can one conduct a war and have newspapers publishing anything they like? They don't let their soldiers choose whom they will or will not attack. I encounter it unfathomable."

The following day he wondered if he understood the German mentality. Hitler sent him another car. It was parked in the courtyard of the Palace and von Stohrer walked around it with Franco. It was a closed sedan, seating seven people. ". . . and has eight cylinders, forty horsepower, turbo compressor, weighs four thousand four hundred kilograms [9,680 lbs.], has a capacity to hold two hundred and fifteen liters of gasoline and is roughly six meters in length.[11]

"The *Führer* sends you this heavily bullet-proofed automobile as one friend concerned for the welfare of another. He said to tell your Excellency that in times such as these one cannot be too careful."

When von Stohrer had left, Franco told his security chief, "Check it for 'firecrackers.'"

CHAPTER NINETEEN

S PANISH INTELLIGENCE REPORTED UNUSUAL ACTIVITY AT THE ROCK OF GIBRALTAR. ALLIED CARGO SHIPS WERE DISCHARGING LARGE LOADS OF HEAVY, CRATED MATERIALS AND LEAVING BEHIND INCREASING NUM-bers of military personnel.

El Caudillo told Count Jordana that he would receive Sir Samuel Hoare, who had just returned from London.

"Excellency," said the British Ambassador, "I am authorized to give full assurance that a large-scale military build-up that will soon be visible at Gibraltar will have nothing to do with Spain or Spanish territory. Categorically, Spain is not involved, and need have no fear of aggression from Great Britain and its allies, despite prevalent rumors that obviously are German inspired.

"I am also happy to inform your Excellency that during my recent visit to London I had long and profound discussions with Mr. Churchill, who is keenly aware that Spain is dependent upon the resources of Great Britain and its allies, and he has authorized me to inform your Excellency that His Majesty's Government are at this moment considering a program of exports covering Spanish needs of petroleum, wheat, rubber and cotton.

"However, Excellency, if the program is to proceed it is essential that the Spanish government avoid serious incidents with Great Britain, and that existing causes of friction are removed."

"Specifically what causes of friction?"

"Axis activities in the strait. They must be stopped if our economic program is not to be halted by people in the government who will be resentful of Spain's indirect aid to the Axis."

"I will certainly do my best to stop non-neutral activities in the strait," Franco said. "However, you must take into account that unfortunate incidents might sometimes occur inadvertently or as a result of corruption."

Listening to the translation Hoare was stunned to hear *El Caudillo* calmly admit to the existence of corruption, and he did not conceal his perplexity.

Franco explained, "We do not live in Utopia. Corruption is a fact of life that we do everything we can to eliminate, but we have not fully succeeded. Nor do I believe it would suit your Excellency if we did succeed, because the only difference between German and Allied covert activities in Spain today is that while the Germans bribe Spanish officials, the Allies intrigue with Spanish reds."

On October 24th a convoy of Allied warships ships left England, bound for Gibraltar. On October 25th a second convoy departed for the same destination.

Battleships, destroyers, landing craft for personnel and others for tanks, aircraft carriers, freighters, tankers and minesweepers—millions of tons of armor and firepower, these four hundred warships and more than half a million British and American soldiers were on their way to carry out Operation Torch, with the desire to change the course of the war and the destiny of the free world.

By October 26th an all-American fleet of some two hundred and fifty more ships was crossing the North Atlantic, bound for Casablanca, bearing General Patton at the command of the landing forces. But there could be no certainty that the landings would be tried from the Atlantic side until the ships had physically arrived and the weather could be seen, not merely forecast, to be favorable or not. If not, the alternative was to take the whole force through the Strait of Gibraltar and land on little-known beaches close to the frontiers of Spanish Morocco.

An RAF Spitfire appeared in the sky above Gibraltar and landed on the just-completed 1,000-yard-long airfield that in more frivolous days had been a race course. From the landing strip the Spitfire taxied to a parking zone to make room for another to come in.

Along the southern coast of Spain, at Estepona, Algeciras, Cádiz and Tarifa, Spanish Intelligence officers counted the planes and made note of their types: bombers, fighters, reconnaissance, troop transports. In eight hours there were fifty airplanes on the Rock of Gibraltar.

CHIEF OF THE SPANISH STATE LONDON
OCTOBER 25, 1942

EXCELLENCY, I HAVE CONFRONTED CHURCHILL, EDEN
AND SIR JOHN ANDERSON. ALL THREE DENY ANY
ALLIED PLAN TO INVADE SPAIN OR SPANISH TERRITORY.

ALBA

Abwehr agents, watching from the hills of Algeciras and Cádiz, reported to their Tangier headquarters, which radioed to Berlin: ". . . now numbering three hundred and twenty-seven airplanes and still arriving at a rate of one every ten minutes . . ."

Adolf Hitler stood at his desk, placing miniatures of Allied aircraft on a map of the field at Gibraltar. Then he moved a convoy of ships out of the English Channel into the Atlantic. This would be Figaro. He had a happy cat-and-mouse feeling in which he was the cat who owned the biggest mousetrap in the world.

CHIEF OF THE SPANISH STATE LONDON,
OCTOBER 25, 1942

EXCELLENCY, FURTHER TO MY EARLIER MESSAGE, I HAVE
JUST LEARNED THAT A SECTION OF BRITISH INTELLI-
GENCE IS IN CONTACT WITH SPANISH REDS FOR POLITI-
CAL ENDS, AS A CARD TO BE PLAYED BY BRITAIN SHOULD
SPAIN ENTER THE WAR ON THE SIDE OF THE AXIS. IN
THAT EVENT THE BRITISH WOULD SUPPORT A REPUBLI-
CAN TYPE MOVEMENT INSIDE AND OUTSIDE OF SPAIN.
PLEASE REFER TO MY REPORT OF FEBRUARY 10, 1942.

ALBA

El Caudillo delved into one of two stacks of papers on his desk and re-read the Duke of Alba's report.

"Negrín has just opened something called Home For Spaniards. It has around five hundred members, Spanish exiles, making a formidable group of anti-Nationalist Spain voices bunched together in London . . ."

Alba's cable explained why the British had now begun tolerating Negrín's political activity. Franco reasoned that the British forming a contingency plan in the event of Spain joining the Axis was a fair confirmation that there really were no Allied plans against Spain.

It was little consolation because assuming that the Allies were not planning to attack Spain, then where *were* they planning their offensive? He suspected it would be French North Africa, which would trigger Operation Ilona and bring the German divisions pouring over the Pyrenees.

Count Jordana told Hayes, *"El Caudillo* has asked me to say that he will consider it an act of friendship if you could let us know in what direction the Allied offensive is going to go."

"Excellency, I can only repeat that I know only that it is not going toward Spain or Spanish territory."

CHIEF OF THE SPANISH STATE LONDON
OCTOBER 26, 1942

EXCELLENCY, FURTHER INFORMATION TELLS ME THAT
THE ALLIES INTEND TO INVADE NORTH AFRICA, PUSH
TOWARD ALGERIA AND TUNISIA, THEN USE THE
NORTH AFRICAN SEABOARD FOR AN INVASION OF
EUROPE ON THE MEDITERRANEAN SIDE. SPAIN WILL
NOT BE TOUCHED.

ALBA

On November 2nd Hitler was informed that the large armada of Allied ships had entered the Mediterranean and that the airplane count at Gibraltar had now passed eight hundred.

He moved the Allied convoys on his desk map, from the Atlantic into the Mediterranean, facing them toward Sardinia and Sicily.

Count Jordana summoned the American Ambassador to the Ministry. "Allied ships have now spilled over from the Bay of Gibraltar into the Bay of Algeciras. They are in Spanish territory and we have the legal right to fire upon them. *El Caudillo* is not looking for technicalities. He is comfortable in the belief that they will be moving away from Spain and not toward her. But the urgent question is when? The German Ambassador will soon be asking how we can allow our neutrality to be violated by the Allies in our waters, while we are still refusing to admit German troops onto Spanish soil in the north. We must be able to say that we have ordered those ships away and that they are leaving on such and such a date. If not, what can we reply when they insist on installing their own aircraft in our Valencia airfield?"

"Excellency, I truly don't know when. I am only able to assure you that Spain is not involved."

"*¡Ojala!* May God grant that!" Franco murmured, hearing it from Jordana, knowing that there was almost no way for Spain not to be involved. He was concerned that he had not already heard from von Stohrer. The Germans were not likely to sit back and do nothing about the wide-open build-up, or about Spain's tolerating violation of her waters. Von Stohrer's silence suggested that the Germans had concluded that words alone were useless with Spain.

He called the General in command of the garrison at San Sebastian, and the army of guerrillas in the north of Spain. "Any attempt by the Germans to violate our neutrality is to be resisted."

He telephoned to the General in charge of the guns of Tarifa, which commanded the Bays of Algeciras and Gibraltar. "Any attempt by the Allies to violate our neutrality is to be resisted."

He called the General in command of the one hundred and fifty thousand Spanish troops in Tangier. "Do not involve us in any action not directed at Spanish territory. Be careful of firing upon landing craft that might, by navigational error, mistakenly land at our shores instead of the French."

Two more double, direct telephone lines were installed connecting the Palace of El Pardo with Tarifa and Tangier, as had earlier been done with the garrison at San Sebastian, and they were kept open for the purpose of a single call. To be doubly certain about communication with Tangier, which was not always reliable by telephone, a shortwave radio transmitter and receiver were installed at the Palace.

There were now one thousand airplanes packed wing to wing on Gibraltar and four hundred warships containing one hundred and seven thousand men floating in the water between the Rock and Spain.

A man's body washed ashore was seen by two *Guardias Civiles* patrolling the beach at Cádiz. When they reached him they found that he was dead. He wore the uniform of a British naval officer.

In Madrid Sir Samuel received a top-priority message informing him that a courier from General Mark Clark to the Governor of Gibraltar, carrying final details concerning Figaro, had not arrived and must now be considered missing. He was urgently instructed to try to learn what had happened to him and to the plans.

Playing his role in the pretense, but confiding the facts to no one, Hoare summoned Yencken and the Embassy's military, naval and press attachés. "We must all devote ourselves exclusively to trying to learn if he has been found by the Spaniards; each of us through our own sources, but with the utmost discretion. We dare not indicate anxiety or we could trigger a manhunt by the enemy."

It was the naval attaché who came up with the news. "Excellency, a British naval officer answering our description was found washed up onto the beach, dead of drowning, they say, and is in the possession of the Spanish naval authorities."

"Can we demand the body and personal effects?"

"A corpse is legally claimable, the war's over for him. But legally ours or not, they might want to keep him. For exactly the same reasons we'd like to get him. We can only request—and hope."

"At least it's the Navy and not the Army or Air that's got him." For some reason, perhaps the prestige of the Royal Navy, or the pro-Allied sentiment of the Minister, Admiral Moreno, Hoare got along better with the Naval chief than with General Vigón or the new Minister of the Army, General Asensio.

Asking for an appointment to see Admiral Moreno on a personal matter Hoare was received promptly.

"I'm saddened to be here on this matter, saddened to say the least," Hoare explained, "but I'm informed that the son of a personal friend of mine, a British Naval officer, was lost overboard in the strait and that his body had been found by the Spanish police. If it would be possible to claim the body so that I could return it to be buried by his family in England . . ."

A British doctor and Intelligence officers were waiting at the Embassy when the body was delivered.

The doctor said, "It looks like drowning . . ." After a quick examination of the lungs he confirmed it.

Removing the clothes from the corpse the Intelligence men discovered a watertight pouch strapped around the man's waist beneath the clothing. Using a jeweler's loupe and a strong light, both Intelligence officers studied the package.

"It appears not to have been tampered with. Quite possibly the Spanish didn't search him. With all that Navy out there they might not have found it curious that one man fell off a ship and drowned. The tape, the string and this lead seal on the string, the wax seal on the inner enclosure, the packet are all British products, and the packet is made in precisely the way it left London. Every knot is correct. On the other hand the Gestapo would know where to obtain the materials, and they might very well know the packet 'code' and it could have been opened and perfectly remade." Hoare fervently hoped so.

They opened the package. The documents were intact. There was no indication that anyone had seen them since they left London. But, fortunately for Allied interests, one of the two couriers carrying the false landing plans had fallen into German hands.

Fear was rendering the American Embassy's staff useless. American Foreign Service officers who had been invaded or bombed out of their previous posts—Warsaw, Amsterdam, Belgrade—and had found safety in the Madrid Embassy, now anticipated the Nazi nightmare to descend on Spain. With no work to do they sat around the Embassy talking about what it had been like, demoralizing and frightening the Embassy staff to the point of making incredible errors in the simplest tasks.

Hayes gathered them together hoping to boost their morale. "I know that you have heard every conceivable rumor. But I can assure you that Allied plans are known to me that, if I could divulge them, would give you reason to relax and have confidence in the force of Allied military strength, as I have, and as I assure you that President Roosevelt has . . ."

Pleased that he had steadied them he returned to his office. The chief of communications was waiting with a cable from Washington.

CONSULT PARAGRAPH 25 IN STANDARD FOREIGN
SERVICE REGULATIONS.

Hayes now learned that his own nerves were shot as he heard himself scolding, "So? Consult them and handle it. Why bother me with this?"

"Excellency, excuse me, sir, but Paragraph 25 is: Procedure to be Followed When an Embassy Must Be Vacated in Emergency Flight From Advancing Enemy Armies."

In London Generals Eisenhower and Mark Clark were being frustrated in their attempts to travel to Gibraltar to command Operation Torch. Twice, foul weather kept them grounded. Time was short for it was now too late for Torch to be postponed. As their third attempt loomed close and the weather remained unchanged the officer commanding the six Flying Fortresses assigned to take their party to Gibraltar told General Eisenhower, "Sir, I give you my technical advice not to make this flight, and I ask you to make the decision as to whether or not I should take off."

It was the only time in his life that Ike was faced with that situation because normally the air commander's decision is final. Eisenhower thought that it did not seem a propitious omen for the great adventure, but they had to go through with it. "Take off," he ordered.

Once in the air the weather was so bad that they flew at an average height of one hundred feet all the way from England to Gibraltar. At the end of the long, tense trip, as finally the great Rock loomed out of its concealing haze, Ike's pilot commented, "This is the first time I have ever had to climb to get into landing traffic."[1]

Eisenhower observed the airfield jammed with fighter craft, every inch taken up by either a Spitfire or a can of gasoline. All this was exposed to the enemy's reconnaissance planes and there was no way to camouflage such bulk. The airfield itself lay on the Spanish border, separated from Spanish territory only by a barbed-wire fence.[2]

He and Mark Clark made their headquarters in the subterranean passages of the Rock that provided the sole available office space and housed the signal equipment by which they expected to keep in touch with the commanders of the three assault forces. The eternal darkness of the tunnels was here and there partially pierced by feeble electric bulbs. Damp, cold air in blocklong passages was heavy with the stagnation that did not noticeably respond to the clattering efforts of electric fans.[3]

"Paco," Carmen Polo said, "everybody is so nervous . . . my sister was here today and all she could talk about were the rumors of the Allies invading us, and Negrín . . . Paco, is that possible?"

"It's not likely. The rumors are a German propaganda tactic. They want us to become so fearful of the Allies that we will beg the *Wehrmacht* to come in to protect us."

"Isabel said they're saying that the Allies are taking into account Wellington's peninsula campaign and have chosen Spain as the easiest road into Hitler's 'Fortress of Europe.'"

"Everybody chooses Spain as their easiest access to whatever it is they want. In 1920 Lenin told the Second World Congress of the Comintern that Spain would be the scene of '. . . the second successful proletarian revolution.' We have the unfortunate condition of seeming to be weak but in fact we are quite strong. I sometimes think how much easier life would be if one were to appear very strong, when in fact he is very weak."

"But, the Allies are friendly with Russia. Stalin does want to get back into Spain. Everything they say makes sense."

"Carmelita, it wouldn't be good propaganda if it didn't make sense."
She saw him starting to doze off. "Paco! How can you fall asleep?"

He opened his eyes. "Everything has been done that can be done.
Rest is what is necessary now."

While he was breakfasting, *El Caudillo* was brought a sealed envelope
from the chief of Spanish Intelligence:

Excellency,

> *We have just learned that General Eisenhower arrived at Gibraltar
> from London in the middle of the night.*
>
> *Another American General, not identified, is with him. We sur-
> mise, repeat, surmise, that it would be Mark Clark.*

> *Martínez-Campos*

Franco told his wife. "Whatever it is that's going to happen will be
happening soon."

In Madrid each hour that passed was another opportunity to hear
still another rumor, and for the imagination to dwell on the worst.

Franco wondered how long it would be before Germany would take
action. And would the action be directed only toward the Allies, or
would it include revenge on Spain?

Hayes wondered how it was possible for the Germans to know of the
giant force massed at Gibraltar and not immediately send the *Luftwaffe*
to try to bomb them out of existence. They were packed so tightly
together that there was no way a bomb could miss hitting something, and
the explosions within one ship would chain-react, igniting its neighbors.
It would be a massacre. And if *he* knew that then why would not the
Germans?

On the Rock of Gibraltar, Eisenhower and Clark stared at the barbed-
wire fence between them and the Spanish border. Politically, they
thought, Spain was leaning toward the Axis, and, almost physically, leaning against the barbed-wire fence were any number of Axis agents. Every
day the American Generals expected a major attack by hostile bombers,

and as each day went by without such an attack they went to bed puzzled, even astonished.

Their only explanation for it was that Allied measures for deceiving the enemy were working well.[4] Better than they knew. For, like Hayes, they could not know that Hitler was hoping to trap and own all of that war power for himself.

As they lay in their beds, through the arched ceilings came a constant drip, drip, drip of surface water that faithfully and drearily ticked off the seconds of the interminable, almost unendurable wait that occurs between completion of a military plan and the moment action begins.[5]

CHAPTER TWENTY

A TOP SECRET, TOP PRIORITY CABLE ARRIVED AT THE BRITISH EMBASSY IN THE BRITISH CODE, ADDRESSED TO BOTH THE BRITISH AND THE AMERICAN AMBASSADORS. THE DAY WAS FRIDAY, NOVEMBER 6, 1942.

The British Ambassador's car arrived at the American Embassy and Hayes got into the back seat with Hoare. The two men made small talk only. They got out of the car at Madrid's principal park, El Retiro. Walking together, away from anyone's earshot, Hoare said, "Torch is very close." He gave Hayes an envelope. "This is a communication from President Roosevelt that you are to present to General Franco himself. To no one else. That was emphasized. I have a similar message from the Prime Minister that I will subsequently present to Count Jordana. Upon receipt, by either or both of us, of a cable with the single word 'Thunderbird' in cipher, followed by a date and hour, we are to concert immediately and arrange to present our letters as soon as possible after the time given, which will be the time of the start of the landings in North Africa.

"When you have handed your letter to General Franco you are to cable the code word 'Jelly' *en clair*, to Washington, Gibraltar, Tangier and Lisbon. When I have given my letter to Count Jordana I am to do the same, substituting London for Washington." [1]

Returning to the Embassy, Hayes called in his Counselor, Mr. Beaulac, and Mr. Outerbridge Horsey, a Third Secretary in whom he confided the secret of Torch. [2] He told them of the message regarding the preparation of the Embassy for evacuation. He had held this off until the last moment because though he had complete confidence in his two top assistants and could rely upon them to execute their duties without panic, if any of the others suspected anything, it would give just cause for further alarm that could result in a security leak. Further, if Horsey and Beaulac were to interpret it as a lack of confidence on the part of the President then the less time they had to dwell on it the better for them.

According to instructions in Paragraph 25: all confidential documents were to be burned; codebooks were to be prepared for quick destruction at the last moment; gasoline was to be stockpiled in the Embassy basement in sufficient quantity for all Embassy cars to be ready to drive nonstop to Lisbon or Gibraltar, carrying Embassy personnel, in a race against Nazi forces coming down from the north.

Hayes directed, "Extract the documents during the day, but burn them at night, in the fireplaces in my quarters."

The final detail would be for the Ambassador to call on the Swiss minister and entrust him with the protection of American interests. But that could only be done at the last moment or it would certainly signal that something was about to happen.

At the German Embassy the von Stohrers were having a banquet. As they dined, a Spanish Naval officer said, "I believe that the Allies are going to strike at North Africa."

Von Stohrer disagreed. "I have the best possible information that their destination is Italy and the eastern Mediterranean."

"I acknowledge the outstanding Intelligence organization at the disposal of your Excellency, and perhaps you are correct. Nevertheless I maintain that it will be an attack against North Africa."

"What would you like to bet?"

"Nylon stockings," sighed the Spanish officer's wife.

Von Stohrer feigned horror. "I was suggesting a small sporting wager, not fortunes . . ."

The following morning, December 6, 1942, von Stohrer reported the conversation to Berlin, emphasizing that it was simply a personal guess made by a Spanish Naval officer, and that German Intelligence chiefs in Spain and Tangier agreed unanimously that there would be no attack on the African coast.

On Saturday, November 7th, just after noon, Hayes was called to the code room.

THUNDERBIRD, SUNDAY, NOVEMBER 8,
TWO A.M. (2: A.M.) SPANISH TIME.

Walking through *El Retiro* park with Sir Samuel, he said, "I plan to contact Count Jordana just after one A.M. and hope to reach General Franco immediately after two."

Hoare said, "In the mood of near-hysteria that exists in Madrid the most constructive thing I can do is proceed with my day as scheduled. If you need to contact me I shall be shooting wood pigeons with the Count of Velayos."

Paintbrush in hand Franco studied his face in the bathroom mirror, preparing to capture the expression in his eyes. But what he saw was not what he wanted to put on canvas. For his self-portrait he wanted the eyes to be noncommunicative, tranquil, as they were normally, when he was in command of the situation. He put down the brush and palette. Those were not the eyes he saw in the mirror.[3]

Ambassador and Mrs. Hayes dismissed the servants after dinner and went upstairs to a small sitting room whose heavily curtained windows would keep the outside world unaware of the all-night vigil that lay ahead. They were accompanied by Mr. Beaulac and Mr. Horsey.[4]

Mr. Beaulac said, "As I was filling the cars and the extra jerry cans, and thinking about us roaring out of here with our privileged supply of gasoline . . . well, it didn't seem very valorous to be leaving the ordinary civilian Americans behind."

"That's a commendable thought," Hayes replied. "But bear in mind that your brain and Mr. Horsey's and mine are filled with secrets and information that could be most useful to the Germans. Remaining here to be captured would serve no one but the Nazis. The valorous thing is to avoid being captured."

Mrs. Hayes asked, "What do you suppose General Franco is going to do?"

Her husband was grim. "If he defies us then only a quick Axis victory can save Spain from starvation. On the other hand, if he defies the Nazis, Hitler might well order his troops to overrun Spain and occupy her."

As November 7th became the 8th they waited in silence, reflecting on the multitude of unknowns: Had the Spaniards found the information on the paratrooper or the drowned British officer and passed it on to the Germans as desired? Would German troops massed in the Pyrenees descend on Spain? Might it actually be a race to Lisbon and Gibraltar? Was the German air force in Bayonne at this moment preparing to strike at the collected forces in Gibraltar?

But above all was the unknown quantity of General Franco's reaction to Torch. He held the power. For, while the British Spitfires could stave off, if not entirely chase away, an attack by the *Luftwaffe*, there existed nothing that could, quickly enough, silence the guns at Tarifa if Franco should order them to fire.

Whose side was Franco really on?

Just after midnight the aide entered the chapel beside the Francos' bedroom to announce a call on the Tarifa line.

"*Mi General*, the Allied ships have begun to move out, away from Spain. Not a single vessel is headed in our direction. They are surely enroute to Africa. Airplanes are taking off at the rate of one every minute. It's a magnificent military spectacle. I regret that your Excellency is not seeing it."

Hanging up, Franco alerted General Orgaz, the Spanish High Commissioner in Morocco.

What were the Germans at Hendaye doing in response?

Calling the Commanding General in San Sebastian, he was told, "Nothing, Excellency. No movement at all."

Now there was only to wait.

At Wolfsschanze, General Jodl's voice quivered, "*Führer* . . . my *Führer*, the armada at Gibraltar has begun moving . . . but not toward Italy; they are moving toward Africa, *Führer* . . ."

Hitler frowned. The Allies, then, had fooled him. "Jodl, relax your-self. They cannot make successful landings on the French African coast without the agreement of the French. And after the noble treatment we have given France you can be certain they will wish to repel the Allies."[5]

At one-ten A.M. Mr. Beaulac called the home of the Minister of Foreign Affairs, Count Jordana, whose home telephone number was pro-vided to all Ambassadors, to be used at their discretion.

In reply to a servant saying the Minister had retired, Beaulac insisted, "I request that you inform him that the Ambassador from the United States of America begs to call on him on a most urgent matter . . ."

Wearing pajamas, robe and slippers, his face devoid of color, the Minister led Hayes and Beaulac to a sitting room.

"Excellency," said Ambassador Hayes, "I have been instructed by my government to seek an immediate audience with General Franco for the purpose of giving him personally this urgent communication from President Roosevelt."

"Can you give me an idea what the message is?"

"I'm sorry, but I am strictly instructed to divulge the communiqué to no one other than to General Franco."

"But, I cannot call *El Generalísimo* at one-forty in the morning with-out some information . . ."

"Excellency, I prevail upon you to trust me, that this is a most urgent matter and that General Franco would want to be awakened."

Count Jordana hesitated, then gestured to chairs, "Please make your-selves comfortable." He left the room and went to the telephone in an adjoining hallway.

He had seen the tension on the American's face and noted the enve-lope that he was holding, and Jordana had no doubt that it concerned the force at Gibraltar and that *El Generalísimo* would very much want to receive the information. But he also knew that *El Generalísimo* would want to know more of its nature before receiving Hayes.

Franco picked up the telephone on the night table and he listened for a moment to Jordana. "I can not receive him until I have some idea what it's about."

"He insists that he is instructed to divulge that only to your Excellency."

"Try again."

Count Jordana returned, visibly distressed. "*El Generalísimo* is away from the Palace at a partridge shoot and will not return until early morning . . ." His voice came forth in nearly a moan, "I can hardly believe this . . . a monstrous war machine is at Gibraltar, President Roosevelt has sent a letter to *El Generalísimo* with obviously crucial information . . ."

Sitting down, he appealed to Hayes, "I respect your instructions, and I will not pursue this further than to ask if you can give me an indication . . . clearly it must relate to the forces gathered at Gibraltar . . . if you could just give me an idea . . . that it is something favorable or unfavorable . . ." A tiny man, barely five feet tall, sitting back on the couch his bedroom-slippered feet did not touch the floor and he appeared even smaller now, as if shrunken by strain and alarm.

Hayes looked at his watch. It was two-fifteen A.M., the landing was under way. He handed Count Jordana the letter. "I give this to your Excellency to read as a trusted friend."[6]

As the Minister read the letter the anxiety, the fear, the tight skin of his face visibly relaxed. "So . . . Spain is not involved."

He stood up. "*El Generalísimo* will return by early morning. If you agree I will pass by your Embassy at eight-thirty and drive you to the Palace." Extending his arms he gave Hayes an *abrazo*. "I am grateful for your extreme kindness."

The moment the Americans had left, Jordana was dialing the phone. "Excellency, it's alright . . . we're not involved. They are landing in French North Africa."

Carmen Polo, sitting on the bed beside her husband, watched his face as he listened to the contents of the letter as Count Jordana remembered it.

On board the *Führer* train, Hitler was sleeping as the first Allied troops approached the beaches of Morocco and Algeria. In the middle of the night the radio car of the train began receiving reports of the landings which indicated that the French were repelling the Allies.

Reading the reports at breakfast with Jodl, Keitel and von Ribbentrop, Hitler took full advantage of the moment. "How is it that only I knew? Why must I make every decision myself, including the most important decision, that is not to pay attention to my best advisors? Why?" Then, as if surprised by the question, he shrugged, "That is why I am *Führer*."

Sunday, November 8th, the sky was overcast as Jordana, Hayes and Beaulac drove to El Pardo, arriving at nine A.M.

El Caudillo, waiting for them with the Barón de las Torres, offered his hand to Ambassador Hayes, who said, "I am grateful to your Excellency for seeing me on such extremely short notice."[7] He presented the communication from President Roosevelt.

As the Barón de las Torres opened the envelope, Hayes studied Franco's eyes. *El Caudillo* showed no sign of tension; he was waiting with interest.[8] Not wishing to stare, Hayes turned and found himself facing the three photographs. He tried to focus on the Pope and to overlook Hitler and Mussolini.

The Barón de las Torres translated aloud:

THE WHITE HOUSE

Dear General Franco,

It is because your nation and mine are friends in the best sense of the word and because you and I are sincerely desirous of the continuation of that friendship that I want very simply to tell you of the compelling reasons that have forced me to send a powerful American military force to the assistance of the French possessions in North Africa.

We have accurate information to the effect that Germany and Italy intend at an early date to occupy with military force French North Africa.

With your wide military experience you will understand clearly that in the interests of the defense of both North America and South America it is essential that action be taken to prevent an Axis occupation of French Africa without delay.

To provide for America's defense I am sending a powerful army
to French possessions and protectorates in North Africa with the sole
purpose of preventing occupation by Germany and Italy and with the
hope that these areas will not be devastated by the horrors of war.

I hope you will accept my full assurance that these moves are in
no shape, manner or form directed against the Government of Spain
or Spanish Morocco or Spanish territories—metropolitan or over-
seas. I believe the Spanish Government and the Spanish people wish
to maintain neutrality and to remain outside the war. Spain has
nothing to fear from the United States.

I am, my dear General, your sincere friend.

Franklin Delano Roosevelt

Franco nodded. "Please convey to your President that I appreciate and accept the guarantees stated in his letter. And, as a soldier I admire the strategy. I will repeat this to President Roosevelt in a letter that I will ask your Excellency to transmit."

In Washington, London, Gibraltar, Lisbon and Tangier cablegrams arrived with the single word message: JELLY.

"What?" Hitler demanded of von Ribbentrop. "What . . . what? Are you crazy? How dare you tell me such a thing?"

He had made a speech in Munich at six P.M. and had just returned to his train. Von Ribbentrop's voice trembled as he read aloud the latest reports stating that the Allied landings in North Africa were resoundingly successful. "'The Allied forces struck with such might and precision that the French were unable to prevent their penetration into French Morocco and Algeria . . .'"

"Unable? Unable you say? The word is betrayed! I have been betrayed by the French. Read it again."

"*Führer* . . ."

"I have ordered you to read it again," Hitler bellowed. "Are you stupid? Or have you betrayed me, too? Read it. I command you."

Von Ribbentrop's eyes found refuge from Hitler's scarlet face as he looked down at the report and read it again.

Hearing the bad news once more, Hitler cut him off. "Stop reading. I can't stand to hear your voice." He strode up and down the railroad car, his outrage growing as he realized that he had been doubly wrong: not only had he been deceived by the Allies with their now-obvious subterfuge, Operation Figaro, but he had been betrayed by the French. And he was embarrassed by remembering his own gloating over the world's largest mousetrap. "So! I am the mouse."

"*Mein Führer?*"

"Yes, yes . . . oh yes, that is precisely the thought in your mind. 'The *Führer* is the mouse.' And that's what Raeder and Jodl and Keitel are thinking." He glared at von Ribbentrop. "Admit it."

"*Mein Führer?*"

"What are you afraid of? A mouse? You mouse!" Abruptly he stopped. "Summon Laval to Berchtesgaden. Send for Mussolini. Instantly! I want the *Duce* here for an emergency conference. And get me Goebbels, get me Goering . . . and . . . get out of my sight."

Understanding, von Ribbentrop's voice was gentle, "*Mein Führer*, I am at your command and I vow my loyalty until death."

Hitler slumped onto a sofa. "I know," he said. "Thank you." He was quiet for a while. When he spoke his voice was flat. "The god of war has turned from Germany and gone over to the other camp."

Von Stohrer entered Count Jordana's office in the manner of a German Mark IV tank. "I have an urgent message from my Minister. It is mandatory now that German troops in the Pyrenees are given immediate free passage through Spain as well as all aid. The *Führer* demands it."

Jordana had courteously met von Stohrer at the door to his office. The German Ambassador was literally fourteen inches taller than the Minister, who had to tilt his neck sharply backward in order to look into von Stohrer's face. On occasions when they'd had to have a picture taken together Jordana had stood on a stone. Especially at this moment Jordana did not enjoy being dwarfed by this unpleasant giant. He went to his desk and sat down. "Your Excellency will surely understand that since *El*

Caudillo has just accepted President Roosevelt's guarantee of nonaggression toward Spain, we cannot possibly compromise our neutrality."

Von Stohrer's emotions had been thrown completely asunder since the moment of hearing of the landings. He had not been able to erase from his mind his humiliating No-attack-on-Africa cable. He slumped in his chair. Drained of his usual swagger he appealed, "May I ask you to arrange an audience with *El Caudillo?* At least I can try . . ."

Franco received the German Ambassador, who said, "Excellency, the *Führer* is eating the walls. He is in a constant rage that you did not let us come in here two years ago. If you had, then this would never have happened. You have changed the course of the war. He demands that you come into it now, while the Allies' positions are not yet secure. With your help our troops could pass through Spain in a matter of days and we could counterattack effectively. There is literally not a minute to lose. The *Führer* calls upon you to keep your promise. If you do not, I fear the worst. He is nearly mad with fury. And Jodl and Keitel—all of them are urging him to invade Spain."

Franco said, "Few diplomats in the world walk into the offices of the Chief of State as easily as you do mine. This has been because we have a personal relationship. On that basis can you tell me that it is in the best interests of my people to enter this war now?"

Von Stohrer, who had been looking into Franco's eyes as he spoke, now looked away. He did not reply.

"Look, Eberhardt, I understand that it was your duty to deliver that message . . ."

Von Stohrer looked up gratefully.

". . . but my message to the *Führer* can only be that if German troops attempt to enter Spain they will be resisted forcefully. Further, it is Germany's turn to give Spain the same guarantees in writing as the United States and Great Britain have given us."

Too late to prevent the invasion Hitler sent two parachute regiments to impede Allied progress in Africa, troops he had planned to use to reinforce Rommel. He sent advanced elements of the 10th Panzer Division, and he recalled four hundred operational aircraft from the Russian front for use in this Theater. One-fourth of the *Luftwaffe* was now in the Mediterranean, compared to one-twelfth eighteen months earlier.

Overnight Madrid was in the red-hot center of the war. Despite the success of Torch, in fact because of it, Spain was going to be the neighbor of heavy aerial and submarine warfare.

Hitler was going to want, now need, Spain's help with increasing intensity. In the Pyrenees, the twenty *Wehrmacht* divisions remained motionless. But Franco could, more than ever, consider them crouched to spring.

CHAPTER TWENTY-ONE

THE GERMAN HIGH COMMAND ASSEMBLED IN THE SALON AT BERGHOF, DREADING TO FACE THE *FÜHRER* WHO HAD NOT BEEN BEARING THE ACCIDENTS OF LIFE WITH DIGNITY NOR GRACE.

Admiral Raeder spoke, "My *Führer*, today more than ever it is of the utmost strategic importance that we occupy the Iberian Peninsula. We are unanimous in the belief that despite Roosevelt's promise the Allies' next action will be to occupy the peninsula.

"And, if we do not take it over before they do then Germany will be deprived of one million tons of iron ore, three thousand five hundred tons of wolfram, two hundred tons of lithium, one thousand tons of tin, in addition to mica, beryllium, citrus fruits, cork, ad infinitum."

Hitler was disbelieving, as if Raeder had been on vacation for the past two years. "But my dear Grand Admiral, we still have that same little problem in Madrid, and without his help the occupation of Spain is an enterprise for which we cannot conveniently spare the military forces or the economic resources. But even if we could successfully overpower Spanish resistance in the impossible terrain, even if we could, there is not enough food on the peninsula to support our armies. Spain is not the well-stocked grocery store we had in France. We would need to import foods from Germany that we neither have, nor could hope to deliver safely to our troops under constant guerrilla warfare. The invasion of Spain at this moment is not practical. No. We must try to strengthen the neutrality of Spain and Portugal. However, if the Allies do land in Spain then Germany must and will seize Spain and Portugal regardless of the economic sacrifice it will cause."

"In that case," Jodl said, "we are back to the need for an invasion. Operation Ilona."

Hitler grimaced. "Obviously the name Ilona has reached the ears of our Spanish 'friend'—and I use the word bitterly as it catches in my throat—causing the sudden Pyrenean installations. Gisela will be the new name." He looked viciously at each man. "And may I suggest that those of us privileged to know such high level secrets will also be so clever as to keep the mouth shut." He turned to Jodl. "Begin drawing Gisela. She will have to be a more complicated lady than Ilona, and she will be merciless simply because of the Spaniards' installations.

"We will meanwhile try to accomplish Spanish neutrality diplomatically. But if we see that we are failing, we will be prepared to strike, and strike we will." He turned to von Ribbentrop. "Begin thinking of someone to replace von Stohrer. Someone tougher who can be effective with Franco."

Hayes wrote to President Roosevelt, on December 7, 1942:

> The most important news from Spain, in my opinion, is the emphatic assurance given me last Monday afternoon by the Foreign Minister, Count Jordana—which I promptly telegraphed to the Department—that General Franco and his whole government are determined to pursue a policy of "impartiality" toward the two sets of belligerents, to maintain the partly mobilized army strictly on the defensive within present Spanish frontiers, and to resist forcefully any attempts by any foreign power to invade Spanish territory. This is a long stride for the government here to take . . .
>
> Thanksgiving Day was observed by the American colony in Madrid with special fervor this year. We had so much in recent developments to be thankful for. At both the Mass in the Catholic church and the service in St. George's Protestant church, your proclamation was read and "America" and "The Star Spangled Banner" were sung. In the afternoon, in the Embassy Annex (Casa Americana) we had a showing of the film, "Abe Lincoln in Illinois." And in the evening, at the Embassy, there was dinner for everybody with turkey—Spanish turkey (which is excellent) . . .[1]

On January 23, 1943, Ambassador von Stohrer was recalled and replaced by Hans Adolf von Moltke, who had been the last Nazi Ambassador to Poland, and whose reputation was for hastening the doom of countries that displeased the *Führer*.[2]

On April 11, 1943, Admiral Doenitz conferred with Hitler. "*Führer*, granted that the Allies have not occupied the peninsula as anticipated, but I fear that they have a Gisela, that they are simply waiting for us to invade Spain. I have a plan of concessions that we could offer to Franco to win his consent . . ."

Deutsche Botschaft in Spanien

April 20, 1943

P r o-M e m o r i a

In the last discussions, the Spanish side, especially the Spanish military authorities, had expressed repeatedly that they were eager to enter the war as quickly as Germany would supply them with arms and munitions. Despite the fact that these negotiations with respect to the supplying of Spain have not yet reached an end, the German Government is disposed to begin shipments of various materials immediately. The arrangements with respect to commercial conditions and reciprocal supplying by Spain to Germany will remain open for the economic negotiations, the initiation of which have just begun.

For the immediate supplying the German Government would begin with the following:

a. ARMY

1. Until May 25, 1943 there could be delivered:

The list went on for three pages offering supplies for the Army, Navy and Air Force, from bullets to bombers, but all with dates after which time they could not be supplied. The letter ended by saying that shipments could begin immediately provided that Spain's decision to enter the war occurred before the expiration dates, which varied from ten to eleven days after the date of the letter.[3]

Franco looked over his reading glasses at the members of the High Command who had been doing the negotiating. "In other words, we must eat the ice cream before it melts."

He stood up. "Keep them talking."

Reed Rosas—the name on the false passport by which Admiral Canaris first entered Spain in 1916—said, "Your Excellency will be amused to know that Herr Hitler, in an effort to have you assassinated or overthrown, has turned the project over to Schellenberg, who has been actively trying to accomplish exactly that against Herr Hitler.

"There have been two major attempts on his life within five days. Still, he remains touched by an incredible luck. He knows he is surrounded by traitors. Now conferences take place in a little hut. He will no longer shake hands with Jodl, probably his most loyal man. Nor will he dine with him or with any staff officer. He lunches and dines alone, with only his dog Blondi. And before he will eat a morsel it must first be tasted in his presence by an SS man.

"His emotional condition—constant fury, often hysteria—is a disaster for a wartime Chief of State. After accusing Admiral Raeder of inaction and the Navy of lacking the will to fight and take risks, he accepted Admiral Raeder's resignation, replacing him with Admiral Doenitz, who is excellent with U-boats but knows little of the use of surface vessels, so as a result he concentrates on the U-boat warfare and now the Navy really is inactive!

"Hitler's bad humor is infectious. Goering insults von Ribbentrop; Generals argue openly among each other . . .

"Jodl gave a secret speech in Munich to around one hundred carefully selected Party officials. He told them of our terrible defeats in Russia. In the last twelve months we have suffered 1,680,000 casualties there. They could not even be buried in the frozen ground . . . our best German boys. The draft law that exempted the youngest, or only, son of a family has now been abolished, and the age for service has been raised to fifty. Veterans of World War I are now eligible for service. Poor Germany . . . poor Fatherland.

"Your Excellency will be interested to know that among Jodl's topics was his bitterness over the inability to bring Spain into the war and thus take Gibraltar.

"I will, of course, continue to inform your Excellency as best I can. But every day I am finding it more difficult to obtain information; the Gestapo has begun a dossier on me and I intuit that I am being kept away from sensitive information until they finally discover something or do not discover something. Many of us are suspected of being traitors, but I . . ." he raised his eyes slightly, ". . . am not exactly clean." His face showed the sincerity of a child. "I have neither fear nor regret. There is nothing I have done that I would not do again. I simply hope that I have been more careful than Himmler is clever." He made a speculative face. "I have been very careful . . . but Himmler is very clever. And ambitious. Being the chief of the SS and the Gestapo is not enough. He wants the *Abwehr* as well."

Admiral Canaris opened his silver cigarette case and began re-applying the goatee, mustache, wig and tinted glasses of Reed Rosas. "I am tired of war. Tired, finally, even of espionage. How nice it will be when one day the killing is over. I look forward to retiring in the south of Spain and growing something. I have entered here as a 'tourist' hundreds of times in these twenty-odd years. What a pleasure it will be to really be a tourist."

It was the first Franco knew of Canaris' plan to retire to Spain.

Bidding farewell to the Chief of the Spanish State, he said, "I think it cannot be much longer now . . . hold on, Excellency . . . hold on . . ."

"And you. The days pass slowly but the months fly by."

When the door had closed behind him *El Caudillo* thought, *Y que vaya con Dios*.

CHAPTER TWENTY-TWO

ADMIRAL DOENITZ MET WITH HITLER AGAIN ON MAY 14TH. "*FÜHRER*, THE ATTACK ON SPAIN IS VITAL TO EASE THE STRANGLEHOLD ON OUR U-BOAT OPERATIONS IN THE BAY OF BISCAY . . ."

Hitler raised a hand. Respecting this man, understanding that he had not been present at the conferences with Raeder and Jodl, he explained, "Doenitz, the occupation of Spain is not exactly a new idea. It has been studied thoroughly and without the consent of the Spaniards it is out of the question."

"My *Führer*, we are talking about the weakest nation in Europe."

"Weak? No. They are without food and supplies, but they are not without courage. Even their women! The Spaniards are the only tough Latin people and they would carry on guerrilla warfare until the last Spaniard or German was dead."

"But if their leader made a treaty with us . . . and surely little Franco will capitulate to your orders, *Führer*."

"'Little Franco'? 'Little Franco'?" Hitler's voice was nostalgic. "In 1940 . . . perhaps then it might have been possible to have forced him to accept German military presence in Spain. But he would not let us into Spain then, when we were invincible. Why should he do it today?

"No, my dear Doenitz, forget about Spain and Gibraltar. And as for 'Little Franco' . . . he is a brave spirit who has a talent for making himself easy to underestimate. The *Duce* did it in '38 during the Spanish Civil War when he told Ciano, 'I prophesy the defeat of Franco.' And I did it at Hendaye . . . in fact until almost this very day. Yes, Doenitz, the *Caudillo* makes himself very easy to underestimate . . ."

CHAPTER TWENTY-THREE

June 20, 1943

THE TWO *GUARDIAS CIVILES* AT THE CUSTOMS BARRIER AT IRÚN
STOOD AT THEIR POSTS, LOOKING INTO FRANCE AT THE GERMAN
TANKS AND TRUCKS AND HALF-TRACKS, AT THE FIELD ARTILLERY AND
the thousands of tents that housed the hundreds of thousands of men of
the *Wehrmacht*. They stared at them as they had stared at them in never-
lessening terror for one week short of three years.

Then they heard the sound of engines starting up, in a low and distant roar. They saw a heavy cloud of dust rising and heard the roar deep-
ening as more and more engines awakened. Then, through binoculars
they could see the vehicles moving, turning . . . away from Spain.

Still watching, to be absolutely sure before they could report what it
seemed certain was happening, they saw tents being dismantled, hundreds of rows, what had been a city of tents that were being folded.

They listened to the sound of the engines increasing, they stared at
the cloud of dust that now was vast. They called their Sergeant and the
three soldiers watched. The black mass that had hovered over Spain was
moving away. "*Se están marchando.* They are leaving."

The Sergeant wanted to run, to toss his hat in the air, to shout, laugh,
jump with joy. But he was a Sergeant in the Spanish Army and so he
walked to his office, where he telephoned his superior. "*Mi Capitán, las
tropas Alemanes, se están marchando,* the German troops are leaving."

The Captain hurried to the frontier to see it with his own eyes. Then
he too contained his desire to run.

271

"Mi General," he told the garrison commander, "se están marchando . . . se están marchando. . ."

The people of Irún and San Sebastian had come to the border. They stood in silence watching the miracle.

The church bells of Irún and San Sebastian began ringing, calling the people to Mass, and there was not enough space within the churches to contain all those who came to give thanks; the word spread to Bilbao, Pamplona, Vitoria, soon all across Spain, and all day and into the night the bells tolled on.

El Caudillo entered the library, ready for lunch. His wife and daughter and two aides were awaiting him. In the dining room he spoke to his wife, but for all to hear, "They are leaving, Carmen, the German troops are leaving . . ."

One of the aides, a Lt. Colonel who for three years had been privy to the pressures from the Axis and the Allies, wanted to congratulate El Caudillo. That was impossible. At least raise a glass of wine. Also impossible. He inclined his head most formally, and said, "¡Mi General!"

Franco acknowledged with a hint of a nod.

Carmen Polo was looking at Carmencita, longing to say, "Do you understand what Papá has done for Spain and all Spaniards who will not see this war? Your father stopped Hitler. He had no guns, he had no matériel, he had no food . . . but God gave him courage and such love for his country . . ."

But she knew that her husband would not want that. Well . . . he would not really mind it, if she could accomplish it discreetly. Certainly not with him present. Carmen Polo looked forward to when she could take Carmencita aside and explain, "Your father has saved Spain."

Returning to work at five P.M. upon entering his office Franco noticed the photographs of Hitler and Mussolini. Though he had seen them there nearly every day for years he had hardly discerned them after a while. He knew that they were irritating to the British and American Ambassadors. He stood before his desk looking at them, considering removing them. He decided, not yet . . . not quite yet.

The End

Note

On July 23, 1944, Gestapo investigators found, in the ruins of a bombed house, diaries that implicated Admiral Canaris and other important officers in a nearly successful bomb attack on Hitler's life.

Canaris was arrested, interrogated for eight months and two weeks, then on April 9, 1945, he was executed by hanging, with piano wire.

General Franco contacted the Admiral's widow in Bavaria and invited her to live in Spain as a guest of the Spanish State for the rest of her life.

APPENDIX I

PEOPLE WE HAVE INTERVIEWED

*   Interview was tape-recorded
\#   Subject has requested anonymity—now working
for the present Government.

Carmen Polo: widow of General Franco *

Carmen Franco Polo, Duchess of Franco and Marquesa de Villaverde: daughter
and only child of General Franco, owner of all of his papers and possessions *

Dr. Cristóbal Martínez-Bordiu, Duke of Franco (consort), and Marqués de
Villaverde: son-in-law of General Franco *

Francisco Franco Martínez-Bordiu: eldest grandson of General Franco, named
after him with permission of his father and by act of Parliament *

Ramón Serrano Suñer: former Minister of the Interior, Chief of the Falange,
former Minister of Foreign Affairs during the time in which this book takes
place. He is the only surviving participant (there were four) of the Hitler-
Franco meeting at Hendaye. He is Franco's brother-in-law but was fired by
Franco as Foreign Minister, which caused a permanent breach in the family *

Isabel Polo: sister of Carmen Polo and sister-in-law of General Franco *

Pilar Franco: sister of General Franco *

General Fernando Fuertes Villavivencio: Chief of the *Casa Civil*

Colonel Don Eusebio Torres: was chief of security at Franco's Palace of El
Pardo. Presently chief of security at Spanish National Radio and Television

Derek Couvel: Information Officer, British Embassy in Madrid.

Felipe Propper: son of the Spanish Minister-Counselor in Vichy, Eduardo
Propper y Callejón, whom Franco ordered to issue Spanish passports to all
Jews fleeing the Nazis.

Count and Countess of Romanones. He is the grandson of the three-times Prime Minister Romanones (under King Alfonso XIII). She is American, OSS agent who worked in Spain in the forties *

Marqués de Santa Cruz: Minister-Counselor under the Duke of Alba in London during World War II and later succeeded Alba as Ambassador to London. He is the only surviving member of the Embassy in the war days of luncheons and meetings with Churchill and principal British Cabinet members.

Barón de las Torres: Chief of Protocol, Interpreter for Franco at Hendaye when Franco met Hitler.

The present Barón de las Torres: son of the above and heir to his papers *

Pedro González Bueno y Bocas: a member of Franco's first cabinet and author of the Franco government's first labor laws *

Major Steven M. Butler: Military Attaché, American Embassy, Madrid.

Nicholas Revenga: Director General Office of Information, Ministry of Foreign Affairs.

Lt. General Rafael Lopez-Saez: Captain General (commanding) of the Air Force in Madrid *

Margarita Orfila: intimate friend of Carmen Franco *

Nicolás Franco: son of Nicolás Franco, General Franco's brother and Ambassador to Lisbon during our period *

Admiral Cristóbal Gonzalez-Aller: aide to General Franco, commanded Franco yacht, later aide to Mrs. Franco *

Maruja Jurado de González-Aller: wife of the above and lifelong friend of Carmen Franco. Was intimate friend during period of our book *

Alfonso de Borbón y Dampierre, Duke of Anjou and Cádiz, member of the Spanish Royal Family, Pretender to the Throne of France: was married to General Franco's eldest granddaughter "Carmencita" *

Gonzalo de Borbon y Dampierre: brother of above *

Francisco Mata-Suarez: Chief of *Analisis Informativo,* Office of Diplomatic Information, Ministry of Foreign Affairs.

Max Borrell: intimate friend and shooting, fishing and golfing mentor of General Franco *

Countess Alexandra von Bismarck: ex-wife of great-grandson of the Iron Chancellor.

Luis Ballesteros: Chief of Radio and Television, Ministry of Culture.

Anne Williams Domecq: daughter of Mr. Guy Williams, who was British Vice-Counsel at Cádiz at the time of the North African landings.

Lt. Colonel Juan Castillejo, Duke of Montealegre: commanded the Moorish Guard for General Franco *

Lt. Colonel José L. Carasco and Lt. Colonel Luis Bermúdez de Castro: Chiefs of Communication and External Security at Franco's Palace of El Pardo *

Maria Dolores Bermúdez de Castro, Duchess of Montealegre: intimate lifelong friend of Carmen Franco, and whose mother was intimate of Mrs. Franco *

José Solís Ruíz: was Minister Secretary of the National Movement, Chief of the Falange and Head of the National Syndicates (trade unions) *

Federico Silva Muñoz: Minister of Public Works under Franco. In the new democracy, Member of Parliament and active politician *

Duke and Duchess of Tarancón: intimate friends of Carmen Franco and were present in Madrid during time of our book *

Dr. Martin A. Cohen: Professor of History at Hebrew Union College, N.Y. Specializing in Spanish, Sephardic and Portugese Studies. Past President of American Society of Sephardic Studies; Chairman of Committee for National Jewish-Catholic Relations, B'nai Brith.

Mort Yarmon: Secretary American Jewish Committee, New York. We did not interview Mr. Yarmon but received research help from him.

Max Mazin: President Hebrew Association of Spain.

Duchess of Alba: daughter of the then Ambassador to London.

Hy Wallach: Secretary, Veterans of the Abraham Lincoln Brigade, New York *

Gerry Cook: Veteran of the Abraham Lincoln Brigade, New York *

Mariano Calvino y Sabucedo: Permanent National Advisor under Franco.

Ricardo Catoira: Assistant Chief of the *Casa Civil* under Franco and presently the *Casa Real* under the King.

General Juan Castañon de Mena: Aide de Camp to Franco and Minister of War.

Olga Scheldweilk: Information, German Embassy, Madrid. No interview, just answered a few questions.

APPENDIX II

BIBLIOGRAPHY

Accounts written by personalities within our story:

Ambassador on Special Mission by Sir Samuel Hoare, Viscount Templewood, who was Prime Minister Winston Churchill's special Ambassador to Spain during our period (London 1946).

The Ciano Diaries 1939–1943, the unabridged diaries of Count Galeazzo Ciano, Mussolini's son-in-law and Foreign Minister. Ciano was present at all of Mussolini's meetings with Hitler, Franco and Ramón Serrano Suñer (New York 1946).

Crusade in Europe by Dwight D. Eisenhower, who was Commander of the African Theater and thus in command of "Torch" (Garden City 1948).

Entre Hendaya y Gibraltar (Barcelona 1973) and *Memorias* (Barcelona 1977), both by Ramón Serrano Suner, General Franco's brother-in-law and Minister of the Interior, later Minister of Foreign Affairs, both during the period of our book.

España Tenía Razon (*Spain Was Right*) by José Maria Doussinague, who was Permanent Director General of the Spanish Foreign Ministry (Madrid 1949).

The Hinge of Fate by Winston Churchill (Boston 1950).

Report from Spain by Emmet John Hughes (New York 1947) The noted *Time* magazine correspondent was Press Attaché at the American Embassy during our period.

The United States and Spain (New York 1951) and *Wartime Mission In Spain* (New York 1945) both by Carlton J. H. Hayes, Professor of History Columbia University and President Roosevelt's special Ambassador to Spain just prior to and during the Allied invasion of North Africa, "Operation Torch."

BIOGRAPHIES OF GENERAL FRANCO

Centinela del Occidente (*Sentinel of the Occident*) by Luis de Galinsoga in collaboration with General Franco's first cousin and aide, General Franco Salgado (Barcelona 1956).

Francisco Franco by Joaquin Arraras (Milwaukee 1938).

Francisco Franco, Escritor Militar (*Writer Soldier*) by the Spanish Government (Madrid 1976).

Franco by Brian Crozier (New York 1967).

Franco by J. W. D. Trythall (London 1970).

Franco, Soldado y Estadista (*Soldier and Statesman*) by Claude Martin (Madrid 1965).

Franco, The Biography of an Enigma by Alan Lloyd (New York 1969).

Franco, The Man and His Nation by George Hills (New York 1969).

Time magazine cover stories on Franco: August 24, 1936, September 6, 1937, March 27, 1939, October 18, 1943, March 18, 1946, January 21, 1966, December 11, 1972, October 13, 1975.

ON GERMAN-SPANISH RELATIONS

Canaris, La Guerra Española y La Guerra Mundial II (*The Spanish War and World War II*) by Andre Brissaud (Barcelona 1973).

Canaris, Patriot Im Zwielicht by Heinz Hohne (Munich 1976).

The Civil War in Spain by Robert Payne (New York 1970).

Documents on German Foreign Policy Series E Volumes III, IX, X, XI, XII, XIII. Translated into English and published after WW II by the British and American governments, using all the Foreign Ministry's documents captured by the Allies when they took Berlin.

España y Los Judíos En La Segunda Guerra Mundial (*Spain and the Jews in the Second World War*) by Federico Ysart (Barcelona 1973).

Historia del Franquismo (*History of Francoism*) by Ricardo de la Cierva (Barcelona 1975).

La Cara Humana de un Caudillo (*The Human Side of a Leader, 401 Anecdotes*) by Rogelio Baon (Madrid 1975–1976).

Palabras del Caudillo (*Words of the Leader*) (Madrid 1943).

Politics and the Military in Modern Spain by Stanley G. Payne (Stanford 1961).

Raza (*Race*) by Francisco Franco under the pen name Jaime de Andrade (Madrid 1942).

Spain, the Gentle Anarchy by Benjamin Welles (New York 1965).

The Spanish Labyrinth by Gerald Brennan (New York 1943).

The Spanish Revolution by Stanley G. Payne (New York 1970).

OF GENERAL VALUE:

The Abraham Lincoln Brigade by Arthur H. Landis (New York 1968).

Action This Day by Archbishop Spellman (New York 1943).

Adolf Hitler by John Toland, two volumes. (New York 1976).

And I Remember Spain, an anthology edited by Murray A. Sperber (New York 1974).

Appeasement's Child by Thomas J. Hamilton (New York 1943).

Counterfeit Spy by Sefton Delmar (New York 1971).

FDR: The Other Side of the Coin by Hamilton Fish (New York 1976).

Forging of a Rebel by Arturo Barera (New York 1946).

Franco Means Business by Georges Rotvand (New York, not dated).

The Grand Camouflage: The Communist Conspiracy in the Spanish Civil War by Bernard Bollotin (London 1961).

Guernica by Gordon Thomas and Max Morgan Witts (New York 1975).

Half of Spain Died by Herbert L. Mathews (New York 1973).

Heroes and Beasts of Spain by Manuel Chaves Nogales, in novel form (New York 1937).

In Franco's Spain by Francis McCullagh (London 1937).

International Solidarity with the Spanish Republic 1936–1939 (Moscow 1975).

The Masquerade in Spain by Charles Foltz, Jr. (Boston 1948).

Men in Battle by Alvah Bessie (New York 1939).

Mis Conversaciones Privados Con Franco (*My Private Conversations with Franco*) by Lieutenant General Francisco Salgado-Araujo (Barcelona 1976).

Modern Spain by C.A.M. Hennessy (London 1965).

My Mission to Spain by Claude G. Bowers (New York 1945) Bowers was U.S. Ambassador to Madrid 1933–1939.

My Truth by Edda Mussolini Ciano (New York 1977).

OSS by R. Harris Smith (California and London 1972).

Pensamiento Politico de Franco (*Franco's Political Thinking*) (Madrid 1975).

Red Terror in Madrid by Luis de Fonteriz (London 1937).

Rise and Fall of the Third Reich by William Shirer (New York 1960).

Rock of Contention: A History of Gibraltar by George Hills (London 1974).

Spain 1809–1939 by Raymond Carr (Oxford 1966).

Spain Resurgent by Sir Robert Hodgson (London 1953).

Spain: The Unfinished Revolution by Arthur H. Landis (New York 1972).

Spain: The Vital Years by Luis Bolin (Philadelphia 1967).

Spain's Ordeal by Robert Sencourt (London 1938).

The Spanish Civil War by Hugh Thomas (London 1961).

The Spanish Red Book on Gibraltar (Madrid 1965).

They Shall Not Pass: The Autobiography of La Passionaria" (original title in Spanish: *No Pasarón*) by Dolores Ibarruri. This autobiography by the former President of the Communist Party in Spain was written in Moscow, where she went into exile following the Spanish Civil War and remained until Franco's death in 1975 (International Publishers USA 1966).

Three Faces of Fascism by Ernest Nolte (New York 1969); in paperback, Mentor (NAL).

Yours Is the Earth by Margaret Vail (Philadelphia 1944).

APPENDIX III

SOURCES

PROLOGUE

1. Hills p. 374 (Schmidt, Toland 735)
2. Toland p. 730
   Documents XI 93–98
3. Toland p. 738
4. Toland p. 731
5. de la Cierva p. 184
   Brissaud: Canaris
6. Hoare p. 18
7. Hoare p. 15, 16
8. Hoare p. 121

CHAPTER ONE

1. Duchess of Franco, Carmen Franco, daughter. In interview.
   Also, Lt. Col. Juan Castillejo, Duke of Monteallegre, Commander of the
   Escolto Moro, Franco's Moorish Guards
2. Whiting *Canaris*
   Heinze Hohne *Canaris*
3. Duchess of Franco
4. Lt. Col. Juan Castillejo
5. Duchess of Franco
6. Ibid.
7. Ibid.
8. Ibid.
9. Ibid.
10. Ibid.

11. Ibid.
12. Ibid.
13. *Marqués de Villaverde*, Franco's son-in-law
14. Whiting
15. Duchess of Franco
16. Hoare
17. Hoare p. 18
18. Hoare p. 19 for message cable form: Mr. Derek Couvel, Info. Officer, British Embassy, Madrid
19. Hoare p. 19
20. Hoare p. 26
21. Hoare p. 27
22. Hoare p. 31
23. "The Voice of Winston Churchill," a recording
24. Hoare p. 19
25. Duchess of Franco
26. Former Minister of *Organización y Acción Sindical* (labor) Excmo.
    Sr. D. Pedro González Bueno
    Also: Former Minister of *Secretaria General de Movimiento*, Excmo.
    Sr. D. José Solís Ruíz
    Also: Former Minister of *Obras Publicas*, Public Works, Excmo.
    Sr. D. Federico Silva Muñoz, all in tape-recorded interviews.
27. Francisco Franco Martínez Bordiu, Franco's eldest grandson, so named by an act of Parliament with permission of his father, *Marqués de Villaverde*, D. Cristobal Martínez Bordiu.
28. Former Minister Solís Ruíz
29. Franco speech
30. Duchess of Franco
31. Ibid.
32. Ibid.
33. Ibid.
34. Ibid.
35. Ibid.
36. Ibid.
37. Ibid.
38. Ibid.
39. Ibid.
40. Hoare p. 19 for content of message
    cable form: Derek Couvel
41. Hoare p. 19

42. Hoare p. 21
43. Hoare p. 21
44. Hoare p. 22
45. Countess of Romanones, presently *Viuda Condesa de Romanones*
46. Descriptions of Spain in these pages have been put into dialogue by the authors. The details come from conversations with the Duchess of Franco, Count and Countess of Romanones, Duke and Duchess of Tarancon, *Marqués de Santa Cruz*, the Duchess of Alba and an article in *Town & Country Magazine*, "The Spanish Nobility", November 1976 by Selwa Roosevelt.
47. Hoare p. 22
48. Hoare p. 31
49. Documents on German Foreign Policy Series E, Volume IX
   UN papers
50. Hoare p. 24
51. Hoare p. 22
52. Hoare p. 22
53. Hoare p. 44
54. Hoare p. 54, 103.
   Brian Crozier Franco, p. 424, 425
   Hamilton, p. 239–242
   Hughes, p. 119
   Conversations: Duchess of Franco, Countess of Romanones
55. Hoare p. 54
56. Hoare p. 30
57. Hoare p. 40
58. Hoare p. 50, 51
59. Hoare p. 51
60. Hoare p. 55
61. Hoare p. 50
62. Hoare p. 50
63. Ricardo de la Cierva Historia del Franquismo, p. 234
64. Hoare p. 66
   Crozier p. 317

CHAPTER TWO

1. Hoare p. 25
2. Description of Moor Escort is from the man who commanded it, Lt. Col. Juan Castillejo.
3. Barón de las Torres

4. Material in this scene is from the present Barón de las Torres, son of the then Barón. Description of the Palace is authors' observations.

   Contrary to Sir Samuel Hoare's statement that the reception took place in the Throne Room (Hoare p. 25) the official records put it in the ante-Throne Room.

5. Hoare p. 45
6. Hoare p. 25
7. Hoare p. 15
8. Hoare p. 25
9. Described by Lt. Col. Castillejo
10. de la Cierva, p. 172
11. Carmen Polo, widow of Franco, in recorded interview. This quote also appears in de la Cierva, p. 172 and *Wartime Mission in Spain,* by then-U.S. Ambassador to Spain Carlton J. H. Hayes. The rest of this conversation is from Carmen Polo excepting the precise Churchill quote, which she remembered only sketchily and which we were able therefore to trace. It appears on "The Voice of Churchill." The Duchess of Franco was present during this and all interviews with her mother, Carmen Polo.
12. Hills, p. 342
13. From an interview in *Le Figaro,* Paris, June 12, 1958, quoted in *Franco* by J. W. D. Trythall, p. 165
14. Duchess of Franco
15. Trythall, p. 162
16. Claude Martin, p. 368, from interview in *Arriba,* Feb. 25, 1951
17. Carmen Polo

CHAPTER THREE

1. Hayes, pp. 112, 113
   Carmen Polo and sister Isabel Polo in taped interview.
   Felipe Proper, son of then-Consul General in France
2. Carmen Polo
3. Shirer, p. 743
4. Hoare, p. 61
5. Hoare p. 47
6. Duchess of Franco
7. Ibid.
8. Hoare, p. 48
9. Hoare, p. 49
10. Duchess of Franco
    Appears in numerous Franco books.

11. Hoare, p. 48
12. Lloyd, p. 172
13. Hoare p.157

CHAPTER FOUR

1. Hoare, p. 38
2. Doc. Vol. X, p. 291
3. Carmen Polo

CHAPTER FIVE

1. Doc. Vol X, p. 396
2. Hamilton
3. Doc. Vol X, p. 443
4. Doc. Vol X, p. 542

CHAPTER SIX

1. Document in hand from Franco's personal papers, translated into English by authors.
2. Doc. Vol XI, p. 38
3. Doc. Vol XI, p. 81

CHAPTER SEVEN

1. Doc. Vol XI, p. 83
2. Doc. Vol XI. p. 89
3. Doc. Vol XI, p. 100
4. Doc. Vol XI, p. 90
5. Doc. Vol X, p. 98
6. Doc. Vol XI, p. 91
7. Doc. Vol XI, p. 84
8. *Memorias*, Serrano Suñer
9. Serrano Suñer, interview with authors
10. Serrano Suñer, interview with authors
11. Felipe Propper, in conversation with authors. This is also mentioned in Hayes, p. 123, as occurring in 1943.
12. Doc. Vol XI, p.106
13. Doc. Vol XI, p.153

CHAPTER EIGHT

1. Serrano Suñer, interview with authors
2. de la Cierva, *La Historia del Franquismo*

CHAPTER NINE

1. A document given us from the archives of Franco's *Casa Civil*.
2. Bolín, *The Vital Years*, p. 90
3. Carmen Polo
4. Daughter of Lola Collantes de Bermudez de Castro: Maria Dolores Bermudez de Castro, Duchess of Montealegre, interview
5. Maruja Jurado de González Aller, interview
   Duchess of Franco
6. Serrano Suñer, interview
7. Duchess of Franco
8. Toland, p. 731
9. Serrano Suñer, interview
10. Doc. Vol. XI, p. 372
11. Toland, p. 730

CHAPTER TEN

1. Toland, p. 730
2. Toland, p. 734
   Doc. Vol. XI, p. 414
3. Toland, p. 738
   Doc. Vol. XI, p. 213, 250
4. Toland, 731
5. Toland, 734
6. Toland, 734
7. Doc. Vol. XII, p.767
8. Toland.p.
9. Doc. Vol. XII, p. 765
10. Serrano Suñer, interview
11. Document written by Barón de Las Torres
12. *Memorias* by Serrano Suñer
13. Trythall, p. 341
14. Carmen Polo

CHAPTER ELEVEN

1. Doc. Vol. XI, p. 514
2. Doc. Vol. XI, p. 575

CHAPTER TWELVE

1. This interview is based largely on German Doc. Vol. XI, doc. no. 352, pages 598 through 606, which is notes taken of the meeting. Also, Serrano Suñer in interview.
   Doc. Vol. XI, p. 599
3. Serrano Suñer interview
4. Doc. Vol. XI, p. 599
5. Doc. Vol. XI, p. 600
6. Doc. Vol. XI, p. 601
7. Doc. Vol. XI, p. 604
8. Doc. Vol. XI, p. 602

CHAPTER THIRTEEN

1. Doc. Vol. XI, p. 725
2. Doc. Vol. XI, p. 739
3. Canaris
4. Doc. Vol. XI, p. 782
5. Doc. Vol. XI, p. 788
6. *Canaris*, by Whiting
7. Carmen Polo
8. Doc. Vol. XI, p. 814
9. Doc. Vol. XI, p. 817

CHAPTER FOURTEEN

1. Crozier, p. 232
2. Marqués de Santa Cruz, interview
3. Crozier, p. 332
4. Marqués de Santa Cruz, interview
5. Ibid.
6. Doc. Vol. XI, p. 991
7. Toland
8. Doc. Vol. XI, p. 1130
9. Ciano's Diaries
10. Ibid.
11. Doc. Vol. XI, p. 1158
12. Doc. Vol. XI, p. 1171

13. Doc. Vol. XI, p. 1175
14. Doc. Vol. XI, p. 1184
15. Doc. Vol. XI, p. 1217
16. Doc. Vol. XI, p. 1223
17. Doc. Vol. XII, p. 37

CHAPTER FIFTEEN

1. Doc. Vol. XII, p.131
2. Doc. Vol. XII, p.190
3. Doc. Vol. XII, p.176
4. Doc. Vol. XII, p.665
5. *Wartime Mission in Spain*, Hayes, p.176
6. *Ambassador on Special Mission*, Sir Samuel Hoare, p.113
7. Marqués de Santa Cruz, interview
8. Ibid.
9. Document from Franco files in possession of authors, who made the translation from Spanish.

CHAPTER SIXTEEN

1. Marqués de Santa Cruz, interview
2. Ibid.
3. Ibid.
4. *The Spanish Civil War* by Hugh Thomas

CHAPTER SEVENTEEN

1. *Wartime Mission in Spain*, Hayes, p. 11
2. Ibid, p. 30
3. Ibid, p. 30, 31
4. Ibid, p. 31
5. Ibid, p. 134
6. Ibid, p. 166
7. Ibid, p. 35, 36
8. Ibid, p. 54
9. Ibid, p. 54

CHAPTER EIGHTEEN

1. *Hinge of Fate*, Churchill, p. 529
2. *Crusade in Europe*, Eisenhower, p. 90
3. *Hinge of Fate*, Churchill
4. Hoare, p. 173

5. Countess of Romanones
6. *Wartime Mission in Spain*, Hayes, p. 73
7. Ibid, p. 87
8. Ibid, p. 137, 137, also 257 and 258 for further example of Government-in-Exile propaganda.
9. *Wartime Mission in Spain*, Hayes, p. 247
10. Countess of Romanones
11 Details of car from the archives of the *Casa Civil*

CHAPTER NINETEEN

1. *Crusade in Europe*, Eisenhower, p. 97
2. Ibid, p. 95, 96
3. Ibid, p. 96
4. Ibid, p. 96

CHAPTER TWENTY

1. *Wartime Mission in Spain*, Hayes, p. 89
2. Ibid, p. 89
3. Carmen Polo
4. *Wartime Mission in Spain*, Hayes, p. 90
5. *Wartime Mission in Spain*, Hayes, p. 90
6. Ibid, p. 91
7. Ibid, p. 92

CHAPTER TWENTY-ONE

1. *Wartime Mission in Spain*, Hayes, p. 93
2. Ibid, p. 96
3. Document in hand, given to the authors by Carmen Franco

APPENDIX IV

The Chancellery
Berlin   September 18, 1940

Dear *Caudillo*,

Minister of Interior Serrano Suñer has brought me your letter, and I cordially return your greetings and the friendship they express. We have entered into an exchange of ideas regarding the problems which at the moment affect not only Europe but probably the entire world. The suggested conferences as well as those which have just taken place and those still going on with your Minister Serrano Suñer prompt me, my dear *Caudillo*, to describe my thoughts to you on these problems in a few points. The opinions of my General Staff are entirely the same as those set down here.

1. The war will decide the future of Europe. There is not a country in Europe that can avoid its political and economic effects. The end of the war will also decide Spain's future, perhaps for centuries. But even today Spain is suffering, though she is still not a participant in the war. The virtual blockade imposed on Spain by England will not be loosened as long as England herself is not conquered, but will only become more severe. In the face of this, any measures for economic assistance can only be of an emergency and temporary nature. But the mere expulsion of the English from the Mediterranean will convert it into an inland sea withdrawn from English interference and again open for commerce. This alone would provide a radical solution to Spain's supply problem. And this aim can and will be attained rapidly and with certainty through Spain's entry into the war.

2. Spain's entry into the war on the side of the Axis powers must begin with the expulsion of the English fleet from Gibraltar and immediately thereafter the seizure of the fortified Rock. This operation must and can be successfully carried through within a few days, if high-grade well-tried, modern means of attack and attack troops are employed. Germany is willing to provide them under Spanish command in the quantities needed.

3. Once Gibraltar is in Spanish possession the western Mediterranean is eliminated as a base of operations for the English fleet. Aside from the threat from isolated British submarines, then possible only to a limited extent, a sure connection will have been brought about between Spain and North Africa. The Spanish Mediterranean coast itself will then no longer be endangered.

4. Aside from the blockade, which for all practical purposes has already been imposed on Spain, England will then have only the possibility of operating against the Atlantic coast of Spain. Defense of this coast by heavy batteries could only be assured—and even then only to a limited extent—if quantities were used which neither Germany nor anyone else can make available.

The best—in fact, the only—sure protection consists in placing dive-bomber units in the vicinity of the coast; these are more effective than heavy coastal batteries as experience from Narvik to the Spanish border has shown, and thus they appear to be the only suitable means for keeping enemy naval forces far from the coast in all circumstances.

In this regard, too, Germany gives assurance of support.

It would be all the more futile to install medium and heavy coastal batteries at this time since their installation would require such extensive and time-consuming preparations that:

    I. The purpose of the procedure would not remain secret but would
       certainly be betrayed, and

    II. the protective effect would occur much too late.

5. Considering the military situation of England at the present time it is out of the question for England to try a landing operation on the Spanish coast or on Portugal. Should such an attempt nevertheless be made, Germany gives assurance in this case, too, of all necessary support on land and in the air to any extent desired.

6. It is more probable, however, that after losing Gibraltar England will try instead to seize a naval base in the Canary Islands. Therefore the defensive power of the islands in the Canary group which might be considered for naval bases must be strengthened in so far as possible before the start of the battle. Either before or at the latest at the same time as the beginning of the battle it will in my opinion be necessary to transfer German dive-bombers or long-range fighters to Las Palmas. Past experience has shown that they provide the absolute certainty of keeping the British ships far away. Preparations for this should best be made before the beginning of the operation.

7. If Italy should also succeed in getting so close to Alexandria in the course of this winter that these British naval bases could be eliminated at least by means of air attack, then the entire strategic position in the Mediterranean will be lost to

the English. The Spanish Merchant Marine in the Mediterranean could then supply Spain freely in a manner quite different from present possibilities. In case of necessity, large parts of the Italian and German fleets could be united in the Atlantic. North Africa would be delivered up to seizure by Italy, Spain and Germany. The danger that a North African area detached from France might unite with British forces would thereby be definitely eliminated.

8. Germany is willing, as already stated, not only to make the necessary military means available under Spanish command for this purpose, but also to provide economic help to the greatest extent possible for Germany herself. These conversations in this regard are now being held.

These, dear *Caudillo*, are, briefly stated, the ideas concerning the decisive character of a Spanish participation in a conflict whose outcome will in any case decide the future of Spain for a long time to come.

In case Spain decides for intervention in this struggle, Germany is resolved to stand exactly as loyally and firmly by her side until a victorious and successful conclusion as we did earlier during the Spanish Civil War. It is a matter of course that this success will be brought about. At most it can only be a question of time. But Spain's entry into the fight will help to show England more emphatically the hopelessness of continuing the war and force her to give up once and for all her unjustified claims.

Please accept, my dear *Caudillo*, my most cordial regards.

In comradely affection,
Adolf Hitler

APPENDIX V

El Pardo, September 22, 1940

My dear *Führer*,

I received your letter in which you stated to me your view and those of your General Staff in connection with the problems with respect to Spain which are arising from the war, views which with the exception of small details match my thoughts and plans and those of my General Staff.

I must thank you for the cordial reception which you and your people prepared for my Envoy, Minister Serrano Suñer, who reported to me about your conversation and about your esteemed ideas, which satisfy our wishes, and with which we believe ourselves to be in complete agreement as you will see from the content of this letter. In spite of complete agreement with your words, communicated to me by my Minister, "to recognize the Spanish claims to Morocco with the one limitation of assuring Germany through favorable commercial agreements a share in the raw materials of this area" there is to be sure one point where they are inconsistent, namely in the wishes of Herr von Ribbentrop, expressed in the form of a proposal during the conversations between our Ministers for the establishment of an enclave for German bases by occupying both the harbors of the southern zone. In our view these are unnecessary in peacetime and superfluous in wartime, because in this case you could not only count upon these harbors but upon all that Spain possesses, since our friendship is to be sealed firmly for the future. The advantages which these bases could offer would counterbalance neither the difficulties which this type of enclave always produces nor the harm which they cause to those areas for which they constitute the outlet to the sea.

I thank you very much for your idea, put before Minister Serrano Suñer, of providing me with an opportunity for us to meet near the Spanish border, for, apart from my eager wish to greet you personally, we could have a more thorough and more direct exchange of ideas than our present communications make possible. Meanwhile I should like to give you my opinion about the individual points about your letter.

1. In regard to your train of thoughts set forth in point One concerning the political and economic effects of the present struggle, I can only say to you that I have agreed from the first day with the view which you have expressed here. Only our isolation and the lack of resources most indispensable for our national existence made action by us impossible.

2. I agree with you that driving the English out of the Mediterranean will improve our transport situation, although it is obvious that all Spain's problems of supply will not thereby be solved, since many products and raw materials which Spain lacks are not to be found in the Mediterranean basin.

3. I am likewise of the opinion that the first action upon our intervening, must be the occupation of Gibraltar. Since 1936 our military policy in the straits has been shaped in this sense, in that we are forestalling the English intentions of expanding and protecting their bases.

4. I agree with your view that it is possible to achieve the success of this operation within a few days by the use of modern equipment and tried troops. In this sense the equipment which you offer me will be of great effect.

5. For our part we have been preparing the operation in secret for a long time, since the area in which it is to take place has no suitable network of communications. With respect to the special conditions of the Rock, points of resistance can withstand even the strongest action from the air, so that they will have to be destroyed by good and accurate artillery. The extraordinary importance of the enterprise would, in my opinion, justify a strong concentration of resources.

6. The fall of Gibraltar would actually protect the western Mediterranean and rule out any danger, except for the temporary dangers which might arise in case de Gaulle should succeed with his plan for rebellion in Algiers and Tunis.

A concentration of our troops in Morocco will prevent this danger.

In this respect it would be useful if your control commissions increased precautionary measures to the utmost.

7. I completely share your view about the effectiveness of dive-bombers for the defense of the coast, as well as about the actual impossibility of establishing fixed artillery emplacements with heavy material on the vulnerable points on the coast. Evidently a mistake has crept into the transmittal of my wish, for my wish concerns not stationary guns of larger caliber, but mobile pieces of about

20 centimeters. I consider these to be further necessary, and indeed in rather large quantities, because of the condition of the terrain which is mountainous and irregular. The possibility of constructing airports is therefore extraordinarily limited. In most cases, these will lie far removed from the coast and from the objects to be defended. Furthermore, one must reckon with the limitations which necessarily result from the storms and rains frequently occurring there.

In any case, the strong air forces offered by you are indispensable.

8. At the present moment there is actually little probability of the English undertaking a landing attempt on the peninsula. Even if this should be the case, our own resources and those which you offer me would quickly ruin this plan.

9. The possibility of a surprise attack on the Canary Islands by the English in order to provide a naval base to protect their overseas connections has always been a worry of mine. So far as we are able to do so, we are placing there supplies of food, ammunition and the modest artillery material which we are getting from other, less threatened, regions; we have effected a partial mobilization several months ago, and also have sent arms for the entire island group. We have transferred a fighter group there which would no longer have been able to get there once the war had begun. I am of your view and consider the presence of dive-bombers and long range fighters in Las Palmas extremely useful, for which bomb material and spare parts must be sent in advance.

10. Obviously freedom of movement in the western Mediterranean is dependent upon Italian successes in Alexandria and Suez, by which the destruction of the English fleet in these waters will be made possible. At such a moment a great part of our provisioning problem would be solved.

11. I consider the offer for our undertaking contained in your point Eight as extremely useful and absolutely necessary. For the economic aid which you with such foresight offer me, to the greatest extent possible for Germany, is just as important as the military equipment. For our part, I offer you reciprocal aid of the same type and to the greatest possible extent, considering our potentialities.

In the meantime I consider it my duty to point out to you that in my opinion the conversations hitherto conducted by our specialists have largely taken the course of strictly commercially oriented negotiations. In setting out to settle old matters, and by striving to solve the economic problems and the postwar exchange of commodities they have deviated from the main subject, which affect both parties equally and which will find its complete solution in the statements of your letter, with which I completely agree.

I would like to thank you once again, dear *Führer*, for the offer of solidarity. I reply with the assurance of my unchangeable and sincere adherence to you personally, to the German people, and to the cause for which you fight. I hope, in defense of this cause, to be able to renew the old bonds of comradeship between our armies.

In the expectation of being able to express this to you personally, I assure you of my most sincere feelings of friendship and I greet you.

Yours,
Francisco Franco[13]

APPENDIX VI

SECRET PROTOCOL

Hendaye, October 23, 1940

The Italian, German and Spanish governments have agreed as follows:

1. The exchange of views between the Führer of the German Reich and the Chief of the Spanish State, following conversations between the Duce and the Führer and among the foreign ministers of the three countries in Rome and Berlin, has clarified the present position of the three countries toward each other as well as the questions implicit in waging the war and affecting general policy.

2. Spain declares her readiness to accede to the Tripartite Pact concluded September 27, 1940 among Italy, Germany and Japan and for this purpose to sign, on a date to be set by the four Powers jointly, an appropriate Protocol regarding the actual accession.

3. By the present Protocol Spain declares her accession to the Treaty of Friendship and Alliance between Italy and Germany and the related Secret Supplementary Protocol of May 22, 1939.

4. In fulfillment of her obligations as an Ally, Spain will intervene in the present war of the Axis Powers against England after they have provided her with the military support necessary for her preparedness, at a time to be set by common agreement of the three Powers, taking into account military preparations to be decided upon. Germany will grant economic aid to Spain by supplying her with food and raw materials so as to meet the needs of the Spanish people and the requirements of the war.

5. In addition to the reincorporation of Gibraltar into Spain the Axis Powers state that in principle they are ready to see to it, in accordance with a general settlement which is to be established in Africa and which must be put

into effect in the peace treaties after the defeat of England—that Spain receives territories in Africa to the same extent as France can be compensated, by assigning to the latter other territories of equal value in Africa but with German and Italian claims against France remaining unaffected.

6. The present Protocol shall be strictly secret and those present undertake to preserve its strict secrecy, unless by common agreement they decide to publish it.

APPENDIX VII

BERLIN   MADRID, NOVEMBER 29, 1940
TOP SECRET
FOR THE FOREIGN MINISTER PERSONALLY.
WITH REFERENCE TO MY TELEGRAM NO. 4074 OF NOVEMBER 28.

FOR YESTERDAY'S DISCUSSION OF FRANCO'S POSITION ON THE QUESTIONS DISCUSSED AT BERCHTESGADEN THE SPANISH FOREIGN MINISTER HAS MADE WRITTEN NOTES WHICH HE READ TO ME. THE PASSAGES BELOW WHICH ARE IN QUOTATION MARKS ARE GIVEN VERBATIM.

1) "IT IS AGREED THAT THE PREPARATIONS FOR SPAIN'S ENTRY INTO THE WAR ARE TO BE SPEEDED UP AS MUCH AS POSSIBLE."

2) "THE TIME REQUIRED FOR THIS, HOWEVER, CANNOT TODAY BE DEFINITELY DETERMINED BECAUSE IN CONNECTION WITH THE G (GIBRALTAR) ACTION THE MAN WHO ORDERS THIS MUST ALSO RECKON WITH THE POSSIBILITY OF OTHER IMPORTANT MILITARY ACTIONS WHICH HE HAS TO FACE FULLY PREPARED."

3) "FOR THIS PURPOSE FRANCO REQUESTS THE DISPATCH OF GERMAN MILITARY EXPERTS WHO WOULD GET IN TOUCH WITH THE SPANISH MINISTRIES OF THE ARMED FORCES. FRANCO WOULD BE ESPECIALLY GRATIFIED IF, IN ADDITION, AN OFFICER ENJOYING THE FUHRER'S SPECIAL CONFIDENCE, WITH WHOM IT WOULD BE POSSIBLE TO DISCUSS ALL QUESTIONS FRANKLY, WERE ATTACHED TO THEM AND SENT TO SPAIN."

FOR ECONOMIC QUESTIONS (DELIVERIES, DISTRIBUTION OF FOOD) AS WELL AS TRANSPORTATION QUESTIONS FRANCO LIKEWISE REQUESTS THAT EXPERTS BE SENT.

5) FRANCO IS OF THE OPINION THAT SIMULTANEOUS WITH THE G-ACTION ANOTHER ACTION SHOULD BE CARRIED OUT IN THE EASTERN MEDITERRANEAN FOR THE PURPOSE OF CLOSING THE SUEZ CANAL.

FURTHER CONSIDERATIONS, PARTLY IN RESPONSE TO INQUIRIES FROM ME, ALSO BROUGHT OUT THE FOLLOWING:

REGARDING 1) AND 2): SPAIN WOULD BE PREPARED EVEN NOW FOR THE BEGINNING OF THE G-ACTION; HOWEVER, THE SPANIARDS FEAR ENGLISH COUNTERACTIONS AGAINST THE GALICIAN COAST (VIGO, LA CORUNNA, ETC.) BILBAO, CADIZ, THE CANARY ISLANDS, THE POSSESSIONS IN WEST AFRICA AND TO A LESSER DEGREE AGAINST THE BALEARIC ISLANDS, WHICH COUNTERACTIONS THEY DO NOT WISH TO FACE UNPREPARED. THE SPANIARDS HAVE LITTLE FEAR OF ENGLISH ACTION AGAINST PORTUGAL, BECAUSE THE PORTUGUESE GOVERNMENT IS DETERMINED NOT TO PERMIT ANY LANDING AND WOULD IMMEDIATELY REQUEST SPANISH (AND HENCE GERMAN) AID. NICHOLAS FRANCO, THE SPANISH AMBASSADOR IN LISBON, WHO HAPPENED TO BE IN MADRID FOR A SHORT WHILE YESTERDAY, EMPHASIZED THIS VIEW OF THE FOREIGN MINISTER'S TO ME, POINTING OUT THAT PORTUGAL HAD PROMISED FULL INFORMA-TION ON ANY ENGLISH DESIGNS AGAINST PORTUGAL OR SPAIN THAT CAME TO LIGHT. PORTUGAL WILL, HOWEVER, DO EVERY-THING POSSIBLE TO REMAIN NEUTRAL TOWARD BOTH SIDES.

THE SPANIARDS FEEL THAT THEY ESPECIALLY NEED ANTIAIR-CRAFT ARTILLERY FOR DEFENSE AGAINST ENEMY AIR ATTACKS ON THE ABOVE-MENTIONED AREAS.

REGARDING 3): SINCE IT WOULD BE QUITE IMPOSSIBLE TO KEEP VISITS OF NUMEROUS GERMAN MILITARY MISSIONS SECRET, THE MINISTER REQUESTS THAT FEW AND ONLY KEY OFFICERS BE SENT. THEIR VISITS, TOO, WOULD BECOME KNOWN TO THE ENEMY BUT WOULD NOT HAVE SUCH AN ALARMING EFFECT AND WOULD GIVE ENGLAND LESS JUSTIFICATION FOR PREMATURE ECONOMIC, NOT TO SPEAK OF MILITARY, COUNTER MEASURES. THE HIGH MILITARY PERSONAGE THAT FRANCO REQUESTS BE SENT SHOULD IF POSSIBLE COME HERE UNDER AN ASSUMED NAME, WELL DISGUISED AS THE PRIVATE GUEST OF SOME GERMAN PERSONAGE.

REGARDING 4): THE QUESTION OF TIRES FOR TRUCKS IS CAUSING SPECIAL CONCERN; THOSE AVAILABLE ARE ALREADY VERY WORN AND THERE ARE NO RESERVES. FOR PERSONNEL CARRIERS REQUISITIONED TIRES OF PRIVATE CARS LAID UP FOR THE TIME BEING FOR LACK OF GASOLINE WILL SUFFICE.

REGARDING 5): THE SPANIARDS FEAR THAT THE PRESSURE FROM ENGLAND WILL BE TOO STRONG UNLESS THE ENGLISH FLEET AND OTHER MILITARY MEANS IN THE MEDITERRANEAN ARE PARTLY TIED DOWN IN THE EASTERN THEATER OF WAR.

THE FOREIGN MINISTER FINALLY CALLED ATTENTION TO THE IMMEDIATE AID REQUESTED FOR SPAIN IN THE FORM OF GRAIN MADE AVAILABLE VIA PORTUGAL AND THE FRENCH BORDER. I CONSIDER ACCOMMODATION IN THIS MATTER EXTREMELY DESIRABLE AND REQUEST AN EARLY DECISION.

STOHRER

APPENDIX VIII

The Chancellery
Berlin

February 6, 1941

Dear *Caudillo*,

If I write this letter I do so for the purpose of setting forth once more as clearly as possible the individual phases in the development of a situation which is not only of importance to Germany and Italy, but might have had a decisive significance to Spain as well.

At our meeting it was my aim to convince you, *Caudillo*, of the necessity of joint action by the states whose interests, in the final analysis, are indissolubly conjoined. For centuries Spain has suffered persecution by the same enemies whom Germany and Italy are forced to fight today. To the earlier imperial aspirations, which were hostile to our three countries, have now however, been added antagonisms of an ideological nature. Jewish international democracy, which rules in these states, will not forgive any one of us for having adopted a course which tries to secure the future of our nations in accordance with national postulates rather than principles entailing a commitment to capitalism. As to Germany's determination to see this fight through to the very end, I need not waste a single word. Nor is the *Duce* of a different mind. The Japanese people, too, will be unable in the long run to avoid this conflict, save by way of a surrender that would sacrifice the future of the Japanese people. I am convinced that the same fate now confronts Spain, too. If you, *Caudillo*, were successful in your struggle against the elements of destruction in Spain, then it was only for the reason that the attitude of Germany and Italy forced your Democratic opponents to move with caution. But never, *Caudillo*, will you be forgiven that victory.

Nor has England the intention, once she again has the power to do something about it, to permit you to remain permanently established in North

Africa, opposite Gibraltar. Spain's seizure of the Tangier Zone—that, *Caudillo*, is my firm conviction—will in that event have been only a transitory episode. England, and probably America as well, will do everything to make their control of that entrance to the Mediterranean in the future if anything more secure than in the past. It is therefore my most sacred conviction that the war which Germany and Italy are fighting today will decide Spain's future destiny as well. Only in the event of our victory will Spain's present regime survive. If Germany and Italy were to lose the war, however, there would be no future whatever for a truly national and independent Spain.

For that reason I have made an effort to convince you, *Caudillo*, of the necessity of joining forces, in the interest of your own country and the future of the Spanish people, with those states which earlier sent soldiers to help you and which today, too, are of necessity fighting not only for their own existence but indirectly also for the national future of Spain.

At our meeting we reached an agreement that Spain would proclaim her willingness to sign the Tripartite Pact and enter the war. In setting the date, we never contemplated, far less mentioned, periods in the remote future, but always spoke only in terms of a very brief period during which you, *Caudillo*, believed you would be able to carry through various economic measures for the benefit of your country.

I personally have been skeptical from the outset about the hope that it would still be possible for Spain to obtain substantial economic advantages in the immediate future:

1. England has no intention whatsoever of giving Spain any real help; England's only endeavor is to postpone Spain's entry into the war and to put her off in order thereby continually to increase the distress in the country in this way and thus be able to overthrow the present Spanish regime.

2. Even if England should want to think differently, however, in a fit of sentimentality (which would be unprecedented in British history) she could not really help Spain in any circumstances. With respect to shipping alone she is in no position at all to help any other country at a time when she herself has been forced to submit to the most stringent restrictions in her standard of living. And the shortage in shipping space will not become less but rather more difficult as the months go by.

Although, as I said before, I was absolutely skeptical about this from the beginning, I had full understanding for your efforts of at least trying to have food shipped to Spain from overseas countries before entering the war.

Germany, on the other hand, has stated her willingness to supply, among other things, food grain—on the greatest possible scale as soon as the date for Spain's entry was fixed. Germany, furthermore, declared that she is prepared to replace the 100,000 tons of grain which are lying in Portugal destined for Switzerland, so that these could at once be used for the benefit of Spain. All this, of course was predicated on the condition that Spain's entry into the war was definitely settled. For there is one thing, *Caudillo*, that must be clearly understood: We are engaged in a battle for life and death and cannot hand out gifts at a time like this. Therefore, the latter assertion that Spain was unable to enter the war because she received no advance deliveries is untrue! For immediately upon setting the date of entry into the war, a date, moreover, that would not yet have been apparent to the outside world, Spain would have received her first advance delivery, namely 100,000 tons of grain. I doubt that it would have been possible within that time to ship 100,000 tons of grain to Spain from abroad, even if there had been the will to do so. I doubt, therefore, that this actually happened. The assertion, however, that if our grain had been delivered immediately that fact could have been used in the propaganda to prepare the Spanish people for the entry into the war, is refuted for another reason.

You yourself, *Caudillo*, personally emphasized to me the importance of not making public the accession to the Tripartite Pact because you were afraid that this might have hampered or even frustrated your other efforts, for instance, to obtain more grain. How much less would it then have been possible, therefore, to make open propaganda for entering the war. No, I must state once more that:

1. It was never considered in our conversations that Spain would not enter the war until perhaps next autumn or winter, and

2. Germany was prepared to make advance deliveries to the Spanish Government the moment the definite date for entering the war was set.

When, prompted by the necessity of relieving our Italian ally, I asked you, *Caudillo*, to set the date for the middle or perhaps the end of January—that is, to permit the German concentration of forces against Gibraltar to start by January 10th so that the attack could be launched by the end of January—only then, for the first time, were our negotiators told plainly that such an early date was entirely out of the question; the reasons given were again economic considerations. Thereupon, when I had it pointed out once more that Germany was willing to begin deliveries of grain immediately, Admiral Canaris was finally told that these grain shipments were not the decisive issue at all, for they would have no practical effect whatever if they were delivered by rail. Since we had in the meantime readied batteries for the Canary Islands and intended to use dive-bombers for additional protection, we were further told that this was not decisive either, because from the standpoint of food the Canary Islands could not be held longer than six months.

That it was not at all a question of economic factors, but of those of a different nature, is evident from the last statement informing us that for climatic reasons a concentration of forces could not succeed at this season of the year and would therefore have to be envisaged for the autumn or winter at the earliest.

In these circumstances I fail to understand, to be sure, why one should first have wanted to declare an operation impossible on economic grounds that is now supposedly impossible simply for climatic reasons. I really do not believe that a climate, to which we are not actually unaccustomed, could have interfered with the concentration of the German Army in January. In the Norwegian campaign, at any rate, we successfully achieved our task in quite different circumstances and under difficult climatic conditions in snow and ice, quite apart from the fact that as a result of the participation of German soldiers and officers in your campaign, *Caudillo*, the climatic conditions of Spain are indeed not unfamiliar to us.

I must deeply regret your view and attitude, *Caudillo!* For this reason:

1. I feel duty bound to afford relief to my Italian friend and ally and thus to help him at a moment when he has suffered an unfortunate mishap. The attack on Gibraltar and the closing of the Strait would at one stroke have changed the entire Mediterranean situation.

2. It is my conviction that time is one of the most important factors in war. Months lost can often not be regained!

3. Finally, it is obvious that if our advance units had been allowed to cross the Spanish frontier on January 10th, Gibraltar would be in our hands by now. This means that two months have been lost which otherwise might have helped decide world history.

4. It is my further conviction that the economic situation of Spain would have improved and not deteriorated as a result of what Spain would have received from us in any case; conversely the shipments that have in the mean-while actually arrived from overseas can only be a fraction of what would immediately have been delivered by us in any event.

But leaving all this aside, *Caudillo*, I would now like to make the following comment:

Spain's entry into the war, after all, was not considered exclusively in order to better the interests of Germany and Italy. Spain herself has put forward large territorial demands and the *Duce* and I have expressed our willingness to fill them to any extent compatible with the reorganization of African colonial possessions that would be acceptable to Europe and its states. And I may point out in this connection that the most tremendous sacrifice of life in this war has up to this point been borne first by German and, after her, by Italy, and that both have nevertheless raised only very modest demands. In any case, the date of military operations can be proposed in the main only by the one who will bear the largest burden in the battle and who therefore must include them in the calculations of his total plan for a military conflict which is, after all, on a worldwide scale. That I, myself, have no other goal in mind than our common success is certainly understandable. Yes, it is my urgency in this instance, *Caudillo*, which proves the depth of my sense of responsibility also to my allies. For whatever difficulties should arise in the course of this war, it will be my unshakable will to bring aid and I am determined to repair in the final settlement that which at one stage of the war or another may temporarily miscarry. That also applies to Spain. Spain will never have other friends than those represented by present-day Germany and Italy, unless, of course, a different Spain should come about. Such a different Spain, however, would be but a Spain of decay and ultimate collapse. For this reason alone I believe, *Caudillo*, that we three men, the *Duce*, you, and I, are linked to one another by the most implacable force of history, and that we should therefore, in this historic conflict, obey the supreme commandment to realize that in grave times such as these nations can be saved by stout hearts rather than by seemingly prudent caution.

For the rest, *Caudillo*, this war has already been decided—no matter what transitory success the British may believe they can achieve somewhere along the periphery. For regardless of this, the fact remains that England's power in Europe has been broken and that the world's most tremendous military machine stands ready to fulfill any task with which it should be confronted. And the future will show how good and reliable that instrument is!

Adolf Hitler

APPENDIX IX

MADRID   FUSCHL, FEBRUARY 22, 1941 9:10PM
RECEIVED BERLIN FEBRUARY 22 11:15PM
NO.430 OF FEBRUARY 22
FROM THE FOREIGN MINISTRY SENT FEBRUARY 22 11:55PM
SECRET FOR OFFICER IN CHARGE

IT IS UNEQUIVOCALLY CLEAR THAT SPAIN IS NOT READY TO
ENTER THE WAR ON OUR SIDE. THIS IS CONFIRMED FOR US ONCE
AGAIN BY THE CONTENT OF THE INFORMATION GIVEN TO US BY
THE ITALIANS CONCERNING THE COURSE OF THE TALK THAT
MUSSOLINI HAD WITH FRANCO AND SUNER IN BORDIGHERA. AT
THIS TIME THE SPANISH GOVERNMENT TOOK THE POSITION, AS
I AM POINTING OUT FOR YOUR EXCLUSIVE, PERSONAL AND
STRICTLY CONFIDENTIAL INFORMATION, THAT SPAIN COULD
ENTER THE WAR ONLY IF

1. THE QUESTION OF GRAIN WAS RESOLVED BEFOREHAND, IN
WHICH CONNECTION SUNER ALSO EMPHASIZED THAT SPAIN
WANTED THE GRAIN NOT ONLY FOR TODAY, BUT FOR AS LONG
AS SHE WAS DEPENDENT UPON IT;

2. THE SPANISH GOVERNMENT WAS EXPLICITLY ASSURED OF
THE FULFILLMENT OF ALL OF THE SPANISH TERRITORIAL
DESIRES IN AFRICA IN MODIFICATION OF THE SECRET PROTOCOL
OF HENDAYE;

3. THE GIBRALTAR OPERATION WAS CARRIED OUT SOLELY AS
A SPANISH OPERATION AND NOT AS A GERMAN ONE, SINCE THE
SPANISH COULD NEVER ALLOW OTHER TROOPS TO TAKE OVER
THEIR PLACE. IN THESE CIRCUMSTANCES SPAIN COULD NOT SET
A DATE FOR HER ENTRY INTO THE WAR.

FROM THIS POSITION TAKEN BY THE SPANIARDS IT IS QUITE EVIDENT THAT FRANCO HAS NOT THE LEAST INTENTION OF ENTERING THE WAR, BECAUSE THE CONDITIONS STATED ACTUALLY POSTPONE AD CALENDUS GRAECAS THIS ENTRY INTO THE WAR; OR, THEY MAKE THE ENTRY INTO THE WAR COMPLETELY PROBLEMATICAL, BECAUSE IT IS MOST LIKELY TO FRANCO, TOO, IN SPITE OF HIS THINKING, WHICH IS EVIDENTLY UNTROUBLED BY MUCH MILITARY EXPERIENCE, THAT SPANISH TROOPS WOULD NEVER SUCCEED IN WRESTING GIBRALTAR FROM THE ENGLISH.

SINCE EVEN THE STATEMENTS OF FRANCO AND SUNER REGARDING YOUR DEMARCHES COULD BE EVALUATED ONLY AS NEGATIVE ANSWERS TO OUR QUESTION REGARDING THE WILL-INGNESS OF SPAIN TO ENTER THE WAR IMMEDIATELY, ALTHOUGH YOU FOR YOUR PART NEGLECTED TO CONFRONT BOTH MEN EXPRESSLY WITH THIS FACT DURING YOUR TALKS, TODAY THE MATTER IS TO BE CONSIDERED CLARIFIED COMPLETELY IN A NEGATIVE SENSE. WE DO NOT INTEND TO CHARGE THE SPANISH GOVERNMENT AT THIS TIME WITH HAVING BROKEN ITS PROMISES MADE IN HENDAYE, OR TO DRAW ANY FURTHER CONCLUSIONS FROM THIS WITH RESPECT TO GERMAN-SPANISH RELATIONS.

IN GENERAL I REQUEST YOU TO EXERCISE RESERVE TOWARD THE SPANISH GOVERNMENT; YOU SHOULD ACT IN PRINCIPLE, IN AN OBJECTIVE AND FRIENDLY MANNER BUT BE COOL AND RESERVED WITH RESPECT TO THE QUESTION OF SPAIN'S PARTICI-PATION IN THE WAR. NOW THAT THE SITUATION HAS BEEN CLARIFIED, PLEASE PROCEED NO LONGER ON THE ASSUMPTION, EVEN IN YOUR REPORTS, THAT THROUGH SOME ACTION OR OTHER WE MIGHT STILL INDUCE SPAIN TO ENTER THE WAR.

YOUR PROPAGANDA EFFORTS IN THE LOCAL PRESS, ETC., TO COUNTERACT BRITISH PROPAGANDA, ARE TO BE MAINTAINED AS BEFORE.

RIBBENTROP

El Pardo
February 26, 1941

Dear *Führer,*

Your letter of February 6th causes me to send you an immediate reply, for I consider it necessary to present a few clarifications and confirmations of my loyalty.

I am convinced, as you are, that we are indissolubly linked in a historic mission—you, the *Duce* and I. It has never been necessary to convince me of this; as I have said to you more than once, our Civil War, from its very beginning and throughout its development, was more than proof of this. I also share your view that the position of Spain on both sides of the Strait forces us to look upon England, who aspires to maintain her domination there, as our greatest enemy.

Our attitude of the past has not changed—we are resolute and of the firmest conviction. Do not doubt, therefore, the absolute sincerity of my political ideas and my conviction that our national destiny is linked with that of Germany and Italy. With this same sincerity I have, since the beginning of these negotiations, explained to you the circumstances of our economic situation, which are solely responsible for the fact that so far it has not been possible to set the date for Spain's intervention.

If you consider the difficulties of our post-war situation, you will recall that I have never fixed such a very short period for our entry into the war. Permit me to say, *Führer,* that the time that has so far passed has not been completely lost. Though we have not been able to obtain grain in sufficiently large quantities to permit us to build up our stocks we have at least a part of the bread necessary for the daily sustenance of our people. Otherwise a large part of the people would have perished of starvation.

Moreover, it must be admitted that in the question of supplying food Germany did not make concrete offers of effective aid until very recently. We are now only beginning to deal with concrete facts, and in view of this I have no other desire than to hasten the negotiations as much as possible. For this purpose I sent to you some days ago data on our needs as to foodstuffs and requirements in general economic and military fields. These data are subject to renewed examination, classification, verification and discussion for the purpose of reaching a speedy solution in which we are both equally interested.

You will undoubtedly understand that a time during which the Spanish people are suffering from extensive starvation and are experiencing all possible privations and sacrifices is certainly not propitious for me to ask new sacrifices of them, unless my appeal is preceded by a betterment in this situation; this would make it possible to carry out beforehand skillful propaganda concerning the constant friendship and effective aid of the German people, so as to arouse anew in the Spaniards the sentiments of sincere friendship and admiration which they have always had for your nation.

My remark regarding our climate was simply a reply to your suggestions, and by no means a pretext for putting off indefinitely what at the proper moment will be our duty.

Only recently in the interview at Bordighera I gave proof before the world of my determined attitude. This conference also served as an appeal to the Spanish people marking the direction in which lie its national obligations and the maintenance of its existence as a free nation.

One consideration I must still express: the closing of the Strait of Gibraltar is not only indispensable for the immediate relief of Italy but probably a prerequisite for the end of the war. In order to give this closing the significance of a destructive blow, however, it is also necessary that the Suez Canal be closed at the same time. Should this latter event not take place, we, who would like to offer you the effective commitment of our military strength, have to state in all sincerity that Spain's position in a prolonged war would be extremely difficult.

You speak of our demands and you compare them with yours and those of Italy. I do not believe that one could criticize the Spanish demands as excessive. The less so if one considers the tremendous sacrifices of the Spanish people in a struggle which was a glorious precursor of the present war. An appropriate statement concerning this point is still lacking in our agreements. The Protocol of Hendaye—permit me to say this—is, in this respect, rather vague and you undoubtedly remember the motives, which do not exist today, for leaving matters vague and open. The facts in their logical development have today left far behind the circumstances which in October brought about this Protocol, so that it can be considered obsolete at the present time.

These, my dear Führer, are my replies to your statements. I wish to dispel thereby any shadow of suspicion and declare my readiness to be completely and decidedly on your side, united in a common destiny; to desert it would mean surrender for me and betrayal of the good cause which I have led and which I represent in Spain. There is no need to assure you of my faith in the triumph of your cause, of which I shall always be a loyal supporter.

Your sincere friend,
Francisco Franco

APPENDIX X

FRANCO AND THE JEWS

Because fifty years of Comintern propaganda has taught us to think of Franco as an anti-Semite, a friend of Hitler and an anti-American, the authors offer the following documentation in order that one can read this story with an open mind.

- James Michener in *Iberia,* 1968, page 547: ". . . Generalissimo Franco is highly regarded by Jews; during the worst days of World War II, when pressures from Hitler were at their heaviest, Franco refused to issue anti-Jewish edicts and instead provided a sanctuary, never violated, for Jews who managed to make it to Spain. Many thousands of Jews owe their lives to Franco, and this is not forgotten."

- In *Resolutions* of the War Emergency Conference of the World Jewish Congress, Atlantic City, New Jersey, November 26–30, 1944, page 15: "The War Emergency Conference extends its gratitude to the Holy See and to the Governments of Sweden, Switzerland and Spain . . . for the protection they offered under difficult conditions to the persecuted Jews of Hungary . . ."

- In *The Congressional Record* of January 24, 1950, Representative Abraham Multer quotes a spokesman for the Joint Distribution Committee: "During the height of Hitler's blood baths upwards of 60,000 Jews had been saved by the generosity of the Spanish authorities."

- *Newsweek,* March 2, 1970: ". . . a respected U.S. rabbi has come forward with surprising evidence that tens of thousands of Jews were saved from Nazi ovens by the personal intervention of an unlikely protector, Spain's Generalissimo Francisco Franco, in so many other respects a wartime collaborator of Adolf Hitler. 'I have absolute proof that Franco saved more than 60,000 Jews during World War II,' says Rabbi Chaim Lipscitz of Brooklyn's Torah Vodaath and Mesivta rabbinical seminary."

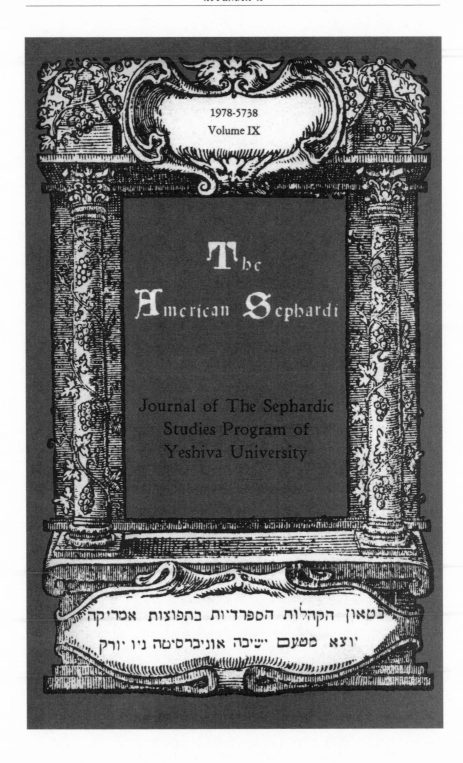

1978-5738
Volume IX

The American Sephardi

Journal of The Sephardic
Studies Program of
Yeshiva University

בטאון הקהלות הספרדיות בתפוצות אמריקה
יוצא מטעם ישיבה אוניברסיטה ניו יורק

215

IN MEMORIAM

Francisco Franco (1892-1975), Benefactor of the Jews

Generalissimo Francisco Franco, Head of the Spanish State, died on November 20, 1975. However general history may judge him, in Jewish history he shall certainly occupy a special place.

In contrast with England, which shut the borders of Palestine to the Jews fleeing Nazism and destruction, and in contrast with democratic Switzerland which sent back to Nazi terror the Jews who came knocking at its gates for help, Spain opened its frontier with occupied France, admitting all refugees, without distinction of religion or race. Prof. Haim Avni of the Hebrew University, who has devoted years to studying this question, concluded that a total of at least 40,000 Jewish lives were saved from the German gas chambers, either through direct Spanish interventions by Spanish ambassadors and consular officials or thanks to the open border. (Cf. Haim Avni, *Yad Vashem Studies on the European Jewish Catastrophe and Resistance,* Jerusalem, 1970, VIII, 31-68; *id., Contemporary Spain and the Jewish People,* Jerusalem, 1975, 292 pp.; Federico Ysart, *España y los judíos en la segunda guerra mundial,* Barcelona, 1973, 231 pp).

On October 23, 1940, at the darkest moment of European Jewish history, when Hitler's troops were deployed along the Spanish border after the fall of France, Franco met Hitler in the French border town of Hendaye and refused to give in to any of Hitler's demands, including the institution of anti-Jewish legislation. Instead, several months later, Franco founded in Madrid and in Barcelona the "Benito Arias Montano Institute of Jewish Studies." Its learned journal *Sefarad* continues to be one of the world's finest Jewish publications and the only one outside of Israel to be entirely subsidized by a national government.

In the autumn of 1953 *Yamim Nora'im* services were conducted in Madrid by Rev. D. A. Jessurun Cardozo of New York. Those services, to which Franco gave personal recognition, were the first to be officially authorized in Spain since the expulsion of 1492. (Cf. D. and T. de Sola Pool, *An Old Faith in the New World,* New York, 1955, 86-7.)

Beginning in 1945, Franco permitted the Jewish Agency to work on Spanish territory to facilitate the illegal immigration of concentration camp survivors to Palestine, which was then sealed to Jewish immigration by the British. After Israel's Suez Campaign of 1956, Moroccan Jews were prohibited from emigrating to Israel. The Haham, Rabbi Dr. Solomon Gaon, was received in private audiences by Franco, and

Spain created facilities for them to transit *en masse* to Israel by way of the Spanish Sahara, with the tacit approval of the Moroccan Government. (Source: Haham Gaon)

In 1960, at the close of the magnificent International Sephardic Bibliographical Exposition held for a month at the National Library in Madrid, Generalissimo Franco bestowed upon Haham Gaon the high honor of Spain: "Commander of the Order of Alfonso the Wise." In response to Haham Gaon's discourse in Judeo-Spanish, Franco, wiping away his tears, declared: ". . . the Spanish Government is proud to have been able to save Jewish lives during the Second World War and wishes to do everything possible to develop cultural bonds between the Sephardim and Spain." (Cf. *Kol Sepharad,* [London], no. 15, June 1960.)

The "First Symposium of Sephardic Studies" took place in Madrid from June 1 to June 6 in 1964. Jewish scholars from all over the world were invited by the Spanish Government to read papers on aspects of Sephardic culture. A 781 page volume of *Actas* was published at Spanish government expense in 1970, an indispensable tool for Sephardic scholars and perhaps the most important work in Sephardic studies to have appeared during this century.

In the aftermath of the Israeli-Arab war of 1967, Franco gave orders to his ambassadors in the Arab countries to distribute to as many Jews as possible Spanish passports and visas. Generalissimo Franco personally intervened on behalf of "stateless" Egyptian Jews arrested by Nasser and interned in inhuman conditions. During 1968, 110 such persons were permitted to depart for Spain. (Cf. Joseph A. Hasson, "Jews in Arab Countries," *The American Sephardi,* III, 1-2, September 1969, 102.)

In 1965 Franco was the first Head of a Spanish government since 1492 to receive in audience delegates from Jewish congregations in his own country. At Franco's instigation, on December 14, 1966, nineteen million Spaniards voted in favor of the law proposed by Franco to grant freedom of worship to all non-Catholic denominations. Official permission to hold public Jewish services ensued immediately. On December 16, 1968, the first synagogue since 1492 was consecrated in Madrid. To mark this occasion, the Ministry of Justice, at the behest of the Head of State, confirmed the abrogation of the Edict of Expulsion of 1492. The document was delivered by special courier to Señor Samuel Toledano of the Madrid Congregation and a copy sent to Haham Gaon in London. (Cf. *The American Sephardi,* I, 2, 1967, 26; *ibid.,* III, 1-2, 1969, 126-7.)

On June 13, 1971, to fulfill a long cherished wish of Generalissimo Franco (cf. his Decree 874 of March 18, 1964, reproduced in *Actas,* 613-5), the ancient "Tránsito" Synagogue of Toledo was officially "restored to Judaism." In the absence of a Jewish community, it was made into a splendid Jewish Museum while awaiting its future reconsecration as a House of Sephardic Jewish Prayer. At the inauguration of the museum, Haham Gaon and the Spanish Minister of Education presided. (Cf. *The American Sephardi,* V, 1-2, 1971, 143-5.)

When Tangier and Tetuan were incorporated into Morocco, the Spanish Government invited all the Jewish inhabitants of these cities to resettle in Spain. At present, the Jewish community of Málaga numbers over 2,500 members. At the order of Francisco Franco a Jewish artist was commissioned to sculpt a statue of Ibn Gabirol, which was erected in a special park in the City of Málaga, where the poet was born. On April 21, 1972, a magnificent ceremony was organized in Málaga to celebrate the poet's 950th anniversary. Specialists in Jewish literature from the Spanish universities and abroad were invited to read papers. Thanks to Franco's efforts, by 1972 Spain was the only country outside of Israel where all State Universities have a Department of Jewish Studies.

Due to Franco a continuous stream of scholarly publications dealing with Jewish culture has been flowing from Spanish presses during the last thirty years. Spain's great contribution to Jewish scholarship under Generalissimo Franco, carried out well-nigh exclusively by Spanish gentile scholars, is a phenomenon unique in the history of the Jewish people. (Cf. *The American Sephardi,* VI, 1-2, 1973, 66-69.)

On *Sabat Vayislah,* 18 Kislev 5736 (November 22, 1975), the co-editors of *The American Sephardi* went before the ark of the historic Spanish and Portuguese Synagogue in New York City to make an offering for the repose of the soul of Generalissimo Francisco Franco. The mention of his name was followed, at their request, by the Hebrew phrase: *sehu ᶜazar ha-yehudim bime hamilhama hagedola* ("for he helped the Jews during the Great War").

Winston Churchill, in his famous memoirs, affirms that the last possibility of Hitler's triumph was foiled by Franco whose "policy throughout the war was entirely selfish . . . He thought only of Spain and Spanish interests . . . This great danger had . . . passed away, and, though we did not know it, it passed forever. It is fashionable at the present time to dwell on the vices of General Franco, and I am, therefore, glad to place on record this testimony to the duplicity . . . of his dealings with Hitler . . . I shall presently record even greater services which . . . General Franco rendered the Allied cause." (Cf. Winston S. Churchill, *The Second World War*, II, *Their Finest Hour*, New York, 1949, pp. 519-530.) There is *not one word* in the four volumes of Churchill's memoirs about the fate of the Jews in occupied Europe.

Putting to one side any other considerations, Jews should honor and bless the memory of this great benefactor of the Jewish people . . . who neither sought nor reaped any profit in what he did.

INDEX